MIDNIGHT CATCH

A NOVEL

NORMAN GILLILAND

The street called Palm Terrace in this book does not represent a place with that name in Gainesville, Florida, or in any other Southern town, but is merely an avenue into a world of the author's imagining. Similarly, no character in this work of fiction depicts any actual person, living or dead.

Published by NEMO Productions
P.O. Box 260079
Madison, WI 53726-0079

Publisher's Cataloging-In-Publication Data
(Prepared by The Donohue Group, Inc.)
Gilliland, Norman.
Midnight catch : a novel / Norman Gilliland. — 1st ed.

p. ; cm.

ISBN-13: 978-0-9715093-5-1
ISBN-10: 0-9715093-5-2

1. Depressions—1929—United States—Fiction. 2. Debtor and creditor—Florida—Fiction. 3. Smuggling—Florida—Fiction. 4. Alcoholic beverage law violations—Florida—Fiction. I. Title.

PS3607.I4455 M53 2012
813/.6

Library of Congress Control Number: 2012902326

Printed in Charleston, South Carolina
For information about quantity discounts,
please call NEMO Productions at (608) 215-4785,
email us at: nemoproductions@hotmail.com,
or visit our website at www.sandmansions.com

For My Brother,
Charles Herbert Gilliland, Jr.,
who turned a sliding board into a rocket ship.

MIDNIGHT CATCH

CHAPTER 1

The blackberries of summer were gone, but the woods by the pasture pulled at Rex Holliman with the promise of small game to be felled by a boy with a BB gun, and he followed the tracks with his weapon cocked. He had hoped to receive a real rifle for his thirteenth birthday, but June of 1929 had come and gone without progress.

His mother had repeated the ancient story about J.J. Ward, who had grown up without two fingers and part of a third because of an accident with a Winchester. "You can't even keep your shoes tied and you're asking for a firearm," she had said at last. "Thirteen is too young."

"What if I talk to Dad about it?" Rex had spoken in a firm but respectful voice on the verge of breaking.

"Go right ahead," his mother had said, "if you can find him. I expected him home for dinner half an hour ago. I guess some cow between here and Tallahassee needs him more than we do right now."

That was how she always sidetracked the request for a rifle, with some complaint about his father's absence. What his father thought of guns was anyone's guess because Charles Pomeroy Holliman was rarely home long enough to discuss them, and often when he was home, he had gotten there so late that Flora had locked him out of the house, leaving him to catch what sleep he could in his wreck of a Model T.

Like his father, Rex thrived on being out and about, but he was better at getting home before his mother lowered the boom. On this delicious, cool, dry September afternoon he had walked almost as far as the old Bailey house, to the paddock where his father kept a white one-eyed mare named Lucy who had been payment for some veterinary miracle. When Rex rode her, she was slow and uninspired, and yet, when she was on her own, Lucy was full of life. She liked to jump the fence and wander through town, day or night. An equally restless spirit, Rex maneuvered her through his explorations with one of his father's contrivances, a rope halter fitted with an alligator belt on each side. He rode bareback with his feet dangling and the loaded BB gun perched upon Lucy's high, worn withers.

The access to the pasture was rough ground, a scrap of scrub his father had bought with cash in 1919 with the idea of selling it for a fat profit after ten years, but in 1926 a hurricane had knocked down houses and land prices all over Florida, and last year's douser had killed Pom Holliman's fading hopes for real estate. So at the ten-year mark the woods waited, smelling of nearby Herefords that grazed where a wire fence separated grass from a hodgepodge of blackberry bushes, beggar-weed, and granddaddy oaks.

Today, though, the woods bore the ripe, heavy scent of decay that came when one of the cows had died, even though all twelve of them grazed in plain sight.

Then there were the tread marks. For the life of him, Rex couldn't figure out why the bald ruts of his father's Model T bore the overlay of crisp tracks left by a heavier car.

He tied the horse to the wide, dragging gate and followed a curve in the shallow road down to a patch of palmettos that fanned out beneath a lone live oak. At his approach, a handful of crows scattered in raucous flight and, as he followed one with the barrel of the BB gun, it dropped low and darted behind the big oak, leaving him face to face with the things bound to the tree.

His first thought—odd for a boy inclined to skip Sunday school—was of the crucified Christ wearing his crown of thorns. But in an instant Rex could see that this man was crowned with barbed wire that wound around the tree and took in also a shorter form that once had been a woman.

The man, strangely formal in a brown suit and cheerful blue and yellow tie, leered at Rex with filmy eyes set in a blotchy purple and gray face. His black mouth was open as if he were about to speak, but a shot to his forehead had bottled his words forever. His companion seemed to be gazing down at the ground as if looking for a pin that had fallen from her matted black hair.

Rex couldn't stop looking.

A shot to the woman's throat had spattered the lace collar of what had been a respectable black dress. A shot to her heart had stained a stylish pearl necklace. Her red lips curled back from brown teeth as if in response to some joke whispered by blown leaves.

When he came to his senses, he noticed the flies.

In his haste to get away, Rex tripped over a shoelace and went down hard, launching the BB gun into the fallow blackberry bushes, but he was up again in a heartbeat, running for the mare that chewed vaguely at the grass by the gate. Once he had snatched apart the loop in the reins, it took him two tries to throw himself onto her back and then, kick as he would, he couldn't get her to take the first step. In a fit of desperation, he unbuckled one of the belt reins and slapped her sloping rump, jolting himself toward the road with a shaky grip on the halter as the resentful mare broke into a lopsided lope. Half a mile or so toward home Lucy collided with a fence post, shaking Rex back to his senses. He heaved up his ham and collard greens, slapped her onto the path again, and kept her pounding down the road until they had clattered all the way home, clear up the brick walk to the front porch.

(HAPTER 2

A t first Pom thought the knocking was inside his head, but as he settled back under the piece of canvas he heard whistling, a tune that ended with a loud bang on the door of the Model T.

He threw back the canvas, sat up, and rubbed his eyes. "Am I dreaming? It's Richard Ward up before noon. How's the wrist?"

Except for the five o'clock shadow, Richard looked like he was dressed for a lawn party, in a blue blazer, pressed gray trousers, and a blue and yellow striped silk tie. With a tilt of his blue-banded boat hat, he nodded toward the house and smiled.

"The wrist's fine. It's just a bruise. You get locked out again?"

Pom yawned as he rubbed the memory back into his balding head. "I was on my way to a farm up toward Paradise when I ran afoul of Trent Walker. He's making juice with some real sparkle to it."

"He ought not to be making hooch."

"Yeah, well, he probably wouldn't be if I hadn't advised him to buy a farm back in '23. Now the fruit flies have eaten it all up. I think I lost a night in there somewhere."

"I tell you, Pom, there's a reason that's stuff's illegal."

"I attended that sermon too—in 1919. That church bell hits like a hammer. Must be the Baptists."

"On Saturday? Pom, I've got an opportunity for you."

"That Richard, always the salesman. What is it, a house on Palm Terrace?"

"You'd be pretty lonely. No, this is a way to *make* some money."

"Thanks, but my state job keeps me busy enough, along with a little moonlighting."

"Isn't that against the rules?"

"Only if they catch you."

After glancing down the driveway, Richard put a hand on the car door. "Pom, I need some help with my boat."

"Didn't know you *had* a boat."

"Got it last spring. A twenty-eight-footer. I keep it down around Cedar Key."

Pom yawned and rubbed his forehead with the heel of his hand. "I'm working on one of my own now—an old wreck of a sloop I've got out at Lake Santa Fe." He rolled back the canvas and stuffed it where the backseat once was, a cavity long since filled with bait buckets, tackle boxes, and assorted tools of the veterinary trade. "This is the jib for it. I got it for curing some horses of the worms, and I'm going to get it all fixed up and give it to Rex for Christmas, if he wants it." He squinted up at his bedroom window without seeing any sign of life. "I'd like to help you, but I've got to stay here and do penance."

Richard pushed his skimmer back, freeing a shock of thick black hair. "Shoot, Pom, this wouldn't take long. I just need you to go down and put some spark into that engine of mine. It's only getting twelve knots and it ought to be more like eighteen."

"Eighteen! You trying to catch fish or run over 'em?"

"I'll be glad to pay you, but I'm in kind of a hurry."

"You usually are. You keep your money. I'll be glad to help you when I can, but I just can't get down there today. If I earn forgiveness, maybe Monday or Tuesday."

A dusty black Chevrolet glinted as it turned into the driveway and pulled up behind Richard's Packard sedan. A frowning heavyset man climbed out and slammed the door without a backward look. His white shirt and new brown worsted britches were freshly-pressed, his black tie was taut behind a fully buttoned tan vest, and a round felt hat sat square and tight on his broad forehead. His stride was all business. The .45 on his hip was strapped into a black holster shiny from use. His belt buckle and his badge caught the light as he came forward.

Pom sat up. "I'm popular today. Morning, Avery."

Richard nodded and put his hands in his pockets. "Mr. Mecum."

"Gentlemen, how you doing?" The sheriff took a pack of chewing gum from a vest pocket, waved it in the general direction of the other two, and helped himself to a stick. "Pom, I'd thought I'd give you a progress report. Here we are at the end of a week, and we still don't have much. Coroner says the victims were out there two or three days before Rex found them, killed probably about September twenty-fifth, but we still don't have much more than the labels in their clothes and some tire marks. We've got five slugs the coroner dug out of them, plus one from the tree, and we know now that they came from a Luger."

"A Luger?" The sail was starting to unfold and Pom crammed it down and secured it with a cane fishing pole. "There can't be too many of those around here. You know anybody with a Luger, Richard?"

Richard was looking down, scuffing the polished toes of his brown and tan wingtips in the pine needle driveway. "One of those queer-looking German guns? I wouldn't think so."

The sheriff shifted his hat back and rubbed his forehead with his thumb. "This one just doesn't add up. I'm tempted to turn it over to the Bureau of Investigation."

Pom watched Richard scraping his foot in the pine needles. "The Bureau of Investigation?"

The sheriff smacked his gum. "It's a new outfit up in Washington. I guess they've got all kinds of tricks. But once you get the feds involved, things can get out of control, so for now I'm keeping this thing close to home and going on hunches."

"I'm a big believer in hunches," Pom said. "More than once I've been saved from having my head knocked in because I got a hunch by looking some horse or cow in the eye."

"Then here's one for you. The killer was working with someone. Somebody held a gun on those two while the other one wound that wire around them. There's nothing earth-shaking about that. The shooter was standing close. Luger shells flip up in your face and these were all within a few feet of each other, not twenty yards from the victims."

With the back of his hand, Pom rubbed the stubble on his chin. "If he was that close, the guy must've been a lousy shot. Or maybe he wanted to hurt their feelings before putting 'em down."

The sheriff stopped chewing. "Could've been drunk. Or maybe he was hit, but we found no blood except at the tree. Left $32 in the man's hip pocket. There wasn't any billfold. We've shown some morgue shots around. Nobody recognizes 'em."

Richard started scuffing in the pine needles again. "Maybe you ought to put their pictures in the paper."

"That sort of thing hasn't caught on around here like it has up north. But we'll have the pictures at the jail for anyone who wants to come down and see 'em. We're putting up five hundred for this one, for information leading to an arrest."

Pom reached over the seat, peeled back the sail, and pulled a jar of grainy coffee out of the tangle of fishing tackle on the floor. He shook it, unscrewed the lid, and took a swig. "All of that sounds solid to me, Avery. Doesn't sound like a hunch in there."

The sheriff took the gum from his mouth, folded it into the wrapper, and tucked it back into his vest pocket. "All right. Then here's one. One of those killers is still around here somewhere, maybe both of 'em. One of 'em might even be from here. But the other one's an outsider for sure."

Richard gave him a sidelong look. "How do you figure?"

"Because nobody around here would set a man and woman up like that. That's a northern thing, maybe even a foreign thing. And I'll tell you something else, gentlemen. If everybody in this town keeps an eye out and comes forward with what they know, we'll have those killers within the week." He motioned toward the end of the driveway. "All the information we need is out there in those houses and gas stations and stores. We don't need the Bureau of Investigation. We just need for people around here to start talking to me. Between you, you know about everybody in town. Listen. And if you hear one peep that sounds out of place, you come to me."

Pom glanced over at Richard. "We'll keep an ear to the ground."

"How's Rex holding up?"

"He's okay. Some of the boys at school keep bringing it up."

"Idle hands," the sheriff said. "I'll see you in a day or so." He straightened his hat and turned toward his car.

As Richard watched him walk back down the driveway, Pom said, "Be nice to get 'em before they do it again. The next time it could be somebody we know."

When the sheriff had backed out to the street and turned toward the Courthouse Square, Pom climbed out of the Model T. "Something's making you itchy, Richard."

"I didn't say anything."

"No, but you were fidgeting the whole time Avery was here. Tell you what. Have another go at that engine today or tomorrow, and if you're still stuck, I'll break loose and go down to have a look at it. Monday or Tuesday maybe."

Before Richard could answer, a large pot-bellied man came ambling up the driveway. He had his hands in the pockets of his plaid trousers and his shirtsleeves were rolled up above his elbows. His golf cap looked a little too small. He smiled as he approached.

"Well, didn't I hit the jackpot?"

Richard turned out his hip pockets. "I wouldn't' say so. Ladies and gentlemen, hold your money tight. It's Mr. Buddy Cole."

Buddy smiled as he fanned himself with his cap. "Warm one, isn't it?"

Pom rubbed at a kink in his neck. "Not if you're sleeping in a car. Fall is in the air."

Richard put his pockets back in order. "You've got a garage, Pom. Why don't you sleep in there?"

"It's got a couple of hogs in it right now. I keep getting paid in kind."

"You're too soft," Richard said.

Buddy was eager to get a word in. "In all seriousness, gentlemen, does either of y'all know where I might make a few dollars? I'm riding on the rims."

Richard turned his palms up. "And I'm running on the *axles*. Everything I've got is in lots in Hollywood-by-the-Sea. Easy terms. What do you say?"

"Sure, if you'll take an IOU."

"How about just putting down a binder?"

Buddy patted him on the back, a little too hard for sheer affection. "You've got it backwards. *I'm* the one hurting for dough and I'll do damn near anything to get it. You always look sharp. You're getting cash flow from somewhere."

Pom had been digging under the seat. He handed Buddy a creased, oil-stained five-dollar bill. "Get you through the day at least."

Buddy pressed the bill to his chest. "Pom, you're all right. I'll pay you back by Tuesday, promise. How's Rex holding up?"

For the first time all morning, Pom was serious. "He needs something to take his mind off this deal so he can move forward. He's been building a radio, but I don't think he's gotten too far with it. Catching those guys would sure help."

Richard started scuffing his feet again. "Well, Buddy, you still playing Yankees for suckers on the golf course?"

"Can't find any more. Word's gotten around I guess."

"Well, you lettered in four sports, didn't you? You ought to be able to make money doing *one* of 'em. Work up another exposition. You always like to put on a show."

"Those days are gone, Hey, you want to pay to see me swim? Or maybe just to watch me change into my trunks?"

Richard smiled and touched the brim of his hat. "I'll call you if I feel the urge." With a slap of the car door, he started down the driveway. "See you Monday, Pom."

"Or Tuesday," Pom called after him. "I'll keep you posted."

Buddy rammed the five into his plaid pocket. "Thanks again, Pom. Come Sunday, I'll put ten percent in the collection plate."

"You do that, and put in a good word for me."

"You going to get back into Flora's good graces today?"

"Well, time is short. I promised to look at some hogs at a place off the Dixie Highway."

Buddy gave him a mischievous smile. "Maybe tonight then."

Pom headed toward the house. "No, not tonight either. She's having her friends over for some crazy table-tipping game, something to do with the murders. I'm going to make myself scarce."

CHAPTER 3

〰️●〰️

The long narrow parlor was private, but a cramped place for
a séance.

After twenty years of haphazard use by the Holliman family, it had become a repository of dead dreams, a cluttered and
musty mausoleum smelling of wood rot and mildew, shielded
from the harsh light of day by loblolly pines and the deep overhang of the porch. The weak overhead electric bulb had long
since broken in the socket, so the ladies had hung a kerosene
lamp above the green felt field of the poker table that dominated the room. The circle of its uncertain amber light revealed
a large wicker chair with a burn hole in one arm, an assortment
of cane and rush seats and, propped against one wall, a weathered wooden sign saying *Larrabee Motors* in old-fashioned block
letters. The five ladies sitting around the table were so crowded
that they touched at the elbows and knees.

Because a week had brought no insights into the grim dis-
covery at the pasture, Mavis Ward was losing sleep, and now she

was dead set on identifying the victims and the killers through spiritualism.

The other four conjurers had their doubts.

Flora Holliman resisted Mavis' attempts to create the right atmosphere for spiritual contact because she felt foolish waiting for a cold draft or the movement of an ethereal hand. She said again that she would have preferred their usual Canasta or even the absurdity of mahjong to this foolishness.

"Give us a sign," Mavis begged the bead board ceiling in a low chesty voice. "Please give us a sign."

Ainsley Harper was there because she thought there might be a story in it to add to her string of successes with *The Ladies' Home Journal* and *Collier's*. Ainsley said that she had heard of the dead talking through mediums at a crossroads called Cassadaga, and thought that tonight the barrier between living and dead might crumble right here in her own hometown.

"And if the spooks don't show," she told her fellow necromancers, "the story will be about *y'all* trying to talk to them, which is almost as scary."

Rachel Holliman, at sixteen, was three years older than her brother Rex, and had all the magic she needed in the voices that came from the Brunswick phonograph that stood in the dining room. A boarder ducking his rent had left behind two discs, one by Enrico Caruso and the other by Paul Whiteman, and she had just about worn the shellac off a jumpy tune called *Whispering* on the Whiteman record. She saw no need to talk to anyone other than the living, and many of *them* she could do without, but her mother had drafted her for the séance with a sense of civic duty not to be denied.

Roberta Barbour was at the table by dint of being inseparable from Rachel. She was so soft-spoken that at school she was rumored to be mute and, indeed, she did much of her talking through Rachel. Her round face hung like a harvest moon over the dark doings of the felt-topped table, and her luminous brown eyes traced the shadowy corners of the room as if watching for the appearance of ghostly script.

So there they sat—Flora, Ainsley, Rachel, and Roberta—each resisting what they had come to find, while Mavis closed her eyes and waited for a sustaining wave from the spirit world.

The flickering of the kerosene light suggested that she was onto something.

Feeling the table tremble, Ainsley leaned over to investigate and resurfaced in time to see the lantern flame die down to a single mean strip of light at the tip of the wick.

"Give us a sign." Mavis pleaded with upturned palms in a husky, alien voice.

"Give us a sign."

As Mavis pressed for a response, the air in the parlor became heavier. Roberta fought an asthmatic cough. A pearl of sweat traced the edge of Rachel's powdered nose. Ainsley's slender, short-nailed index finger twitched and, after a moment of breathless expectation, the women dropped back into the spell of Mavis' measured voice, their eyes glazed, their settling shadows playing larger than life on the mottled wallpaper.

Was that the small, sweet tinkling of an otherworldly bell? Ainsley looked from one pair of lowered eyes to the next for confirmation, but didn't find it.

In the wall behind Roberta something rattled and popped.

Mavis' face fell back, her open mouth a dark portal to the dimension of the dead.

"Give us a sign!"

Now she got one.

A sharp rap shook the window, and the shade shot to the top of the frame with a slap that toppled Mavis from her wicker throne to a chorus of shrieks. Someone collided with the lamp and it swayed in a drunken loop, spinning crazy silhouettes as the ladies tumbled over each other on their way to the door.

"Jesus Ch-*rist!*" Suddenly Ainsley was all the way across the front room. She had one hand on the mantel and the other on her heart. "Jesus Christ! I saw a *face* at that window."

"Do you *swear?*" Roberta stared into the dizzy shadows of the parlor.

Now the knocking rattled the screen door.

Flora steadied herself against the round table in front of the fireplace and peered into the yellow light of the front hall. "Get the door, Rachel. You're always so eager."

The older women burst into nervous laughter, but Rachel clung to Roberta. "Not me, Mama."

"Oh, all right." Flora straightened, touched her auburn hair as if to make sure the wave was still there, and ventured forth. With a deft twist of the knob, she got the door past the sticking point and opened it all the way so as not to be alone with whatever was there.

Squinting through the patched screen and the yellow light of the porch was a compact, fair-haired man of about thirty-five. He was a day or so overdue for a shave and a change of clothes, the button was torn from the throat of his shirt, and his leather vest was cracked at the shoulders, but he was brushed and smoothed and he minded his manners. He worked the visor of his cap with chafed thumbs in a way that reminded Flora of a vagrant offering to do chores for table scraps, except that his gaze was direct as he looked from face to face as if to assess the disarray.

"I turned the doorbell," he said in some kind of northern accent, "but it seems to be frozen up. Mr. Holliman said there might be a room I could rent for a few days. He said I should speak to someone called his keeper."

Hearing her husband's humor come through the mouth of a stranger threw Flora's thoughts back to the séance and made her all the more uneasy. Her arm barred the door as she appraised the man through the patchwork screen.

"Mr. Holliman said you could have a room here tonight?"

"Yes, ma'am. He said you're mighty picky, but said you should make an exception for me."

"An exception? Why?"

His hands continued to work the visor. "Well, if I may say so, he referred to me as a stripe above the breed of cat that generally walks in off the road."

The rest of the ladies had ventured closer, and over her shoulder Flora could hear Ainsley say, "You can tell he's been talking to Pom all right."

She came forward and put her hand on the doorjamb. "What else did Mr. Holliman say?"

The stranger stood straight, with his feet spread and his hands quiet on the cap now. "He talked about cattle mostly, and rabies. Said he'd be home just as soon as he tended to one little thing."

She sighed. "I don't doubt that he did."

"He stopped and gave me a lift on the Dixie Highway. My name's Jim Rhodes. I'd just like to stop over for a few days on my way back north."

Flora moved her hand to the screen door. "Most of the travelers we see at this time of year are going south, Mr. Rhodes. Why would you be headed north?"

When he shifted into the light from the front hall, a healing cut showed through a tawny bruise on his right cheek. "Well, there's no work down south, so I'm going back to Wisconsin for a few days. Then maybe I'll look for a job in Chicago."

Her hand tightened on the doorjamb as she continued with strained formality. "You say you're between jobs. What was your last position?"

His thumbs went back to work on the visor, harder now. "I was a reader, ma'am, down in Tampa, Ybor City to be exact."

She cocked her head. "A reader?"

The stranger shifted something slung behind his shoulder. "I was a reader in a cigar factory. The leaf rollers are sitting there all day, day in and day out, and they need something to improve their minds, so the management brings in somebody to read to them and, when they're short-handed, the reader takes a place on the bench along with everybody else."

Ainsley whispered to Mavis. "Kind of short, but not half bad to look at, is he?"

Keeping her eyes on him, Mavis replied, a little too loud. "I don't care if he looks like Douglas Fairbanks. I wouldn't let him into *my* house until—"

As if in defiance, Flora opened the screen door a crack. A moth fluttered in. "I'll need two nights rent in advance, two-fifty a night."

The traveler pulled a few bills from his hip pocket, unfolded a five, and handed it to her through the slot.

Mavis turned so that only Ainsley would see her open-mouthed disbelief. She lifted her handbag from a ladder-back chair by the fireplace. "Well, we chatted away the evening and settled down to business too late. I don't think we were quite in the spirit of it anyway. Are you coming with me, Roberta?"

Flora tucked the money into the pocket of her house dress. "We've already had supper and the stove's cold, but we can get out a few things for you. Just wait here a moment."

"Sorry for the trouble." The traveler shifted the burden on his back and it caught the light as he moved away when Flora opened the screen door for her departing guests.

"A guitar," Ainsley said to Roberta as they followed Mavis down the steps. "We have a wandering minstrel here."

The traveler waited hat in hand by the door as the ladies escorted the frustrated medium down the broken brick walkway and offered her words of encouragement. But Mavis was eager to change the subject, and by the time she and Roberta climbed into her dented Chevrolet, she was telling them again about the stolen silverware that had been in her family since her grandmother's wedding. As she repeated the story of its burial under the corncrib during the siege of Petersburg, Flora took her leave.

Ainsley broke away and caught up with her halfway to the porch steps. She murmured her misgivings. "Listen, if you're short of cash, I can—"

Flora turned. "You're an angel, but we do rent rooms."

"At least let me stay till Pom gets here."

"Ainsley, who knows when he'll show up."

"Then I'll spend the night. I'll just tell Mavis that I'm staying."

As she turned, Flora caught her by the elbow. "No, really."

"You sure?"

With closed eyes, as if shutting out her doubts, Flora nodded. She favored her husband's given name over his nickname, as if using it would somehow improve his conduct. "If Charles says that man's okay, that's good enough for me, for a couple of nights anyway. In fact, I'm going to lock the doors at ten whether Charles is here or not."

As Rachel approached from the car, Ainsley leaned closer to Flora and scarcely more than breathed the words: "You're going to lock Pom *out* and that guy *in*?"

Flora was unmoved. "Maybe it'll finally teach Charles to come home on time."

"Well, call me. Call me anytime. I don't care if it's the middle of the night."

"I'll call you in the morning. I have some more magazines I meant to give you."

CHAPTER 4

———◦◦◦———

As Rachel trailed behind, Flora crossed the porch and led the stranger into the house as far as the front hall, where she excused herself long enough to give Rachel some instructions in the kitchen. By the time she came back, he had drifted into the front room and stood playing a few notes on the piano. It was tinny but in tune. He broke off when the creaking floor announced her return.

"I'll show you your room," she told him. She ushered him upstairs and went through the house rules.

"My husband's up at all hours," she said at the end. "I hope you're a sound sleeper."

"I'm kind of a night owl myself," he said. He apologized again for startling Flora and her friends.

She glanced out the window into the darkness. 'It's been a difficult couple of weeks. A few nights before the murders, they found poor Mr. Howard dead in the woods near the depot. I suppose my husband told you?"

"He told me the old man was a friend of your son's." Jim Rhodes paused as if to add something, but as he put a large black book on the dresser, he knocked over a small swaybacked horse carved out of soft pine. Setting it back on its feet, he noticed a framed photograph of two grinning bearded old men posing beside a trophy mackerel.

"My father and Ainsley's," Flora told him. "After a trip to Seahorse Reef."

"Well, they look stout-hearted," the traveler said. "I hope I get to meet them.

"I'd like that," Flora said with an air of mystery. She turned toward the door. "Well, such as it is, dinner should be on the table by now."

He followed her back downstairs to the dim dining room, where Rachel had set a plate of fried chicken, mashed potatoes, and collard greens at Pom's place at the head of the table. He was just sitting down when Rex burst through the back door and pumped himself a drink from the kitchen tap.

The boy was calling his mother and wiping his hands on his jeans as he came into the dining room. He stopped short when he saw the stranger at the head of the table.

Flora introduced Rex with an apology about the racket.

The traveler rose to shake hands. "Your father said you were a dynamo."

Rex looked down at the dark oak floor. "I never know what he means by that."

"He told me about your friend, Mr. Howard. I'm sorry for your loss."

The boy looked away to the open window. "Well, at least he died on his own terms."

Flora took away some of the romance. "He died in a tarpaper lean-to in the Porter's Quarters, a rail corridor. Of pneumonia."

A shadow thrown by the headlamps of a passing car crossed the traveler's face as he sat back down. He sliced into his chicken.

"The same thing's happening all over southern Florida, you know, people turned out, living in their cars, living under bridges, but nobody in power wants to see it, let alone do anything about it."

The boy was intrigued. He had never seen anyone eat chicken with a knife and fork, and this man Jim Rhodes was very precise with them, even though the knife was dull.

Flora pretended to discover a burn hole in the table cloth, a blemish that had been there for untold years. "Have you been in Alachua County for long, Mr. Rhodes?"

He looked up from his cutting. "I just got here today. Spent last night in some little town on the Dixie Highway. Place with a funny name, started with a K."

Rex blurted it out. "Kissimmee?"

His mother touched him on the shoulder. "Let Mr. Rhodes answer, Rex."

The boarder seized on the name. "Yes, that's it. I spent the night with a real estate salesman—a *former* real estate salesman—who's been sleeping under a tarp inside a circle of azalea bushes."

His defensive tone suggested that the subject of his travels was closed.

Flora said something about men being out of work since the hurricane.

"But that was just the last straw," the traveler said. "It came on top of runaway land speculation with absolutely no hard money behind it. And what has Mr. Hoover done about it? No more than Mr. Coolidge did. They seem to think that these things will take care of themselves. They seem to think that people in need don't want help from their government."

Rex had never heard anyone speak disrespectfully about the President of the United States. He thought this man might be a traitor. He asked what the people in power could do.

The traveler's hazel eyes flashed. "Plenty. They can set up temporary housing. They can provide food from the agricultural surplus. They can subsidize medical and dental care. They can provide jobs on public projects. They've got a workforce down there in south Florida. They ought to put it to work."

For a boy accustomed to wry small talk at home and rote repetition at school, this man's assertions hit like a breaker at Flagler Beach.

With a deft turn of the knife, the traveler severed thigh from drumstick and went on. "Up in Wisconsin we have a progressive tradition, the belief that government should be involved in the welfare of the people every day."

Remembering a headline, Rex grabbed at what he thought was a safe, distant topic, a recent newspaper headline. "Is Wisconsin where they just had that shipwreck?"

Flora told him to stop asking questions and let their guest get on with his dinner.

The man seemed not to hear her. His eyes lit up again. "Yes, that was Wisconsin, and we'll have more shipwrecks. The owners push their luck in the autumn storms. They lose ships and they lose men. They figure both are expendable. The crews are going to be organizing though."

Rex wasn't sure he should be having this conversation. "You mean unions?"

"Exactly." The boarder snapped his fingers. "They'll stop the exploitation just like that."

Flora had been listening for the rasping approach of Pom's Model T. She crossed the room and turned on a corner lamp that just made the shadows worse. "And if the unions get too strong," she said, "what's to stop them from striking until the whole country breaks down?"

The boarder leaned back to make eye contact. "Fair wages, Mrs. Holliman. That's all it'll take. No one wants the country to break down. They just want a living wage."

She began to lose patience with him. "And with work so scarce down here, especially in the south part in the state, why did you come to Florida in the first place? Why not some northern state?"

His answer smacked of an oft-repeated justification. "I heard that the cigar makers at the Perfecta Company were getting the short end of the stick, that they were breaking their backs to make the factory owners rich. I wanted to come down and see for myself, to see if there was anything I could do to get them a square deal."

Flora came to her place at the far end of the table and put her hands on the back of her chair. "For the past three years there've been plenty of people who could use a better deal, including the employers. But if you go talking union to the cigar workers, you'll probably just get them all laid off, and there are plenty of hungry people down there ready to take their places, people willing to work for whatever they can get."

Rex became uneasy whenever his mother got that tightness in her voice. Hoping to change the subject to something completely safe, he said something about replacing the burned out bulb in the parlor.

But the traveler was not to be distracted. "Oh, the rest of the workers at Perfecta are secure enough for now," he said. "*I* was the one they laid off. *Fired,* to be more precise."

Flora didn't understand. "For reading? What were you reading to them, Mr. Rhodes?"

He set the knife down and touched his fingertips together as if accepting a challenge. "When I was fired? *The Communist Manifesto.*"

The room fell silent except for far-off barking and the rhythmic squeak of a backyard pump. Flora repeated the words carefully, the way she did when her husband mentioned an unfamiliar disease. "*The Communist Manifesto.* Are you a communist, Mr. Rhodes?"

His eyes held hers. "No, I'm a socialist. But I believe in airing all political points of view."

"What do you suppose the new person's reading to them?"

"Nothing. They replaced me with a radio."

For Rex, it was as if a secret word had unlocked a roomful of thoughts. He pulled out his chair and sat down, thrust his elbows onto the table, and leaned forward. "I built a radio in my room from a diagram in the Sunday supplement, not just a crystal set—a *real* radio. It gets a lot of static, but think of it—on the radio somebody a hundred miles away can read to you—and to hundreds of other people all at the same time. You won't even have to pick up a book."

The boarder dismissed the idea. "I'm all for radio. I've worked with it a lot. But I don't think it'll ever replace books."

At the sound of tires in the driveway, Flora went toward the front door, but the light faded as the automobile backed out with grinding gears and retraced its route down the tree-lined street.

The man rose and pulled the napkin from his collar. "I'm sorry if I'm making you uneasy."

She turned abruptly. "How much did my husband tell you about the couple in the pasture?"

He twisted the napkin in his chafed fingers. "An execution of some kind apparently."

"And no suspects. You can understand if we're all on edge."

At ten o'clock, as Rex was getting ready to go to bed, Flora came into his room and showed him how to block the door by wedging a chair under the knob.

"Jim's all right," the boy protested. "Didn't Dad say so?"

"Your father isn't here," she reminded him. "Rachel will be in with me."

He set aside his algebra book and sat at his desk, trying to figure out where he'd gone wrong with the radio diagram as he listened to her make her nighttime rounds of the house.

He heard her lock the doors, front and back. He heard her come upstairs and lock the door to the master bedroom. He heard the murmur of voices, hers and Rachel's. Heard the opening of a drawer and, and then, faintly, a new sound that he was slow to identify, the loading of a pistol.

CHAPTER 5

A scream from the house shattered Pom's dream of cornering a rabid dog.

He thought at once of the hitchhiker he had sent to Flora for a room. He jumped out of the car, ran up the back steps and tried the door, but it was still locked, so he bullied it open with a twist and a yank and burst into the kitchen. He pulled so hard at a sticking drawer that the face of it came off and an assortment of cutlery spilled at his feet. He grabbed a butcher knife and bounded up the stairs two at a time.

When he rounded the corner at the top of the stairs, Flora was staring at him.

"What in the world are you doing with *that*?" she said. "Has everyone around here gone mad?"

He lowered the weapon and paused to catch his breath. "What was all that racket up here?"

"Up here? It sounded like a cyclone hit the kitchen."

"From way out in the yard I heard a scream."

"Just give me the knife and go take care of things. By the way, how did you get in?"

He brushed past her. "Tell you later."

He found Rex at his radio with his hands clasped to a headset made from two telephone receivers.

Rachel was stifling a scream with a fist pressed to her mouth. When she saw Pom, she took him by the sleeve and pointed toward her room. "There's a big one on my wall and Rex won't get it."

He patted her hand. "Oh, now, come on. You're too old to be scared of roaches."

"It was on my *pillow*."

He looked past her to the radio. "Okay, okay. I'll take care of it. But first, let me take a gander at this."

Jim Rhodes was tightening the antenna wire, a bright copper line that ran from the face of the radio to the window frame. He turned and stood with the bearing of a soldier "Good morning, Mr. Holliman."

"Call me Pom. Glad to see you found the place, Jimmy."

"Thanks again for the lift last night—and for putting me up."

Rex bounced in his chair. "That's it! The signal's back!"

Flora had already returned to the room. "He found 'the place' a lot faster than you did."

Pom chuckled. "Well, it sounds a little strange, but after dropping Jimmy off, I was most of the way to Paradise and that radiator gave out again. By the time I got to a phone it was too late to call you."

She looked at him askance. "Someday when you get a new car, whatever are you going to use for excuses?"

He put his hands in his pockets. "All right. I'll give it to you straight. Truth is I'm seeing another woman."

She raised a brow. "Now there's something I can understand."

"Yup. Cute as a kitten. Wears a fox-fur boa that winks at you when she dances the Charleston."

Rachel laughed. "That I'd like to see."

Flora sighed. "Well, I just hope she gets to see more of you than we do."

Pom had a good look at the radio. "It's hardly more than a coffee can and a speedometer hooked to a few feet of baling wire. Can you really hear all the way across the country with it?"

"You can now," Jim said. "At breakfast he told me that he kept losing the signal. We figured out that the contact arm of the rheostat was bent and he had a break in the antenna. Tonight he should be able to get more than just the local station."

Pom rubbed a neck still stiff from a second night in the car. "Looks like the novelty's here to stay. But what's the point of spending all that time listening to somebody you can't see?"

"It can be a force for bringing people together," Jim said, "a powerful force. When there's one of these in every house, the president can talk to everyone in the country at the same time. And let's hope that he has something worth saying."

As Jim turned back toward the antenna, Flora whispered to her husband. "Do *not* get him started on politics."

Pom bent down for a closer look at the tuner. "That the idea? One in every house? Along with the chicken in every pot and the car in every garage?"

"There's music on it too," Rachel reminded him. "And I'd like to hear some of it. But Rex is never going to let go of that thing."

Pom went on playing the devil's advocate, a role he relished. "You get singers and orchestras off the Brunswick, don't you? What do you need a radio for?"

Rachel rolled her eyes. "Daddy, you're missing the point. These singers are *right there* while you're listening to them, except that the *whole country's* hearing them along with you. It's like a big party."

"Well, I understand that. But can't you pretty much do that with the telephone? We've already got wire strung all over town for that. We could have one big party line."

Flora cleared her throat to signal her impatience. "Charles, don't be so contrary. You sound just like my father when the telephone came along. He thought we'd be better off just shouting out the window—at least that's what he said. Did you see Avery yesterday?"

With the radio as a diversion, Pom felt more at ease talking to the wife he had forsaken for the past two nights. "No. There's nothing new since Saturday. The best clue he's got is that Luger and the way those two were set up. Something foreign about it."

Rex pressed the headset with his palms and shouted something about a farm report, forcing his mother to step back to hear what Pom was saying.

Flora was watching Jim wrap a wire around the base of the radiator in fast precise coils. "I don't know which would be worse—to have it be a stranger or someone we know."

Rex pressed the headset all the tighter in an effort to shut out his parents.

"Last night we had a bunch of women downstairs talking to dead people," Pom said, "and now we've got Rex up here listening to somebody on the other side of town. It's going to get so that we'll listen to anybody but the guy who's right there looking at us."

But after squirming through Sunday school, Rex did plenty of listening to someone right there. As Jim sat on a cane chair and picked out bluesy tunes on his guitar, the boy pumped him with questions about radio—what made it work and how did Jim come to know so much about it?

The performer propped the guitar against the dresser. "I have the U.S. Navy to thank for teaching me the mysteries of radio." As he sat back in the chair, he knocked over the framed photograph on the dresser and, righting it, studied again the image of the two bearded, grinning old men standing beside the giant mackerel.

Rex couldn't resist another look at the cheerful faces. "The one smoking the cigar and wearing the derby is old Bob Harper, Ainsley's father. The one wearing the Saratoga hat is my grandfather Larrabee."

Jim turned it away from the glint of daylight that filtered through the loblolly pines in the backyard. "They look like the best of friends."

"They were," Rex told him. "They ran a boat together way back when Paynes Prairie was a lake. For his seventieth birthday Bob got himself a 22-foot Cadet, and they loved to go fishing out in the Gulf. A year ago September they went out for mackerel and didn't come back. My dad says they went down in a storm, but Mama still waits for 'em to come back. Sometimes you'll see her looking out the window at suppertime as if they'd only been gone since breakfast. How can we pick up more stations with less static?"

Jim smiled at the boy's nimble hopping from one subject to the next. "You've already got a vacuum tube radio. The rest is in the tweaking, the antenna—and the weather."

"Can we get Atlanta and Charlotte?"

"Sure. And New York. And as more stations come on, it'll get easier and easier. It's the wave of the future. Radios won't always be just for a few people. Before you know it, everybody in the country will have one and then you'll see some changes."

"You mean better signals?"

"More than that. You'll see a change in the way people think about how the country ought to be run, about how the resources are shared. Whenever the workingman's getting a raw deal, word will get out just like that, and you won't have a few capitalists getting fat while the guys doing the work are scraping for their next meal. You'll see a revolution."

Rex wasn't sure what Jim had in mind, but the visitor from the north seemed so calm and logical in the progression of his ideas that the revolution he spoke of began to make sense.

On Monday Rex got so swept up in algebra, keeping clear of
the lunch bag predator Ollie Holiday, and running to the train
station in time to sell boiled peanuts to the passengers on the
6:39 that he collapsed in bed and fell asleep before the house
had quite settled down for the night, which made him all the
more keen to get his hands on the radio when Tuesday morning
came around. He pried himself away from it at the last minute,
bounded downstairs, and gobbled up his biscuits and grits,
thinking all the while about getting a logbook to keep track of all
the stations he could pick up with his improved radio. "That way
I'll know just when and where on the dial to get them again,"
he said, half to his mother and half to the wind that scattered
magnolia leaves across the front walk.

School was a torment, partly because he was so eager to get
back to the radio, and partly because some of the boys were still
asking him graphic questions about the dead bodies wired to the
oak tree. The biggest of them, the notorious Ollie Holiday, made
a mockery of the horror by tripping Rex and tying his hand to
a fence with a snotty bandana, then rifling though his lunch bag
for a prized piece of pecan pie.

As Mrs. Campion chalked up the blackboard and boomed
out the fundamentals of solving for x, Rex daydreamed about
an antenna that could pick up every station in the country
with such a strong, clear signal that he could hear script pages
turn and floorboards creak in those distant studios. The finer
points of binomial equations slipped past him as he thought
of stringing copper wire from tree to tree all around the yard
and pulling in remote signals that brought new voices men-
tioning exotic places alive with exciting events that he could
call in to the newspaper. Or what if he ran his wire to West
Main Street and secured it to the railroad track? The whole
country would be his antenna. Without so much as setting
foot outside his own room, he would have his finger on the
pulse of the world.

As the school day progressed and binomial equations gave way to levers and fulcrums and the distinction between effort and work, Rex tried to reconstruct what Jim had told him about the unseen wonders of wireless communication. It started with an announcer whose voice vibrated a carbon ribbon. The carbon ribbon somehow turned the words into a flow of electrons that jumped through a vacuum, shot through a wire to a tower and then flowed through the air in waves that rose and fell like invisible water, bounced off the sky, struck antennas all around the country, and somehow re-emerged in his headset. These radio waves were going through everyone all the time whether they knew it or not, beaming right through their clothes and their internal organs, wherever they were, whatever they were doing, every minute of the day and night, going right through doors and walls, and yet you couldn't begin to hear them without that little box of metal and wire and glass tubes.

How did they ever keep those radio waves from crashing into each other in a big wash of meaningless sound? In his excitement about picking the voices out of the air, he ached to jump up from his desk, run home, and ask Jim to unveil the mystery.

By the time his head cleared, the class had moved on to social studies. The subject was the Great War, and Mrs. Campion, who was related to the cattle ranchers on Paynes Prairie, spoke of the conflict with the commanding voice of someone accustomed to working with large animals. She had been asking questions all through algebra and science and had somehow overlooked Rex, but now she bore down on him with an inquiry about the causes of the recent conflict.

He rallied his intellectual forces and was just as surprised as anyone at what came out.

"It was all about the capitalists controlling the means of production."

Mrs. Campion blinked as if one of the cows had kicked dirt into her face. "Would you mind repeating that for us, Rex?"

The budding radical rubbed an ancient groove etched in his desktop by some long forgotten, perhaps dead, student, hoping that a genie would emerge and give him an acceptable answer. "It—it was all about controlling the means of production. The masses were doing all the work, but the bankers and industrialists—the capitalists—were controlling the means of production. They got the workers to fight the war while they got rich selling the weapons. So the masses were being kept poor while the—the capitalists just got richer and richer off the sweat and blood of the workers."

He became aware of twenty faces turned around staring at him.

"Well, I mean, that's one way of looking at it," he said.

After school he and Mrs. Campion had a little chat.

The young dissenter was ready to recant everything just so he could run home and get back to the radio, but Mrs. Campion wasn't interested in confessions. She wanted to know causes. "It's never enough to know *what* happened," she was fond of saying. "It's important to know *why* it happened. We know very well that people get ringworm, but that does us very little good unless we know *why* they get ringworm."

As Mrs. Campion closed the door to the eighth grade classroom, Rex scanned the walls for inspiration, counted the stars on the flag, and studied the pale impassive features of George Washington. Finally his eyes rested on a photograph of the smooth-faced, squinting Charles Lindbergh. He wished that he too could climb into the *Spirit of St. Louis*—and fly away from the probing to come.

She had him sit at a chair by her desk. It doubled as the dunce's perch.

She sat in her swivel chair, moved a can of pencils, and put her fingertips together.

"You shared some interesting ideas with the class today, Rex."

"Yes, ma'am."

"It's always been my impression that the war was fought to help a nation in distress, to make the world safe for democracy."

Rex thought he had heard those words in a song somewhere. "Yes, ma'am."

"Do you have some reason to think otherwise?"

He started to say something but thought better of it. "No, ma'am."

"Where did you get those ideas about capitalists and masses and all that?"

"Well, ma'am, I guess I must've made 'em up."

"Oftentimes when we think we've made something up it's really just something we've heard without remembering it. Might you have heard those words somewhere?"

"Maybe. I forget, ma'am."

Mrs. Campion studied his face as she thought for a moment. "I see. You may go then."

Rex got up as quickly as he dared. He was halfway to the door when she stood up and called out to him. "Perhaps your parents will have something to say about this."

He measured his steps to the door and, when he got to the hall, he broke for daylight and ran all the way home.

(HAPTER 6

When he bounded into the front hall, he discovered that
Pom had hired a maid. Mavis Ward had fired Amelia for
stealing the family silver, an accusation Amelia had denied
with a raised hand as a lifelong member of the African Methodist
Episcopal Church, but to no avail, and, after three days, she still
burst into tears whenever the subject came up.

Jim was following her around as she dusted. "That's what
we're seeing now—the death rattle of the capitalist system, just
as Marx predicted. Next stop, the new order—and your people
will be better off in it."

She swiped at the round table with an old undershirt of
Rex's. "I don't know about any capitalist system, Mister Rose.
All I knows is that my *personal* system's all out of whack. As a
Christian, I'm working through it and I forgive Miz Ward for
doing me wrong. But as a person with a reputation and a person
needing cash money, I'm feeling more than a little put out. I
don't even know how I'm going to pay for the BC Powder to take

this pain out of my head. I'm so strung out I've been waking up my husband talking in my sleep."

He pursued her around the table. "Don't you see though? Under socialism you'd have a guaranteed income. You wouldn't have to work at all if you weren't able to."

She screeched. "Not work at all? Ain't I stuck with that man of mine enough without settin' on the porch all day every day? I wouldn't' know what to do with myself."

"Well, of course, you could work if you wanted to. That's the beauty of the system. You can always make more money if you want a higher standard of living, but this way you'd have everything you need if you got laid off. You wouldn't be at the mercy of people like the Wards."

She went over to the mantel, picked up a pair of pewter candleholders, dusted them, and polished the long oak ledge. "That has some appeal, but if it wasn't for the need to work, I wouldn't know what to do with myself. And Luther would never even leave the house! Three years ago he got a hundred dollars reward for snitching on a chicken thief and he lived off it for most of a year, underfoot night and day. No, sir, I don't believe I can swallow your socialism in one gulp like that."

Rex stood in the front hall, fascinated. Amelia was giving Jim a run for his money. He wanted Jim to tell her about how the capitalists had tricked the masses into fighting the Great War. He wanted him to win her over to the socialist cause with new facts that would come in handy for keeping the overbearing Mrs. Campion at bay.

Jim waited for Amelia at the end of the mantel. "There's a force at work in America and change is in the air. We can fight it or we can see it for what it is and roll up our sleeves and work with it to make this a free country for everyone, not just for the guy with money and property. When the bulkheads of capitalism come crashing down—the banks and the automobile manufacturers and the steel barons and the railroad plunderers—when the market crashes and capitalism writhes in its death throes, then the way will be cleared for real democracy—democracy that represents the working man—and woman—not just the power brokers who control the Congress. It's coming, Amelia. It's just around the corner. You can read about it in the papers every day now. Let's not fight that force, let's work with it."

The maid dabbed at her temples with the clean end of the rag. "Mister Rose, I don't know what you just said, but I sure like the way you said it! You oughts to be a preacher—or a politician at the least, like that man that gives the Cross o' Gold speech. If you can dust as fancy as you can talk, take this rag and we'll whip through this house like a whirlwind!"

On his way into the room, Rex tossed his schoolbooks on the stairs to announce his arrival. His family had never employed a maid, so he wasn't sure what to make of Amelia handling his undershirt.

"You got home in good time," Jim said, not the least self-conscious about his impassioned speech. "How was school?"

"It's been better," Rex told him. He skipped over the confrontation with Mrs. Campion. "For one thing, I was eager to ask you how the radio stations put the signals in the air without mixing 'em up with other stations."

"I could tell you that, but the best way would be to go down and see it firsthand."

"Go to the radio station?" The thought had never occurred to Rex.

"Sure. Why not? Radio stations are just people doing a job."

"You think they'll let us in?"

"The worst they can do is say no. We can go down there any-time you want."

"Now?"

"Well, I suppose so. If it's okay with your parents."

At that very moment, Pom clattered through the back door.

The boy's face brightened and he beat a path for the kitchen, where he found his father pawing through the cupboards.

Pom pulled at another stubborn drawer. "You seen the small funnel, Rex? I could've sworn it was right here next to the strainer."

"Jim and I are just on our way to the radio station. Do you think the weather will hold?"

"Well, I think that cloudbank is moving off to the west, so you should be okay. Boy, this thing sticks. Too much junk in here."

"I'll take care of my homework and everything as soon as we get back."

Pom tugged at the next drawer, which came open at the second try. "There's that little bugger. Who put it in there? Just don't be late for supper or we'll both be sleeping in the car."

As they scraped through the front gate and passed into the shadows of arching oaks, Jim glanced back toward the house.

"I'm not sure that constituted permission. Your father was kind of preoccupied."

Rex quickened his step. "Yeah, but he was there at least. I guess Amelia wasn't buying what you had to say about not having to work."

"People can be so resistant to what's good for them. She doesn't understand that under socialism she won't have to come in through the back door."

Rex stooped down to pick up something shiny in the dirt, only a bottle cap. With a sidearm throw he hurled it over a wire fence. "What's wrong with the back door? I go in that way all the time."

They walked to University Avenue, past the new Florida Theater and the Presbyterian Church and west, where simple, solid old houses sat among tall straight pines. At the train tracks they turned south, following the rails through the brush and scrub of the Porter's Quarters, behind the strangely popular LaRue warehouse. The right-of-way was cluttered with bottles, bits of old cardboard, and corrugated tin.

Rex left the tracks and poked his foot through the debris.

Jim followed at a respectful distance. "Did you lose something here?"

"Yeah, kind of." Rex flipped over a tattered piece of tarpaper. "A friend of mine used to live down here."

"Mr. Howard."

"We took him in when he was sick, but as soon as he felt good enough to walk, he left us and came back down here. A man trying to jump the train found him. Dr. Willis said he died from exposure. I thought maybe he left something down here. I've sorted through this stuff a couple of times, looking for—I don't know." He flipped the tarpaper over again and walked back down to the rails. "There's a rumor going around that he left a will with lots of money for somebody. But nobody seems to know for sure. He kept to himself so much. Anyway, I don't care."

"You've had a rough couple of weeks," Jim said.

"The pasture used to be a good place to pick blackberries."

"And it will be again someday. You know, after the good outweighs the bad, places get back their value. The whole state's in a slump right now, but it'll get back on its feet."

"After the revolution, you mean."

"Maybe. But tell me how Mr. Howard came to be living down here."

"He used to own orange groves and timber and a store on the Courthouse Square. He went broke when they put the university here instead of in Lake City. For a long time he and my granddad were enemies. But when he was dying, we took him in. That was after my granddad disappeared."

"What if he'd had a comfortable place to live? Not fancy, but secure, safe from dying in a cardboard lean-to at the edge of the tracks. Would that be worth a change of thinking?"

"Well, I think Mr. Howard had his own ideas about comfort. He seemed to be happy down here, almost like it was his purpose."

Jim walked the ties while Rex teetered along on the rails. "For reasons of their own, some men prefer the simple life, but somebody has to speak up for the people working under the thumb of the company store, for the sharecroppers and a lot of others who don't have a choice and don't have a voice."

Rex was already on to the next thing. "I can't wait to see the radio station. There's this one kid they have in a show called *Brian and Petey*. He gets out of more scrapes. He even flew an airplane one time. 'Speedy as a sprinter, tough as a tackle.' That's what they say at the beginning of every show."

The tracks angled to the southwest and took them across the highway that ran south to the prairie. Someone passing by in a Packard sedan honked the horn and waved as he turned west onto the Archer Road. Seeing that it was Richard Ward, Rex waved back, and then he and Jim cut north along a wooded path up a long slope. The trees gave way to a broad pasture dotted with strolling sandhill cranes. A set of gray ruts between the woods and the pasture brought them to a house that was a two-story hodge-podge of half-timbered Henry the Eighth and work-a-day red brick.

"So this is it." Jim said "Let's go in and see if they're friendly."

Rex couldn't stop staring at the photographs on the walls of the cramped lobby. It was as if he had come to some kind of pantheon of all the people he had heard on the radio. Radiant in glossy black-and-white was the agriculture reporter. Next to his picture was the dignified face of the evening organist, Claude Murphree. Then there was a beaming bandleader posing in front of his dapper ensemble, the Floridians. From a gold frame, the Story Time Lady looked at him with a coy smile, as if challenging him to guess her real name. In a group photo, the members of the Philharmonic Society awaited the downbeat as their conductor stood with raised baton. There was the good-time grin of Tommy Berardo, captioned "the tenor with tipple," the regal baritone G.O. Hack, and, in glamorous soft focus, Mrs. Elizabeth Watts Tyler, soprano.

In the past few months all of them had become both celebrities and household guests to Rex. He could scarcely believe that they inhabited the same town as that marauding roughneck Ollie Holiday, breathed the same air as the irksome Rachel and her moon-faced sidekick Roberta, shopped in the same stores frequented by the gossipy Mrs. Ward, and walked the same streets as the deranged wanderer, Crazy Joan Leary.

A skinny college boy plucking at his bow tie came into the lobby, asked them their business, and introduced himself as Skip. He went to ask the manager for permission to show the visitors around the station and, through a double-paned window, Jim and Rex could see him talking to a middle-aged man with a pencil mustache and a desperate comb-over. The man put away a pocket watch, threw out his hands in exasperation, and left the room.

"Well, okay," Skip said as he came back into the lobby. "Mr. Bennett says I can give you a quick look before the five-thirty talent shows up. Then you'll have to skidoo." He pointed to a dark rectangle over the door. "Once that sign lights up, we're on the air."

On their way to the studio they brushed past a short, bald, fortyish man lighting a cigar.

Turning around and walking backward, Skip said "Hello, Johnny. Didn't expect to see you today."

"Just came to get my pay envelope," the man said in a high boyish voice. "The ex has been giving me hell about the alimony." The cigar fell from his fingers and he stooped down to snatch it off the floor. "Damn. See you next week."

Looking back as he walked, Rex tripped over his own feet. "I *know* that guy."

"Everybody knows him," Skip said. "Or his voice anyway. That's Rupert St. John. He plays all kinds of characters in our shows. He does Petey and—"

Rex continued to stare, even after St. John had left the building. "*That's* Petey?"

"Sure. He also plays the grandfather and the pirate captain and—"

"He's a *grownup*."

"Gone through two wives. Great guy though. Let's go. We've only got a couple minutes till air time."

"There's *no* Petey." Rex tumbled into the studio when Skip pushed the door open.

As they stepped over a tangle of thick black cords and squares marked off with dark brown packing tape, Rex was so careful getting around the grand piano and a table full of musical instruments that he bumped into one of several microphones that jutted up like cornstalks.

Skip steadied the precious device and glanced back to make sure that the station manager hadn't seen.

Jim began explaining again how the sounds from the room went through the microphones, turned into electrical impulses, traveled by wire to the transmitter, to the antenna tower, and then out into the air in waves that traveled with specified properties.

Skip was so impressed that he forgot all about the tour. "How do you know all that?" he asked, absentmindedly smoothing his bow tie.

"I was in the Navy," Jim said. "Now, as to your question about keeping the signals clear of each other. Each wave has a specific amplitude and—"

A gangly man in a string tie ambled into the lobby. Mr. Bennett rushed forward and snagged him by the elbow.

"This isn't Vaudeville," he said as he all but pushed the arrival into the studio. "This is radio. And punctuality is of the essence. We're on the air in one minute and ten seconds."

Skip seemed more relaxed now that the talent had arrived. "This guy's great," he told Jim. "We saw him over at the Lyric Theater last Friday. Boy, can he sing up a storm. Had the audience eating out of his hand. And wait till you hear him yodel. He cracks great jokes too. Said that when the stores started selling his songs, they had *record-breaking* crowds."

Before anyone could leave the studio, the On Air sign lit up. Mr. Bennett stepped up to the microphone and, in a voice an octave lower than his own, signed on, concluding, "And now, fresh from Gainesville's own Lyric Theater, this is Caleb Callahan, the Yodeling Gypsy."

"He doesn't look like a gypsy to me," Rex whispered.

"Doesn't have to," Jim whispered back. "It's radio. Everybody out there is *imagining* a gypsy."

Grinning and scratching his head with bony fingers, the Yodeling Gypsy approached the microphone, took a harmonica from his back pocket, and opened his mouth.

Nothing came out.

Mr. Bennett took a step toward the microphone and made an encouraging gesture.

Skip leaned forward, thinking perhaps, that the gypsy was beginning on a very soft note.

The gypsy wiped his mouth with his sleeve and swallowed. His bony fingers tugged at the knot in his string tie.

With fluttering hands, Mr. Bennett encouraged him again.

The gypsy stared at the microphone.

"Hell," he drawled. "I ain't singing into that thing." He backed away and turned toward the egress. The On Air sign winked out.

Horrified by the profanity but hell-bent that the show would go on, Skip took the Yodeling Gypsy by the shoulders and tried to spin him back toward the microphone, prompting the panicky star to swing a bony fist that clipped him on the chin. Skip lowered his head and butted him so hard that they both went over and, in an instant, they were down among the cords, grabbing and kicking at each other in a strange horizontal dance that knocked a ukulele off the table with a hollow *twang*.

Jim swept it out of harm's way and plucked at it to be sure it wasn't broken. He adjusted a tuning peg, set it back on the table, and tugged Rex toward the door. "Let's get out of here before that light goes back on."

Mr. Bennett caught him by the shoulder of his leather vest and spoke into his ear in a humid undertone. "Can you play that thing, mister? If so, play it now and play it loud. But *play!*"

Jim wasn't sure what he meant.

Mr. Bennett swung him around and maneuvered him up to the microphone. "Just—anything to get us to six o'clock."

The On Air sign lit up again. Jim stared at the microphone.

Mr. Bennett seemed frozen at his side. Behind them, the Yodeling Gypsy had risen to one knee and had Skip by the ear. Rex looked back into the adjoining control room. The engineer shrugged, put on a headset, and pointed through the window at Jim, who looked around the studio, licked his lips, and addressed the microphone.

"Ladies and gentlemen," he said, "there is a force at work in America and change is in the air."

Rex felt the color drain from his face. He had gotten into trouble over those words before, and now the whole town was going to hear about the capitalists exploiting the working class.

"Ladies and gentlemen..." Jim became aware of the nervous boy beside him and hesitated. "There is—there is a force at work in America. It's—it's called *radio* and we're going to put it to work for you tonight." Then, as if noticing the ukulele for the first time, he raised it to the microphone, stroked the strings, struck up a lilting melody, and sang in a surprisingly high tenor voice. He played a song called *All Around the Water Tank* that Rex had never heard, giving the ends of the lines a little lift that raised the tips of Mr. Bennett's pencil mustache. At the end of the song, the Yodeling Gypsy jerked free of Skip and stumbled toward the exit with a lurid malediction that the audience of three covered up with lusty applause.

Jim held the ukulele by the neck at an arm's length as if it might bite. He looked over at Mr. Bennett and the battered Skip, who were nodding and gesturing with enthusiasm.

He stared at the microphone for a moment and then began playing again. *Drill Ye Tarriers, Drill.* It was a forceful song and, before he was finished, the strings lost most of their tone and took on a rough, grating sound. Without turning around again, he re-tuned and went into another song, something more soft and lyrical. He played work songs about railroad men and cowboys and miners and steelworkers. It was as if the microphone had tapped some vein in him, and the music flowed rich and strange until Mr. Bennett came in and announced in a breathless baritone, "Ladies and gentlemen, you've been listening to—to the Shirtsleeve Troubadour, a new program on this radio station. We hope you'll join us Thursday evening at 5:30 for more of his fine songs."

The On Air light went off and organ music started pouring from a speaker on the wall.

"The ukulele really is not my instrument," Jim said. "I kind of favor the guitar."

Mr. Bennett took him by the shoulders. "Mister, I'll pay you fifteen dollars a week for two shows a week through the end of the year. What do you say to that?"

Jim laid the ukulele on the instrument table. "I'm going to be moving on in a few days."

Mr. Bennett locked him in a moist handshake. "Well mister, think again! Bring in that guitar and be back here Thursday at 5:15. Like you said, radio is a powerful force—and the Shirtsleeve Troubadour can't disappoint the people."

CHAPTER 7

n hour earlier, as Richard had turned his Packard onto
Archer Road and waved at the man and boy walking the
railroad track, he wondered why Rex was out alone with
the suspicious northerner, but his thoughts quickly went back to
money and the boat in Cedar Key.

He was passing Lake Kanapaha, making good time on new
grading, when a tire went flat.

Swearing under his breath, he guided the Packard to the
shoulder and got out, eager to get at the patch kit so that he
could be on his way to Cedar Key again. He was pulling off the
spare when he saw the other car shining through the pines.

Hell, he said to himself, *some help would make this go faster.*

He propped the spare against the bumper and walked the
edge of the road to the turnoff.

*Damn fine machine. Somebody's done very well. Maybe they've got
some money to invest.*

He'd never seen anything quite like it, a big eight-cylinder Graham-Paige Phaeton with a black roof and fenders and a body painted oxblood.

The turnoff was hardly more than a track through the palmettos and, with nobody in sight, he was hard-pressed to figure out what such a gem was doing out there in the woods at the edge of a swamp. He ventured toward the abandoned car with a mix of curiosity and suspicion.

Suspicion. That was the last thing he remembered.

He came to on his back with something pressing on his chest and a sharp pain in his ribs. When the dizziness wore off, he realized that the collector was sitting on him. Today he was wearing a houndstooth coat, a doughboy hat, and glasses. Alligator shoes. Richard could smell the leather. The feet were small to be carrying such a load. The man was riding Richard sidesaddle, knees spread, poking him with that gun, some kind of automatic. Richard couldn't get a good look at it.

"Where you been, Richard? You're late with your September payment." The accent was Cracker. The words pulled like taffy.

A swallow flitted through the trees with a shrill *cheet-cheet*.

"I said, where you been, Richard? I waited for you last night."

The man was amazingly quiet and light on his feet for somebody with his build, barrel chest and stubby legs. Half of him face. And heavy. Richard coughed under the weight. "Damn. I never heard you coming."

"You didn't think that flat tire was by chance, did you? I wasted a lot of time at Porter's Place waiting for you."

In a voice forced and shallow Richard said, "I'm getting paid tonight. Just give me another day. Money's tight."

The gun probed his ear now, tickled like a fly. "Not my problem, Richard. My problem is when you don't pay and I'm supposed to get the next installment out of you or prove that you're dead. You know, fingers, ears, that kind of thing. What part should I take tonight?"

"I suppose a death certificate would be too formal."

The collector waved the gun in the general direction of the woods. "I'm getting tired of coming up here. The roads are lousy. Next time we do this, you know what'll be different? No, that's okay. I'll talk for both of us. The next time we'll be just like this, you and me, except that you'll be under that much water. Just that much." He got up and dusted the seat of his pants. "I'm giving you till tomorrow night at eight to come up with the next payment, Richard, the eight hundred. If you're a minute late, one minute late, I'll find you and I'll start cutting your acquaintance."

When the collector was well out of sight, Richard brushed himself off, changed the tire, and drove—the only way he seemed able to think. He had spent the eight hundred from his mother on the new boat engine. And the only way to pay the collector the other forty-two hundred was to keep that boat ahead of the Coast Guard and whoever else was out there. But the engine wasn't giving him the eighteen knots he needed. Coast Guard boats could do sixteen or seventeen and so could some of the more predatory people in the Gulf. Anything less than eighteen and somebody was going to catch up to him. When they did, going to prison would be the least of his worries.

He got a new spare in town and was on his way to Cedar Key again when he caught sight of a flatbed truck going into his father's woods. Four years back, J.J. Ward had subdivided the sandy acreage of oaks and pines and called it Palm Terrace. For four years Palm Terrace had been nothing but woods and a sinkhole pond, but now Richard saw a road roughed out in stakes and string. He turned off, bouncing over the old hunting track, and parked at the pond. To his surprise, the stakes went all the way around the sinkhole and on into the woods. Walking the path, he noticed that other vehicles had come through recently, breaking down the brush and scrub. He followed the trail another hundred and fifty yards and came to the flatbed truck and a pickup. Several men were tramping through the woods above the swamp where Hogtown Creek wound its lazy way between wooded hills. Others were packing up, putting saws and axes into a pickup. Barehanded, a Negro was coiling rusty barbed wire cut from the old cattle fence that had joined the oaks at the back edge of the lot.

Richard approached the two coming back from the creek.

"Gentlemen, may I ask what the hell y'all are doing?"

"We're clearing this here lot," one of the men said as he stopped to pull a hatchet out of a stump.

"I guess I can see that," Richard told him. "What I'd like to know is why and on whose authority."

One of the white men tramping through the leaves came over and sized him up. He was heavyset and sweaty and carried a pine stick like a weapon. "You the son, ain't you?"

"My daddy owns this property, yeah."

"Then it's your daddy sent us out here. Didn't he tell you he's building a house on this lot?"

Richard pushed back his hat. "A house? That's the craziest damn thing I ever heard. Y'all must be in the wrong place."

The man tossed away the stick and took off his cap long enough to wipe his brows with a brawny forearm. He pulled a paper from his back pocket, unfolded it, and pointed with a dirty forefinger. "You see that there? That's the creek. This here's the hill you're standing on. If you keep on standing here, the house is going to go up right on top of you. Fifty-two feet on a side, two stories high. Clapboard. None of that —"

Just then another flatbed truck rumbled through the trees, trailing smoke. J.J. was behind the wheel. He leaned out the driver's window and spoke over the throbbing of the engine.

"Better get out of the way. I'm going to park this over there at the back of the house."

The man with the blueprint folded it up and started yelling something at one of the workers. Richard backed away and looked up at his father. "What gives? The man says they're building a house."

"Cappy Kincaid wants a home for his son. So we're going to put one up and sell it to him."

"Kincaid's building a house for Spencer—on Palm Terrace?"

"I didn't say that. He likes the location, and if he likes what we put up, he'll buy it."

"So it's a spec house?"

"Call it whatever you want. It's the best thing we've got going. There's plenty of cheap labor around these days. It'll go up fast."

"This is kind of a surprise. Just a week ago we waited at the pond most of a morning for buyers from Atlanta who never showed up. If we can't sell lots, how are we going to sell a house, let alone a whole street of 'em?"

"We're going to give 'em something to look at. Once we get the house up and the road in, they'll be able to see how the whole street's going to take shape. Once Kincaid buys, we'll get people talking about it and advertise the lots in some of the northern newspapers. There may not be any money left down here, but they've still got it up there."

"What are the flatbeds for?"

"The palm trees."

"The palm trees?"

"It's going to be Palm Terrace, remember? We're going to put up a tree for every house. Royal palms for the most expensive. Coming all the way from Miami. Cabbage palms for everyone else. That'll get some attention too. Maybe we can get Ainsley Harper out here to write it up for the national press."

"It's kind of risky, isn't it?"

"What isn't? We can grab life by the horns and wrestle it down or let it run over us."

Richard looked down the track. Over the rattle of the truck he could hear the clattering of tools. "Where's the money coming from?"

"Your mother's got eight hundred left in her inheritance. I haven't talked to her about it yet, so don't you mention it, you hear?"

Fifteen minutes later, Richard parked the Packard at the usual place, an old tobacco barn a few miles outside of town, and got into a farm truck stacked with hay. An hour later he pulled up at the long wooden wharf in Cedar Key and walked to a gray boat called the *Sun Dog*. It was hardly more than a twenty-eight-foot shell with a seven-foot beam. He climbed down into the cramped compartment aft and had a good look at the eighty-horsepower car engine that was supposed to get him out of debt, trying all the while to figure out how he could get more than twelve knots out of the thing.

It was the best he'd been able to buy with his mother's eight hundred.

He drove the truck down to a lonely landing on the Waccasassa River and parked it a few yards into the scrub. He walked back up to the road, and within an hour had hitchhiked back into Cedar Key. He walked from a side street to the wharf, set out the fishing tackle on his boat, put on an old touring cap and khaki pants, and bought a bucket of mullet on ice. By the time he was ready to go, he looked and smelled like a fisherman.

The clouds hung low in a darkening sky as he followed his compass beyond the last of the tall wooden channel markers and took a course of 300 degrees. He figured that with any luck he could get past Seahorse Reef to the rendezvous point and back up the road to Baldwin in six hours. He eyed the slate clouds for signs of rain, pushed the throttle up full, and slapped through the chop. He had the water to himself. During the weekend, the sportsmen would come out this far and farther, the eight miles to Seahorse Reef and a mile or two beyond if the sky was clear and the Spanish mackerel were biting. But you could never trust the weather. The sky had been clear at this time last year when the old men, Bob Harper and Nathaniel Larrabee, had ventured out for mackerel, and they hadn't been seen since. A hurricane had whipped up right in their faces.

He pressed on, listening to the steady gurgling of the engine. He had been around boats all of his life, fishing with his father in flat-bottomed hulls among the mangrove islands outside Cedar Key, scaring up trout from Shell Mound to Crystal River. But hooking trout wouldn't get you arrested and nobody got killed over a boatload of fish.

As the western sky dimmed and the swells built and pitched, Richard began to think about the size of the Gulf and the likelihood of finding the whiskey boat without landmarks. In four months he hadn't failed yet, but this was the first time he had tried it alone.

He followed his compass at full throttle. A northeast wind came up in that forlorn spot beyond the reef, and he kept the boat turning in a rectangle that he estimated to be the size of a football field, taking comfort as he thought of himself back in college, laying odds on a head-busting game at Fleming Field. As the wind rose and the swells grew under the disappearing sky, he began to doubt his chances of getting back to shore alive, let alone with his cargo. But just as he was thinking that even the whiskey boat wouldn't venture out in such slop, he saw the light. It approached from the southwest, small at first, and then growing into a steady white glow with multiple bright points appearing as it turned. He thought of going toward it, but decided to sit tight, not to give them an inch. Let them come to him.

He wasn't expecting something so big. What he saw this time was a small freighter, and it was moving with good speed.

Although it seemed absurd with just the two boats in an unbroken sea, Richard waved his flashlight in a broad arc. The freighter slowed and pulled up beside the *Sun Dog*. Without anyone exchanging a word, Richard held up half a dollar bill. Bracing himself with his foot in a scupper, a dark-bearded man on the freighter held up the other half and they tied the two vessels together, riding with a lopsided roll.

The man jumped onto the deck next to him and began jerking down what was lowered over the side.

He talked the way he moved, fast and punchy. "You're wasting our time working single like this." He sounded like a Yankee, a New Yorker maybe.

Richard wasn't about to take a scolding. He grabbed a gunnysack from him "My man went jumping between boats the same way you just did, and now he's down in Pinellas County with a peg leg and a tin cup."

That shut him up. But in the rough water it took the two of them the better part of an hour to load the seventy-five sacks into the hold.

Richard cast off the lines, turned toward the east, and pushed the boat to full throttle, all of ten knots, he figured.

He held tight to his compass for what seemed more like two nights than one. Although the Gulf was getting rougher, the clouds held steady, so he felt confident about reaching the coast, but he wasn't so optimistic about his navigational skills bringing him back to the Waccasassa, and he dreaded the thought of running out of darkness and being stuck after sunrise with a slow, overloaded boat full of incrimination. If the Coast Guard caught sight of him, he wouldn't have time to dump the bottles. His only chance would be to abandon ship, and then he'd be out close to ten thousand dollars worth of merchandise, risking his neck in uncertain water, with the collector waiting to kill him for not making his payments.

He set his thoughts on the eight hundred and twenty-five he'd make if he got the load all the way to Baldwin.

The seas continued to build and the swells took on edges that shattered against the boat and threw out a cold spray. Richard kept under the overhang of the cockpit as much as he could and still the water caught him. He stuck to his heading with the thought that his life might depend on it and pointed the bow into the waves as best he could to avoid getting broadsided by the powerful surges that built behind him. The comforting rasp of the engine was almost lost now in the sound of the sea, and he began to think about a thousand things that might happen if the pistons stopped.

The *Sun Dog* took a beating. The water swept across the open stern, swirled over his feet, and circled back out. The bottles, wrapped in straw and stuffed in gunnysacks, slid and clanked until the sweet smell of whiskey mingled with a mash of gasoline and engine smoke and seawater. The timbers creaked and popped and a cold rain beat down on man and boat, but Richard stood at the wheel with his chin set against the chaos, watching through the streaked glass for the first sign of land.

He felt it before he saw it, the bar invisible in the wash of the half tide. The flat bottom of the boat scraped from bow to stern and then shuddered free, and he knew that he would survive the surge to shore. The rain let up and the wind dropped and he ran a flashlight from island to inlet until he found the familiar features of the bay. With fingers cramping on the wheel, he felt his way into the mouth of the river.

He swung the light freely now, more certain of the channel. The eddies and dead ends fell away as the main channel presented itself, and he worked the turns without error, one by one, until the water opened up, revealing the black line of the dock.

It took him two nerve-wracking tries to tie off and, as it was, the planks took a bite of the bow before he had the heaving boat under control. He wasn't going to do this solo again, he told himself.

The work ashore was slow and tiring, and he seemed still to be aboard the boat, his blood rolling from side to side with the shifting sea. Soaked to the skin, he hauled the load, bag by bag, stashing the whiskey under the hay in the truck until the cargo was hidden and secure. When he got onto the seat, he took a deep breath. Then he pulled onto the muddy track and eased his way up to the graded road.

He drove without stopping, through one sleeping town after another, peering though the darkness at every approaching light until he arrived at the railroad siding in Baldwin.

At the squeaking of the brakes, two shadows tumbled out of a red Duesenberg and hurried toward him. In front, a gaunt man in a camel's hair topcoat carried a flashlight. The coat was open and showed a salmon pink silk tie and a three-piece serge suit. The other was a bear by comparison, muscle gone to gut under a pilly gray sweater and a shapeless brown sport coat.

The clotheshorse rapped the flashlight on the shoulder of his companion. "Train won't wait forever, Archie. Hop to it."

The big man moved away to avoid a second prodding. "Take it easy, Ralph. I'm a lot faster than you think."

Richard set the brake and lit a cigarette. He was trying to figure out where he'd seen the big man a year, two years ago. He got out of the car.

"It's blowing stink out there, Ralph. You ought to pay me double for this load."

The clotheshorse tapped the flashlight in the palm of his hand and smiled. "Except that you damn near missed the train. So let's call it a wash." The light played across a jagged scar that ran from the man's jaw to his eye socket.

Richard slammed the car door, loud enough to make the man glance around to see if anyone had heard. "Okay then. Seventy-five cases. That's eight hundred and twenty-five dollars."

As Ralph came closer, the scar went pale. His breath smelled of peppermint schnapps. "The sooner you unload, the sooner you get it. You're staring again."

"Just impressed. Somebody must've really landed one on you."

The man ran a finger the length of the mark and twisted the corner of his mouth into a smile. "Belgium. Hand-to-hand. I did the other guy with a sledgehammer. Train won't wait. Hop to it now, Richard."

As Richard moved the truck closer to a Seaboard Airline box-car, he saw Ralph walk down the railroad tracks and stoop down beside a small dark form. He swept back his camel's hair coat and poked at the thing with his toe, then flipped it up so that for a moment the profile of a cat showed clear, standing on stiff legs, its back arched, and its tail frozen straight. He let the carcass fall and nudged it onto the glinting rail.

By the time the cargo was packed into the boxcar, it was well hidden in a load of two-by-fours. Ralph climbed back into the Duesenberg, pulled out a flask, and took a quick drink. The big man reached into his coat and pulled out a roll of bills. He peeled off sixteen fifties and pressed them into Richard's palm.

Richard pocketed the money and brought his hand back out. "Where's the other twenty-five?"

"Take it easy." Archie took more bills from someplace inside his coat and handed them to Richard. "Spend it on a faster boat and some help. When you're late, Ralph gets edgy and you don't want that. He told you, didn't he, that in the war he killed a guy with his bare hands."

"Wasn't that the deal? To kill Germans?"

With the flick of a finger, the big man flipped Richard's hat off kilter. "Who said it was a German?"

(HAPTER 8

After a few hours of shallow sleep, Richard woke up to the sound of his father banging on his bedroom door. He gazed at the tan plaster walls still covered with childhood pictures of racecars and football players, looked at the balsa wood biplanes dangling from the ceiling, and took comfort in his refuge. At a hard rap, he jumped out of bed and was stuffing himself into a pair of wrinkled trousers when his father came in.

"What's this about your mother writing you a check?" A streak of sunlight pierced the curtains and crossed his father's face.

Richard rubbed his unruly hair and smiled at the awkwardness of his situation. "Mama never could keep a secret, could she? To tell you the truth, we were going to surprise you."

"Well, you damn sure did that. Where's the money, Richard?"

"Like I told Mama, I only needed it for a few days, until this deal in Miami came through."

"The bottom falls out of the real estate market, but you still have your deals. And they're always in some far-flung place, aren't they? Is there a reason you never have any deals around here?"

"Hey, wherever I can find 'em." Richard pulled on a shirt, one of the new ones with the collar attached, and began buttoning it.

"Where's the money? Without it Palm Terrace dies today. All those men have been working on faith and promises and this is payday."

"I tell you, that deal in Miami got a little complicated."

"They always do, don't they? Without that money we're in real trouble. You knew that, but you went on throwing our money into the clouds."

"Well, you know, some of 'em *do* have silver linings."

"Don't bait me, boy. Either you've got the money or you don't. Now which is it?"

"Which do you think it is?"

As J.J. came forward, a second streak of light crossed his face. "God damn it, Richard. Where's your spine? The man out there cleaning the street's making more money than you are. At least he brings home a few dollars a week, every week. What do you have to show for all your deals in Miami? Noth—"

Richard reached into his hip pocket and pulled out the wad of fifties. He fanned them until all sixteen showed.

His father coughed at the sight of them. "I apologize. I misjudged you."

"Take it. It's yours and Mama's. Like I told her, I was just borrowing it for a few days. I imagine there'll be more in a couple of weeks. I guess Miami's not washed up yet. Of course, I've got some irons in the fire up in Georgia too. I'm not Nelda Ward's grandson for nothing."

J.J. smoothed the bills and held them tight. "I'd say you got your grandmother's knack for wheeling and dealing, all right. And if Palm Terrace pans out, we can all be proud of it. I believe we'll get through the rough patches just fine."

As his father left the room Richard said, "Sure we will."

Then he put his mind to coming up with another eight hundred dollars for the collector by eight o'clock that night.

He got cleaned up, went into the kitchen, kissed his mother, and had something to eat. With a backward glance, he got into the Packard and drove to a hill tucked away in the woods north of Palm Terrace. The curving driveway lined with border grass and azaleas opened into a broad lawn shaded by towering pines and live oaks that parted to reveal a full-blown Italian villa. Kincaid's Castle was what Buddy Cole called it. Its stucco walls and tile roof overlooked a sleepy stretch of Hogtown Creek that flowed through a deep swamp. Richard walked to the back of the house and strode into the big bright tile kitchen.

A thin black man in a white double-breasted chef's jacket and popover hat looked up from the roast beef he was slicing.

"You come to help, Richard? Chop some of this here lettuce."

"I'm not cutting any lettuce and neither should you, Cleveland. It turns brown on the edges."

"You know that and I know that, but Mr. Kincaid doesn't care. That's the way he likes it, so that's the way he gets it."

"I'll straighten him out. He's just the guy I'm here to see."

Cleveland balanced the knife on his pink palm. The beef was rare in the middle, downright bloody. "And whom shall I say I'm throwing out?"

"Am I not invited to the shindig?"

"Looks like he passed over you again. Want me to sneak something out the back door to you?"

"Thanks just the same, but last time I looked I was still white."

"He's in the pool. But I wouldn't go in there—and I never saw you."

Richard headed for an arched hallway. He turned and backed his way in. "You come back to work for us when the slump is over."

Cleveland smiled as he sawed off another slice. "Yes sir. Soon as Palm Terrace is sold out and the Dixie Hotel is finished, I'll be at your back door. But, hey, first you re-hire Amelia. She didn't take that silver. She's an honest woman."

Richard paused in the high doorway. "Sure she is. It was all a mistake. No doubt about it."

The tile and stucco corridor echoed with the sound of splashing, and the light from the water danced across the walls as Richard approached a bulky, balding man in a striped trunk suit whose labored breaststroke was thrusting him toward the shallow end of the pool. Not until the swimmer turned to begin a new lap did he see his visitor. He stopped short and made for the far side of the pool with a hand clapped to his head.

Richard stood with his weight on one foot and his hands in his pockets. "I think you look great without it, Mr. Kincaid."

The swimmer's hand came down to the side of the pool. The lapping water resonated through the roofed courtyard.

"How did you get in? Didn't your parents teach you any manners?"

"I came over to set up an appointment and somehow I wound up in here. It's such a big house it's easy to get turned around."

"Well then you can just turn around and beat it."

"I know you're expecting company. But I've come with a favor in mind."

Kincaid pressed the water from his pennant mustache, a remnant of bygone style. "Well, I'm not in a mood to do you any favors. Ask me sometime when I've got my damn clothes on."

Somewhere toward the deep end, a frog let out a shrill chirp that reverberated beneath the pale vaulted ceiling.

"Actually, it's a favor *for* you. A flick of the pen and you double your money."

Kincaid pinched off the water dripping from his nose. "Don't waste my time."

"Eight hundred today brings you sixteen a week from today. Can't find many deals like that anymore."

"What is this? Land in Miami? Fort Lauderdale?? Hollywood? Forget it. Those days are over."

Richard turned his palms up. "I got out when the getting was good. Now I'm ready to put my money into something more solid."

"Like Palm Terrace."

"No, that's Daddy's baby. This is interstate commerce."

"Well, I don't have any money for that, whatever it is."

"All I'm asking for is eight hundred and one week."

"Look, I appreciate what you did for Spencer, but I'm not giving you any eight hundred today."

"Some would call it perjury, Mr. Kincaid. Some would say it made the difference between getting him off and putting him away. Truth is, I came into the yard just a second too late to see who pulled a gun first that night, but since the other guy was dead, I gave Spencer the benefit of the doubt."

With a watery sweep of his hand, Kincaid ejected a drowned cricket from the pool. "All right, Richard. Here's the deal. I'm throwing a party on New Year's Eve. New Year's Eve. You come and show me you've got *five thousand*—not eight hundred, but five thousand—to invest in this thing, whatever it is, and I'll match it. How's that? Carte blanche." He waved his hand as if to ward off a fly. "I didn't get where I am throwing money into every wildcat scheme that came along, but you show me you've got something to work with and I'll match it. That's liberal. That's the best I can do for you."

Richard stepped to the edge of the pool. "I need the eight hundred a lot sooner if this deal's going to work. I need it today."

Cappy Kincaid's reply was all but lost in the wash of sound. "Talk to me on the thirty-first of December."

Turning his back, he launched into a sidestroke that thrust him toward the deep end of the pool as the frog resumed its overblown song.

(H Я P T E R 9

Ten minutes later, Richard was back in town, rapping on the screen door of a sagging bungalow that had been at the forefront of fashion fifty years ago. During his twenty-four years, the house had remained unaltered by vogue and convenience. The small sunken yard was always mowed short, and the dark green border grass had always lined the bunchy three-by-three pattern of the brick walk. The rocking chair and an assortment of porch furniture were forever in their familiar configuration, except in the worst storms. The whitewashed stucco walls retained the same stress cracks at the bottom corners of the windows. So far as he could remember, the black-framed screen door had always hung just a little crooked in front of the rusty crank of the bell. Like Nelda Larson Ward, the bungalow was worn, but rock steady.

Putting her weight on her two canes, she came to the door and ushered him into the stuffy living room, from which he could see through the cramped kitchen to a stone terrace at the edge of the shallow, hedged backyard. It was the perfect house for Nelda now that her arthritis kept her from climbing stairs

He tipped his hat. "Hey, Gramma. I was wondering if you'd like to go to the cotillion with me tonight."

She made a little *clip-clop* with the canes and adjusted her shawl. "Richard, you get fresher every day. Come on in and sit down, boy."

Before he could get to her to help, she plopped down on a pale green horsehair sofa half covered by a sheet. She wore a shapeless green cotton dress and fuzzy brown wool stockings turned down short of her knees. The wattles of her throat mocked the chic folds of the cowl at her collar. Her wispy hair, pinned and plastered to her round skull, was as black as it was gray, and her large brown eyes sparkled with wit.

One of the canes began to slip. She let it hit the floor and folded her spotted hands over the stick that remained.

"All right, Richard, give me your pitch. Or am I selling you short?"

He pulled a rush chair a little closer and sat down. "How's that, Gramma?"

Nelda leaned forward and punched out the words as if her grandson were hard of hearing. "I said, have I sold you short or have you indeed come to make some kind of a pitch for cash?"

Richard laughed. "A pitch? Now, come on, I just—"

She waved him off. "Spare me, Richard. I may be old, but I haven't lost my marbles—yet. I haven't made it to almost eighty-nine without picking up a little savvy."

He listened for a moment to the faraway whistle of a train passing through the Porters Quarters. Then he reached forward and took a ball of yarn from the couch. "What's this you're knitting?"

"It's a sweater for Rachel. If my hands quit cramping up long enough, I may have it done by Christmas. Otherwise it may be the Fourth of July. Fat lot of good it'll do her then."

Richard dumped the yarn into his lap and began working the needles.

His grandmother fell back and let out a thin, wheezing laugh.

He was fast and deft. Hand over hand, the points of the needles darted. "You know I'm going to do it right, don't you, Gramma, because I had the best teacher in the world."

Despite its rasp, her laugh had something girlish about it. "That was *years* ago! I'd forgotten all about it. That time you had the influenza. You had some hours to kill."

"And the hands don't forget. Isn't that what you told me? Once you get the moves and the rhythm in your hands, they remember? 'Course, I've been known to sneak in a little knitting every now and then just to keep sharp. It drives Mother crazy. She can't for the life of her figure out how she keeps jumping ahead on things." He put up a finger. "Now don't you tell her! I can keep the joke going for a hundred years."

Nelda was laughing so hard that she had to reach into her dress somewhere for a handkerchief to touch to the corners of her eyes.

"You are one awful boy! Where did you come from? Neither of your parents is like that. I haven't seen your daddy so much as crack a smile for thirty years."

Richard worked the needles a little faster, with small, precise strokes. "Okay, now, Gramma, here's the pitch."

She wiped away a tear. "Oh, sure. There's no getting around that, is there?"

The knitting needles clicked faster. "You know, it takes a little money to make money."

"Where have I heard *that* before? Why don't you just tell me how much you want?"

He set the knitting aside and pulled his chair closer. "Gramma, give me a thousand today and I'll give you twice that by New Year's Eve."

She let out a pained laugh and waved her hand as if clearing a cobweb. "Oh, Richard, my dear Richard! You and I are talking different languages! You've come a long way from getting a penny a stroke for churning butter. You know that I gave most of my big money to the university for the endowment." She waved toward the back door, to the west. "That's where your thousand dollars is—in bricks and mortar, either a pharmacy school or a gymnasium. I don't recall exactly what they did with it. Now, whatever I give you, I hope you'll do something sensible with it. Your father would like to see you settle down and do something solid."

He put his fingertips together. "You mean like Palm Terrace and the Dixie Hotel?"

She leaned forward, clasping her hands over her lumpy knees. "First of all you should know that your father has always been cautious, and while he may have missed out on an opportunity or two because of it, he's done about as well as anybody could have, given the circumstances." Her dentures clattered as she went on. "Nobody knew that land would go bust like that. They all made the same mistake, and I wouldn't be surprised if the whole country's in for it. And unlike a lot of them, your daddy isn't in it out of greed. All he wants to do is make a living. That's one thing he got from your grandfather and me. We did very well, but we came along at the right time. We worked hard and we made a living—a good one. Never broke the law. Never put one over on anybody. We just bought and sold." She settled back and took a rattling breath. "Now I'm going to lecture you, Richard. There's an old-fashioned word that people used in my day." She picked up a yellowed photograph in a gilt frame. The light from it caught Richard in the face before he recognized the image of his grandfather as a young man, dressed in Confederate finery, scowling behind crossed pistols. "We used it and we lived by it and your grandfather put his life on the line for it. Do you know what word I mean?"

"Gramma, I just enjoy listening to you."

"Well, now, he may have ridden for the wrong cause from the way history looks at it, but you know he and his fellows came charging down the street out there even though the Yankees way outnumbered them because they took it as a matter of *honor*. There's your word, Richard. Honor. Men used to kill each other over it. You'd have to go a long way to find a man who would do that today. The word honor has been replaced by another word and you know what that word is, Richard—*money*."

He shrugged. "I'm just trying to make a living too. Can't do that without money."

She had started to lean back and now she came forward again. "Richard, there are things people do for money and things people *don't* do for money. And then, putting honor aside, there are things that get you money—until you get thrown into the penitentiary, or killed."

He patted her cold, knotty hand. "Now, it ain't as bad as what you hear. All you need is a fast boat and a little sense of timing. And what I'm doing—what a lot of guys are doing—is what was perfectly honorable in most of the country till ten years ago. There's no difference. A drink in 1919 isn't any different from a drink tonight. It's the same stuff, isn't it? I don't deal in *moonshine*. That's what's killing people. The stuff I move is fit for kings and presidents."

"Richard, you know this foolishness is going to end before long. There are too many people getting killed over it—and for nothing. They're going to roll it back because it's foolish. Would you want to be the last man killed before the end of Prohibition? And would that be any way for your parents to find out what you've been up to? Your mother would die of grief and shame."

He stood up and looked at her with a lopsided smile. "Well, every day is a new day. Who knows? Maybe I'll quit tomorrow."

"And maybe the dog will have kittens, Richard." She crossed one brown wool foot over the other. "Now be a dear and get me the Florida atlas, will you?"

He looked around and saw it on a corner table. The heavy worn leather volume was pressing roses. He brought it to her and set it down on the sheet beside her.

She ran her finger over the gold lettering. "Eighteen-eighty. That was a lovely year. The hat business was really starting to take off. Anna Newhouse won a horse in a foot race against a million boys."

"It's a fine old book."

She opened it carefully, as if the binding would fall apart. Great oak leaves lay pressed between its vast pages. Here and there flashed the peach and gray of Confederate bills, twenties, fifties—all of the same value now. Then she came to some real money, oversized greenbacks. She counted out a sheaf and handed it to him.

Richard folded it once and stuffed it into his hip pocket. "It's a start. It'll spend. Thanks."

A smile crossed the creases of the old woman's face. "Fine and fast. I imagine it'll spend fine and fast. Come back sometime for a social visit."

He bent down and kissed her on the cheek. "Well, maybe you'd like to go for a boat ride sometime."

"Thanks, but I think you'll go too fast for me, Richard."

"Not so fast. In fact, I'm going to see a man now about putting a little more kick into it."

He found Pom at the paddock on the road to the old Bailey house, down on his haunches, cleaning Lucy's hooves.

"You come looking for some reliable transportation, Richard?"

"As a matter of fact, I have, but not this kind. If you can get down to Cedar Key now, I'd really like to get that extra speed out of my boat."

Pom looked up and the horse tried to pull her hoof away. "Today? Hold on, Lucy."

"I'm supposed to meet a guy tonight at eight. He wants to buy into the boat, make some money fishing. I'd like to be able to tell him that I can get out to the reef and get back before the weather can turn on me. I can sure use that eighteen knots."

Pom put down Lucy's right hind hoof and ran his fingers over her shaggy fetlock. "And you're getting twelve? What kind of boat did you say you have?"

"Twenty-eight foot. Eighty-horse engine."

"Eighty! Then I'd say you ought to be getting more. That's a lot of power for a twenty-eight-foot boat."

"If anyone can get eighteen out of it, it would be you."

Pom moved to the other hind leg and wrestled with Lucy until she relaxed and let him rest her hoof between his knees. "You ought to be able to jump circles in it."

"You thought you'd be able to have a look at it today."

"I know, but it's getting late and Flora damn near skewered me for letting Rex go to the radio station with Jim yesterday. Things are just now starting to get back to normal at home."

Richard squatted down beside him. "Pom, getting that boat up to speed today is worth plenty to me. If you can fix it up, there's cash money in it for both of us."

Their eyes met and then Pom went back to picking the hoof. He smoothed the rim and picked a piece of gravel from the *V* as Richard watched and waited. When he was done, he let go of Lucy's leg, brushed off his lap, and stood up. "Like I said, forget the money. I'll be glad to have a look at it tomorrow. As long as I get back home ahead of the divorce lawyer."

When he got back to the car, Richard counted his grandmother's greenbacks again. Less than half of what he needed by eight o'clock.

Two-thirty. He drove to a genteel neighborhood that spread along both sides of East Main Street where a linear retention basin had been dredged out of the Sweetwater Branch. Among the shaded Queen Anne houses of thirty and forty years ago, a few newer designs had sprouted—elf houses with steep roofs and flagstone walkways, half-timbered Tudor fantasies, and the barn of the White House Hotel chopped in half and turned into a pair of respectable Dutch colonials. Richard parked the Packard at the high red curb in front of a two-story manor house thick with ivy on the near side. He ambled through the live oaks and whistled through his fingers. After a second signal, an upstairs window slid up and a blonde looked down at him between raised forearms.

"The coast is clear. You could've come in the front door."

He leaned against a tree. "Not as much fun. How's your dance card looking tonight?"

She smiled. "Father's in Tallahassee. Won't be back till after eleven."

"Well, isn't that a shame."

She ruffled her blonde hair. "I feel like being happy. Take me to Porter's Place."

"You got a little *too* happy last time, Edith."

The hands came down to the windowsill. "You didn't seem to mind. When do I get another driving lesson?"

He fanned his face with his hat. "Well, you've got the parking mastered."

She shushed him. "You'd better come in."

He sauntered up the curving stone pathway and, with a backward glance at the street, went through the arched portico, took off his skimmer, and let himself in. He ran a fingertip across the leather-bound volumes in the built-in bookcases, studied the angular faces of the oils on the dining room wall, picked up a gold humidor and helped himself to one of the cigars inside. He was so light-footed on the stairs that he startled her when she saw his face in the mirror of her vanity. She swung around on the bench. Her camisole was crooked and she still had a pink lace garter in her hand.

He tossed his hat onto the dresser and stuffed his hands in his hip pockets. "That's a hell of a way to get dressed. Don't most girls fix their face *after* they put their stockings on?"

She gave him a suspicious smile. "How would you know?"

He shrugged. "I do a lot of reading."

"Sure you do." She fastened the garter and pulled on her other stocking. "You know, if father found you up here, he'd shoot you."

"That's what makes it so much fun." He closed the door.

She stood up and looked at him wide-eyed. "What on earth are you doing?"

"Fortifying in case your daddy comes home early. What kind of hardware does he use anyway?"

"What kind of—oh, I don't know. But he keeps it in his bedside table. It's ugly. That's why we're—"

Before she knew it, Richard's warm hands were on her cool bare shoulders. He bent down and kissed her.

"Going in a minute," she said.

"In a few minutes," he told her.

Her blue eyes looked up at him. "So what about it?"

"What about what?"

"Porter's Place?"

"It's no place for a girl like you, on the rebound from a brush with drink."

"I told you, it was my roommate's bottle. I got thrown out for not snitching."

"At Florida State. What about Radcliff?"

"That was for grades."

He put his nose behind her ear, smelled her perfume. "I stand corrected."

"At least I was trying. What about you?"

"I changed my priorities."

"You change them fast, don't you?"

"Don't know what you mean."

"Didn't you tell me you walked out in the middle of class and never came back?"

"Yeah, well, I did all right down in Miami during Christmas break that year. Got off the northbound train and went straight to class, still carrying my suitcase. Sat down and listened for all of five minutes. Put my hat and coat back on and walked out. Wasn't your old man's fault. I always did think chemistry was a bore."

"Don't let father hear you say that."

She had her clothes on now. She motioned toward the door. "So then?"

He went to the window, took a quick look at the street and the yard, and lowered the shade. "There's no place like home."

"Are you kidding? If father ever finds out—"

"About that gun," he said. "I'd like to borrow it tonight."

CHAPTER 10

H e woke up in the dark to the sweep of headlamps and the sound of a car pulling up to the curb. He kissed Edith and tumbled out of her sleepy embrace in time to see Professor Milford Thompson driving down the street in his blue Nash Roadster.

"Oh, damn," she whispered. "He's early. He really will kill you."

Richard patted the Browning .25 semi-automatic in his hip pocket. "Not unless he's got another one of these." He stripped the bed, leaving Edith to cover up with the comforter, whipped the sheets into tight twists, tied them to the bedpost, rappelled out the window, and dropped several feet into a camellia bush. He ducked behind it long enough to tuck in his shirttail and sweep his hair back. He looked up in time to catch his hat.

He was still straightening his tie as he ambled past the professor on his way to the Packard. When he got to the car, he got a glimpse of the professor glancing his way before going into the house.

He took a roundabout route to get home, past the court-house, through the narrow roads of the deserted campus, and into the woods on the far side of Palm Terrace, a devious route indeed, but not devious enough.

Richard saw the collector too late. Tonight he was dressed like a preacher. He was driving a Buick and he was quick to run the Packard off the road. He had the whole outfit on, right down to clerical collar and the black felt hat. By the time Richard thought of pulling the Browning, it was too late. Reaching inside his blazer would get him shot for sure. Next time he would be faster, he told himself.

Next time. That's a joke.

The collector came up to the car from behind and stood at the window.

"This is it, Richard. I guess you know that."

"Well, I guess I just missed you somehow."

"Why don't you come on out of the car?"

The suggestion had the relaxed authority of a doctor in the examining room, a doctor about to launch into a personal and painful procedure.

Richard did as he was told, smoothed his trousers and brushed the sleeves of his blazer as if he were on his way from croquet to the dining room at Kincaid's. The collector motioned him into the woods and followed him through a tangle of palmetto and swamp lilies.

"I've got three-eighty," Richard said, fighting the impulse to reach into his blazer. "I can get another—"

The collector put a gun to the back of his head, reached around, helped himself to the Browning, and tossed it into the swamp. He got the money and put it in his pocket.

Fast hands for a preacher, too fast.

"I knew a man," he said, "also named Richard as it turns out. A young guy. Handsome as all get out. He was making great money down in Miami, you know, selling binders on lots. I mean, not even selling property, just the right to lock in the price of the property so some other guy could buy it and make a killing on it. Quick money."

At a turn in the path Richard stole a look at the gun. It was a .38, so ordinary, just a tool, for God's sake.

"Well, this handsome young guy borrowed a lot of money to buy his binders, was going to double it or something practically overnight, so what did he care if he didn't have any money in the first place? Right?"

Richard tried not to listen, tried to come up with an idea. Now he could feel the .38 in his back.

Just keep him talking, wait for a break. "Look, I'm getting eighteen knots out of the boat now, maybe twenty. I mean, going that fast I can get the rest of the eight hundred by tomorrow. Right?"

Shouldn't have said that. It sounded like mockery. Get yourself killed that way.

"Step lively, Richard. We're not there yet. So about this other Richard. He borrowed a lot of money. And in '26, when the crash came, he couldn't pay his debts. What do you think of that?"

"Forgive us our debts as we forgive our debtors, that what I say."

"I killed him, Richard. I marched him out into the woods and killed him. A polite young guy. Handsome as all get out. But I said that. He pleaded, of course. Who wouldn't if he had all that going for him? He was a newlywed, lived with his wife in the prettiest little cottage you ever saw, with green shutters and a garden just spilling with roses. He and his bride were inseparable. They'd worked on that garden together, but he didn't tend to business, and after all that gardening, he died in some rotten little stand of woods. He wept. He got on his knees and begged me for his life. He just couldn't believe it was ending so soon. He had plans. He'd made assumptions. But he had to pay the price to set the example for others. So in that sense, he was performing a public service, wouldn't you say?"

They had come to the swamp that stretched all the way to the foot of Kincaid's hill.

Stall him. Just stall him until you can think of something.

Richard stopped and turned slowly, hands spread, palms up. "What about the girl? What about the bride?"

The collector shrugged and poked the .38 into Richard's chest.

"Well, didn't I say they were inseparable? Now turn back around and walk over there."

Richard took slow steps toward the stew of brackish water and shapeless catching undergrowth.

"You know, I never will be able to pay you back if you fill me full of holes."

"Keep walking, Richard, or the holes will be a lot bigger and sloppier."

After the first few steps, the muck sucked off his polished brogans. His pressed khakis turned to mud. He slogged forward, not daring to glance back until a clump of sawgrass cut off his view of the man with the .38.

Then he noticed dark forms moving under the water.

The voice that came through the darkness was strangely flat and dull. "I'll be at Porters Place tomorrow night. See to it that you are there with the four-twenty for September's payment. Plus a hundred in interest."

Richard stood waist deep in the dark stink until the mosquitoes found him.

At daybreak he picked up Pom and sped through the construction on Highway 13, sixty miles to the long plank bridge over the tidal flats that ended at the wharf in Cedar Key.

Pom descended into the engine compartment of the *Sun Dog* and came back up smiling. "She's got an eighty all right, a Marmon with double ignition on all six cylinders. You open her up all the way and you'll burn gas like a fart on a match, but you ought to get at least fifteen knots out of her."

An hour later, as they were working their way out the channel, Pom listened to the engine and looked out toward the choppy green water of the open Gulf.

"Doesn't smell much like a fishing boat, does it?"

Richard turned around to be heard. "I like to keep it neat"

"Room for a lot of fish on here. Probably *could* go commercial, you and your partner."

"That's what I said, isn't it?"

"How long have you been in the trade?"

Richard responded as if to the most casual turn in the conversation. "Since spring. I was about to get killed by this guy out of Miami, a bill collector. My last deal down there turned bad right after Coleman du Pont dropped out. That was in '26. The IRS started taxing paper profits and that damn hurricane blew away a thousand squatters. Lots dropped to ten cents on the dollar and I fell behind on my loan payments. Been paying ever since. The collector comes out of the woodwork every now and then to keep me on track, last night included."

"That what happened to the wrist?"

"He's very affectionate. Back in May I was down in Cedar Key just trying to get away for a day when this big guy, Archie, comes up to me on the wharf. I've seen him before somewhere, but I can't for the life of me figure out where. Anyway, he asks me if I'd like to make some quick money."

"Just like that?"

"I was on the wharf, so he figured I had a boat, and I let him think it. I thought he was nuts. I never heard of anyone bringing hooch into Cedar Key. Seems like a roundabout way when you can run it in from Bimini, but who was I to argue? I rented a boat and did what the man said. Delivered the stuff to a guy on the Waccasassa for six hundred. Bought time for the bruises to clear up. I liked that. Scraped up the money to buy this thing and then a couple weeks ago the guy on the Waccasassa didn't show up. I'd heard him say something about running the stuff up to Baldwin, so I sneaked back into Cedar Key and loaded about thirty cases into my car and drove it up there myself. It didn't take me long to find Archie and his pal Ralph up there. I thought, what the hell, it's that much more money. I put some of it into the truck and since then I've been doing the land route, too, for a couple hundred extra, all the way from the reef to the rail yard in Baldwin. I got Theron Purdy to put heavy springs in the car just in case. It gets complicated doing it on my own, but it's hard to find someone I can trust."

"So you ought to be flush by now, Richard."

"Except that I've got to put most of the money back into the boat to keep it fixed up and a lap ahead of everyone else. And the collector's gotten most of what was left. If I drop a load, I get behind in a hurry. Then a couple weeks ago Denny Maggard got his leg squashed between the two boats. Boy was that a mess. I damn near missed the train. If I'm short when the collector cómes around, I'll make myself scarce. I favor Magnesia Springs for safe hiding in a crowd. But tonight I'm going to play straight with him and cash in to the tune of five hundred and twenty bucks—my granddaddy's dueling pistols and the last of his life insurance."

"Well, life insurance," Pom said. "That seems fitting."

When they had put the islands and the last channel marker behind them, Richard shoved the throttle and the *Sun Dog* lurched forward, forcing Pom to grab at the wall of the pilothouse for a handhold.

He righted himself. "Well, she's got fire in her belly all right, but I believe you can get more out of her."

Richard laughed. "Show me what you can do!"

"You've got the wind on your nose. That makes it seem like a damn hurricane. They call it apparent wind. 'Course if you want to let it go at this it's all right with me."

"Whatever you can get out of her, Pom. Lay it on."

"Okay. When I give you the signal, you head the boat straight out that way and come over here and stand where I am now."

"You mean it?"

"Soon as I give you the go-ahead. Just make sure we aren't pointed at anything. I can get another knot or two out of her."

Pom lifted the hatch cover and climbed down into the engine compartment. He poked around for a while and determined that only one set of plugs was firing. Then he started fiddling with the ignition wires. He stuck his head up and yelled back to Richard.

"Okay! One hand on the pilothouse and the other up like this to test the wind!"

Richard stuck a crowbar in the wheel and went to the side of the boat. He steadied himself with one hand and held the other aloft.

Pom chuckled. "You look pretty, standing there like the Statue of Liberty."

Richard looked back, smiling, his black hair whipping about his forehead. "That's me! Free as the wind!"

Pom smiled and nodded, climbed back down into the engine compartment and stuck two ignition wires together.

The *Sun Dog* jolted into the chop, slamming Richard into the rail. He was on his way over the side when jamming his foot into a scupper threw him back into the boat.

His gleeful scream drowned out the wind as the shattered waves sprayed past.

Pom emerged from the engine compartment, greasy faced and grinning. "Got two sets of plugs—may as well use 'em both!"

Richard was looking out to the open sea as the untended wheel rocked slowly from side to side. "To hell with the divorce lawyer, Pom. Let's take her all the way to Mexico!"

That night, when he met the collector at Porter's Place and paid him for September, the encounter at the swamp was still vivid in his mind. He thought about the slain speculator and his bride, thought about unleashing the sheriff on the collector, and kept his hands on the table to keep them from shaking.

CHAPTER 11

The blackberries of summer are gone. The pasture is rough ground, a scrap of scrub smelling faintly of cattle, sprouting saplings and beggar weed. Only tonight, it has the close, heavy, scent of rot. He ties the white horse to the wide, dragging gate, follows the tire tracks into the woods, and walks a curve in the old road through a stand of jack pines in an uneven corner of the wooded wedge, to the shadow of a sprawling live oak. Startled, a handful of crows scatters in raucous flight, leaving him face to face with the things wired to the tree. The barbs make him think first of the crucified Christ with his crown of thorns but, coming closer, he sees fencing wire wound round the tree, circling the swollen forms that used to be a man and a woman. The man stares at him with filmy eyes. His companion gazes down at the ground as if looking for a pin that has fallen from her matted black hair. The boy turns and runs, but something cold and black, thick as tar, has descended on this place, drawing him to the tree and pinning him beside the dead.

Rex threw off the blankets and sat sweating on the edge of the bed. A cold draft came through the open window, but he wasn't ready to get up and do anything about it. He stared at the moonstruck walls of his room, finding little comfort in familiar objects. The map of the United States beside the wardrobe was dark except for a strip of light along the East Coast. The display case of shark teeth and arrowheads cast a jagged shadow by the door. He looked down into the front yard, able to see no more than a pale rectangle blotched by the dark shapes of trees, split by the brick walk that led to the gate and the vacant street. Familiar by day, in the night it seemed an alien place where dead men might walk and killers roam free.

When he turned back around, he saw the radio that he and Jim had built. It was his best hope for escaping his nightmare and fear. He closed the window and went to the desk, sat down and pressed the cold headset to his ears. By moonlight and by touch, he turned the tuning dials. The big stations, the familiar stations, were off the air, and he heard nothing but a wave of featureless noise as he eased the dial from left to right. It was like listening to an ocean wash, an endless breaker never receding from the beach, as he edged the dial through the arc of numbers. But even in that lonely sound he took some comfort because it came from so far away, from a place free of the terrors of his night. Then, high above the positions of the daytime and evening stations, he heard a staccato patter of rusty tones. He listened for some time, staring at the dim silo of the receiving set without detecting any repetition of the pattern. He found an envelope and a pencil and began writing down what he took to be the dots and dashes of Morse code, but he was slow and uncertain and the result was a meaningless jumble of letters and numbers.

He abandoned the radio and put on his grandfather's frayed plaid robe. He left the room and walked the perimeter of the hall, past the little sewing alcove and Rachel's room, past the musty room once occupied by his grandfather and scarcely touched in the year since his disappearance. Jim's room, the one that led to the summer comforts of the sleeping porch, was at the head of the stairs. There old John Howard had passed some of his last days, but long before, when the house was new, a preacher had lived there. He had been related somehow—a second husband to Rex's mother's mother, perhaps—and the couple, sometime in the remote past, returning home from missionary work in China, had been lost at sea, just as his Grandfather Larrabee had been lost scarcely a year ago. In the next room, the northwest corner, Rex's parents slept. That had always been the master bedroom. Years ago as a young man, Grandfather Larrabee had slept there with his bride, Anna, always a bride, for she had lived to be only twenty-two.

He heard whispering, complaint and reassurance, something about the visit to the radio station? He leaned closer, hearing nothing now but his father's thin snore.

The wanderer shivered in his robe, feeling the loss of his grandfather to the Gulf, a grandfather merely missing, Flora said, too full of life not to come clomping up the porch with some fantastic tale of adventure in the skirt of a hurricane.

Gone for good, Pom confided, lost to the sea like the old preacher and his wife, gone like countless other fishermen who had ridden the channel toward Seahorse Reef, never to be seen again.

At this cold hour of the deep night, the house seemed more a repository of ghosts than the happy, sunlit home of the living. Evil outweighed good, death got the upper hand over life, darkness engulfed delightful day.

He descended the groaning stairs, bumped into the ancient wicker chair that his mother defended against his father's muttered threats, and went into the kitchen. He dipped a cup into the basin and washed his face, hoping that the chilly water would give him resolve in this hour of doubt. He wondered what had become of the two bodies wired to the tree. He supposed they were still in some dreary locker in the recesses of the stucco hospital. Were they twisted and stiff in their bloody clothes or had they been peeled down to their violated skin and somehow flattened to conform to marble slabs?

And were the killers moving through the woods again tonight, forcing another man and another woman against another tree?

He drank deep from the cup, avoiding the sight of the black window above the sink. The smell of flour gave him courage. He listened to the wind and what seemed to be the breathing of the house. He thought about what he might have to do to drive the corpses from his dreams. He saw himself walking through the night to the paddock, climbing onto Lucy, and riding the roadside to the sagging gate. He pushed the image further, down the curving ruts, through the jack pines to the dark tree. It would be a grisly game of tag. The cautious approach, hand extended. Looking over his shoulder, inching closer. The scattering of the crows or whatever spirits loitered there. Placing his palm on the rough, stained bark—banishing the things that haunted him.

Whatever living monsters remained and moved in the night would no longer trouble him. They could be felled by the forces of day—the sheriff, vengeful hunters, bright-banded coral snakes.

He was exhausted at half past six when Flora shook him awake, but happy to see the sunlight washing his room. The smell of bacon and grits and coffee drifted up from the kitchen where Rachel and Pom were in some kind of discussion with Amelia. The sound of their voices, the stuttering of automobiles, the sharp call and response of children, and the barking of dogs made the bright day all the more glorious.

Were they a dream or a memory, those whispered words between his parents? Something about that walk to the radio station with Jim. His father's voice low and reassuring in response to his mother's pointed complaint. He decided to bring the issue into the daylight, to make his case and ask if he could go back to the station with Jim.

His mother sat down at the head of the table, at Pom's place, and counted off the conditions on her fingers, routine conditions, with raking the yard added on. His parents *had* talked. Whatever her misgivings, she had already come to terms with them during the night.

He dozed during algebra and took a ribbing for it during recess. Ollie Holiday pushed his sunburned face at him. "You know what they call a guy who sleeps too long?"

Rex was caught off guard just long enough for Ollie to slip a dirty hand on his shirt pocket, so that when he broke free the seams gave way.

"Rip! They call him *Rip* van Winkle!"

Rex pictured a variety of fights in which he would pound Ollie into the dirt, but he settled for avoiding him for the rest of the day because he had already done time after school for scuffling, and a win—an unlikely win—would be too costly, would just bring him more unwanted attention. As it was, word had already begun to spread about the confrontational politics of his friend from the north.

"Yellow!" Ollie called after him. "Yellow loves a Red."

By the time Rex got home it was nearly time to leave for the return performance of the Shirtsleeve Troubadour. Jim was in his room warming up on his guitar. Rex waited at the door, listening, admiring the way Jim's left hand moved up and down the fingerboard, linking chords with scattered notes. "I've never heard that one," he said at the end of the song.

Jim glanced up. "I'm not sure I have either. I think I just made it up."

Rex looked at the tawny face of the guitar, which was worn from years of strumming. "I never would've thought you could get such a pretty sound out of that thing."

Jim hit a low chord and pulled hard at the strings. Something rattled. "It has its limits. That's for sure. This fret needs filing. Actually, I'm not even sure that'll take care of it. This guitar's got a lot of miles on it. It's a giant step beyond that ukulele though."

"Where do you get all those songs?"

"I don't know exactly. They just sort of stick in my head, and usually it's nothing to pick them out on the guitar. Not just the way you'd hear them in the field or find them in a book, you know, but close enough. What happened to your shirt?"

"I caught it on something. We've got to go, don't we, if we're going to get to the station by five?"

Jim stood up, holding the guitar, and pulled something green out of his hip pocket. It looked like the neck of a Coca-Cola bottle. He stuck his left index finger into it and started playing again, running his left hand up and down the neck, tapping his foot while he strummed and plucked with his right, and the music took on a striking metallic slide that reminded Rex of a cylinder player winding down.

Rachel came up the stairs and joined Rex at the door to Jim's room. She swept her auburn hair back behind her ears and watched, fascinated, as the troubadour's hands worked their magic. The sliding warble was a long way from the Diabelli piano sonatinas she had labored through lately, for that matter a long way from the calculated frenzy of Paul Whiteman's Orchestra.

"It sounds kind of *earthy*," she whispered to Rex. "I like it."

She wasn't the only one. When the Shirtsleeve Troubadour slid and jangled to the end of his second broadcast, the telephone at the radio station rang. An unidentified woman wanted to know all about the performer. Mr. Bennett put her off, promising to include introductory remarks at the beginning of Tuesday's program. Three similar calls followed in rapid succession.

A fourth caller took issue with Jim's closing statement about the need for unity among workers.

As Rex and Jim walked the railroad tracks on the way home, the Troubadour was thoughtful. He adjusted the guitar on his back. "Well, that's one week."

"Fifteen dollars a week," Rex marveled. "Week after week. You'll be rich!"

Jim stopped to pocket a penny left on the rail. "I don't know about rich. Sooner or later, people are bound to get tired of the Shirtsleeve Troubadour."

Wobbling on the rail, Rex waved his arms to keep his balance. "How can they? They've never heard anything like it. Even Rachel likes it. I wouldn't be surprised if she was in my room hogging the headset for the entire program."

"Rachel likes it?"

"Yeah. She said it sounds dirty."

Jim laughed and shifted the guitar. "I guess it kind of does at that. It's the music of field hands and hobos, so it's close to the ground all right. I'm not sure the bourgeoisie will be as accepting though."

"The what?"

"The bourgeoisie. The middle class, merchants and shop-keepers, smug in their bungalows, with their minds made up."

Rex turned something shiny with his toe, another bottle cap. "What's a Red?"

Jim went on for a few steps as if he hadn't heard and then stopped and looked down the tracks. "Rex, you have a remark-able family and I'd hate to put you all on the spot."

"What do you mean?"

"Maybe you're right. Maybe the Shirtsleeve Troubadour will be a hit. I'm almost afraid that he will."

"Huh? How come?"

"Because that's not what I'm here to do. I see my purpose as making life better for people."

"Cripes! Isn't that what you're doing? Music makes people happy. It lit Rachel right up and she's about the sourest person I know."

"Music is an immediate thing, Rex. I'm talking about more than a tune on the radio."

Suddenly Rex remembered the mysterious radio signal in the night. He described it. "I've practiced my Morse code plenty. I know it pretty well, just not well enough I guess."

"There's going to be more and more new stuff on the radio every day," Jim said. "And there are other codes besides Morse. You probably ran into one of them. Why were you up in the middle of the night?"

"I was thinking, I guess. How are you going to spend your $15?"

"I hadn't given it any thought. Money's kind of a curse, you know."

"Kind of a blessing, too, if you need it. My dad says if the love of money is the root of all evil, he's willing to take it off anyone's hands for their betterment."

Jim adjusted his cap and smiled. "I can see I won't gain any easy converts among the Hollimans."

"Well, I think everybody likes your music. But they're not so sure about the revolution."

"Give it time," Jim said. "Give it time."

CHAPTER 12

When they got back to the house, a welcoming committee was waiting for them. Ainsley Harper, Mavis Ward, and several other ladies were on the porch, smiling and applauding as the dusty pair came through the front gate.

Jim gave Rex a questioning look and saw that the boy was also surprised. Inside the gate he balked, standing with the guitar behind his back as if to conceal what had brought him all the attention. After a moment's hesitation, he followed Rex up the walkway.

"Wonderful show," Ainsley said, "with an editorial too. We have just one request. We darn near crippled each other fighting over that headset. Can you fix it so we can all hear at the same time?"

When show time came around the following Tuesday, the enthusiastic ladies gathered in a semi-circle around the radio in Rex's room. At five-thirty they broke off their discussion of picnic hams at Piggly Wiggly and stared into the shiny brown fluted cone that honked out Mr. Bennett's crackling sign-on.

The Shirtsleeve Troubadour began with *Casey Jones,* the ballad about a heroic railroad engineer who sacrificed himself for the lives of others in a fatal train wreck. He said some things about an international workers movement and sang his way through the rest of the half hour with a request or two, and then one of the latest popular songs, *I've Got a Feeling I'm Falling.* He was in the final chorus when something happened that made him the talk of the town. He was singing

> *Hey, mister parson, stand by-y-y,*
> *For I've got a feeling I'm falling,*
> *Falling for nobody else but you.*

And just as he got to the final *you*, a brown calf with a blaze face poked his head through the studio window and bellowed out a loud *o-o-o-o* that blended perfectly with the end of the Troubadour's chorus. The timing and pitch were so perfect that Jim repeated the chorus with the Hereford joining in whenever he felt like it. Rex looked from the calf to the other side of the studio glass where Mr. Bennett was daubing his shiny forehead with a handkerchief. The engineer, who relished any setback, laughed so hard that he choked on his chewing gum.

At the end of the repeat chorus, the calf raised his face and sounded a final blast of approval, and then turned and trotted back toward the pasture.

It was all the Troubadour could do to get through the last song of the program. He chose *The Streets of Laredo,* giving added stress when he got to the line "get along little dogie," and by the time the show closed, even Mr. Bennett was cracking up.

"The singing is so grand," he said as Jim and Rex were leaving, "you hardly need to, you know, provide commentary.'

This time their walk back along the tracks was less than peaceful. Somehow complete strangers knew that Jim was the man on the radio. As he and Rex crossed the paved road to the prairie, somebody in a yellow McFarlan Roadster honked and waved and hollered *Troubadour!* And when they emerged from the brush of the Porters Quarters, someone hailed them from the depot on the other side of University Avenue.

"Hey, great show, Troubadour! Next time how about playing *Red River Valley?*"

Jim waved in response and watched the car speed away. "This is getting a little out of hand. How does everybody suddenly know who I am?"

Rex shrugged. "Maybe it's the guitar on your back."

Down the street, the ten-story shell of the Dixie Hotel gave the Troubadour a curious notion. "I might just as well climb up there and start yelling at the whole town."

Rex failed to see the tormented humor. "It wouldn't be at all the same. On the radio it's like you're in people's parlors and living rooms. You're talking right to 'em like you're a member of the family."

The guitar slid onto one shoulder and Jim elbowed it back into position, nudging a protest from the low strings. "Now that I've actually been on the radio, it doesn't seem quite right somehow. I like to see people when I'm talking to them and I imagine they like to see me. It doesn't seem right floating into their bedrooms and bathrooms that way."

"Well, it would be hard to do it any other way with a cow," Rex reminded him. "You going to play *Red River Valley* for that guy on Thursday?"

"Why not? It's only five chords. Better still, I can teach it to you and you can play it on Thursday."

"You kidding? I'm so bad that my piano teacher paid my mother *not* to give me lessons. It's you they want to hear."

Jim walked with his hands in his vest pockets, scattering dogwood and magnolia leaves as he scuffed along. "All right. If it helps them to forget their troubles for a while."

This time the house was full of fans. Ainsley met Jim and Rex on the front walk and declared that she wanted to interview the Shirtsleeve Troubadour. She favored him with one of those wide white smiles of hers. "I don't know which magazine will print it, but you can be sure that one of 'em will. How soon can you be available?"

The Troubadour hedged. "I was kind of thinking Rex and I could tweak the radio reception."

She came close and gave his arm a squeeze. "There can't be much room for improvement because it sure sounded great tonight. In fact, if it gets any better, you're going to have to put a loudspeaker on it and play it at the hardware store like the World Series."

"They would surely run me out of town if that happened."

"I want you to tell me about your songs and how you came out of the blue like this. What have you been doing all your life? What have you been doing all of *my* life?"

The crowd on the porch began to disperse. On their way past, people slowed down to pat the Troubadour on the shoulder and congratulate him on the show. He was ill at ease with the praise but gracious in his acknowledgement of it. Ainsley slipped a tablet and pencil from a macramé handbag and began taking notes.

"Now, where are you from, Jim? May I call you Jim?"

"I'm from one place and another now. From Madison, Wisconsin, originally. Have you lived here all your life?"

"Not yet!" When he failed to follow her humor, she brushed the question aside "Oh, yes. I'm from right here. I was born in a farmhouse at the edge of Paynes Prairie—just after it became a prairie."

"I'm afraid I don't understand."

"Which part?"

"About the prairie."

"Oh. It used to be a lake. Alachua Lake. Things have a way of changing around here—things you might think would be permanent."

"Oh, yes, I've heard about the disappearing lake. You've lived here all your life then, on the prairie?"

"All my life, yes, but not on the prairie. I live in town now, close enough to my neighbors that I can hear their kids carrying on and their dogs barking. Now back to you. Where did you learn all those songs—in Wisconsin?"

"Some of them, sure. *Pinery Boy* for one. But the rest of them, I mean, they're kind of our national treasures, aren't they? They come from the working people—except for the popular songs. Those I just pick up here and there. Some of them I hear on the radio."

She was getting behind in her note taking. "Not so fast. You must have traveled around quite a bit. Do you support yourself as a troubadour?"

"Not by a long shot. I work. I've worked in the fields and canneries, in the mills and mines and feedlots. That's the only way you can learn the kind of music I play. But, you know, the music is just the icing on the cake."

She looked up from her note pad. "Really? How do you mean?"

"Well, the songs are just the voice of the people, the people on whose backs the country rides. Their backs get mighty sore. That's where the songs come from."

"I would imagine so. Are you saying that the songs have a kind of a—a political message?"

"Absolutely."

"And is that why you sing them?"

He thought for a moment, glanced toward the house with its complement of cheerful visitors. "I sing them because each man, woman, and child can find something of his or her own in them. It's up to them what they find. That's why the songs endure. They offer something to everyone. I just sing them. I let the people who hear them get what they can. "What do you get out of them?"

Caught off guard, she smiled and looked away. "I get real pretty tunes and some sweet guitar picking and that thing that you do with the sliding. It gives me shivers all up and down my back."

He chuckled "Is that so? Well—"

She turned as a man drove up in a Model A. He got out and slammed the door with his foot. With a quick twist of his fingers he mastered the latch and wire, yanked the gate open, and slapped it aside. His dark red hair was wet with sweat and his flushed face unshaven. He trimmed a thumbnail with his teeth as he strode up the walkway.

"What you doing over here, Ainsley?"

She closed the notebook and put it back into her handbag. "This was my last stop on the way home."

"I was about to drive all the way down to your mamma's looking for you."

Jim looked at her for an explanation.

She was vague. "Jim Rhodes, this is the man I married. This is the one and only Theron Purdy."

Theron came forward, tan and sinewy, the taller of the two by half a head. He pumped Jim's hand.

"You the guy on the radio? The one that talks politics and plays the guitar?"

"For now."

"Just traveling through?"

"That's right."

"That's good. Traveling's good."

Ainsley ran a finger through her necklace, a simple gold chain. "What are you doing back so soon, Theron? I thought you were hunting for the week."

He rubbed a ring of peeling skin from his sunburned nose and put his hands in his back pockets. "Was. I got what I was after."

Sheriff Mecum pulled up in his black Chevrolet and parked in front of Theron's Model A, close enough to pen it in. The conversation waited while he came through the open gate and up the brick walk.

"Do you have more news?" Flora asked.

He took off his hat. "Wish I did. I've been looking for you, Theron. I guess you know your neighbor's got a bone to pick with you."

"I've been fox hunting with some guys from Tampa," Theron said. "Maybe we'd've got him if you'd come along."

"She's fit to be tied, after what you did."

"Damn fox got away," Theron said. "He doubled back and ran right between our feet. Dogs went crazy trying to find his scent after that. You should've seen it. I like to died laughing. Got me a possum though. From about a mile away. Ask the guys from Tampa."

The sheriff had listened with folded arms. "You've been complaining about her dog barking."

"Been keeping Peachy here awake at night. Isn't that right?"

Ainsley blushed and looked away. "What's he done, Avery?"

The sheriff put his hands on his hips. "Mrs. Faust spent the last few days looking for her cocker spaniel. Came home this afternoon and found him on the porch—stuffed."

Theron laughed. "Well, he's quieter now. Looks nice too, Very lifelike."

"You're going to owe her some restitution," the sheriff said. "She's talking about taking you to court."

"She'll have to find me first. I'm going fishing—for grouper. You ought to come."

"Thanks just the same. I don't much care for grouper."

"That's 'cause you've never had it right. You know what the best part of the grouper is? It's the cheeks. Fix 'em up right and they're a real delicacy. You know what a delicacy is, don't you?"

"Pay her for the dog, Theron, or go to court. Sorry to interrupt, ladies."

The sheriff nodded, put on his hat, and walked back to his car.

Theron was cheerful, as if he had won some kind of victory. "Got a surprise for you, Ainsley. It's at the house." He reached for her arm.

She drew back. "Well, it sounds like you're full of surprises today. But I can't come just now. I'm working."

"Looks to me like you were just visiting."

"Believe it or not, for me sometimes they're the same thing. I'll be along as soon as I'm through here."

He smiled and made an awkward courtly gesture toward the car. "Can't wait till tonight. The surprise is better in the daylight." He caught her by the wrist.

Jim propped the guitar against the porch rail and moved toward Ainsley. "If you'd like to continue later—"

She glanced at the people gathered on the porch, tossed her head, and started toward the car. "Yes, I'd like that." Theron jerked her off balance and she cast a backward look at Jim. "It's been a pleasure. Maybe we can finish the next time I'm in town. Meanwhile—" she flashed him one of her trademark smiles— "I'll be listening."

Jim followed as far as the gate and watched as she climbed into the Model A. When it had rattled out of sight on the tree-lined road, he came back to the porch, picked up the guitar, and gave the rail a little rap on his way into the house.

(HAPTER 13

On Saturday morning Rex was teetering after another night of bad sleep, but he was eager to go with Jim to find some songs for Tuesday's radio show.

First he had to convince Flora to let him go, and the debate went on in hushed tones while she dusted the headboard in the master bedroom. He had his work cut out for him because, just the night before, Rachel had come home well after dark with the excuse that she and Roberta had lost track of the time while they were at the Duck Pond gathering specimens for their botany project, and were intent on finding some Resurrection fern when they noticed the daylight beginning to fail.

"That was Rachel," Rex reminded his mother. "And she was with that screwball Roberta. What do you expect? This is me and I'll be with a grownup."

Flora paused in passing the dust cloth over the top of the headboard. "With Jim."

"Yeah, with Jim. What could go wrong?"

She gazed out the window to the stand of pines where her mother had kept a horse long ago, and her mind jumped to her own adventures at twelve, when she had hopped a train in the Oklahoma Territory to come to Florida looking for her father. In that light, the boy's request seemed reasonable, maybe even necessary.

"Your father trusts Jim, so I guess I do, too. But if you're home even a minute past five, I'll send the sheriff after you and you'll be under lock and key till you're twenty-one."

He hardly heard her last words. The sound of Jim tuning his guitar drew him like the song of a siren.

He watched the Troubadour tighten a set of new strings "Can you can really learn a song after hearing it just once?"

"Most of them are pretty simple and straightforward," Jim said. A string groaned as he turned a peg, warbling it up to the right register. "They express a state of mind or an emotion, and the tunes are as straightforward as a locomotive."

It seemed to Rex that the Troubadour was inventing lyrics as he talked.

Jim went on to the next string. "You know, I'm not sure it's such a good idea for you to come with me today. And anyway, I'm only going over to the Millhopper Road to that chain gang. They may not be in a very musical mood. It could be a big waste of time."

"I got Mama to give me the okay and Dad says he'll drive us all the way to the cutoff. That's going to save us a lot of walking right there—or hitchhiking."

"Never you mind about hitchhiking. That's not a way of life you need to know, at least not till you're older." Jim stood up and shouldered the guitar. "All right. But only because you'll find out that being a troubadour isn't all it's cracked up to be. If we get one good song for half a day's work we'll be lucky."

Right after breakfast they wedged themselves into the cluttered Model T. Jim fastened the passenger door with a piece of wire while Rex climbed into the back and squeezed in edgewise with his feet resting on a bait bucket.

Pom set his wilted gray touring cap at an angle. He was on his way to the Campion farm, way out overlooking the prairie, so he dropped them off at a Cracker house with a dustpan roof where the Millhopper Road cut north from the segmented highway west to Fort Clark and Newberry. As they walked the shoulder, the occasional automobile sped by, rattling gravel. Jim was strangely quiet.

Rex tried to keep a conversation going with talk about the radio traffic he had been tracking at night when he couldn't sleep, and he mentioned again the odd code that eluded the logic of Morse, but Jim replied with single words and phrases.

"You aren't mad at me for coming?" Rex asked at last.

Jim patted him on the shoulder and adjusted the guitar on his back. "No, I'm just having second thoughts about bringing you out here. There are safer ways to get an education."

The chain gang was where Jim had hoped it would be, about a hundred yards south of a little country church and burying ground by the crossroads at the edge of deep oak woods. The song hunters had to come within fifty yards of the men before they heard any singing, and then it was a single Negro at the head of the group, half moaning, half humming a mournful minor-key tune. Jim stopped and listened.

The gang was a mishmash of black and white men, dogs, horses and machines. The workers were in sun-bleached gray and white stripes, each with a heavy black x on the back of his unbuttoned shirt. A uniformed trusty lounged against a pickup truck and drank from a canteen. One deputy watched on horseback with the barrel of his shotgun resting on the pommel of his saddle. A second deputy stood a few yards ahead of the line with his double barrel cradled in the crook of his arm. The men were digging heavy muck out of the drainage ditch without any particular unity or rhythm. The lone singer kept the beat with the thrusts of his shovel.

"Some words would help," Jim said.

"You could take down the music and come up with your own words," Rex suggested.

"Not in a million years. To do that I'd have to go through what that man's been through."

"You mean, go to prison?"

"Everything. The backbreaking work in the fields, the beatings, the hunger."

A gray Chrysler sedan passed by, slowed down, and sped north on grimy whitewalls.

Rex thought for a moment. "But you can sing his words without going through all that?"

"Yes, I can go that far. I can put myself into that man's shoes if I know his words, but I can't make up the words for him."

As if on cue, the man began to sing.

Jim edged up a little closer on the far side of the road with Rex following. He took a small notebook from his vest pocket, put on a pair of wire-rim glasses, and started writing. Rex took a peek but couldn't make any sense of it.

"Is that English?"

Without looking up, Jim shook his head. "My own form of shorthand. Comes in pretty handy in this line of work."

They stood there listening until Rex's feet started to hurt. He wasn't one for staying still.

"What's he singing?" he asked at last.

Jim made a face and shrugged. "Can't make out a word of it."

"I think he's missing some teeth," Rex said. "The words aren't coming out quite the way I'm used to. It sort of reminds me of that code on the radio."

Jim raised his hand for silence. He closed his eyes, his head rocking gently to the singing. The man was repeating the first line and then adding a second. It gave Jim a double opportunity to pick up the words. He started humming along, short bursts of notes followed by a phrase that rose slowly and dropped hard. He made more notes in shorthand.

"Let's go," he said when the convict had stopped. He put his glasses and notebook back in his vest pocket. "I want to get this down before I forget it. We can go up to that church long enough for me to marry the words to the chords."

"To marry," Rex repeated. It struck him as a peculiar word with the chain gang passing by.

As the convicts shoveled their way south, Jim and Rex hurried to the little crossroads church at the edge of the woods. Jim pulled off his guitar, sat down on the wooden steps and went to work, but the chords were trickier than they seemed, and he wrestled with the tune as Rex took a seat on a mossy tombstone and listened.

The gray Chrysler squealed into the crossroads on its bald tires, its cracked windshield glinting as it slid into a left turn and disappeared.

"I wish I could hear that song again," Jim said as if speaking to the guitar. "There's something not right here." He put his glasses on and wrote a few chords in his notebook.

After knotting his fingers into one wild chord after another, he stood up and put his glasses back in his vest pocket. "I think I'm going to have to let it breathe for a while."

Rex got off the tombstone and looked at the guitar as if it were some kind of genie's lamp. "They're going to love that song when you finally get it. You can be sure they've never heard anything like it. Not unless they've done prison time."

As they walked toward the back of the church Jim offered advice. "Don't let your mother hear you talking like that or this'll be the last time you'll—"

He found himself face to face with a heavyset man in a white hood. The man was tapping an ax handle in the palm of his hand.

"Hello, Red."

Jim leaned the guitar against the clapboard wall of the church.

"Leave the boy out of it." He spoke as if he knew what was coming next.

The ax handle came up to eye level. "Sure. He's gonna have to pick up the pieces."

Jim turned around as far as he dared. "Go on, Rex. It'll be okay."

The boy swallowed and stood his ground. "He can't get both of us. If he raises that thing at me, I'll bite his hand off." As Rex uttered his defiance, his voice broke.

Jim kept his eyes on the man with the ax handle. "Rex, you need to be out of the way for this. Just let me take care of it."

Through the rattling leaves of laurel oaks a second hooded man approached Jim.

No ax handle at least, Rex thought through the pounding of his heart. *There's a mercy.*

He backed up, all the way to the front of the church, where he bumped into a third arrival carrying a tire iron.

Jim kept his eyes on the one with the ax handle. "Does it take three of you to fight a singer?"

With the toe of his shoe, he flipped the guitar into the air, and the hooded man swung. The ax handle flashed in the sunlight, broke the neck, and sent the twanging wreck skyward. Jim grabbed the weapon at the end of its arc, caught the attacker off balance, and slammed him into the wall of the church, then rammed the handle into the base of the man's breastbone, throwing him belly up, sucking for air.

Rex ducked just as Jim hurled the ax handle, which smacked the second man in the forehead. The tire iron dropped as the man went into a drunken spin that turned into a clumsy, gravel-scratching run for the road.

The empty-handed man was fast. He staggered Jim with a cracking punch to the base of the skull, thrust both hands under his arms, and pressed against the back of his neck

"Come on now," he called to the others, "come and get him!"

Fists clenched, Jim shot his arms into the air, stepped forward with his left foot and dropped to his right knee while bringing both elbows down to his sides and leaning back slightly, breaking the grip of the fingers locked on his neck. With a quick turn to the right, he felled the man with a fist to the cheek.

The man swung again and connected above Jim's ear, dropping him to all fours, and then lifted him with a kick to the stomach. A second kick flattened him face up, and the man dropped down with his knee on Jim's chest. His fist was back to deliver a hammer blow to the face when he felt the boy on his neck and the stinging bite on the back of his hand.

The Chrysler came around again and the stunned man ran toward it with newfound agility as the winded man stopped and yelled at the man who turned to slap Rex to the ground.

"Leave him! Come on! You know the deal!"

The man hesitated, pushed Rex away, and ran for the car.

Jim got to his feet and pulled Rex around the corner of the church.

Just then they heard a loud pop.

"That way! To the woods!" Jim gave the boy a rough tug on the shoulder that spun him toward the little churchyard.

"Were they *shooting* at us?" The words were little more than wind coming from the boy's lungs as he ran.

They bounded across the road and into the trees and caught their breath under an arching canopy of branches and Spanish moss.

Gasping, Rex stopped and leaned against a gray old elephant of an oak.

Jim coughed and rubbed the back of his head. "Probably just a backfire. Are you okay?"

"Why would the Klan come after us?"

"It wasn't the Klan. I've seen enough of them in Wisconsin to know them when I see them. I'm not sure what they were after. Could you see the one who was driving the car?"

"To tell you the truth, I was too scared to notice, but I think he was wearing a hood too."

"I think so." Jim rubbed the back of his head again and looked at his hand. "The last one was wearing a ring. I can tell you that much. Got a heck of a rock on it. I'll bet he's done some wrestling, too, from that grip he had me in."

"Wait'll I tell everybody about this. How we beat all three of 'em."

They started walking down the leafy corridor. "That's not such a good idea. I'm not asking you to lie if the subject comes up somehow, but I don't want people thinking I'm some kind of thug. I should probably be moving on."

Rex halted at a large branch that had fallen across the trail "What for? Everybody's crazy about your show, and there's so much to do with the radio and all the songs to learn."

Jim took a deep breath and patted him on the shoulder. "I won't be going today. Today can be just the way we want if we put our minds to it."

They followed the tree tunnel to the east, listening all the while for the choke and whine of the returning Chrysler. They crossed the gravel road a hundred yards north of the church, followed a double sand track south through tall grass and knotty pines and, after about half a mile, emerged on the packed lime rock road. Looking back from time to time and taking each oncoming car for the Chrysler, they walked the shoulder, going east for most of two miles. They walked in silence up a long grade, to a T intersection with a gravel road that led south toward town, and when they got to the top of it, Jim stopped and pointed toward a fallow cornfield.

"Look at that. At first I thought it was a man, but it's a scarecrow. He's so lifelike."

Rex watched the dry stalks fluttering in the breeze. "That corn isn't worth protecting."

Jim smiled. "Yes, he's out of work just like everyone else. Still, it's kind of curious that he'd be looking so well-kept when the farm's obviously been untended for months."

"Want to go have a closer look?" Rex moved toward the side of the road.

"No, no. Come back here. We don't have time. We've got to get you home or your parents will throw me out for sure, especially after Rachel and Roberta came in late like that. As your father said, we can't have young people wandering all over the county."

Rex put his hands in his pockets and smiled. "Later on, my mother said it to Rachel a lot stronger than that."

They began walking the sloping road south to town. A gray sedan came over the crest and they hurried into the cover of tall grass, but it was just a harmless Buick, and soon they were on their way again. Rex gazed down at the sandy edge of the road, following a set of powdery prints. He came to a standstill and knelt down for a better look.

"Rachel," he said. "Rachel's been coming out here."

Jim watched him trace the prints with a lowered finger. "Are you sure? Those tracks are pretty faint."

"But they say a lot." Rex moved his hand over the sand as if to elicit a secret signature. My granddaddy showed me how you can tell one horse from another by the print. Lucy has this kind of a wide frog—that's the *V* there in the hoof. You'd have to look at a lot of horses to find another one with a frog like that, and anyway there aren't that many horses on these roads anymore.

Jim smiled. "You sound seasoned beyond your years."

"So what was she doing way out here?" Rex moved his hand to another print in the soft ground at the edge of the shoulder. "Look, there's another one, a newer one, going the same way. She came out here with Roberta that time."

"Now I *am* impressed. How do you know it was Roberta?"

"I don't, but she had some extra weight, and who else would get on a horse with Rachel?"

"Spoken like a true brother."

"So what were they doing way out here?"

Jim started walking again. "When we finally get home, you can ask her."

At dinner Pom had a hard time keeping the conversation alive. He asked Rachel how Lucy was doing.

"Fine." She hardly looked up from her ham and raisin sauce. "She's fine."

"She needs the work or she'll go sour. How far you taking her?"

"I don't know. Not too far."

Rex began to say something but thought better of it. He waited to hear what else his sister would say.

"Well, where all are you going with her then?"

"Oh, you know. Just around looking for ferns and things. Out on University Avenue and to some of those roads off there. I just sort of let her follow her nose."

Pom listened to the 6:39 rumble and hiss its way up West Main Street. "I can see that we're not about to get a travelogue here. That grapefruit salad sure looks good, Rex. Thanks, you got the hint. Can't say as I have much to report either. Went out to the Campions' and talked calves. Went down to the Duforges' and talked to Martha about the hog cholera. Barkley's walking more hunched over than ever. I told him if he was a mule I'd recommend less heavy lifting, but seeing as how he ain't a mule but only as stubborn as one, he's going to keep right on hauling those logs and throwing his back out. How about you, boys? How was your walk up the Millhopper Road?"

Rex gave Jim a quick look. "Fine. It was fine."

"Flora, have you noticed how our children spent their first thirteen or fourteen years talking our ears off and now it's like pulling teeth just to get a word out of 'em? Have you used up your lifetime allotment of words? Is that how it works?"

Later that night, as he climbed into the sagging bed, Pom asked his wife if she had any idea what was going on with their children.

The springs squeaked as she shifted away from the depression in the middle of the bed. "They're thirteen and sixteen years old, that's what."

Pom smiled and rubbed the side of his head with his forefinger. "Yeah, I know. I'm *that* connected. And Rex has had a few tough weeks. I hear him in his room in the middle of the night sometimes, working that radio, I guess."

"Jim's become a good friend for that."

"Yeah. It's just the diversion Rex needs right now. Jimmy's all right, even if he is a Red. I guess they can't all be bad."

"You were gone a long time today. Were you down at Campions' all that time?"

"Well, I meant to mention that. I took a little trip to Lake Santa Fe. There's a man up there who's having trouble weaning a foal."

"So you spent the rest of the day working on that?"

"No, now you're getting ahead of me. My main reason for being up there is that I'm working on a boat."

"A boat? You've already hired a maid we can't afford. How can we pay for a boat?"

He plumped his pillow and sat up against the tall headboard. "Paying is not what it's about. It's not costing us anything but some odds and ends and my time. It's a sailboat, an eighteen-footer, just right for two brave seafarers. I was thinking I'd give it to Rex for Christmas if he wants it. If I get it done in time."

"He could use something lasting. Jim won't be around forever."

"On my way back from the lake I saw Theron. He's got a new car, can't be more than a year or two old, a pretty one, a dark blue Studebaker."

"You're not jealous of Jim, are you? I mean all the time he spends with Rex. They've become almost inseparable."

Pom flopped up to a higher part of the bed. "Jealous ain't in my vocabulary. Oh, all right, maybe just a little. But Rex ought to have friends outside the house. That's the nature of things. He'll be picking and choosing his ideas and his friends and you can be sure we won't approve of all of 'em. Didn't you tell me you and your dad crossed words when you were that age?"

"I was raised by a deranged aunt until I was twelve. Rex is doing a little better than that."

"But he still needs something to get him going forward again while this business with the killings is settled."

Flora put her hand on the lace curtains as they fluttered in the sweet night breeze. "But you don't always *get* things settled, do you?"

He came down from the high edge of the bed and dropped to one elbow. "I know it's hard, but we might never know what happened to your dad out there on Seahorse Reef. We might have to take what we've got and just move on."

"I'm not ready," she said, "and I won't be—not till I know."

Sometime in the middle of the night Pom woke up and went downstairs. He fished a well-folded letter out of his inside coat pocket, took it into the wood room, closed the door, and turned on the light. He wanted to be sure that he had read it right. There was the official Florida seal, the blocks of text just as he remembered, and the gist of it all in the first sentence of the last paragraph, taking issue with his moonlighting and removing him from his position as a state veterinarian.

CHAPTER 14

Five days later, Rex was selling boiled peanuts to the passengers en route to Jacksonville on the 6:39, and instead of the usual banter about the wet weather or the endless bribery trial of the former Secretary of the Interior, it was newspaper talk. Copies of the *Daily Sun* were selling faster than the paper boys could hand them over. The eager hands poking out the windows made the train look like an overgrown tomato worm.

Several children got off, herded by a matron in a long coat, forcing the paperboys away from their customers as they trooped along the platform. One of the vendors looked worried as he turned and broke into another bundle. "This ain't one of them orphan trains, is it?"

"Who cares," another boy said through a hunk of sugarcane he was sucking on, "as long as they get out of the way."

"What's your secret to selling so many?" Rex asked the first one, a stout, tough eleven-year-old named Carl.

"No secret," the boy said as he handed a copy of the paper through the window to an eager passenger. "It's right on the front page. See for yourself."

Rex caught only a few words as the paper disappeared into the car, something about the stock exchange and a *mad selling orgy.*

When he got home he asked Pom what it meant.

His father looked up from the front page.

"It means the rest of the country just caught up to Florida."

After dinner he asked Jim.

The Troubadour looked up from one of his gilt-lettered books and took off his glasses. "It means the collapse of world capitalism. It means that men who've been living on imaginary money will now have to make an honest living."

Rex waited for an explanation, but there was none. "Is it the revolution?"

"Time will tell, but no matter what, you'll see some big changes in this country."

"For the better?"

"I believe so. It'll be painful at first, but most change is. The Civil War, the American Revolution, they came with a cost."

During Tuesday's show the Shirtsleeve Troubadour couldn't resist saying a few words about the stock market. He lowered his guitar, a replacement that had cost him two weeks' pay at the music store on the Courthouse Square, and spoke into the microphone as if whispering into the ear of a lover.

"It had to happen," he concluded. "We were rising too fast not to fall. But the country will prevail on a new, more secure footing."

Then he sang *Hard Times Come Again No More.*

Halloween took on a strange, somber tone. With the murders barely a month behind them, many neighbors were still wary of everyone who came to the door at night, and the porch lights seemed brighter this year. The trick-or-treaters were the usual

assortment of pirates and pilots and It Girls more demure than
Clara Bow, but now they traveled in packs and shuffled quickly
from one porch to the next. Rex went to only half a dozen homes
before his awareness of the here-and-now became too keen to
let him play the part of Zorro. He emptied his apples and pe-
cans and chewing gum onto the dining room table, pulled off his
mask and cape, and settled for watching the rest of the revelers
from his bedroom window.

From porches and open windows spilled dark talk of big city
suicides and a market that had never recovered despite the heroic efforts of the Morgan bank and the Rockefeller family. Raising
his voice above a fiddler's practice, someone said that losses for
the week totaled $30 billion; ten times the annual budget of the
federal government.

Rex bit into an apple and found a worm in it.

On his radio he heard news from a Chicago station about a
huge ore carrier that had rammed another freighter in fog off
Port Washington, Wisconsin, with the loss of thirteen lives, the
third fatal Great Lakes wreck in ten days. He heard about huge
profits of the Mid-Continent Petroleum Corporation and the
Continental Oil Company, and he heard about a failed Chicago
businessman and his wife who were found shot to death in a
room in the Ambassador Hotel, an apparent murder and suicide.

The first two reports seemed to bear out what Jim had been
saying—that there would be more exploitation of the workers—
but the report of the failed businessman suggested that the capitalists were beginning to suffer too. Was that progress? How did
these events weigh one against the other? He thought about asking Jim for an explanation, but decided to wait for the newspaper reports in case he had heard wrong through the hum and
static.

Because of the news in the air, Halloween had become strange
and frightening enough without fluttering sheets and soaped
window screens.

Richard sat among the revelers in Porter's Place and slid eight hundred dollars across the table to the collector, who was wearing a pin-stripe suit.

"Scary costume," Richard said, "if you're supposed to be a banker."

The collector got up and slipped the envelope into an inside pocket. "See you right here four weeks from tonight for November's payment. Do I need to remind you?"

Richard kept his hands on the table. "I'll be here." He set his chin. "I'd hate to have you pull your Luger on me."

On his way out, the collector patted him on the shoulder. "You look kind of strung out. Get yourself some rest. The weather gets pretty rough out there at this time of year."

As if to answer Rex's unvoiced questions, at the end of Tuesday night's broadcast, the Shirtsleeve Troubadour closed with a few words about the wrecks on the Great Lakes.

"Only the heroism of the working man kept the loss of life from being greater," he said, now holding his guitar by the neck as if it were doing the speaking. "And as the fate of the nation unfolds in business failures and collapsing profits, it will be up to the working man to be the hero again and shoulder the burden of this country's renewal."

Then he sang *Joe Hill*.

As he left the studio, the station manager intercepted him, still stuffing a damp handkerchief into his breast pocket. "Look, just stick to the singing, will you? We're starting to get complaints."

The Troubadour shouldered his guitar. "And so you should. People are starting to wake up. The singing, the talking, it's all part of the message."

The station manager took a breath as he drew from some inner reservoir of resolve."One of the calls was a death threat. So just sing, will you? What's so hard about that?"

Armistice Day took people's minds off their troubles with the biggest celebration the town had seen, including airplane flyovers at Jarvis Field, boat races on Newnan's Lake, and a big parade down University Avenue to the Courthouse Square.

As if everyone wanted to forget about the collapse, the diversion went on for the rest of the week with Homecoming at the university.

Several hundred townspeople and students crammed into the university auditorium for the Friday night pep rally. Amid honking cars full of revelers, the whole Holliman family walked the mile to the Gothic brick edifice, and while the speeches went on about how the Fighting Gators would trounce the Clemson College Tigers, Rex studied with fascination the carved caricatures of football players that looked down from the high rafters like latter-day gargoyles. Jim had declined to come to the festivities, preferring to stay in his room and write letters to northern newspaper and magazine editors, but Rex imagined him there in the crowd, and wondered what he would have to say about this full-throated zeal for football on the eve of the revolution.

On the morning of the parade, the house on Magnolia Street was empty except for Amelia, who described herself as too old and fat to chase after such entertainments. Ainsley had gotten Jim to agree to give a workingman's perspective of the event for an article to be submitted to *The Progressive Review*. The concept sounded farfetched to him, but she was so fired up that he gave in just for the sake of getting some peace.

With one of her blinding smiles she told him that he would at least like this better than her first idea, which was to talk the radio station manager into putting the Shirtsleeve Troubadour in a parade car.

"I hope you are joking," he said, looking in vain for irony in her face.

She glanced over her shoulder at him and smiled again. "I'll see you at the parade. Please be on time."

Flora had left just after that to join Mavis in the VIP section of the reviewing stands. Mavis and J.J. enjoyed a privileged position there by dint of the endowment J.J.'s mother had given to the university. The talk in town and on campus was that some building or other was going to be named the Nelda Larson Ward memorial something-or-other, or perhaps take the name of her late husband, Pendleton Ward, which seemed less likely because the building would inevitably take his nickname and become known as Penney's.

Rex and Rachel had taken off early to get prime curb real estate at the beginning of the parade route. Roberta had come along as always, but Rachel was also expecting someone new. She wouldn't say who.

So only Amelia remained at the house on Magnolia Street.

As she was in the backyard beating a rug, she became aware of a husky white man standing near the woodpile. His face was shaded beneath a touring cap cocked at a jaunty angle. He rested one hand against a loblolly pine.

"Did they take off for the parade and leave you on your lonesome to do all the work?"

It took her a beat to realize that he was talking to her. Her first thought was that he was a Red, maybe a friend of Jim's, what with that talk about her doing all the work while the white folks took it easy. She wasn't about to get into another of those wrong-headed word dances, and she started to say so when the man spoke again.

"It's a fine, pretty day to be outside doing something useful. I'm out doing a little work myself. Kind of enjoy it when it's quiet like this."

Around the front of the house somewhere a dog started barking. Sounded like the overly fertile dachshund across the street at the Pennell house.

"Is that so?" Amelia adjusted the rug on the clothesline and gave it a good whack with the stick, a retired pool cue.

"Yes, ma'am. I'm out and about looking at places that might need painting. I'm a house painter. I come through town, have a good look around, and then come back and point out some things that might be better for a coat or two of good lead-based exterior. It'll last twenty years, even in this Florida weather."

Amelia thought this man a little odd. The way he called her ma'am. No sober white man was going to call a colored lady ma'am, even as a figure of speech. And also, propped up on the tree was that hand with a pinky ring as gaudy as a cigar band. That didn't seem quite right for a house painter.

She wondered if he hadn't slipped away from the state home up in Chattahoochee.

She kept on beating the rug while the wiener dog yapped away and the man gave the house a looking-over for paint flakes. There were plenty to see.

With upturned face, he went around to the side yard and then came back to report that he'd be getting in touch. He was about to go when he turned around and said, "Say, isn't this the place where old John Howard lived out his last?"

Suddenly the man seemed less of a stranger. "He sure did," Amelia said. "All but the dying. During his last sickness he lived in the room at the top of the stairs and the Hollimans took care of him, just like the Samaritan. They're good Christian people."

"Well, I knew old John just a bit toward the end there."

"Is that so?"

"He told me something about a will."

"What will? He didn't have no money."

The man smiled at her naiveté. "You don't know much about old coots, do you? Shoot, not a week ago I read about a spinster in New York living in a $12-a-month tenement who left half a million in bonds and bank accounts. You can bet old John had some dough, too. And that he left it for the ones that took care of him. I wouldn't be surprised if he left his will right there in that room somewhere. 'Course it ain't any of my business. I'm just telling you what I figure from knowing him. Just seems like human nature, don't it, to do right by those that take care of you?"

Amelia allowed that he seemed to be onto something.

He tugged at his touring cap. It was too much to believe that he was actually tipping it.

"Well, you enjoy the day now. I suppose when the folks get back they'll tell you all about the parade."

Despite her dismissal by Mavis Ward, Amelia was known around town as an honest, hard-working, loyal African Methodist Episcopalian whose only weaknesses were pecan rolls and curiosity. She went up to Jim's room with the best of motives—to do a little light dusting. It was an informal rule in the houses she cleaned that a maid could go anywhere and pick up anything for dusting as long as it was in plain sight. That meant no opening of drawers and no unlocking of wardrobes or closets. At the Wards' house she had even picked up piles of cash and had always replaced them exactly as she found them.

She had never even touched that silver.

So why not give Jim's room a once-over? After all his talk of equality, he'd surely not mind.

And if by some chance she should come across the lost will of Mr. John Howard, leaving his hidden fortune to the Hollimans, well, that would be more than all right, wouldn't it, to help the ones that had taken her into their home?

The room was distressingly neat and dust-free, but when she ran a fingertip over the dresser, a thin line appeared, and so she picked up the photograph of the old fishermen and gave it a pass with her rag. Then she moved on to the brass bed frame and the windowsill. And then there was the bookcase, a dust collector if ever there was one. She went tiptoe and swiped her cloth over the old leather bindings and gilt pages up there and moved down shelf by shelf to the books with the strange gold letters that reminded her of old hymnals. Unlike the higher books, these were pulled forward on the shelf so that a fair amount of space remained behind them, space where a dying old man might have tucked an important document.

As she dusted, one of the books came forward and fell at her feet, startling her. She looked up and caught sight of a cigar box wedged behind the remaining volumes on the shelf. She reached in and pulled it out. Yes, a will could surely fit into a cigar box, but this was a heavy one. Before she had time to debate, she had raised the lid, folded back a soft gray cloth, and beheld not a will at all, but a grim black instrument of death.

She put it back, replaced the books as well as her shaking hands would permit, and hurried downstairs, repeating random words from scripture all the while.

Then she hurried home to steady herself with a glass of plum bounce, resolving not to let her tattletale husband know what she had seen.

(H A P T E R 1 5

The parade was different this year, at least for Rex. The floats were the usual colorful crepe paper contrivances, interspersed with bands, policemen, and firemen sounding their sirens, Sheriff Mecum tipped his hat from atop a big borrowed Palomino, and various city and county facilities participated with cardboard signs tied to trucks crammed with waving functionaries and politicians. As usual, when the prison farm truck went by sporting a few model inmates, the children in the crowd held their fingers in front of their faces like jail bars.

But then there was that boy Gene, who swept Rachel up onto his fraternity's float and danced the tango with her while Rex marveled at how supple and flowing her movements were. He wondered if she hadn't been practicing with Roberta at home, to those jumpy phonograph records of hers, but he couldn't picture that, so he imagined some secret life his sister had that was full of late-night revels. He concluded that if she ever learned how to drive an automobile, there was no telling what she might do.

And then there was Rachel's new friend, a slender, braided, sweet-faced girl named Kim who was at the parade with her kid brother Carl—the boy who sold newspapers at the depot. As all of them stood on the curb and watched the parade, the sun broke through a cloud, and suddenly Rex was smelling the warm scent of Kim's golden brown hair.

He had been looking forward to the football game most of all. He loved the sound of leather hitting leather and the grunts of the players as they achieved superhuman feats. He loved the scarring of the sod as the game ground on, and wished that he could clasp that rough ball to his ribs and butt his way through a wall of defenders.

But now all of those things shrank when he thought of Kim, of slender Kim with the gray-green eyes and warm hair, who talked with the hard edge of a boy and yet moved with the grace of a ballerina. Late at night, after the parade had passed and the game was won, he lay in bed, listening to the slow rhythms of an unseen chorus of crickets, wondering if there was some secret message in their pulse, wondering if it would remain mysterious like the unfathomable code that brought the radio to life long after the house had gone quiet. And those two mysteries led him to a third that he saw in those gray-green eyes, wise beyond thirteen years, but sometimes frightened. As he lay with his fingers laced behind his head, he wondered about the secrets that lit those eyes. What did he know about her? Only threads of conversation—a fondness for key lime pie, a big book she had read over and over—what was it—*The Tin Woodman of Oz,* a knack for making clothes. Rachel had made Kim's acquaintance while buying a tomato from her. Why? Rachel had never bought a tomato in her life.

When he thought calmly of the things she had said, she seemed an ordinary girl who would be a part of the well-behaved herd in Mrs. Campion's class, angels of the blackboard, shallow and obedient. But then Kim slipped the loop and took on the shape of someone altogether different, unique and mysterious, her gray-green eyes once, twice meeting his. He traced his feelings back to what now seemed some gossamer mythical past, although it had been only a few hours ago, when the scent of her hair had suddenly made him aware of his surroundings. His heart had sunk when, at halftime, she had said that she and Carl had to leave. Suddenly his time with her was cut short and all the brilliant colors of the game turned to shades of gray.

He tried to remember what she looked like, what she had been wearing, but the image was lost to him, as were her first words, so that she seemed now to have been there always. Rachel had been vague about where Kim lived, where she went to school, what her parents were like, and the certain result of any inquiry on his part would be ridicule. So, as the crickets chafed out their cryptic communiqués, he settled for speculating about the girl's origins and life, settled for speculating and yearning until sleep carried him to some plane of freer thought.

For the first time in weeks, he slept through the night, through the strange incomprehensible sputtering of radio code, and paid no terrifying dream visits to the desolate oak tree at the edge of his father's pasture. When he woke up, he was grateful to the girl for freeing him.

Late on Sunday afternoon, Rachel took Lucy for another of her rides and, after a few minutes, Rex hauled his bicycle out of the garage and took up her trail. He maintained a position a hundred yards or so behind the swishing tail and rolling haunches of the mare, biked west through town, then north, and up the slope until Rachel turned Lucy east again and disappeared beyond the trees. He stood and pumped away on the pedals, following the sandy hoof prints until the familiar straw man appeared in the fallow cornfield. He pumped his way along the weedy ruts of the driveway and right up to the sagging porch of the weathered farmhouse. He leaned the bicycle against the rail, climbed the steps, crossed the creaking porch, and banged hard on the warped front door. He waited, listening for muffled footsteps and muttering deep in the house, tried the knob, then elbowed the door open, and ventured past the arc it had scraped in the pine planking of the musty front room.

Had he heard someone go out the back door? He walked through the bare kitchen and looked into the yard where scraggly privet swayed, moved by the wind—or had someone just passed by? He stood there, smelling kerosene and ashes, started up the narrow stairs by the back door, but thought better of going up. He went outside and followed a path through a tidy tomato patch to the sagging barn, tugged the worn door aside, and listened to the twittering of invisible swallows while he waited for his eyes to adjust to the darkness.

The floor was packed dirt with a scattering of cornhusks and straw. The rails of the stalls had been scooped long ago by the cribbing of horses and showed no recent activity, except for the corner where Lucy stood poking at strewn hay. The only other sign of life—or death—was in a back corner where the straw and walls were caked and spattered with rust that smelled of spoiled meat and threw the boy's thoughts back to the rot in the pasture.

Something stirred in the rafters. He stood listening, smelling the decay and the sweet mustiness of old hay. Then he climbed the ladder, testing each worn rung as he went up until his face cleared the floor of the loft. He reached for a hold and his fingers closed on something cold and sinewy, a hand.

He spun on the ladder, dizzy and sick, dropped most of the way to the ground and landed on his knees. When he got to his feet, he saw a shape moving in the doorway. The face took form in streaks of light from the cracks between the barn boards.

His voice was slow to come. "Rachel?"

She looked strangely stern and unyielding. "You shouldn't be here."

He steadied himself against the ladder. "What is this place?"

"It's where I live."

Rex felt his neck snap at the sound of the second girl's voice. Kim came out from behind the horse. At the top of the ladder, Carl appeared in the loft.

Rex was at a loss for words. He spanked the grit from his knees. "You live *here*?"

She knelt down and tied her shoe, strangely angelic amid the dirt and gore. She tossed her head and her light brown braids flew about her shoulders. She kept her distance and her words came tough and unwelcoming. "Swear not to tell. Do you swear?"

More secrets. His head seemed to be flooding with them. "I swear," he said. He watched the strips of light play across Rachel's face as she came near. "Just tell me why you've been coming out here."

His sister was a little too quick, a little too cheerful in her reply. "I brought some leftovers from home, for a picnic." Then that demand again. "Don't you tell *anybody*, you hear me?"

The word *forsaken* came into his head. This was a forsaken place. He went to the girl standing beside the horse. "Where are your folks?"

"They're on a trip," Carl said from the loft. "A long business trip, but they'll be back any day, any minute really."

During his next late night radio session, Rex began listening to music. He could pick up big Midwestern stations that stayed on the air an hour later than those in the Eastern Time zone, and suddenly he favored high tenors that sang shameless love songs. He had bicycled to the dilapidated farmhouse three times since the Homecoming parade, had brought food sneaked from his plate, some repulsive vegetables, but also some gems—a chunk of pot roast with glazed carrots, onions wrapped in waxed paper— and a precious piece of key lime pie.

He noticed that on more humid days Kim's fine brown hair rose from her part like amber sparks. In the sunlight the freckles that bridged her nose appeared like a constellation, remote and mysterious in the night sky. Her hands and nose and mouth had the thickness of a child's, but her figure had begun to fill and curve and she moved with a beguiling grace.

On a Friday night, as lightning cracked the sky and a curtain of cold rain showed silver in the glare of the porch light, Rex was listening through the static to a variety show called *Radio Vaudeville* on WBT in Charlotte, North Carolina, when he heard a car come to a squeaking halt at the front gate. He went to the window and peered through the rain at the black Chevrolet, unable to make out the faces of the men in dark slickers and broad-brimmed hats, until a white flash lit up the features of the sheriff and one of his deputies. They hurried up the walkway and then he lost them under the slope of the porch roof. He propped a ruler under the window to provide some air without letting in the rain, and went downstairs.

Pom was already at the door with Rachel right behind him. "Sorry," he was saying as he pulled the knob away from the door-jamb and gave it a sharp inward tug. "This thing sticks some-thing fierce in damp weather. Sometimes I wish the whole place would just go up in smoke. Come on in and dry off."

By now Flora had joined them from the front room. She took the men's slickers and hats and went back to hang them in the wood room.

"Got some news?" Pom asked.

The sheriff swept a hand over his thinning hair. "Pom, I figured I could do this legal or I could do it friendly and I chose
friendly, so I don't have any papers." His eyes followed the line
of the banister and stopped at the door at the top of the stairs. "If
you don't mind, we'd like to have a look in one of your rooms."
He nodded toward the deputy. "I guess you know my deputy,
Leonard. Is your boarder in tonight?"

"Jim? Sure. He's been in all night."

"He's been working on songs for Tuesday's broadcast," Rex
told the dripping visitors. "He's finally figured out a song we
heard up on the Millhopper Road."

The sheriff motioned toward the stairs. Pom led the way up
and tapped on the door. From the room came the muffled sound
of steely chords sliding up and down the neck of the guitar. Pom
tapped again. "Jim?"

He came to the door, guitar in hand. His sleeves were rolled
up. He had a pencil stuck behind his ear. He had opened the
door wide, apparently without any expectation of trouble. When
he saw the tall sheriff and his frowning deputy, he propped the
guitar against the bureau and looked from face to face. "What
gives?"

"The sheriff here would just like to have a look in your—in
the room," Pom said. "I don't suppose you'll be too long, will
you, Avery?"

Jim put a hand on the doorjamb. "I suppose you know that
without a warrant this is unconstitutional."

"We can get the warrant if we need to," the sheriff said. "And
in the meantime, we can make sure that nothing leaves this
room, including you. But I was kind of hoping to do it without
bothering the folks who've been kind enough to put you up."

"Would you mind telling me what it is you're looking for?"

"You'll know soon enough if we find it."

"What made you want to come up here? I haven't done anything but sing on the radio."

"That'll come out too. Are we square then?"

After a moment of hesitation, Jim moved away from the door. "Suit yourself."

The sheriff stepped past him and the deputy followed. He stood in the middle of the room, his hands on his hips, and spoke as if Jim weren't even there. "Is he the only boarder been in here lately?"

"Before him it was just old Mr. Howard," Flora said. "During his last illness."

Pom thought back. "Before that, nobody in a coon's age. Some college guys from time to time over the past fifteen years."

The deputy started to back into the guitar. Jim whisked it to safety and laid it on the bed. "Maybe I can save you some time if you'll tell me what you're looking for."

Avery dropped to one knee and poked around under the bed. The butt of his .45 stood out like a club. "You want to check the drawers, Leonard?"

"Do y'all mind?" The deputy gestured toward the bureau.

"Help yourself." Jim joined everyone else at the doorway and watched with folded arms.

The deputy opened each drawer as if it were booby-trapped, lifted the meager piles of clothing without interest, and eased it shut.

"Do you know what they're looking for?" Jim asked Pom.

"Beats me," Pom said.

The sheriff ran his hand along the bookcase. Most of the books were dusty old relics left by previous inhabitants. On one shelf there was a chunk of coquina, rich with fossil shells. Beside it stood a leather-bound book with gold Gothic letters on the binding. The sheriff picked it up and puzzled over the title.

"*Das Kapital*," Jim said. "Take it and read it if you want—if you read German."

The sheriff tossed the book onto the bed, barely missing the guitar. Behind a dictionary he found a small notebook, which he flipped open. "What's this?" He showed the pages of small symbols to Jim. "Looks like some kind of ciphers."

"I use a form of shorthand for taking down songs," Jim explained. He kept his arms crossed as if standing guard. "It wouldn't be of interest to anyone else."

The sheriff slipped the notebook into his shirt pocket, helped Leonard pull the bureau out from the wall, and bent over to test the dust apron of the bookcase. The deputy jumped back from the bureau and bumped into him. Arms flailing, they nearly toppled over.

Everyone fell back from the doorway. The sheriff straightened and slapped his hand on the butt of his .45.

"Damn roach." The deputy stomped at it and missed as it circled and darted toward the corner. He pushed the bureau back against the wall and coughed as if to break his tension and embarrassment. "I hate those things."

The sheriff said something under his breath and returned his attention to the bookcase, following the edges of the remaining books with his fingertips. His hand had been there for only a moment when he reached back and removed some books. Then he brought out a cigar box. He flipped the lid, folded back a gray cloth, and displayed the contents to the people in the room.

Flora angled for a better view. "What is it?"

"It's a German automatic pistol," the sheriff said. "Something called a Luger."

(HAPTER 16

⟨⟩uddenly Ainsley Harper had a big story, whether she wanted
it or not. Four days after Jim's arrest, she dragged a heavy
wooden chair up to the door of his cell and took in the bare
gray and green walls and high barred window.

"The district attorney's building a case against you, mostly on
hearsay so far."

The pull-down bunk was too far away for polite conversation,
so the prisoner stood before her. He planted his feet and folded
his arms like a soldier at parade rest, but apparently that seemed
too severe, so he shifted his weight to one foot and rested a hand
on the bars.

"That Luger might not be through killing people," he said.
"Don't write that down."

She hadn't yet taken out her notebook. "Any idea how it got
in your room?"

"Somebody wanted to frame me."

"Because of your politics?"

"Well, in my case it's hard to separate the political from the personal."

"The personal? Do you have any enemies here in town?"

"Pretty clearly."

"I mean do you know who they are?"

"Not exactly."

She came to the edge of the chair. "You do have enemies here though. Plural. What can you tell me about them?"

"Nothing." Seeing her frustration, he told her more. "All right, here it is. But this is off the record too."

She closed the notebook and crossed her legs. "I've pretty much given up on a story with any substance for now."

He told her about the three men at the church, adding, "One of them called me *Red*. So it wasn't just some guys out for a lark."

"So if you could find them...."

"Maybe we'd have something."

"In the meantime, the least they could do is let you have your guitar."

"Don't be so sure. I could use a string to strangle somebody." He came toward her and curled his fingers around the bars. "You see? I'm starting to think like them. I tried reading to the other prisoners but that didn't go so well."

"What about your politics, Jim? What's this revolution you've been talking about?"

"You've been doing your homework."

"It's a small town. Word gets around. What about the revolution? Do you espouse the violent overthrow of the U.S. government?"

"If the government is going to change as much as it needs to, violence might be unavoidable. Do I want it to happen that way? No, I don't. But look at the real changes this country has undergone, the radical improvements. The abolition of slavery and the subordination of the states to the central government— that took a civil war. The throwing off of the government of taxation without representation—that took a revolution. Even the Haymarket massacre back in the eighties made its point and had a positive effect. Maybe this time we'll do it right. I hope so."

"But now—don't you think that the government represents the will of the people?"

He pushed his hands against the bars. "Ever heard of Victor Berger?"

She thought for a moment. "No, I don't believe so."

"He was a socialist, elected repeatedly by Wisconsin's fifth congressional district right up until last year, and twice the U.S. House of Representatives refused to seat him just because he opposed our entry into the war. So, no, the government doesn't necessarily represent the will of the people."

She opened up the notebook again. "Is the Luger the murder weapon?"

"The lab in Jacksonville can't tell for sure. They can't get a match. The bullets were too deformed. The caliber's right though. Nine millimeter. If the murder weapon had been a seven-point-six-five instead of a nine, I'd be home free."

"Fingerprints?"

"I can guarantee you, they won't find mine on it."

"What about that cigar box the gun was in?"

"It wasn't from Perfecta. So they can't use it to prove a connection to me."

"Well, one way or the other, the truth's going to come out, don't you suppose?"

Jim tightened his grip on the bars. "Unfortunately, the truth *doesn't* always come out. When people run scared, the first thing to get trampled is the truth. Look what happened to Joe Hill."

Ainsley's face took on a faraway look. "When people run scared, the first thing to get trampled is the truth. That's poetry. It's like a line from a song. It wouldn't make a bad caption either. What if we did a story about the politics of fear? There's an angle. We could—"

He put up his hand. "The last thing I want is to be part of a newspaper circus. Look what happened at the Scopes trial—a complete zoo, a total distortion of the fundamental issue. I don't want a horde of people who don't even know me to start writing a lot of things that aren't true. I wouldn't want to be misrepresented."

Ainsley sighed and stood up. "It's hard dealing with a person who has principles. I'm just not used to it in my line of work. Okay, I'll see what I can do to get the facts out un-sensationalized. In the meantime, just don't...."

He came as close as the bars would allow. "Silence would also be a misrepresentation. If I have something to say, I have to speak out."

A deputy came into the corridor and she put the notebook into her handbag. "You know, they searched this before they let me in here."

He dropped his hands from the bars and took on a more formal tone. "Maybe next time I'll be able to give you something more useful."

Pom and Rex came during the afternoon. Pom turned the heavy chair around backwards and straddled it, sat with his thick forearms resting on the curved back while Rex stood with one hand on a cool bar of the cell door.

"Life keeps flaring up in our dull little town," Pom said. "Avery treating you okay?"

A deputy opened the door wide enough to slide in a meal on a tray. Sliced ham, black-eyed peas, collard greens, and cornbread. Water in a blue enamel mug. The door clicked shut.

"We get along." Jim set the tray on the bunk. "I think I'll let this soften up."

"They put the organist on the radio where you were," Rex told him. "I hear they've gotten some complaints too. We think they ought to let you out on Tuesdays and Thursdays to do the show."

"Thanks for the thought," Jim said, "but I can't see the Shirtsleeve Troubadour becoming the Jailhouse Troubadour. It would be hard to keep a following, let alone find a sponsor."

Pom had been thinking about the case. "I hate to say it, but that public defender's getting too senile to sign his own name, and the district attorney's an up-and-comer. Of course, he's got to prove you were connected to the victims."

"Well, I guess I'm connected to them now." Jim swept his hand toward the back of the cell. "Just like I'm connected to all the names on these walls. Sometimes it's almost as if they're talking to me. See that big one in the corner? *Michael Kierens, '91* and something in Latin. There has to be a story behind that. But how will we ever know what it is? And over here is one too faded to read, except the date, '79. I haven't made up my mind about adding my own."

Pom listened to the ranting of a prisoner down the gray and green corridor, a man who had blown his wife apart with a shotgun and was strolling down the street whistling when the police caught him. "What if we made this into something political, like Saco and Vanzetti? I bet we could get you a decent lawyer."

Jim let the idea sink in and then shook his head. "I guess you and Ainsley have been talking. As I told her, I wouldn't feel right doing that. I don't think politics is the issue here, or at least not the main one. I think there's something else going on."

For much of the night, Rex paced in his room and thought about Jim pacing in his. He was thinking about the guilty excitement of his first visit to the jail and the dreary confinement that Jim had to put up with all day every day. He thought that, for one who was accustomed to long solitary rambles, the cramped cell must be just short of torture.

He talked with his mother, who didn't know what to believe about Jim.

"He's been a good friend to you," she said as she emptied Pom's pockets before putting his shirts in the washtub. "But people can be complicated and sometimes we see just one side of them."

They both knew that she was thinking of her own father, who had lived an honest life for fifty years after robbing a Missouri bank.

Rachel seemed stung by the arrest. Just as the tender shoots of a relationship with Gene were developing, it turned out that she had been harboring a murder suspect, which somehow cast a shadow over her respectability at school. She hadn't seen Gene since the parade, for more than a week, but in a bitter way, she was glad. How could she face the embarrassment of having lived with the suspect because her father had misjudged him? And had she been duped also? She had liked Jim, maybe still did. But maybe this was a lesson that likable people could hide evil designs, that those who were best at it were the most dangerous. She turned away when her friends attempted to discuss it

She had a dream that the kitchen tap gushed blood.

Of all people, Roberta rose to the occasion. On the walk home from school, she caught up with Rex as he was passing the Florida Theater. He was watching Ben Pennell change the marquee from *Two Black Crows* to an all-talking picture, *The Virginian*, when he felt the hand on his shoulder and there she was, breathless but elegant in a cloche hat and white gloves. He looked down the street in disbelief. Rachel was nowhere to be seen. It was as if Siamese twins had been snipped apart. He was so startled by the novelty of the situation that afterward he wasn't sure what Roberta had said, something about how his family had been doing the right thing by taking Jim in and how the Shirtsleeve Troubadour was too honest to lie about his innocence.

By the time he got home, he couldn't remember what he had said either, nothing gracious, he thought with regret.

He never found out why she was suddenly so dressed up.

After supper Ainsley come by to compare her impressions with Pom's. Rex heard her rich rising laugh in the front room before he came downstairs. He wished that he could face his troubles with humor and conversation instead of pacing and turning his concerns over and over in private like a raunchy picture.

"Anybody who's known Jim for an hour would know that he'd never shoot anybody," Ainsley was saying. "He might talk them to death, but that's never been a crime."

When the house had settled down for the night and the only sounds were the shifting gears of the occasional passing car and Pom's light, rhythmic snoring, Rex stopped his pacing and picked up his compass and let the blue needle drift north. In his mind he flew the miles through the pinewoods, up the sloping road and over the rustling cornfield to the scarecrow and the farmhouse with the sagging porch. He wondered if Kim was a wanderer, too, if, like him, she was inclined to gaze into the night. He wondered if she ever thought of him.

He had no indication that she did. Nothing in her movements and glances suggested that she saw anything magical in him as he did in her, but he couldn't resign himself to her indifference. He felt like a member of a chain gang, moving to the strains of a song that no one else could hear, let alone sing, and at night he would give himself over to thoughts of her gray-green eyes, her wild brown hair and mysterious preoccupations.

He put the compass on the desk and idly turned the rough dial of the radio. On this night the faraway lonesome music was more than he could bear, so he went hunting the strange staccato signals. After a while he found them and did his best to copy down the senseless assortment of dots and dashes.

In the morning, before he left for school, he asked his father to deliver the ciphers to Jim and, after dragging through hours of algebra and history, he hurried home, looking for Pom to take him back to the jail. But Pom hadn't come back yet from a trip to Melrose, so Rex convinced his mother to walk over with him.

"To tell you the truth, I was sort of looking for an excuse," she said as she wrapped her shawl about her shoulders.

Not until they were crossing the courthouse lawn did Flora finally get Rex to slow down enough so that she could keep up. She stopped him beside the statue of the Confederate soldier. "Remember, Jim's not going anywhere," she told him, "and I don't do steeplechases."

The prisoner's response was a letdown. Jim pulled off his glasses, looked up from the paper with a blank face, and handed it back to him. "It's not Morse. That's for sure. It could be somebody testing a transmitter with a random signal." Seeing the boy's disappointment, he took back the piece of notebook paper and studied it some more. "Tell you what. It's just the thing I need to while away the time. I'll give it a good going-over in the morning and, if you like, we can talk again after school."

When Rex and his mother returned the next day, though, Jim had little to report.

"It looks kind of familiar," he said, "but I still can't make anything of it. Are you sure you copied it down right?"

"It was going awfully fast," Rex admitted.

"Do you think it's the same message every night or does it vary?"

"I don't know. Some of it sounds familiar, at the beginning I think. And then it's all over the place. I don't know how I can write it down any faster."

Jim tucked the piece of paper into his pocket. "Well, tonight see if you can get just the first part. Work on that and bring it tomorrow."

In the cell, under Leonard's unblinking supervision, Jim played the guitar for them, but refrained from singing.

"Have you learned any new songs?" Rex asked.

"I haven't quite worked up to that," Jim said.

"But all those people you got your songs from—didn't you tell me that they came mostly from tough situations too? Didn't the singing make it better? And didn't the singing help to get the message out as to what they were going through?"

Jim passed his hand over the gray part of the wall. "Maybe once I get a little more accustomed to this place."

That night a fight broke out at a tourist camp a stone's throw from the Porter's Quarters, and suddenly the sleepy jail filled up. Jim got a cellmate with little appreciation for music and none for literate conversation, let alone political theory. The Troubadour contented himself with reading a ripped-up copy of *Burning Daylight* by Jack London. The last several pages were torn out, but he didn't care.

"I can make up my own ending," he told Rex the next day, "and whenever I get out of here I can find an un-violated copy and compare my ending with his."

"It's got to be pretty boring in here," Pom said, looking at the cells full of surly and sleeping combatants from the tourist camp.

"After a while you begin to scale down your field of vision," Jim said. "You start to take interest in the little things. I'll bet Thoreau had no trouble doing jail time. He had such a penchant for observing the miniature, right down to the ants in his woodpile."

Rex fished in his pocket for the latest coded message. "They ought to let you out for Thanksgiving at least."

"I think we get turkey tonight," Jim said. "Already cut so they don't have to give us knives."

Rex thought that the entertainment value of the code must have faded for Jim by now, so when he pulled the slip of note-book paper from his pocket, he mentioned it only casually. "It's just the beginning, and it probably doesn't even match what I gave you before."

Jim went to his bunk and slipped the earlier page of code from the ragged copy of *Burning Daylight*. He studied the two pieces of paper for a while and then looked up sharply. "They're different all right, but it's the same message—or part of a message." He held up the new copy. "In the first one you were trying to make sense of it as Morse code. In this one you copied down what you actually heard."

Rex pressed against the bars. "Do you know what it is?"

Jim's cellmate had been lying belly up on his bunk with one arm flung across his face. He sat up and glared at the two visitors with bloodshot eyes. "Me being in jail don't mean I have to put up with chiggers like y'all. Would you kindly shut up so I can get some sleep?"

Jim came up to the bars so that his hand was almost touching Rex's. "I think it's Navy code. It's not much different from what I used when I was at sea. That was ten, twelve years ago though. I've forgotten a lot, so it's going to take some time. But I think we can crack this, especially after a good night's sleep."

CHAPTER 17

⁂

As had been their custom for more than fifty years, the Wards came to the Holliman house for a potluck Thanksgiving dinner.

"It's so warm we could almost eat outside," Flora said as she watched Nelda hobble up the front walk with J.J. supporting one arm and the two canes dangling from the other.

The matriarch stopped at the bottom of the steps. "It may be warm to you young folks, but we old buzzards who have lost our stuffing get the chills when it drops below eighty. I shiver just thinking of my girlhood winters in New Jersey."

Pom reached down from the steps with a guiding hand. "Have you joined the Daughters of the Confederacy, Nelda? Seems to me you've turned into a Cracker through and through."

She waved her free hand and the canes bopped her in the side. "No, I'm not that far gone yet, and I give my Confederate widow's pension to the library. I don't have any use for a bunch of silly old clubs. Who's got time for all that hooey?"

"I'm thinking of building a little railroad from the street to the porch just for you," Pom said.

Flora helped her up the steps. "If it takes him as long as putting in the new wiring, *I'll* need your railroad too."

"Never mind," Nelda said, regaining her balance as she reached the porch. "He's just another man with promises."

When the feast was well underway, Pom mentioned that Ainsley was working on a story about Jim's arrest.

Nelda groaned and pushed her upper plate back into place. "Everything nowadays is such a sensation. I don't think things have been the same since the war with Spain."

Richard sawed quietly at his turkey. He was far and away the best-dressed person at the table, dapper in a navy blue blazer, a tie in blue and white regency stripes, and pressed gray trousers. On the way in, he had tossed his gray fedora onto the knob of the newel post.

During a lull, Pom asked him what he thought of the case of the Shirtsleeve Troubadour.

He looked up like a cat caught swallowing a parakeet and paused, either to finish chewing or to give the question due thought. "Whether he did it or not, they'll likely turn him loose, don't you suppose? What do they have for evidence?"

"They've got that gun," J.J. said. "They've sure enough got that German gun that came from his room."

"They ought to get the fingerprints off it," Rex declared. "I'll bet you Jim's prints aren't anywhere on it."

"You're right," boomed a voice from the back of the room. Sheriff Mecum came forward, put his hat on the Brunswick, and joined Pom at the head of the table. "Sorry to let myself in, folks, but I guess you didn't hear me ringing the bell."

"It's on the fritz and we've been making a lot of commotion," Pom said. "As usual when we get these clans together. Won't you have a bite with us? We've got fresh pork and a wild turkey that J.J. shot in the San Felasco Hammock."

"Wish I could, Pom, but I just stopped by to fill you in a little."
Avery swept a hand over his broad forehead. "It looks like we're
going to be holding onto Mr. Jim Rhodes for a while. Seems he
was mixed up in another murder case, in Wisconsin. I'm sorry
to come in here like this on Thanksgiving, but I thought you'd
want to know."

Pom pushed his chair back from the table and took the napkin out of his collar. "What did he do?"

The sheriff placed a hand on the back of Rex's chair. "In 1919
there was a strike up in Wisconsin, in the city of Madison. We
know that Rhodes and a strikebreaker, a man named Fadden,
exchanged words that came to blows. And we know that the
next morning Fadden turned up floating in a lake with his face
knocked in."

Flora put her fingers to her temples.

The floor creaked as the sheriff shifted his weight. "On top of
that, the lab up in Jacksonville has a tentative match between the
Luger we've got and the slug taken out of the woman's throat."
He let the reaction die down before he went on. "The evidence
begins to slide to one side of the scale."

Pom got up and pushed his chair in and pointed to the stairs.
"But you can't tell us how you found out there was a Luger was
up there?"

"It might come out in the trial, but for now, take my word for
it, it's got no bearing on Mr. Rhodes' guilt or innocence."

"Amelia swears it wasn't her."

"It wasn't. End of discussion."

"And you say it was a strikebreaker that got killed up there in
Wisconsin."

"That's right. He was working for a factory owner up there."

"Did Jim go to trial for it?"

"Didn't even get arraigned. A key witness disappeared."

Becoming aware of his tight grip on the back of the chair,
Pom put his hands on his hips. "Seems to me that the murder

up in Wisconsin is about as different as can be from the one in my pasture—and neither one of 'em sounds like Jim. I've never seen him so much as lift a finger in anger." He looked at the faces around the table. "Has any of you?"

Rex gazed past his father's raised hand. He tried to shut out the images of the fight at the church by watching a shower of dogwood leaves flutter past the open window.

Avery took his hat from the Brunswick. "The fingerprints are a wash. That Luger was so clean the lab couldn't get anything off it. They're looking real hard at the rest of those bullets though." He scanned the upturned faces at the table. "Sorry to bust in on your Thanksgiving, but I thought you'd want to know."

After dinner Richard and Pom went out to the driveway to have a look at the Packard. "It's all I can do to get up Kincaid Hill," Richard said for all to hear as they left the house.

When they got to the car the conversation turned. "Pom, I could sure use you on the boat. I need somebody I can trust."

Pom made a point of folding back the hood and poking around as if to look for fouled valves. "You been making trips? I thought you were doing okay."

"I tried working with a guy out of Crystal River, crazy, careless bastard. The other night on the way back he fell overboard when I was below and it took me most of an hour to find him. He's a damn thief, too."

"Imagine that." Pom pulled back and looked him in the eye. "What if you talk to Avery about your friend the collector?"

"And pin what on him? He's a little heavy-handed when I try to shortchange him, but you can't put him in jail for that. All you can do is make him mad. No thanks."

"What if he goes after somebody else, though?"

"That's more second guessing than I can do. And even if Avery could put him away, somebody else would just as likely come along to take his place, maybe somebody even less friendly. Give me time to buy my way out. You want to blow the whistle on him after that, go ahead. For now, I can sure use somebody to help me out on the boat."

"I'm no rumrunner. I'd be a danger to you, to both of us."

"Oh, come on. It's mostly just a boat ride and a drive in the country. But another pair of hands to load and unload and keep the boat going in the right direction would sure make it easier. Somebody steady who won't blab."

"What about Buddy Cole? He sure needs the money."

"Give me a break. His nerves are shot and he couldn't keep a secret if he was underwater."

"Well, now, who says so?"

"*He* did. Look, for now, just don't say no. How's that? There's plenty of quick money in it."

Pom had kept the letter from the state to himself, but it was as if Richard had read it and picked just the right moment to come back to him.

"All right. I'm not saying no. But I hope you'll get someone better lined up before I say yes."

Rex came out to the porch to duck the dishwashing and avoid a discussion about the new skirts that went all the way down to mid-calf. As he listened to the barking of a distant dog and the sharp reply of the dachshund across the street, he wrestled with this new setback, Jim's implication in the Wisconsin killing. It had been a labor quarrel. Jim had locked horns with a strikebreaker and someone had beaten the man to death. Rex might be the only person other than the masked attackers who knew what Jim could do with his fists. It didn't seem right to tell. But on the other hand, it didn't seem right *not* to tell. He was trying to decide what to do when the screen door opened.

"I forgot to give these to Ainsley," Flora said, handing him a slippery stack of magazines with cheerful covers, *The Saturday Evening Post* and *Collier's*. "Will you please take them over to her? Just tell her that if she sells a story I want a finder's fee. And don't dawdle. It's getting dark"

He had no desire to be batting around in the blackness, so he took the shortest of his shortcuts, catty-corner through backyards and over fences, a route with some risk of dogs and snakes, barbed wire and Spanish bayonets, but the going was easy this time, and the magazines made it to her street unscathed.

He came in through the corner of Ainsley's backyard and was on his way to the kitchen door when he heard the voices, Ainsley's and Theron's, in some kind of set-to. He hesitated, bright, chipper magazines in hand, not wanting to walk into a fight that was none of his business, but not wanting to go all the way back home with nothing accomplished, so he wavered there beyond the edge of the light from the kitchen windows, waiting for the voices to stop, glad now that Theron's taxidermy had silenced the neighbor's cocker spaniel.

At a lull he came closer, all the way to the back step, but the voices went at it again, worse than before, so he stood in the shadows, watching through the edge of the window in the door, waiting for his chance.

Ainsley's voice cut through the open window, shrill and angry. "Theron, I don't *want* to go with you. I'm not in the mood."

A chair scraped as Theron came toward her. "Come on, Peachy. You'll be glad you did."

"Do *not* call me that. Look, I don't have time for this. Just tell me what you're up to."

"You've got time to idle away the hours at Pom's house and at the parade."

"I keep telling you, that was work."

"Didn't look like work to me."

After a long stillness she said in a lower, steadier voice, "Has it dawned on you that things have not exactly worked out between us?"

"This is just a bump. Anyway, we're married. Till death do us part."

She came toward him, head lowered. "This is 1929, Theron, and mistakes can be fixed. You can be free to go hunting whenever you want and I can be free to pursue my little rainbows around here. All we have to do is sign some papers. What do you say?"

He stuck his furry jaw toward her. "A deal's a deal."

"Well, I'm ready for a fresh deal. It's called divorce."

He looked at her edgewise. "Don't believe in it. Come on, Peachy, let's just make up. Tonight."

She backed away and picked up her macramé handbag. "The very idea makes me want to, I don't know, to throw myself off the Dixie Hotel. It makes me want to get tattoos all over my body and dye my hair orange so I'll be a different person from the misguided girl that had anything to do with you, so I can have my identity back and start all over again. If you won't go, I will."

Suddenly he had her by the hair. She twisted in his grasp, but he had her fast and close with one arm clamped around her waist so that she had no room to strike at him.

His face was red and the vein in his neck stood out as he curled his hand more tightly in her hair. "Looks like nobody's going anywhere for awhile."

She pulled back and slammed her forehead into his temple and he let go, stumbling backwards. She grabbed at her handbag, but before she could get a grip on it, he came back at her, caught at the strap and broke it, spilling the bag onto the floor. She dove for it but he was faster. He dropped to one knee and pulled it toward him, and she raked her fingernails across his cheek, coming at him again as he struggled to his feet. He swore and swung his fist, splitting her lip and dropping her down hard, still clutching the handbag. She sat up, brushed the hair from her face, and touched the back of her hand to her bloody mouth.

"I ought to pop you again," he said, his chest heaving as he hovered over her. "I've been wanting to do that for eight years."

Ainsley sat on the floor, knees up, heels spread, the hem of her dress thrown above her garters. She pressed the handbag to her chest as Theron stormed out the front door and ran to his dark blue Studebaker. Backing out of the driveway, he knocked over the mailbox and slid into the road. Then he skidded off in a welter of gravel and dust.

Rex waited in the shadows of the back porch, trying to decide whether he should go in and see to Ainsley or leave her alone. As he stood listening to the distant *snip-snip* of swallows, he began to fear for her life, and so he tapped on the window of the back door, strangely formal standing there with his shoulders squared and the cheerful magazines clenched to his hip.

When she failed to appear, he let himself in and found her still sitting on the floor.

Seeing him, she seemed to come out of a trance.

"Oh, Rex, you brought magazines. Thank you." Her smile was a broken relic of what it had been. "Did you just get here?"

He kept his eyes away from the indecency of her legs. "No, ma'am. I was in the yard for a while."

She put her knees down and smoothed her hem, became more limber, but was still clumsy. She picked up the handbag the wrong way, scattering the rest of the contents, lipstick, a notepad, a small pistol. She scooped it all up as if it were everyday spillage.

"Well, you probably know that these things happen," she sniffed. "They're a part of life."

"I can call my folks. They can come and get us."

She smiled again, not very well this time, as he helped her struggle to her feet. "Don't you even think of it. They have plenty to do as it is."

His knees were shaking. He'd never held a woman this way. She was warm and heavy on his shoulder, breathing hot.

"You ought not to be out here tonight. What if he comes back?"

She dragged out a chair and sat at the kitchen table. "Oh, don't you worry about that. I know him. He won't be back anytime soon."

"It isn't safe. You ought not to—"

A ghost of a smile returned to her smudged mouth. She put a finger to his lips. "It'll be all right. You're a very fine man to be so concerned."

"Isn't there anything I can do for you?"

She leaned close and lowered her voice. "There is one thing, Rex. Keep this to yourself, will you?"

CHAPTER 18

———◈———

om asked about Theron's new Studebaker when he and Rex came to the jail to visit the Troubadour.

The sheriff struck a match on the whetstone he'd been using to sharpen his jackknife. "He's good with cars, you know. He fixes 'em up in between stints as a hunting guide and doing the taxidermy." He lit a panatela and rocked back in his swivel chair. "You see him again, tell him I'm looking for him. He's got to settle with his neighbor for stuffing her dog."

Pom bit his lip to keep from smiling. "So I hear. Those cars he works on, they've always junkers, aren't they? I've never known him to have a car like that Studebaker."

The sheriff settled into the chair. "I guess that's his prerogative."

Back in the cellblock somebody began singing loud and off-key, *Halleluiah, I'm a Bum.*

Pom winced. "He's no Shirtsleeve Troubadour, is he?"

"We're packed. We've got all kinds," Avery said. "And on top of that, now I've got these damn federal men nipping at my heels."

"What do they want down here?"

"They're pushing the Volstead Act. Two agents, Thorndike and Lamar by name, breezed in here the other night and accused me of being soft on it. Only problem is, when Congress passed the damn thing they never made any provision for enforcing it, except for giving federal agents all kinds of vague powers. So now they're telling me I'm supposed to take the same handful of men to cover the usual mayhem, plus go chasing down every nickel bootlegger and rumrunner in the county."

"What set 'em off?"

"They're looking for the tail end of a big rumrunning operation that an army of agents broke in New York. So we hauled in everyone we knew of, plus two college boys that hit a pothole in front of Holy Trinity and dribbled Canadian whiskey clear around the Square."

Pom could see that Rex was getting fidgety, so they went into the dank green and gray cellblock to see Jim. Before they got to him, Pom stopped at the sight of another familiar face. He smiled. "Trent Walker. What are you doing in here?"

Trent sat against the wall, wrapping loops in a piece of string. "Seems like somebody talked about my still."

With Rex beside him, Pom spoke in vague terms. "I'm sorry to hear that. Whoever it was probably just meant it as a compliment. Wouldn't've done any harm if the rules hadn't changed."

Trent pulled his hands apart, revealing the neat lattice of Jacob's Ladder.

"Don't give it another thought. Just forget it, Pom."

"At this rate I'll have more friends in than out. I'd get you out of there if I could."

Trent undid his handiwork. "I'm starting to wish I'd stayed and shot it out. That helper of mine got away Scot free."

Pom grew serious. "What happened?"

Trent's gray eyes looked tired. "All of a sudden they decided to come after me. That's all I know. I heard there was some feds in town putting the heat on Avery to bring everybody in, but I thought it was just a rumor."

Pom put his hands on his hips. "Are Elsie and the girls okay? Because—"

Trent looked up from his loops. "They'll be all right for a while. But I need a way out of here before I lose it. I can pace off this floor only so many times."

"Don't think about where you are, Trent. Think about where you want to be, and that'll help get you through. At least you're in one chunk. You came in peaceful then?"

"If you don't count that fool Ernie. He took a shot and ran. Me, I had my hands up before they could even get the words out."

"Then likely they'll let you off easy."

"Hell, the process alone drags on enough to make a man go stir crazy. And you know they've got me dead to rights. I might just as well have put an ad in the paper."

"They'll likely let you off with a fine and give you some time to come up with the money."

"Well, whatever happens, I ain't going back to Raiford." Suddenly he became aware of the boy beside Pom. "That you, Rex? You're so big I hardy knew you. How are things at school?"

The only thing Rex could come up with was the pie thief Ollie Holiday.

Trent began working his loops again. "His family still lives over there at the edge of the Leary Woods, don't they?"

"On what used to be the Dorsey farm." Pom gave Rex an inquiring look. "That's the first I've heard of this."

"I never much cared for the whole load of 'em," Trent said, pulling the string into a Cat's Cradle. "They ran that place into the ground. It was a perfectly good farm till they got a hold of it."

"Jake Jolly helped 'em," Pom said. "They hired him on, but I hear that instead of tending to business, he spends all his time out in the woods peeping in car windows."

When they went back to see Jim, he was at the bars waiting for them.

"What's the news from the outside?"

All Rex could think of was Admiral Byrd attempting to fly to the South Pole.

"Keep listening to your radio," Jim said. "In the meantime, there's this." He went to his bunk and came back with a piece of notepaper. "I've got it all figured out, everything you've given me. It's Navy code all right, just a little different from the one I used. These are ship-to-shore position reports."

The other bunk was folded up against the wall. "Where's your roommate?" Pom asked.

"Bailed out," Jim said. "I would've paid it gladly if I had it, just to have him gone."

Pom put his hands in his pockets the way he did when he was launching into a difficult subject. "Do you think the district attorney's going to make trouble for you with that killing up in Wisconsin?"

Jim was fast to reply. "Let him. He won't find anything. Fadden landed one on me and I put one on his chin before some strikers pulled us apart. That was as far as it went."

"Then who killed him?"

"Could've been anybody. He was a tough and a womanizer. I wasn't sorry when he turned up in Lake Monona, but I didn't put him there. There were plenty of guys in line ahead of me to do that, maybe some women too."

It was as if Pom had opened a tap to ten years of anger, and he thought it best to let Jim cool down. He mentioned some business with Avery, took his leave, and went back into the office.

"Look, get me some more of this," Jim told Rex when they were alone. "There's something strange going on here."

Rex touched the bars of the cell door. "There has to be some way to get you out of here. They can't hold you forever."

Jim gripped his hand to reassure him. "Well, the arraignment went against me and the judge set the bail at five thousand, so it'll take a minor miracle to get me out while I'm waiting for the trial. Next stop—a lot of paperwork and the pre-trial hearing. I don't know how all of this is going to turn out, but I have two great things on my side—the truth and your friendship." He held up the wrinkled piece of notebook paper. "In the meantime, let's see what we can do to get closer to this little scrap of truth."

The cryptic radio messages became hard to find. They welled up at unpredictable times in the middle of the night on different parts of the dial, and Rex resorted to sneaking coffee into his room after supper so that he could stay awake looking for them. The coffee was left over from the early evening, had long since grown cold, and it tasted like mulch, but a cup or two spirited away before Flora could toss it out was enough to keep Rex going until the first birds of morning began to sing. His copying was full of errors because the code was so fast and seemingly random, and he was usually half-asleep when it finally came through.

After five nights, feeling numb and pinched, he began dozing in school. Mrs. Campion was patient with him and did her best to keep the other boys from ribbing him about his friend the Red in jail. Toward the end of the day, he woke with a start as he was falling out of his desk. He brushed away a hand, not sure if it was helpful or hurtful, and stared ahead, as if looking though a tunnel, ignoring the giggles and whispers.

That night he slept through the elusive code and found himself dreaming of another long walk into the dark pasture, a place now devoid of sound except for his own breathing. The tall grass got higher and higher as he followed his feet to the bloodstained oak tree. Gradually the darkness became impenetrable, so that he could tell only that he was going downhill, but the distance was longer than he remembered. Thinking that he might blunder into the tree and its grim companions, he put his hand out and felt his way into the abyss. When his fingers curled into an open mouth, he screamed, but the only noise he heard was a thin rhythmic ringing, two long and one short.

Suddenly his mother was sitting at the edge of his bed. "That was Mrs. Campion on the telephone. She thought you might be sick." The back of her hand was cool against his forehead. She sat back and folded her arms. "No fever. But I think you've come down with something. We need to talk."

Rex wiped his forehead with his pajama sleeve. "I'm okay. Just need some sleep."

She watched him for a moment, as if waiting for him to break out in spots. "Anyone would be exhausted after what you've been through these last couple of months, since the pasture."

The mere word *pasture* had come to sum up so much that she didn't need to say more. He wondered if the word would ever again evoke sweet grass and sunshine.

"And now all this business with Jim." He had forgotten to hide the coffee cup. She saw it behind the radio and picked it up.

"I've been studying a lot," he explained. "Sometimes I need a boost to stay awake."

She set the cup back down and stroked his cheek. She looked tired. "Rex, this won't do. There's more than homework keeping you up all night. You can't go on like this."

"I'll be all right. Really. It's the weekend. I can catch up on my sleep."

She clasped her hands on her knee. She was wearing the same broad-collared dress that she had worn when they had carried Mr. Howard to the room at the top of the stairs, the room Jim had occupied until the arrest.

"Somehow it's all tied up together," she said. "The pasture, the radio—Jim. None of it healthy. It's time to move forward."

He started to say something, but she went on. "The pasture—you just have to put it out of your mind. There's nothing you can do about it and it was just an accident that you happened to be the one to—that you were the first one there."

It was supposed to be so simple, he thought. Just make up your mind and put it behind you. But those images burned into his head had a life of their own. He couldn't control when they jumped out at him.

She looked at the radio, the mysterious working of the commonplace into the exotic. "That's done more harm than good," she said. "We should probably throw it out."

He jolted awake and sat up against the brass headboard. "That radio's the only thing that keeps me going, the only thing that takes my mind off what I saw out there."

She took his hand and squeezed it. "Listen to me. You can put it behind you. Things will take their course. One way or the other, whoever did it will pay for it."

Rex pulled his hand away. "Except that Jim's in jail for it."

"There's a price for everything. He didn't do himself any favors by airing his politics on the radio."

"Don't tell me you think—"

She put her hands up. "I'm just saying that he painted himself into a corner. There's a couple dead—executed—not robbed, not attacked, just executed. It's the kind of thing that happens in Russia or Germany, the places he talks about, the places where people are killed for their politics. The gun that did it is a foreign gun. All I'm saying is that if Jim didn't do it, he made himself the perfect suspect with all that talk about unions and socialism and revolution."

"He couldn't help it. He says what he believes. That's how I know he's innocent. If he had killed those people, he's say so and he'd say why. I don't think he could lie about it if he tried."

"You and your father," Flora said. "You're so sure about people. Remember your first trip to the radio station? When you met that actor, the one that plays the boy? What did you learn?"

"That was dif—"

"You learned that people aren't always what they seem. Didn't you? Well, things will take their course. The truth will come out. And for now Jim's probably safer where he is."

She didn't have to explain. They had both read the recent newspaper account of the prisoner in transit up in Live Oak, the one a mob took from the sheriff, dragged to an oak tree, and did a bad job of hanging.

CHAPTER 19

For the first time in his career, Pom was glad that being a veterinarian kept him away from home so much. He liked the freedom of it anyway, the open road with a new destination each day, whether it was up to Alachua to look at hog cholera or south to Ocala to help with foaling. He liked setting his own hours and steering his life with one hand on the wheel. Now his lifestyle was proving especially fortunate because people were used to him being gone all night, and he could justify disappearing for a day or two with a vague explanation. By the time people found out he'd lost the state job, he'd have enough money to cover expenses until the next job came along. In the meantime, he could use the comings and goings of a veterinarian as a perfect cover for a brief partnership with Richard. The only drawback—other than the risk of getting caught—was getting home in the wee hours, long after Flora had locked him out.

He figured that two trips with Richard, two successful trips, would get Trent out on bail and hire him a lawyer good enough to minimize the sentence for moonshining, and he felt a growing urgency to do it because he had spoken too freely about the wonderful sparkle coming from the still. His care-lessness had surely helped to get Trent arrested. And his ad-vice had prompted Trent to sink his money into a farm at what turned out to be the worst time and place. He was haunted by the hopelessness in his friend's face, and hoped for a few dollars left over to start putting Trent's little scrap of a farm back together. He'd be able to pay Amelia until she could find something better. Maybe he could even clear a hundred for Rachel's college tuition, which ought to put him back in good graces with Flora. And how to explain where the money had come from? Debts paid! Surely there were enough of those to account for a thousand dollars.

And what about Jim Rhodes? Pom had vouched for him from the beginning, had pronounced him sound, and was so cocksure about that judgment that he decided to go out on a limb to get Jim cleared.

He made the rounds and borrowed twenty-four hundred from Laetitia Harper, put up his pasture and cows as collateral for a bank loan, and redeemed some old bonds from Missouri to come up with bail for him. But getting Jim out of jail during the legal process was just a start. The real nut to crack was in the courtroom, and he couldn't imagine the doddering public defender making a case for Jim at the pre-trial hearing and the second arraignment, let alone getting a not guilty verdict from a jury when the case went to trial.

A decent lawyer would require money, and he knew of only one way to get it.

According to Richard, a few more runs to Baldwin would bring them both enough to quit. They were on the boat, following the channel into the Gulf. They were taking a good close look at the shore so that Pom could recognize landmarks at night.

The way Richard told it, the last transaction at Porter's Place was downright routine. He had paid the collector for November. The phantom had worn no disguise for the occasion; just a gray three-piece suit and a damn sharp Panama hat.

Pom watched the tree line recede in the east. "When's you next payment due?"

Richard was fast to answer. "December the twenty-seventh."

"Kind of like paying a mortgage, isn't it, only a little more dangerous if you default. How many more payments?"

Richard smiled. "Just that one, Pom."

"That ought to make you happy."

"Sure, I'll be happy and the collector will be happy. And come December the thirty-first, you'll be on easy street."

"Seems like a couple of details have fallen by the wayside," Pom said.

"Well, you've always got to be able to improvise," Richard told him. "The main thing is, you know the water and you know the boats. The rest of it's just doing the best you can."

"For starters, how about this?" Pom said. "You ever wonder what happened to the guy who was driving the stuff up to Baldwin before you?"

Ahead of them, the water took on a rough edge. Richard slowed the boat and swung the wheel to the left. "Something better came up maybe."

"Or something worse," Pom said.

Four nights later, on the fifteenth of December, Pom made his first run up the Waccasassa with Richard.

It began with the long trip out the Cedar Key channel over choppy water flecked orange by the sinking sun. Pom watched the white wake spreading out behind them in its endless *V* and wondered aloud if they might just as well be trolling for mackerel as long as they had this long ride ahead of them.

"We'll be trolling for bigger fish soon enough," Richard said over the drone of the engine.

"You ever gotten out to the pickup point and not have the big boat show up?"

"The whole thing goes like clockwork. And when I bring it to the pickup point the guys in Baldwin know exactly how much I'm supposed to have. They've got a nice tight little operation."

"As long as they don't show up at my house to do business."

"They don't even know my last name. They always get a hold of me by calling at Porter's Place, formerly the LaRue warehouse. You ever been in there?"

"In a speakeasy? I'll have a drink in the woods or a swig of Martha Duforge's blackberry wine, but I'm not a saloon man. It's too close to home. I don't like the idea of being drug into jail by my ear."

They left the last channel marker behind, and Richard angled to the north, where dark bands of clouds hovered over the horizon.

Pom continued. "Don't you suppose Avery's going to close it down one of these nights?"

"Probably. If he's not on the take."

"Avery? Nah."

"It's just a matter of price, Pom, and he needs money too, same as everybody else. All he's got to do is keep looking the other way. That wouldn't be so hard."

"He rounded up Trent Walker and a dozen other bootleggers in the space of about a week just to make the feds happy."

"Yeah, but those are little guys, Pom. You think they could pay off a sheriff between 'em? The big ones get away with it because they've got the money to move fast or buy their way out."

"So a big guy owns the speakeasy?"

"Not so big and not a guy. Just discrete."

Pom swept the spray from his face. "How about you?"

Richard laughed. "Yeah, discrete. That's me. But you can pull off only so many tricks before people start to catch on. That's why I'm going to cash in big on the last one."

It was a smooth rendezvous. They loaded the liquor without exchanging more than a few words, working in the shadows with quiet efficiency. As he stowed the heavy sacks in the hold, Pom kept an eye out for approaching boats, but the darkness held. When they had the hold filled, Richard pulled the lines from the cleats, throttled up, and steered back to the east.

"*Cristobel*," Pom said as the freighter turned stern to. "Out of Havana."

Despite the speed of the *Sun Dog* and the spray shooting over the bow, he was starting to get groggy by the time they saw the first scattering of lights along the coast.

"Don't fall asleep on me," Richard said. "We're just now fixing to go to work."

Pom broke off a yawn when one of the lights came toward them. "Any idea who that is?"

"It's too late for a fisherman and too close in for a shrimper." Richard slowed the engine and took a pair of binoculars from a shelf behind the wheel. After two or three swells had passed, he turned back toward open water.

Pom took the binoculars but couldn't make anything out of the vague silhouette.

"Better safe," Richard said. "We're going to go up toward Cedar Key and see if we can shake him."

The boat matched their easterly course for a mile and then started moving toward them again.

"He's doing a good job of keeping between us and the shore," Pom said. "How are we doing on gas?"

"Not that good. I was in a hurry so I didn't fill up." Richard brought the engine down to idle and took a hard look through the binoculars. "Cut the lights off."

Pom flipped the toggle switch on the panel by the wheel and the bow and stern went dark. "This is going to take a little imagination."

They steered by flashlight and compass in a zigzag that took them south and east. The yellow light of the other boat slowed, but continued to come at them.

Richard swung back out toward the open Gulf. "Damn! How can he tell where we are?"

"Maybe he's just guessing," Pom said.

"Well, if he keeps on guessing, we're going to run out of gas."

"You want to try to beat him to the Waccasassa?"

"Not much choice since that's where the truck is." Richard wheeled the boat south and throttled forward to about three-quarter speed. "We've got to hit the channel right. If we run aground, we're cooked. Where the hell is that boat?"

Pom scanned the darkness. "I don't know and I hope I never find out."

After speeding blind through the night for a few more miles, they jolted to a halt. The bottom of the boat squealed and shimmied and they sat.

"At least we're close in," Pom said. "But at this rate, the last mile or so might be slow going. He took out his watch and looked at it in Richard's flashlight. "Tide's coming back in now. You suppose we ought to lie low and float off?"

Richard began taking his clothes off. "Let's find out where the water is and go for it." When he had stripped naked, he took a long gaff and slid into the water with it. He made his way to the bow and swam forward with an easy sidestroke. He splashed around a little, dove down once or twice, then swam back and reported that there was plenty of water just ahead.

"It's better than that," Pom told him. "Look over that way."

Not a hundred yards off, at an odd angle, was the familiar silhouette of a channel marker.

"We hit the damn thing head on, Richard. We ran into the dredgings at the edge of the channel."

But by the time Richard was back on board and dressed, the news had turned bad. The light, the relentless yellow light, was coming at them again. Richard backed the boat and gunned the engine, then gave it full throttle forward until the water boiled and kicked around them. They moved forward then stuck again, backed and lunged and stuck.

Pom felt free to raise his voice above the racket. "Well, he sure knows where we are now!"

Richard bit his thumb. "He knew where we were headed all along, don't you suppose? We may have faked him out for a while there, but he knew from the start where we were headed."

The boat rocked and shook. Behind them the yellow light took on the form of a sleek vessel with a high pilothouse. Pom and Richard stood wreathed in smoke, looking from the churning water ahead to the oncoming light behind.

Richard called over his shoulder. "How far can you swim? Can't be more than a mile or two."

"I can swim from here to Sopchoppy," Pom said, "if it'll keep me out of —"

Both of them crashed into the wheel as the boat jerked forward. Richard regained his balance and swung into the channel.

Pom picked himself up and let out a whoop. "Let's burn some water! Just keep her between the markers."

As he spoke, his face lit up like a full moon, and one window of the pilothouse shattered. He and Richard ducked at the same time while splinters flew past them. Crouching, he looked back. "If they're not careful they're going to kill us."

Richard ducked even lower. "That's what they're trying to do!"

"What are you talking about? Don't they just want to take us in?"

"They're hijackers, Pom. They want the booze."

"You didn't tell me about any hijackers."

A bullet whistled past Pom's ear. He dropped down and pressed himself against the bulkhead, shielding his face with his shoulder as he looked back over the stern.

"It's the first time I've run into any." Richard hunched low over the wheel, peering through the spokes to the next channel marker.

Pom expressed a profound wish to be back at the dinner table, talking the finer points of college dating and home repair. Idle talk suddenly had immense appeal.

A slug slammed into the stern, then a second, and the engine started to misfire.

Pom took the flashlight, crawled aft, and lifted the hatch cover. He slid down into the engine compartment and had a look. Gas was spurting from the line in two places. He rummaged through the darkness for the toolbox and closed his fingers over some adhesive tape that he wrapped several times around each break. Just as the engine was recovering, a third bullet pierced the compartment and ricocheted under his arm. He jumped up, hitting his head on the hatch frame, scrambled up the ladder, and rolled onto the deck.

"Get us out of here before they stop us cold."

"See if you can slow 'em down a little with this." Richard had one hand on the wheel and the other on a .32 caliber pistol.

The spotlight swept through the pilothouse again, Pom dropped to his knees with his arm shading his eyes. He fired at the light.

A burst of return fire threw up a shower of splinters.

Richard spun the wheel to throw the pursuer away from his stern, but he was dangerously close to the edge of the channel.

Pom fired at the light again. "I'm going to save the rest of my ammo in case we get into serious trouble."

From the chipped and splintered wheelhouse Richard gave him a skeptical smile. A bullet hole showed black in the glass of the light-struck window behind him.

From another direction a second salvo raked the darkness beyond the glaring light.

"Damn bloody hell," Richard said, roaring down the channel at full throttle. "There's two of 'em on us now! Get ready to swim, Pom. We can't run away from both of 'em. We can dive off the back and let 'em go for the boat. It'll be a while before they figure we're not on it, and by then, they won't care." He straightened the wheel and wedged the gaff against it. Then he steadied himself on the sloping deck and offered his hand. "Well, good luck to us, Pom! Sink or swim, we'll probably not see each other again soon."

Before Pom could reply, the deadly spotlight went out and the sounds of guns and voices began to fade. A hundred yards away now, gun flashes lit up the blackness

"Richard, that other boat isn't after us—he's after *them!* What the *hell* is going on?"

"A golden opportunity, that's what." Richard yanked the gaff out of the wheel and charged for the middle of the channel. "It's the damn Coast Guard going after the hijacker."

Slack-jawed, Pom stared into the darkness.

The hijacker sped out into the Gulf with the government boat closing behind it.

Richard let out a shrill cry and hugged Pom around the neck until they started to fall over.

Pom freed himself and jiggled his fingers in his ears to stop the ringing. "Would that be the Rebel Yell?"

"Learned it from my granddaddy! That and never to give up, no matter how outnumbered you are!"

When they got to the mouth of the Waccasassa, Richard slowed the boat and used the flashlight to probe his way through the several twisting miles to the landing, a forlorn outpost with a sorry little pine pier that creaked beneath the weight of men and bottles. They worked quickly under scant moonlight to transfer the cargo to the hay truck and put the sand ruts behind them all the faster. The tires let out a squeal as they hit the gravel of the main highway.

"I'm about ready to let out a little yip myself," Pom said. "Tell me it's all downhill from here, Richard."

"Be in Baldwin before you know it."

When they got to the freight yard, Pom kept quiet and stayed out of the light while they transferred the load to the boxcar. When the job was done, he kept to himself while Richard dealt with Ralph and Archie.

"Does that big guy look familiar?" Richard asked as he swung the truck around.

Pom sat up and had a good look at him. "No, but I can tell you he's wound up."

"Archie? How so?"

"He grinds his teeth."

Pom got home just as the sky was brightening behind the courthouse clock tower. He tried the kitchen door and went back out to sleep under a moth-bitten buffalo robe that he'd thought to leave in the Model T. Before he settled in, he counted the crisp bills again just to make sure the money was really there, all five hundred of it.

CHAPTER 20

Two days later, Jim Rhodes walked back to the Holliman house with Pom. They were deep in conversation as they passed the Ford dealership, so he failed to notice the horseshoes embedded in the sidewalk, but Pom couldn't help smiling as they followed them. A generation ago, with an accomplice, the teenaged Flora had sneaked them into the fresh cement to advertise her father's livery stable.

"I don't get any of this," Jim said. "I get jailed on suspicion of a double murder I didn't commit and now suddenly I'm out on bail thanks to somebody whose name I don't know. Where did the money come from? You really don't think it's a setup?"

Pom hooked his thumbs in his vest pockets, a habit he couldn't indulge when Flora was around. "Rest easy. It was yours truly."

Jim stopped. *"You?"*

"That's right. And keep it under your hat." He gave Jim a sidelong look. "I got a two-for-one deal for you and Trent. And since it *is* bail, I'm expecting to get the money back as soon as you're cleared."

"Count on it. I'm going to see this thing through—and thanks." Jim clasped his hands behind his back and walked with measured steps as if he were still pacing off a ten-by-ten cell. "I have some news for Rex. Ever hear of a boat called the *Cristobel*?"

Pom tripped on a crack and grabbed hold of a produce display to keep from falling. He collected his wits while chasing several navel oranges into the street. Ahead of him, the silver roof of the giant brick courthouse rose through the oaks on the square. "The *Cristobel* did you say? What about it?"

"Someone's sending coded messages to it every few nights. I've cracked the code that Rex has been hearing on his radio. There are the names of other boats too, and rendezvous positions. But there's more to it than that. As soon as I get back to Rex's radio I'll find out what it is."

When they came in through the kitchen door, Flora dropped the wire brush she was using to scrub the stovetop.

He's on loan till the trial's over." Pom said.

After four weeks in jail, Jim was thinner and looked at least a year older. "Well, we'll feed you proper," she said. "Who put up all that money for the bail?"

"I'm not at liberty to say," he told her. "Someone who believes in the legal system."

"That jail was getting too crowded anyway," Pom said, "with people who actually *belong* in there."

They went upstairs to Rex's room. Pom had Jim stay out of sight and greeted Rex through the half-open door. "How's that algebra coming?"

Rex was bent over a protractor. "It's not algebra, Dad. It's geometry, complementary and supplementary angles. Do you know what a transversal is?"

"The Transvaal? It's in South Africa, isn't it? A Dutch colony or something?"

Rex had been sitting on the floor with his book on the bed. He stood up and stomped the pins and needles out of his foot. "Africa? What's Africa got to do with geometry?"

"Well, why don't you ask somebody who's done some traveling?"

He motioned Jim into the room.

Rex lost his balance and nearly knocked the radio off the desk.

"They let you out!"

"For the time being," Jim said with a tired smile. "I'm out on bail, thanks to a benefactor."

"Even that doddering public defender ought to be able to get you off," Pom said "That Luger was in *my* house. Avery might just as well have picked *me* up for those murders—or Amelia. She's the one who's been cleaning that room for the past several weeks. Without prints on them, that gun and cigar box could've been put there by just about anybody."

That night, as Jim and Rex worked the radio dial, Pom sat by the fire in the front room. He was enjoying the forbidden pleasure of rocking back in one cane chair while propping his feet on another as he read through the Farm and Grove section of the *Daily Sun*. In the dining room Rachel was adjusting the Brunswick to get the right pitch on a new Paul Whiteman record called *Love Nest*. Flora was off visiting Mavis Ward, who had some flash of inspiration about a dress pattern. Pom was reading the lead paragraph of yet another hog cholera story when he heard an automobile stop at the gate. He unstuck the front door and went out onto the porch to greet the visitor.

It was Sheriff Mecum, coming down the brick walk, rolling his big flat-brimmed hat in his hand.

Pom tucked the paper under his arm. "Evening, Avery. Seems like fall is finally catching up to us."

"It's plenty warm in the jail," the sheriff said. "No lack of customers. Cold weather seems to bring 'em in."

"You come to see Jim?"

"No, I'm here to see you." The sheriff came up the steps and sat in the rocker. He hung his hat on one of its ornate knobs and settled in.

Pom took the cue and sat on the swing. "That so?"

The sheriff rocked for a moment, sizing him up. "You know, Pom, you've got a special position around here. There's folks on both sides of the law that know you and respect you. Putting up bail for Trent Walker was the latest proof of that."

Pom began to sway in the swing, back and forth, one foot tucked under the seat, the other anchored to the floor, pushing. "I've known Trent for a good many years. I used to go to cattle auctions with his dad. Trent's okay."

"What I'm getting at is you're kind of walking on a fence. If you go over to the one side too much, the folks on the other side won't trust you anymore. You might have to decide which side to come down on."

Pom stopped swaying for a moment. "A person has to do what's right for a situation, doesn't he? You haven't always done everything by the book have you? There's the letter of the law and the spirit. Haven't I heard you say that?"

"I've said that. But these days we're working by the letter, and those that cross the letter are going to get judged by it. I'm not the law around here in case there was ever any doubt about that. I'm just one of the enforcers. There are others out there that have their own way of enforcing, and they're maybe not as patient or as understanding as I am. When they crack down, you know, I'll have to crack down too, and woe betide the fella that's crossing the law when the hand comes down. I'd sure hate to see any of my friends get slapped."

He stood up and put on his hat and listened to the sounds of voices in the house. Rachel was playing *Love Nest* again, at a lower pitch this time, and the sound of a muted cornet carried on the evening breeze.

"Then there's the guy who bailed out Mr. Rhodes. A person of some means, I suppose."

"I suppose the judge could tell you who it was, couldn't he?"

"If I asked, which I don't intend to. As long as it's honest money, it's no business of mine."

"Well, you've got enough to keep up with as it is."

"Good night. After things settle down a little, let's go out fishing again."

Pom continued to rock in the swing. "Let's do that. With this cold snap, the big ones ought to be coming into Cedar Key."

"And we'll get some."

Pom's next visitor came on foot. He moseyed down the middle of the street as the neighborhood dogs yapped and growled behind their picket fences. When the figure emerged from the shadow of a magnolia tree, Pom recognized the easygoing gait of Trent Walker. He was wearing a new powder blue fedora, but the rest of his clothes were the usual formless gray rags. He fumbled with the latch, pushed back his hat, and ambled up the walkway.

Pom propped his feet up against the porch rail and folded his arms. "Pretty evening to be out."

Trent came into the yellow light of the porch. "*Any* night's a good night to be out. I was starting to see angels in that damn jail cell."

"Well, I'm glad you're sprung."

"I've come to thank you. I'd probably be off my rocker by now if somebody hadn't put up bail for me. I just wasn't sure who it was—till now."

Pom stopped rocking. "All right. You've got me."

Trent set his foot on the bottom step of the porch. "You give up mighty easy. Don't you want to know how I figured out it was you that put up that bail money?"

Pom began rocking again. "Oh, it's pretty clear that I'm rolling in dough, ain't it?" From the dining room the low, throaty voice of a saxophone floated through the cool air like backyard gossip. "Can't you tell? We're running a speakeasy in there. Make some pretty good money."

Trent went on as if he hadn't heard the joke. "It was 'cause you weren't surprised to see me out of jail just now. That's how I knew you put up that money. And 'cause they let that Red out too, and wasn't nobody else in the world going to set *that* boy free, though he ain't half bad when he ain't talking politics. He's a decent sort in his way."

"All right. But just keep it under your hat, will you—and a right nice hat it is too."

"I won it betting on a cat fight. What I can't figure out is where you got the money. You dig up a jar or something?"

Pom began rocking a little harder. "If there's one thing I've learned about money in my too close to forty years it's not to question it when you've got it. You didn't belong in that jail any more than Flora's dad would have thirty years ago for running a saloon. You're not making anybody buy it and you can't help it if the fruit flies ate you out of your farm. The way I see it, we can wait for time or the Congress to fix everything or we can do our best to take care of it right here and now in our own backyard, even if we have to bend the rules a little. Maybe you'll do the same for me when I'm in jail."

"Shoot, Pom. That'll be the day."

"What do you figure to do if they let you off?"

Trent shrugged. "What *can* I do? Just do the same old thing without getting caught I guess. It was buying all those jugs at the same place that gave me away. That and I didn't really expect 'em to mess with me. They never bothered before."

"My timing was off when I advised you to buy that farm," Pom said. "But there's progress being made. The department of agriculture's going to lift that fruit fly quarantine before too long."

"I'll make a go of it, Pom, but I need some seed money, and making liquor's about the only way I know to get it."

"Well, just remember, the rules have changed. If you go back to making the sauce, they'll come after you again, and harder too. You ought at least to lie low for a while."

"Can't afford to. Got to eat. Elsie and the girls got to eat. I ain't going to let my family split up again, Pom. That's one thing I decided while I was in there."

Pom stopped rocking and set his feet on the floor. He glanced over the porch rail to make sure the yard was empty. Then he got up, came to the top of the steps, and spoke softly. "What if you could make it all in a week or two? Five hundred, maybe more. No jugs and no Avery. Would that square it? Would that be enough to get you started up again in farming?"

"Pom, if pennies started raining from the sky it would get me started again, and the one's about as likely to happen as the other."

"Hear me out now. You know the Gulf from Shell Mound to Crystal River."

"I ought to. I've been fishing out there my whole life."

Pom put a hand on his shoulder. "Well, right now that kind of knowledge is valuable, especially to someone like you, who can keep a secret."

Back in the house, life had settled down to a semblance of what it had been before Jim's arrest. Jim and Rex had temporarily given up on the radio because they couldn't find any more transmissions to the mysterious *Cristobel*. So they had fallen into a discussion of books. Jim sat at the desk with his arm hooked over the back of the chair and Rex sat cross-legged on the bed. Jim was telling him about a book by Jack London, *The Iron Heel*. "It's prophetic," he was saying. "It has a lot to do with the fix we're in now."

"Well, I ought to get Mrs. Campion to put it on the reading list for class," Rex said.

Jim leaned down and tightened the ground wire wrapped around the radiator. "I'm afraid you're becoming cynical. There's always *The Sea-Wolf*. It's a great adventure story, but it has some things to say too."

Rex said he wanted to go to sea to throw off all the trusses in his life.

"Oh, life at sea requires even more discipline," Jim said. "There's nothing like the sea for building and revealing character."

Pom had overheard from the hall. He drifted to the top of the stairs and stood there wondering what seafaring was doing to *his* character.

In the morning he went over to tell Richard about his offer to let Trent in on the rumrunning. He regretted spilling the beans to a third partner, but he couldn't help feeling that Trent needed the money even more than he did. And while all three of them stood to lose everything if they failed, he felt certain that Trent had little left to lose and plenty to gain. Pom could imagine him keeping to his old ways and going down in a desperate shootout over a rusty little still in some godforsaken patch of pinewoods, whereas there was a chance this way, just a chance, that Trent could pull his life back together. And anyway, what should Richard care? Trent was tough and reliable. He knew the rivers and the back roads and he knew how to keep his mouth shut. Still, Pom wanted to make the pitch to Richard before the call came for the next trip.

The morning was still chilly and a pink sun was just starting to show through the Spanish moss when Pom pulled up in front of the Ward house. He was surprised to hear that Richard was already up and gone.

"He got a telephone call and threw his clothes on before I could so much as poach him an egg," Mavis said. In her green silk dressing gown and maroon striped turban, she struck Pom as someone who might well talk to the dead.

"Do you know who it was that called him, Mavis? We were both expecting to hear from the same fella—some boat business."

J.J. came in from the kitchen, wiping his mouth with a yellowed linen napkin. "Well, you can rest easy, Pom, 'cause it was a woman. She was dying to talk to Richard and that was that. Fortunately, he sleeps like a cat, so Mavis got him on the phone before the woman had a conniption."

Mavis invited him in for some grits and bacon and eggs, but Pom backed away from the screen door. "Thanks, but I've got to be on my way. Just tell Richard that I need to see him today. If I'm not home, I'll be over at the Sand Hill Farm and then down to the Campions'."

As it turned out, Richard was already most of the way to the Campions', but the ranch was not his destination. He was speeding toward the promontory where he and Edith had sat on their first date, taking in the broad view of the prairie as they caught their breath after snatching off each other's clothes and thrashing through a bout of sweaty love in a prickly bed of palmettos and beggar weed.

They were not quite to the overlook when Edith came out with the news that she was pregnant.

Richard's window was rolled down and his gray fedora had been trying to blow into the backseat for the past five miles. Now it did. His knuckles went white on the steering wheel.

He put on a smile. "Well, congratulations, Edie. That's—swell."

Suddenly her voice took on a commanding tone. "Richard, this isn't an award for best table setter at the Grange. This is me—you and me—having a baby. You can't say we haven't been working at it for the past couple of months."

He felt hot. He wished he hadn't worn his dress coat, even if it did look sharp. "Are you—I mean, are you sure?"

"Richard, I *am* a woman. Shall I spell it out for you?"

After a strained silence, he said the first thing that came to mind. "When is the delivery?"

She moved toward him on the seat. "Richard, Richard, pull over. Pull over now and stop the car."

He looked at her as if she had gone crazy. "We're almost to the overlook. You can almost see the Campions' silo through those trees."

"I don't care. Just stop the car here."

"You're kind of pushy all of a sudden."

She laughed. "*I'm* pushy! *You* were the pushy one or we wouldn't be in this pickle." She put her arms around his neck and pressed her painted lips to his cheek. "But isn't it a lovely pickle to be in? We're going to have a baby. We can be together from now on. Together. Such a glamorous word, such a romantic word! I can't wait till we're together *all* the time!"

CHAPTER 21

W hen Richard got home, he welcomed the word that Pom was looking for him. He gobbled down some reheated poached eggs and bacon, kissed his mother, and took off again.

From the screen door Mavis called out as he hurried down the walkway. "Wouldn't it be easier just talk to him on the telephone?"

He repeated his drive all the way to the Campions'. As he watched the Guernseys and Jerseys grazing on the grassy slope at the edge of the prairie, he planned his next delivery to the men in Baldwin, which might bring in enough to keep the collector at bay long enough for him to get the matching funds from Kincaid and skip town. In his mind he ran the trips around Coast Guard cutters and hijackers to the Waccasassa landing, imagined loading up the hay truck and hitting Highway 13, through town and to the freight yard, all without getting shot full of holes or hustled into prison. Once he had a good wad to show Kincaid, he'd be able to skip town, maybe scrape up enough to buy some beachfront property somewhere before the next boom, and he was convinced that sooner or later there would be another boom, even though the newspapers were continuing to run stories about a burgeoning national collapse.

He spent half the day driving around the county, using his search for Pom as an excuse to get away and clear his head. At the edge of town he stopped by the ramshackle Leary Store, let the screen door bang on his way in to announce his arrival, and ordered a hamburger and a raspberry phosphate. While he waited, he poked around to calm his nerves, freed a loaf of Merita that had glued itself to the shelf, and glanced occasionally into the woods across the road. Except for the Packard, the parking lot remained empty, a void of crushed lime rock, potholes, and oak trees painted white shoulder-high for a festive effect. He ate as he drove the road to Baldwin, taking note of turnoffs and shortcuts where he could shake the collector if he had to. He found three ponds where he could ditch the truck or the Packard if that's what it took to keep alive and out of jail. He stopped at a dismal stand of pines for some target practice and emptied the .32 shooting at a knothole.

He had plans on top of plans, but the unpredictable kept him biting his nails most of the way back from Baldwin.

It was dusk by the time he pulled into town, but he was too keyed up to eat. And he certainly wasn't ready to telephone Edith. He didn't even want to talk to Pom just now. He drove down to the Porter's Quarters and knocked his way into the speakeasy.

The slender brunette behind the bar looked up from the Bourbon she was pouring. "I was beginning to think you'd left town."

"It's been a while I guess." He set his hat on the bar. "Sorry. I should've called."

She hung it on a rack of deer antlers that stuck out over the bottles behind her. "You're looking all wrung out, Richard. Long day?"

"And it ain't over yet." He propped his elbows on the bar and looked into her dark eyes. "Deardra, have you ever considered selling this place?"

She smiled. "Every day. You want to buy it?"

"Not on your life, but I'll bet there's plenty of guys who would. I hear the Baptists need more space."

She laughed. "And?"

"Nothing I guess. But it'd be a shame for a high-born girl like you to land in the clink if somebody was to raid this place."

The noise of conversation and the scrape of people coming and going were enough to cover what he had said. Deardra lit a cigarette. The smoke uncoiled in front of her face as she waited for him to say more.

"Have you heard something you'd like to share, Richard?"

"I hear people talking every day. That's about all they do anymore—talk. What do you suppose you'd do if you could unload this place?"

"Search me. Go back to New Orleans maybe. I kind of miss the pulse and smell of that town. A girl could do worse than nestling down in the fragrant embrace of the Garden District." She tapped her cigarette over an ashtray adorned with a cherub's face.

He let the smoke drift over him. "And once you got there, what would you do?"

"Who knows? It's as good a place as any to meet a man of means. Why the twenty questions?"

"New Orleans." He turned the name over as if it were the answer to all his troubles. "I kind of have a hankering to see New Orleans. Maybe you could show it to me."

She touched her palm to his forehead. "What about your blonde friend?"

He sat back and shrugged. "We knock around together sometimes. I could use a beer."

Her penciled brows went up. "So what gives?"

"Think of it like any other business. There's a time to get in and a time to get out."

"How biblical. What makes you think this is the time to get out?"

"A hunch maybe. Something in the air. Prohibition can't last forever."

She popped the cap from a bottle. "And?"

"And maybe I'll see if New Orleans is all it's cracked up to be. How does next week sound?"

She poured the beer and slid it toward him. "You want to know what I think? I think for what you're after, New Orleans wouldn't be nearly far enough."

"It'd be a start. With you, a really good start."

"I'm flattered. But give a girl a little time."

"Don't you like doing things on the fly? Didn't we have a great time out at Magnesia Springs?"

"Once we got some rules straight, yeah."

"You drove the car like it was a rocket."

"Been doing it since I was ten."

"We can take my car tonight and be in the French Quarter for dinner tomorrow."

She leaned forward with her elbows on the bar. "I love you and your car, Richard, but you move a little too fast for me."

"And you know what I think? I think you're too smart to hang onto this place. Do you like sawdust and peanut husks on your floor?"

"I go back and forth about that. The place has a certain charm about it, a rustic charm. And after all, Uncle Bobby left it to me."

"I remember Bobby LaRue as a stickler for tidiness. How far he fell."

"Well, then let's say I'm falling too. For now."

Early in the morning Richard went to the house on Magnolia Street hoping to find Pom. Instead he found Sheriff Mecum parked at the front gate, standing with his foot on the running board of his Chevrolet. He was smoking a panatela and gazing toward the courthouse. Richard saw him too late to avoid him gracefully, so he pulled alongside for a friendly greeting.

The sheriff pushed back his flat-brimmed hat. "Looks like you and I are both hunting the same man this morning."

Richard had a ready smile. "That Pom. He's everybody's friend."

"To a fault. Flora says he took off for parts unknown a little while ago. Any idea where he might be?"

"Am I my neighbor's keeper?"

"Well, when he gets back, maybe the three of us ought to sit down and have a talk."

"I'd like that. I really would. But right now I've got to track down some other folks. You know how the real estate business is—always tracking folks down to get their *t*'s dotted and their eyes crossed."

Sheriff Mecum let the joke pass. "Could be you're not ready to talk yet. But you will be—and when you are, you come on down to the jail and we'll have a heart-to-heart. In the meantime, be careful, Richard. These are getting to be dangerous times. I'd hate to have anything happen to you because of a lark gone bad."

He threw down the butt of his cigar, ducked into the Chevrolet, and drove toward the square.

Richard was in no hurry to go back home, so he headed out to Lake Santa Fe on the chance that Pom would be out there. He was. He had the hull of the boat nicely finished, caulked and varnished to reflect the brilliant blue sky. He was cranking away on a rusty old windlass, and the foot of a tall mast was rising toward a hole in the foredeck.

With his hands in his pockets, Richard watched the polished pine pole edge toward the target. "When you set your mind to it, you can get more done than any two men I know."

Pom was bent low over the windlass, too low to look up. "You're welcome to share the glory."

He got Richard to guide the mast into the hole while he cranked the windlass. They were a peculiar pair, the tall, dapper young swain in the gray fedora and navy blue blazer, and the burly, balding jack-of-all-trades in dirty denim.

"Will you look at that?" Pom bent back to see the top of the mast and all but lost it in the strong morning sunlight. "We've darn near got us a boat here."

Richard wasn't as impressed. "How fast does it go?"

"We'll find out after I give it to Rex. He's been as restless as a panther, and I want to get this thing out there in a good blow. There's nothing like the fear of God to take the edge off. How's it going with the collector?"

"You've been looking for me, Pom?"

"Yeah. I'm hoping that three's not a crowd."

Richard perched on the gunwale. "We don't need a third. Who is it?"

"Trent Walker."

"Trent? He couldn't even keep out of jail running a still."

"He's that far from losing his farm. He needs the money."

"He needs the money! Well, fine! We'll bring in the whole county, Pom. Except for Cappy Kincaid. He's the only one I know who *doesn't* need it."

"Trent's a good man in a jam. And he knows the Gulf shore better than you and me put together. He was raised in Yankeetown."

"How much did you tell him?"

"Just that we're making some butter-and-egg money."

"Well, he'd better keep his mouth shut or those dry men will tack my hide to the wall—and yours too."

"I know Trent. He's discrete. That whole time he was in jail he never did say who he was working for. You could twist his arm off and he wouldn't squeal—and he'll do anything to stay out of jail."

"Well, he gets half of your share. And as soon as we get the call from Baldwin, he'll have to be ready to go."

"When do you figure?"

"Just be near the phone."

CHAPTER 22

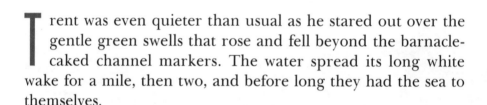

Trent was even quieter than usual as he stared out over the gentle green swells that rose and fell beyond the barnacle-caked channel markers. The water spread its long white wake for a mile, then two, and before long they had the sea to themselves.

"Sorry about the delay," Richard said. "The guys in Baldwin move in mysterious ways."

Pom scanned the empty Gulf. "We had to eat one of the hogs from the backyard the other night. I couldn't tell Rachel we were running out of money. Made up some mumbo-jumbo about culling. Should've eaten it before she gave it a name."

Richard remained cheerful. "Well, Trent, there's one good thing about this business. It can make you rich quick."

Pom watched the new partner for some sign of levity but saw none. "Trent, you may as well enjoy the ride. Once we get back inside the three-mile limit we're fair game, but till then we're twenty-one, white, and free."

Trent continued to stare out at the open water and said that he'd be a lot more chipper once he had the money in hand.

Richard gave up trying to keep his touring cap on, dropped it on the floor of the cockpit, and let it slide back to the stern. "Didn't you make any money with your still?"

Trent pulled a piece of string from his hip pocket and started tying a knot, a monkey's fist. He broke off to brace himself as the boat hit a wave. "The fella making all the money was a professor who bankrolled it and made up the recipes. I passed sixty percent to him."

"Why would he set up a still?" Pom asked. "Don't professors make good money?"

Trent shrugged. "Wants more I guess."

"You were making some pretty fine stuff," Pom said.

"Yeah, well, my so-called partner said it was all just chemistry."

Richard swung around with one hand on the wheel. "He's a *chemistry* professor? What's his name?"

Trent scooped up Richard's cap and pitched it forward. "Don't know and don't want to know. I see his car over by the duck pond from time to time, a cruddy old Nash Roadster. You'd think he'd want to spend some of that dough."

Richard laughed and turned his back to the wheel. The boat took off on a course all its own, shooting over the chop in a shallow arc. A worried look from Pom prompted him to take hold of the wheel again to fix the course. He steered with one hand, not bothering to watch where he was going, getting his bearings by the angle of the orange sunlight on the starboard storage locker. "We're all in it together! Y'all and me and—" He was all smiles and his chin stuck out in that way that dared you to take a poke at him. "Trent, I know your partner. I know his daughter even better. All this time, I thought he figured Edith was too good for me, but maybe he just figures I'm the competition."

They slogged their way through rising seas, north-north-west, as the disc of the sun went scarlet and dissolved in a gray cloudbank. Richard turned on the green and red running lights and the yellow light atop the mast, and all around them the water was suddenly aglow.

"What do you suppose it is?" Trent put his hands on the gunwale and studied the green radiance. "I've seen it a hundred times and it still takes me by surprise."

"It's phosphorus in the water," Pom explained. "There's microscopic organisms, about a billion of 'em, all full of phosphorus, that show up when the light hits 'em."

Trent looked out across the vast radiant circle. "I'm not going back to jail."

Richard remained casual about the course. He settled for glancing down at the compass from time to time until they crossed the broken water of the reef. Then he followed his heading carefully into undistinguished seas and brought the throttle down to idle when they seemed to be in the middle of nowhere.

The little freighter had never been more than half an hour late, but this time they waited. Pom took out his watch and looked at it by the light in the cockpit. "Are your friends in Baldwin going to be sore if you miss the train?"

Richard scanned the dark northern horizon for the tenth time. "If that freighter doesn't show up, they'll have bigger problems than me. And I'll have bigger problems than them."

They waited and paced and smoked for half an hour, an hour, two hours.

"So what do you think?" Pom had only smoked his pipe and the occasional ceremonial cigar, never cigarettes, until tonight. He tossed a butt into the water, spat, and settled back against the gunwale.

"Could be the Coast Guard already got 'em," Trent said. He was finishing another knot, a hangman's noose "What's to stop 'em from grabbing the stuff outside the territorial limit if they've a mind to? Or maybe there was some secret treaty signed and—"

"There!" Richard was looking through the binoculars and pointing to the northwest.

"It's about time," Pom said. "At this rate, it's going to be a week before I get to sleep in the house again."

Richard was less than cordial when the boat finally pulled up alongside. "You took your sweet time. Where the hell you been?"

The bearded man on the bigger boat glared down at him. "We had company. It's a wonder we got here at all."

"Well, maybe you should get a faster engine," Richard said. "Or better help." He was rising and falling with the boat, but he stood with his arms crossed and his feet spread as if he were standing on a stone pier.

"Take it easy." The man gestured toward an antenna on the mast of the freighter. "We already told Baldwin."

With three of them the work went much faster. Trent and Pom grabbed the heavy sacks as fast as the men on the freighter could hand them down while Richard packed the hold and the storage lockers. Then they cast off the lines and the two boats swung apart. The freighter turned stern to, and as the shadow of it crossed him, Pom looked up at the name *Cristobel* and wondered how to spell it in Navy code.

They were silent for most of the long dark run to the river. "We're going to miss the damn tide," Richard said at last. "We'll be lucky if we don't fetch up on some oyster bar."

"That's why we have our boy here, "Pom said. "He knows how to get through those bars."

"I ain't promising you no picnic," Trent told them. "It would help to have some lights."

"Just get us up that river," Richard said.

Once the shoreline took form and Trent got his bearings, he started directing the course.

"Off toward two o'clock," he said. "Now about twelve-thirty. There's going to be three bars, side by side, from about nine o'clock to twelve. You can't go between 'em, you're going to have to go all the way around and the water's deeper at nine."

A soft scraping passed beneath them. Pom held his breath as the boat stuck, slipped, and stuck again.

"I guess that took care of the barnacles," he said.

Richard gripped the wheel with both hands. "Why didn't you call this one?"

Trent kept his eyes on the water. "I don't go over these things loaded to the shoulder with booze. Well, damn. We're on here good."

Pom leaned against the gunwale and folded his arms. "Okay, Richard, you want to sit here and wait for high tide?'

"Like hell."

"You thinking what I'm thinking?"

Richard stared into the shallow water. "Look, we don't have all night. Let's just shut up and do it."

They began hauling out sacks and sliding them over the side. Every now and then, Richard would nudge the throttle forward. By the time the *Sun Dog* slipped forward, a quarter of the cargo was on the bottom of the Gulf.

Richard set his chin as he eased the throttle forward. "I don't want to hear the first damn joke about drinking like a fish,"

Pom tapped Trent on the shoulder and pointed to the east. "You wanted some light, you got it." The rising crescent of the moon was clearing the tree line, shining through a silver cloud.

Richard was studying a dim green light ahead.

"That's onshore," Trent said. "There's a house down in there with a green porch light."

Pom smiled. "That's why you're here."

"Just get me up that river." Richard said again, sliding his hand over the wheel. "Just get me in there and the rest is gravy."

"You're going to have to bear around to two-thirty," Trent told him. "You get past this one and it should be a straight shot. Just don't cut it too close."

They poked their way through the chop, whitecaps showing like shark's teeth row on row. The boat rode low and heavy in the water and the moon came out again as they broke straight for the opening in the shoreline. Richard throttled forward and the water whirled up at the stern.

"The coast is clear," Pom said. "That ground smells mighty good."

They passed through the broad mouth of the river. Richard slowed the boat again and moved down the channel as Trent pointed from the bow with the flashlight. They carried through a few turns and suddenly the dark woods ahead burst into life, slapping and screeching. The boat went dark. Pom dropped to the deck and Richard swung out to the other side of the channel. Several ospreys flew directly in front of the boat, vanished into the woods on the far side of the river, and then doubled back, not more than a stone's throw from the stern.

Pom sat up, leaning against the wall of the cockpit. He got a grip on the window frame and came up to a crouch, let out a breath.

In the bow, the flashlight came on again and cut through top-less trees where the ospreys were beginning to settle back down.

"We ain't necessarily over the hump," Trent whispered. He was still lying on his side, propped up on one elbow. "Something in there set off those birds."

Pom looked around. "Maybe just a coon."

"Maybe not," Richard said. He eased the boat back toward shore. They edged past the ospreys and nosed on down the maze of the river. The shadows of tall bending palms and knobby cypresses passed over them as the rising moon went from orange to pale yellow.

Pom stood hunched over with one hand on the edge of the window frame and the other hanging in front of him, ready to drop again at the first flash or sound.

"I don't remember this river being so long."

"They're always longer at night," Richard said.

The woods were dark and quiet by the time Richard slipped the boat up to the landing where the truck waited in a thicket of scrub oaks. They loaded quickly and without speaking, the only sounds being the occasional clink of bottles and the muffled thud of a sack being stuffed under the hay.

When they had finished, Richard gave Trent a hundred dollars.

"Call this an advance. Come by Porter's Place tomorrow night and get the rest of your cut."

Trent climbed back onto the boat. He looked up and raised his hand as Richard waved him off. "Cedar Key's going to be looking damn good by the time I get there. I'm going to put up in the Island Hotel and sleep till noon."

Richard smiled. "See you tomorrow night."

"That was mighty generous," Pom said as they walked up to the truck.

"Yeah, well," Richard said. "That's me."

He and Pom covered the bottles with quilts and hay and then found out that no amount of tinkering and swearing would get the truck to start. Richard set his hat on the hood and wiped the sweat from his face. "This goddam thing. It's not yet three years old. What the hell's wrong with it?"

They rolled it out of the thicket, through the palmettos, and onto level ground. Richard shoved it toward the road while Pom steered. After twenty yards the engine came to life, and a few minutes later, on creaking springs, they were bouncing along the winding dirt road to the graded highway.

Pom settled back on the seat. "I'm starting to feel pretty good. It's nothing but an automobile ride now."

The words were hardly out of his mouth when the headlights caught a Dodge sedan blocking the junction with the highway.

Richard threw the truck into reverse and, hay bouncing, took off through the woods.

Pom's head hit the ceiling. He gripped the seat. "I feel like a knocked-up sow trying to outrun a wolf. Is there a way through here?"

"We'll find one or make one." Richard jerked the gearshift. The truck snarled, lurched through a ditch, and jumped up an embankment. He turned off the headlamps and swung back toward the road. "You should've gone with Trent when you had the chance."

They struck graded road behind the waiting car and spun to the far shoulder. A cloth bundle fell off the seat. As Pom bent over to pick it up, a bullet crashed through the windshield.

"Richard, I thought we were past this."

"Shoot back. You're holding a damn gun in your hand!"

Before Richard could get it under control, the truck ran off the shoulder.

Pom opened the cloth bundle in his lap and held up the .32, handling it like glass.

"Go ahead, Pom! You don't have to kill anybody! Just slow 'em down some!"

As the dark car came at them, Pom rolled down his window, turned around, cocked one eye, and shot out a front tire. With a spinning screech the car came to an ungainly halt, backside to in the palmettos at the shoulder of the road.

Richard laughed and looked back over his shoulder longer than was safe. "That ought to take the starch out of their collars! I didn't know you were such a crack shot."

Pom was still looking out the window at the rapidly receding car. "My finger twitched all on its own. You suppose that's the end of them?"

"Not till we're home in bed with the money in our shoes."

On both sides of the road, tall pines brushed by in a blur.

Pom folded the .32 into the cloth and set it on the floor. He sat back and let out a big breath. "How often does this happen?"

Richard had the truck going seventy. The occasional heave in the road made them take to the air. "It's all a cockfight, Pom."

"Well, untangle some of this for me. Just who was shooting at us back there?"

Richard shifted his weight to get a firmer grip on the wheel. "Beats me. Hijackers."

"Connected to the ones that shot us up in the channel?"

"Hard to say."

"Are you leveling with me? Are you giving me the whole story?"

"Pom, I don't *know* the whole story."

"But you know that this thing is big. How much do you know about that freighter, the *Cristobel*?"

"I know it holds a lot of booze."

"And works the coast. Did you know they were in radio contact with Baldwin?"

Richard swerved to avoid a set of amber eyes at the edge of the road. "Don't you suppose they have to be in touch somehow?"

"Yeah, but who else is listening in?"

"What?"

"Forget it. A flat tire isn't going to stop those men in the car back there. If they come back at us, we'll have to kill 'em, won't we?"

"Well, Pom, I admit it's a little messy from a strictly Sunday school point of view."

They kept to the graded road, through the dreary ruins of the burned-out Negro hamlet of Rosewood, to Otter Creek and Bronson and Archer, where, glancing over his shoulder, Richard slowed the truck to forty. They sped the length of the wide main street, put the false-front brick business district behind them, and shot past rows of big white houses asleep behind deep porches. The far edge of the community sported a billboard packed with praise for a passing circus.

They were not far beyond it on new pavement when Pom sat up at the sight of a red lantern hanging from a chain across the road.

Richard slowed the car. "Now what."

"Whatever it is," Pom said, "we can't run through it."

Richard bit at a thumbnail. "It's just a chain. We might can."

Pom saw dark figures in the woods on either side of it. "They look like troopers. Even if we get away here, tracking us down's going to be a cinch."

Richard sped up. "Would you rather pay a fifty-dollar fine for running it or get caught right now with about a ton of Canadian Red? I guess you could always just shoot the sons-of-bitches."

"I'm not shooting anybody."

"What if they aren't really troopers?"

Just short of the chain, Richard hit the brakes and brought the truck to a shuddering stop. "Give me the gun and let's find out who they are."

Pom handed over the .32 and Richard slipped it into the pocket of his overcoat. The two of them climbed out of the car and walked toward the lantern.

"Stop right there, both of you."

Coming at them from each side of the road were armed men in black-and-tan uniforms. One of them, gun drawn, flashlight in hand, emerged from the woods to have a good look at the men standing by the truck.

Richard's hand moved to his overcoat pocket.

"He sure looks like a trooper to me," Pom whispered. "And he looks riled."

"It's dark! How can you tell?"

The trooper stopped in front of the truck and walked toward them with his flashlight playing across their faces and glancing across the windshield. Pom put a hand in front of his eyes, but Richard gazed at the oncoming troopers with a questioning look, as if waiting for the punch line of a practical joke.

(HAPTER 23

The trooper moved with the suppleness of a man in his twenties, but he spoke with the rough edge of someone who had spent most of his life doing hard work outdoors. He pointed the flashlight smack into Richard's face. "I guess you didn't see the lantern."

Richard kept his hands in his pockets. "I guess I *did*. Why do you think I stopped?"

"Let me see some identification."

Keeping his right hand on the .32, Richard fished around with his left until he had pulled his billfold from his inside coat pocket.

The trooper brought his gun closer. "Take it out slowly."

Pom was leaning against the truck in an effort to look casual. He edged over enough to keep an eye on Richard's gun hand.

The trooper studied the license under the flashlight and handed it back. "What y'all got in here? You're riding mighty low."

"Bad springs," Richard said. "A fairly new truck and all, you'd think they'd be okay. You can be sure the dealer's going to set it right—and for free."

"Or maybe it isn't built to carry the load you've got." The trooper trained his flashlight into the bed of the truck, which had lost a good deal of hay.

Pom had been listening to the trooper's voice. He squinted toward the flashlight for a better look at his face. "Do I know you?"

The trooper turned his flashlight from the hay bales to Pom. His frown broke into a smile of disbelief. "Is that you, Mr. Holliman?"

Pom squirmed away from the light. "The very same. Now who are you?"

The trooper holstered his gun and tucked the flashlight under his arm. "I'm Ted Richland. I go by T.R. Remember? We lived up toward Newberry. I had a pony with the colic and—"

"Prettiest black-and-white paint you ever saw," Pom told Richard. "He had black circles around both eyes, just like he'd been boxing. How you doing, T.R.?"

"We didn't think that pony would last till morning. He'd been thrashing around most of the day, then got real quiet like he'd lost all his fight. I like to cried myself into the ground. Then you came down and worked on him all night and pulled him through."

"I helped, T.R., but your pony pulled himself through."

"You remember."

"Sure I remember. I just don't recall exactly when it was, except that your daddy said he had to ride a long way to get to a telephone. They didn't have 'em just everywhere back then."

"That was fourteen years ago. Nineteen-fifteen. I'd been riding that pony from the time I was big enough to climb onto him. He died when I was fighting in France." Even in the unsteady beam of the flashlight it was apparent that Trooper Richland had tears in his eyes. He patted the roof of the truck. "Well, I'm sorry to hold y'all up. From a distance y'all looked like you might be rumrunners, riding so low to the ground that way."

"Oh, that's all right," Pom said. "I'm just glad we got to catch up on old times, T.R."

"I tell you, there's many a time I've thought about that night you came over. Look me up next time you're in town. Just ask anybody. They know where to find me."

"I'll do that, T.R."

The trooper was still saying good-bye when Richard put the truck in gear and drove off. Over his shoulder he watched T.R. walk back into the woods to rejoin his comrades. "I thought y'all were going to talk all night. But doesn't that make you feel like a million bucks?"

Pom watched Richard place the .32 on the seat beside him. "No, more like two cents."

"Come on. It was a big break. If your pal had taken us in, we'd be in deep right now, or if he had stood there blabbing all night, the guys we shot at would've caught up to us. But he flat out let us go. Do you know how lucky we are?"

"I'm starting to feel real low on luck, like maybe I've used up my lifetime share in one night. I just want to get back home and sleep in my own—automobile. I need to fit that thing out as a sleeping car. And in the meantime, get a better cover, will you? That hay you've got back there is so moldy it would give any horse the heaves."

They were most of the way back to town and pushing seventy miles an hour again on the new road when they hit the deer. Pom slammed into the dashboard and Richard smacked his head against the windshield. When he pulled himself back onto the seat, Pom discovered that the truck had somehow turned all the way around and cut a swath through a field of saplings. Wafting through the cool night air was the sweet, unmistakable aroma of Canadian Red.

In the moonlight, Pom saw blood on Richard's forehead. He steadied himself against the seat. "As for luck, I'd say we're now running on empty."

Richard wheezed and rubbed his chest. "There ought to be a longer hunting season."

Pom was counting fingers. "You all right?"

"Never been better!" Richard stared at the torn crown of the touring cap, which had taken the brunt of the impact. "My grandmother always did say that everyone should wear a good hat."

Pom pushed the door open and made his way to the front of the truck. Steam rose from the grille. The right fender was bent down against the tire. He hobbled to the back to see what Richard had found.

"Do we have enough bottles left to make it worth going on to Baldwin and risking our necks on the road again?"

"Pom, if there was only one bottle left, I'd get it all the way there. Can you stand up without hanging onto the truck?"

Pom became aware of holding himself up by the door handle. He started to let go and then chose to ignore the question. "We've got some work to do to get this thing going again."

"Then we'd better get to it in case those guys get through the roadblock."

Patching the damage under the hood was hot business, but it took only a few strips from Pom's vest and a shoestring. The bent fender required a heavy hammer and more strength than either man had left, but by pulling together they got the sharp steel to curve away from the tire. Then they both sat down on the running board to catch their breath.

Richard had a good look at Pom. "Your head's beginning to look like a five-cent cantaloupe. You got a story for it?"

"Kicked by a mule at some little farm." Pom sniffled and ran the back of his hand across his nose. "By some chance, none of the places I go to lately have telephones."

"Of course, I'll have the damn truck to explain."

"I have an idea," Pom said. "What if you say you hit a deer?"

Richard laughed. "There's an idea. The truth." He touched his chest and winced.

"It will set you free. You know what I wish?"

"To be home, in your Model T. Sleeper."

"Well, yeah. But I wish Flora's dad was still around. I'd like to talk to him. He robbed a bank one time, you know."

"Old Mr. Larrabee? You kidding?"

"When he was hardly more than a kid, back in Missouri. Got into a shootout and thought he might have killed a man. Got so scared that he ran all the way down here, and all he got out of the whole fiasco was one ten-dollar gold piece. Flora never said word one about it till a few weeks ago. I guess it's starting to sink in that he's not coming back from Seahorse Reef."

"Ten dollars? If that's the best he could do robbing banks, it's just as well he became an automobile dealer."

Pom was exploring under the fender with his hand. He dug deeper and tugged out something long and slender, part of a deer's leg.

Richard got up smiling. "Well, Pom, I'll bet you can patch him up good as new."

They climbed back into the truck and rattled out to the road. Pom tied a strip of quilting around Richard's forehead to keep the blood from getting in his eyes, listening all the while for the sound of the tire scraping against the fender or the hiss of water spraying from the radiator.

Richard adjusted the wrap. "We're going to have to get all the way to Baldwin without turning left."

Pom was looking hard for more deer. One headlight showed the empty road, the other had gone walleyed and lit up fallow cornfields.

Richard started coughing.

"You coming down with something?"

"The damn steering wheel."

"You need a doctor."

Richard smiled. "Or a mighty fine veterinarian."

They took a strange, convoluted route through town, down back roads and through the narrow streets of the colored section with three-point turns that pointed them east and north while keeping them away from the lights of University Avenue and the Courthouse Square.

Richard shifted into third and accelerated. "We've probably shaken everybody off our scent by now, but I'd appreciate it if you'd ride all the way to Baldwin again. Be there before you know it."

"Sure," Pom said, settling back on the seat. "I'm late for dinner but early for breakfast."

The moon was behind them and the first streaks of dawn showed white behind the rail yard. Richard pulled up to the freight office and worked his way out of the truck. "Have that .32 ready," he whispered. "You never know who's around."

The two men came out of their Duesenberg before Richard had taken three steps. The shadows cast by an overhead light danced behind them. The big man was still putting on his coat. A shoulder holster disappeared beneath his lapel.

"You get lost?" Ralph said. "You're more than two hours late."

Richard stood tall, not letting on to the pain he was starting to feel. "Yeah, and you know why if you've been talking to the *Cristobel*. Plus we had a little setback of our own."

With a friendly cuff on the shoulder, the big man made him wince. "Well, you're in luck. The train was delayed. Busted switch. Take about three hours to fix." He hauled a nickel-plated watch out of his hip pocket. "Looks like maybe another half hour."

"So get loading," Ralph said. "Hop to it."

Richard was in no mood for orders. "You want this goddamn stuff, you can sure as hell lend a hand. We're bushed." He got into the truck and drove over to the train. Far ahead, the locomotive throbbed with power.

The man with the scar said something to Archie, gestured toward the train, and poked him with the flashlight. The big man said something to the wind and followed the truck over to the train. Every now and then, when he hoisted a sack, he straightened and put his hands to the small of his back.

"You're a few bottles light," he said. "You drink some?"

Richard stuck out his chin. "Less for you to lift. You got a touch of lumbago there, Archie?"

"Go to hell."

"Maybe a drink would help. It seems to work for Ralph."

"Yeah, well, I can tell you about Ralph."

"So is he the boss because he's smarter than you?"

Archie took it with a smile. He made a gun of his hand, pointed it at Richard, and brought his thumb down like the hammer. "No, he's the boss because he's more dangerous. Just ask him."

When they were done, the big man shoved a stack of two-by-fours in front of the sacks. Then they laid more boards on top of the cargo. The result was what looked like a carload of solid lumber.

Ralph came up and pulled an envelope out of an inside pocket. He made a point of taking out a hundred dollars before he gave it to Richard. "You look like hell. Go home and rest up. We'll be calling again before you know it."

Richard tossed the envelope onto the seat, climbed in, and started the truck. "I'll be right there by the phone."

As they crossed over the tracks and headed toward the setting moon, Pom counted the fifties.

"Honor Bright," he said when he had finished. "The name of T.R.'s pony was Honor Bright."

(H A P T E R   2 4

After two hours of sleep, Pom was up chopping wood, not because the pile was low, but because the work warmed him and made enough noise to get Rachel to come downstairs and unlock the kitchen door.

"I don't know why you don't just have a key made," she said, shivering with crossed arms in her pale blue flannel nightie and green wool socks.

Pom pulled a splinter from his thumb. "Between you and me, I do have a special way of gripping the doorknob to get in during emergencies, but it wouldn't be the same. There's this business of penance that has to be taken care of. If you went to Sunday school more you'd know about that. Your mother still in bed?"

"I think so." Rachel skated across the kitchen floor. When she got to the hall, she caught the doorjamb and swung around to face him. "I wish you could be home at night. It would mean so much to Mama, to all of us."

He rubbed the stubble on his chin. "I'm working on it, kiddo. Just seems like there's always something."

He had been turning away to keep her from seeing the lump on his head, but he forgot himself and she cried out and came toward him. He pulled back, protesting and telling her the story about the mule kick.

"Every now and then when you forget, you get rapped. I don't think it was personal this time, just nerves."

He didn't like lying to her, but telling her about the deer would mean explaining why the Model T wasn't damaged. Soon, he told himself, the lying could stop.

"Isn't there some other job you can do?" Rachel was dampening a dishtowel with water from the kitchen tap.

"We've been piecing and patching as it is. If I give up the veterinary work just because I take a knock on the noggin every now and then, well, I ought to have my head examined."

Her smile was weak. "Can't you just work with small animals?"

He chuckled even though it made his head hurt. "People need their big animals taken care of. A lot of 'em depend on those cattle and horses—"

"And mules."

He kissed her on the forehead. "It's going to be okay. It could've been worse."

He was on his way upstairs when Flora came out of the bedroom. She stood at the top step with her hands in the pockets of her housedress.

He looked up at her, his hand on the banister. "I hope I didn't wake you up."

Her fingers curled around the newel post. "It was time to be up anyway, and I suppose we're going to need the kindling."

"Sorry I was late. There was this—"

She came down the stairs. "Never mind. None of us have been sleeping all that much anyway. What happened to your head?"

"Occupational hazard." He thought that made a good, more-or-less true explanation.

"We have guests, Rachel said, "Carl and Kim. They spent the night."

"They sound like nice kids," Pom said. "I'd like to meet their folks some time."

"They'd like that," Rachel was quick to say. "But their parents travel a lot."

"Well, I know how that is." Pom kissed Flora on the cheek and turned back toward Rachel. "Do your friends like to eat by any chance? Maybe they'd like some breakfast. Grits and bacon and eggs?"

"You're going to have to get the bacon out of the icebox," Rachel told him. "Nobody else will go near it with that dog head in there."

"Oh, yeah." Pom rubbed his chin. "I've got to get to that. It's a case of rabies—a suspected case anyway. There was a boy up near Waldo that got bitten and they think that was the dog. I'm hoping to get that one figured out today."

"Amelia fainted when she saw it," Flora said. "We didn't have any smelling salts, so we touched the tip of her nose with a spoonful of lemon sherbet. She was delirious."

Pom coughed back a laugh. "Ah, well, that's—uh—that's good sherbet. I hope you used a small spoon."

The food brought them together. Kim held back, but Carl tried to take more than his share of bacon, and his sister intercepted his hand with hers and told him to have more grits instead. She gave him a look that left no room for argument.

They skirted Pom's questions about the farm and their parents, although Carl let slip a few words about their parents' dark green Studebaker.

"Theron Purdy got a nice blue one," Pom said. "The cat's pajamas."

"They're fun to ride in," Carl said. "But ours has something none of the others have."

Kim tried to shush him, but he couldn't resist going on.

"I stuck a marble in the dashboard, a yellow cat's eye. You can hear it rolling around every time Daddy takes a hard turn, and he's never been able to get it out of there. He gave me a whipping with a hickory switch."

"My sympathies," Pom said. He looked down the table at Flora as he reached for the succotash." I hear Ainsley's bruises are pretty well healed now."

"There are other things we might talk about," Flora said.

"If she really got 'em from trying to make her way around in the dark, it's a lesson about turning on the light."

"I hope you're not really that naïve. Don't you suppose there might be all kinds of reasons why a person—a woman in particular—wouldn't want the truth to come out about such a thing?"

"Some women maybe, but Ainsley? She's always looking for a good story. How could she resist telling one of her own?"

"Maybe it's not such a good one," Flora said. "Or maybe she's trying to protect somebody."

Jim held the basket of biscuits without taking one. "Are you saying you think someone attacked Ainsley?"

Flora gave her husband a pointed look. "I'm afraid that's exactly what I'm saying."

Jim looked to Pom for some further explanation

"I suppose you're referring to Theron," Pom said. "But why would Theron want to take a poke at Ainsley? Last I heard he was crazy about her. And even if he did, why would she keep quiet about it? Something there doesn't add up."

"That's because there's a lot that you don't know—about people in general and women in particular."

He cleared his throat. "Did you want to elaborate on that?"

"All right. For one thing, it's possible she still loves him."

"Oh, come on. I said *he's* crazy about *her*. But those two were like milk and beer from day one. For her part, I don't think love had much to do with it. It was probably something a lot more basic."

"Charles, for heaven's sake."

"Oh, everybody at this table's old enough to know what's love and what isn't." He looked at Rex. "Am I right?"

Flora persisted. "I'm just saying don't overlook it as a possibility. Women are always falling in love with men who don't deserve it. Some of them even thrive on a certain amount of abuse."

"That doesn't sound like the Ainsley I know."

Flora waved a hand toward the backyard. "I give up. Now what are we going to do with all those animals out there? The garage and the garden look like Noah's ark landed on them."

Pom put his fork down and smiled. "Well, we ate one of 'em and I believe I can take care of the rest today."

Rachel gulped down her orange juice. "Daddy, you're not going to—"

"No, nothing like that. Soon as I can get hold of a truck I'm going to cart 'em all over to the university farm. They're always looking for more animals, and the ones we give 'em are going to live pretty high on the hog."

"I was hoping we could get some money for them," Flora said.

"Oh, we can take 'em off our taxes; that's something."

"As long as you can finish the work on the house and get some of the other things we need around here."

"Soon as I get those animals taken care of I'm going to pick up the rest of the stuff I need for the wiring. I'll have Leon Duforge come over and help me finish it once and for all. He'll be happy to have the work."

"How can we afford to do that? You're always telling me there's no time and no money."

"Well, we're pulling ourselves up by our bootstraps around here, and anyway I've been putting in some time, you know. Every now and then I even get paid in cash! That's the way it's supposed to work, though I'll admit, I'd almost forgotten."

"That all sounds very mysterious, but if the things that need to happen start happening, fine."

Jim had been preoccupied, but now he spoke up. "I took the liberty of replacing the bulb in the parlor socket," he said. "And I know a thing or two about wiring."

"You've got enough to think about," Pom told him. "I've seen that bushel of paper you got from the public defender. And, knowing him, he probably left some out."

On his way to the garage, Pom encountered Amelia at the kitchen door. They exchanged pleasantries on the back steps and then he asked, "How long have you been with us now, Amelia?"

She wiped her hands on her apron. "I don't exactly know, Mr. Holliman. What for are you asking?"

"It just seems like time for you to get paid for your work."

She laughed. "Now, Mister Holliman, you knows that pay or no pay, I'm the kind that's got to be working all the time or I gets fidgety. I hope I'm doing okay for you."

"You're doing fine! The place never looked better." He reached into his hip pocket and pulled out a fifty-dollar bill. "Seems to me it's about time to pay you."

She nearly fell down the steps. "Lord, Mister Holliman! I can't take no fifty-dollar bill!" A nervous laugh turned into a cough. "I'd be afraid it'd burn a hole in my pocketbook. Something bad would surly come of it if I had that kind of money on me. Not that I ain't grateful."

Pom swept a hand over his forehead. "Now *there's* a setback I hadn't figured on. What if I were to give you a couple a day for the next month? Could you handle that?"

She laughed again, more easily this time. "I believe I just might be able to get used to it! Just don't tell that husband of mine. You know he's got his way of spending money and I've got mine and they's two different things!"

Pom smiled. "I know how that is."

She went on. "So did Mr. Howard leave y'all some money in his will?"

"How's that, Amelia?"

"That fella that came around during the parade. He said most likely Mr. Howard left y'all some money in his will out of gratitude for y'all taking him in during his last illness."

"I'm still not following you. What fella you talking about exactly?"

Her smile gave way to a look of concern. "Well, you know. Back then about the time the weather turned and Mr. Rose was on the radio and all, when y'all were at the Homecoming parade, this gentleman come 'round. I was beating the rugs, and he said Mr. Howard must surely have left y'all some money in a will somewhere in the house I just figured y'all had found it."

"Well, we did no such thing. May I ask was this man white or colored?"

"Oh, white for sure and dressed to beat the band. A little fussy in fact. Had a stone in his ring the size of a pecan."

"This fella was here at the house you say?"

"In the yard. Just in the yard, chattering like a jaybird while I beat the rugs."

"Just stood in the yard and talked and then left? Never went into the house?"

"Lord, no! As it was, he seemed a little scared of the dog across the street."

"You mean the dog was barking?"

"After a while, sure. Like to bark her head off for some reason."

Pom gave the screen door a tug, testing a rusty hinge. He made a point of looking at the hinge, not at Amelia. "After this fella left, I suppose you got on with the housework."

"Most absolutely. There's no end of it around here."

"Yeah, we might just as well be running a ranch. After this fella left I suppose you did what you could, though, cleaning upstairs. Jim's room and all."

She began pulling at her fingers. "Just a pass with the dust rag. Not to disturb anything."

The hinge squawked as Pom worked it. "Sure. There's a lot of books in there. They seem to sprout dust."

She pulled her fingers free and balled up her hands. "I can't hold it back anymore, Mr. Holliman. I was the one that found that gun in there. But I was just hoping to help, you know. If Mr. Howard's will was in there, it would be a good thing, wouldn't it?"

Pom looked up from the hinge. "Sure. That would've been good. You were doing the right thing."

"My curiosity done got the best of me though, I've got to admit that."

"You found the gun right after the guy in the yard left?"

"I was tumbling around with what to do about looking for the will. I wasn't expecting to find no *gun* in there! I figured if I told you, which I ought to have done, then you'd have to tell the sheriff, and I just hadn't got that far along in my thinking. I didn't even tell Luther, but he got it out of me on account of I talked in my *sleep!* And he called the sheriff thinking there might be a reward. A *reward!*"

"Don't you give it another thought, Amelia. Just tell me more about the guy in the yard. What did he look like?"

She thought for a moment. "You know, it was a while ago and I was working and all."

"But you said he was well-dressed."

"Yessir. And he had a little mustache that didn't hardly seem worth the trouble. And he was a big fella, but he'd maybe lost some weight on account of his trousers was drooping."

"That it?"

"Pretty near. Except for the stone in that ring. I only noticed it on account of it was so colorful, like a boil ready to pop. It looked like one of them paper rings that comes off a cigar, except it was real and he wore it on his little finger. Ain't that queer? Wearing a ring on your little finger?"

"Did you happen to see where this fella went after he left here?"

"Didn't go much of anywhere. Just away."

"Didn't go next door to the Polks or across the street toward the Pennells?"

"No, sir. Just away. Traipsing down the street, near as I could tell, setting off the dogs again. Didn't have no automobile. I couldn't see past the trees. I'm real sorry about all of it, Mr. Holliman."

Pom made way so that she could get through the kitchen door. "Forget it, Amelia. But do me a favor. Keep this mum for now, will you? And try not to talk in your sleep."

By the time he got the livestock trucked off to the university farm, Pom was ready to get away and do some more thinking. So he told Flora that he was going to work on the wiring after he checked on some suspected hog cholera down toward Rocky Point. He made the stops, but they were really only brief social visits because the threat of the disease had long since passed. Then he pursued his real object. He drove across the prairie to see Ainsley and her mother.

In his planning he had forgotten about Tom and Tim Campion, twins in their twenties who ran cattle on Paynes Prairie. The Campion Ranch sprawled along the northwest edge of the old lakebed. The grass was lush and the range was open, and so the beef herds roamed freely through the sprawling scrub and wetlands. In the nearly forty years since the lake had drained, a road had been cut through the tangle, and in the dry weather of fall the Campions used it to move their herd from one part of the range to the other. Pom guided the Model T onto the prairie and followed the swishing tails of the cattle at parade speed until one of the Campion twins turned in the saddle and caught sight of him.

"I hear that up at the college they're playing polo with automobiles," he said. "So why not use 'em to herd cattle? How you doing, Pom?"

"I guess I'm all right, Tom. What you been feeding those beeves of yours?"

"I'm Tim. Tom's the one over there swearing at his horse. You know that temper of his. Our cows've been eating the same stuff they've always eaten. They just look scrawny for some reason."

They were going down a slope and Pom let the automobile coast along behind the herd. "I thought I'd tap some blood from some of 'em. You have any animals die on you lately?"

"No more than usual." Tom turned his stout buckskin around and gestured toward the rim of the prairie, toward town. "Any word on the killings?"

"You know about as much as I do."

Tom brought his horse around in a tight circle to keep him quiet. "I hear old John Howard left a will."

"That's just a rumor. I don't know how it got started." Pom pumped the brake on the Model T to give Tim and his horse plenty of room. "He'd been living down in the Porters Quarters under a hunk of cardboard and tarpaper. I don't think he had a will or anything to leave in it. Just a place in the bushes."

"Funny how some folks'll do that. Not so different from horses, wandering back to what they're used to. Lost all of his money then I guess."

"A long time ago. I got to like old John. He was straight as pump water."

"You like everybody, Pom."

"I did till a few weeks ago."

CHAPTER 25

—◠●◠—

When they came to an open area, the Campion brothers brought the herd to a stop and hobbled a couple of calves. Pom drew a vial of blood from each and then drove on ahead. When he had crossed the prairie, he doubled back along a sand road that wound through the blackjack to the farms along the western edge of the old lakebed. He pushed the Model T over a little rise and coasted past a herd of grazing Herefords, down to a trim white clapboard house that faced the six miles of scrub and grassland of the prairie. To the right, up the slope, was a stand of red-leafed young dogwoods sprouting among rows of short black stumps. Pom set the brake and walked the sandy path to the gray wooden steps of the porch. The persistent barking of a basset hound carried over the steady *tap-tap-tappa* of a typewriter in an upstairs bedroom.

"What in the world happened to you?" Laetitia asked by way of a greeting.

After assuring her that the bump on his head wasn't as bad as it looked, he gestured toward the rows of decaying stumps, remnants of a grove frozen thirty years ago. "You ever think of growing just a few orange trees?" he asked through the screen door

"Never once," Laetitia said. "Mr. Harper and I got to like it the way it is. Kind of wild and grown over."

He scraped his feet on the mat and reached down to pat the dog. "Wild, huh? Like old Kaiser here."

As she let him into the house, Laetitia's thoughts went back. "I have a clear picture in my memory, from about the time Ainsley was born, of her brother and J.J. tearing through that grove on their horses, throwing oranges at each other. They were always snorting around, those two."

Pom chuckled. "I never thought of J.J. Ward as a snorter."

She smiled up at him. At seventy-four she still had pretty teeth. "He has kind of settled down, hasn't he?"

"Speaking of Ainsley, I'd like to have a little parley with her if she's around."

Laetitia went to the foot of the stairs and yelled to her daughter. "I hate doing that," she told Pom, "but I can't get up and down all those steps the way I used to. Would you believe I was a bride of twenty-one when I moved into this house?"

Ainsley put in an appearance at the top of the stairs. Seeing Pom, she smiled through her bruises and came down. "You parked too far back. I couldn't see who it was. My, that's quite a lump you've got. Are you okay?"

"Never better, thanks." He was careful not to pay too much attention to the fading marks on her face. "My brakes aren't working so well these days, so I thought I'd better not park too close to the drop-off."

She went over to a big leather wing chair and flopped down in a way that made her mother frown. "Well, Pom, you on your way to raise somebody's cow from the dead?"

He smiled at the image. "No, I came down here to see you. Did you ever play chess?"

"Chess? No, can't say as I have. Why, is Flora looking for another victim?"

"Always, but that's not what I'm getting at. It seems to me that this community of ours has gotten to be like a chessboard, with lots of pieces out in the middle of the board and everything very dangerous and complicated. So I'm going to try to move a piece very carefully."

"I never knew you to be so poetic, Pom."

Now he let himself look at Ainsley's healing lip and the shadowy bruise on her jaw. "I don't work on people much. I work on animals. But they do have some things in common, and one of 'em is injuries from fighting—or let's say, from being attacked."

Ainsley sat forward in the big chair and clasped her knees. "I hope you didn't come all the way down here to talk about old news."

"I'm moving a pawn, and that may not look like much, but a little thing just might affect the whole board, a little thing like a pawn—or a bruise. I know it's not exactly my business, but may I ask, did Theron do it?"

Ainsley glanced at her mother, the essence of grace as she sat down straight-backed on the horsehair sofa. "Let's say that he did. What of it? If I wanted to make an issue of it, I'd report it to the sheriff."

Laetitia's dark eyes flashed. "When I was your age, a man would be whipped out of town for that kind of thing, maybe shot."

"Don't be so melodramatic, mother." Ainsley took a deep breath. "So what if it was Theron? What if it was?"

"Well, for one thing it's just possible that Jim Rhodes will go after him. Jimmy's a hard guy to read, but from what I've seen of him—"

"No, no! He can't do that! That's one reason I've been staying out of town. I don't want anybody to know, to avoid that very thing! So please just keep this to yourself."

"I wish it was that simple, Ainsley, but the cat's already out of the bag. Word's going around. You can't stop people from adding two and two."

"If Jim and Theron mix it up, there are only two outcomes—both of 'em bad for Jim."

"Sure, he can beat the stuffing out of Theron and go back to jail looking capable of murder or Theron could kill him."

She dropped back in the chair and put her face in her hands. Her thick brown hair trailed through her long fingers. "I swear I don't know what to do."

Pom drew a breath. "This is where moving those chess pieces gets tricky. The best thing you can do for both of 'em—for everybody—is to press charges against Theron, to make sure he stays in jail till we can get this whole murder business cleared up, till we can get Jim cleared and out of town."

"I don't want to do that. I don't want him to go to jail. I just want him—I don't know."

"What if she does press charges?" Laetitia asked. "And when he gets out, he comes after her? Then what?"

"Maybe once he's in there a while, he'll cool off and we can talk some sense into him."

Ainsley sat up in the chair. "He's not mean. He can be sweet. He just gets his mind set on things."

"Tell you what," Pom said. "If I have to sleep in your front room with Mr. Larrabee's .45, I'll do it till this matter is settled."

"And I'm a pretty fair shot with Mr. Harper's Navy pistol," Laetitia said. "I've kind of lost track of it, but I'll find it if I have to turn over every stick of furniture."

Ainsley got up and went to the closet under the stairs. "Don't bother, mother. I've got it." She took out her macramé handbag and hefted it.

"Well, I wish you'd had it when he came at you that way."

"As a matter of fact, I did."

"Well, for pity's sake, child, if you had a gun, why did you let him do what he did?"

"You mean, why didn't I shoot him dead on the spot? You'd better believe I thought about it, but then I *really* thought about it, and I've thought about it plenty ever since. If I had pointed that gun at him, I just might've used it. And do you really think that taking a few bumps balances with shooting a man to death? Sometimes life just doesn't come out even, but it's a lot more even this way than it would've been the other."

"He still might come back after you," Laetitia reminded her.

Ainsley put the purse back in the closet. "No, that event was a one-time thing. He was really wound up that night. And you can't keep him in jail forever."

"There's pieces here," Pom said. "There's pieces on the board and I don't know what they're up to. But I know one thing for sure. We've got to get a hold of Theron if we're going to make sense of 'em. Somehow he's becoming the key to this whole thing. May I ask what set him off?"

"A stupid car, that's what. I don't know one car from another, but it was something dark and shiny. He wanted me to go for a ride in it. That's how we got into our fight. I was too dense to realize that he just wanted to impress me."

"It's a dark blue 1927 Studebaker," Pom said. "Quite a car. Any idea where he got the money for it?"

"Not from what he makes as a hunting guide and not from taxidermy. His whole year wouldn't bring in enough cash to pay for a new automobile."

Pom stood up. "I'd kind of like to go for a ride in it. All right then. We'll keep him out of jail for a little while. But keep your doors locked, will you?"

In the evening, when he got back to the house on Magnolia Street, Richard was waiting for him in the front room. "Your boy Trent's been talking a blue streak all around town."

Pom stopped in his tracks. "He wouldn't do that."

"So you said, but he is. If this blows up, we're all going down with it. You know him so well. Maybe you know where we can find him."

They caught up with him at Porter's Place. He had four empty shot glasses beside him on the bar and was regaling anyone who would listen about his plans to spend big money.

"God damn," Richard said to the bartender. "Couldn't you shut him up?"

Trent drained his fifth glass and greeted his partners with open arms. "Where you been, gentlemen? I thought we were going for a boat ride."

"The guy's built like an oak," the bartender said. "Deardra doesn't pay me to get my head knocked off. I'll call the police if you want."

"That's real white of you," Richard said, "but thanks just the same." He got Trent by the elbow. "Where can we take him?"

The bartender pointed toward the back of the dance floor. "The office. You can stow him in there the whole night long for all I care."

The office was hardly more than a long closet. The décor consisted of a few coat hangers on nails. One held a bow tie, another a dowdy black dress and an old-fashioned woman's hat, large, round, and feathery. Some of the sawdust and peanut husks had trailed in from the dance floor. An ancient roll-top desk crammed with yellowing papers took up one end of the room. A frayed canvas army cot took up most of what was left. The barred window had been lacquered over and nailed shut. The office was hot.

Pom glanced toward the door to make sure it was closed all the way before he spoke to Trent. "Just where all have you been talking your head off?"

With a supporting arm from Richard, Trent tried to keep his feet under him. "Here and there. I spread my money around pretty good I guess. Folks sure love to get money, don't they? Where's the rest of my five hundred?"

The door opened and Deardra came in bearing the scent of some tropical flower that Pom couldn't identify. "The minute I leave this place, things start to fall apart."

"Guess you two haven't met," Richard said. "Pom, this is Deardra. Pom's a friend from way back. Deardra from not so far back, but we've been making up for lost time."

"Do tell all," Deardra said. "It seems to be the thing to do tonight."

A little rough and impatient, Pom shook hands with her. "Nice place you have here."

"Thanks, but I didn't set it up. I inherited it from my mother's uncle. I don't think he knew exactly what was going on in his warehouse."

Richard still had a grip on Trent. "Maybe we should just chain our boy up till we can dry him out and put him to work"

The brown window lit up and the room began to vibrate, making Pom think that Judgment Day was coming, but it was only the 7:22 freight train on its way into town. The four of them stood silent until it had passed. Through the smoky window, Pom watched it disappear. "How long do you suppose before we get the call, Richard?"

"Could be tonight."

"But I mean, what's the latest it could come?"

"Day after tomorrow. The day after that is pushing it."

"Yeah. That's Christmas. So we've got to keep him under wraps till then."

Suddenly Trent became interested. "What are y'all talking about?"

Richard turned around. "We're talking about you, you damn blabbermouth. You just can't shut up, can you?"

Trent twisted free of Richard and began swearing so color-
fully that nobody was sure what he was saying.

Pom put his hands on his hips. "What'd you do, Trent, drink
up your hundred bucks?"

Trent steadied himself against the desk and grinned. "Hell,
no. Some of it I *wasted*."

Pom punched him in the forehead so hard that he fell backwards onto the cot. With his fist still doubled, he bent over him.
"You damn fool! You want to chop your own head off, go ahead,
but don't you ever put my neck on the block again, you hear?"

Trent tried to come back at him, but Richard held him down
by the shoulder. "This is no time to go crazy. We've just got to
stick it out for a few more days."

Trent rubbed his forehead as if he were coming out of a
dream. "Damn, Pom. I'm sorry. I just needed to cut loose. I
guess the money kind of fogged my thinking."

Pom kicked the cot, nearly knocking it over with Trent still
on it. "So it was all for nothing? Nothing! We damn near got
ourselves killed for that money and you blew a hundred of it in
one night? Is that why I fished your sorry hide out of jail? What
about the farm? What about Elsie and the girls?"

Richard got between them and caught Pom by the shirtsleeve. "Never mind. We've got to make that last trip without
everybody in town knowing about it. We're going to have to lie
low and be ready when the call comes. And when it does, we're
going to need him. He's still our ticket through those islands and
sandbars. Now dry him out and keep his head glued together till
then."

Pom turned around, rubbing his knuckles. "This line of work
is bringing out the worst in me. Look, Trent, you keep your trap
shut. You think I want my wife and kids to find out what I've
been up to? And I sure as hell don't want Avery to find out. I
want to get this last trip done and put all this behind me, and

if you want to keep your carcass out of jail as much as you say, you'd better do the same. Are you hearing me?"

Trent clutched the edge of the cot. "Hell, Pom. I said I was sorry. I guess I just had to let off some steam. Now when do I get the rest of my money?"

Pom kept rubbing his sore knuckles. "Later. Now you stay with me till that call comes."

Headlights turning on the other side of the tracks caught the lacquered window and brightened Richard's face as he spoke. "Aren't you going to attract attention dragging Trent around all of a sudden?"

"Nobody's going to notice another stray at the house," Pom said, "except maybe Avery. Let's go, Trent. We can say Elsie kicked you out. Anybody can believe that."

(HAPTER 26

As the night sky cleared, a cold north wind swept through the woods and streets and sent brittle brown magnolia leaves crabbing from yard to yard. Pom was glad that he got back home before Flora had locked the doors. He found her in the front room setting the screen across the fireplace. She knocked down one of the bright knit Christmas stockings and re-hung it.

"I was hauled away at the last minute," he explained. "I was close enough to smell the liver and onions when the loop dropped around my neck. But nothing was going to keep me away from your avocado and grapefruit salad."

She turned and touched him on the shoulder. "At least your intentions were good. You were in the house for a minute there."

"And the aroma of the best liver and onions in the entire state of Florida—"

With raised hands, she stopped him. "Charles, we set some aside for you and you can warm it up if there's any fire left. Wouldn't it be nice if we had a gas stove?"

He was glad to turn the talk away from his tardiness. "Don't you have any sentimental attachment to the old wood stove? Didn't your mother and your grandmother cook on it?"

"Yeah, they did, and that's why it's about cracked to pieces. One day it's going to blow apart right in our faces."

He was enjoying the safe talk. "Next thing you know, you'll be going on about a new house again."

"Worse things could happen. This one's been a struggle for as long as I can remember. It's been one nuisance after another."

"You mean, if you had the chance you'd really up and move away?"

"Just across town to one of those new ones by the golf course."

"That again. Those don't have anything over this one. All of those houses over there are frauds—little castles and haciendas. This one here is the real thing."

"With real dry rot! As far as I'm concerned, there's nothing wrong with a little style. Anyway, I'm sure that over there the roofs don't leak and the faucet handles don't come off in your hand and the plumbing doesn't choke up and the lights turn on and off."

"I'm working on that last part. And you'll notice that I'm making some real progress. By the way, about that liver and onions, we got enough for Trent?"

"Trent Walker? What's he doing here?"

Pom was vague. "Well, he kind of needed a place to stay for a night or two. You know how it is."

The fire popped and she moved away from the screen. "Were you planning to empty out the whole jail and move everybody in here?"

"It's just for a couple of nights."

"For Christmas? I don't know if I want a moonshiner staying in my house. The neighbors are talking as it is."

"It's going to be too cold to make him sleep in the garage. What if we clear a place in the northeast room? It's either that or have him bunk with Rex."

"I won't have him staying with Rex. And I don't want him in my father's room either." He's a bootlegger."

"You'd be surprised at the caliber of people involved in bootlegging. He needs a place."

"Well, all right. If Jim can stand it, you can put Trent in with him. What's he going to be doing all day? Not plying his trade I hope."

"His trade is *farming*, and just as soon as he gets back on his feet that's what he's going to be doing."

As the moon rose through the pines, the night turned cold, and Pom slipped deeper beneath the quilt, warm in bed beside his wife, thinking more and more about the long miles of chilly Gulf water and the dangerous route between the *Cristobel* and the freight yard in Baldwin. In his mind he retraced the steps that had brought him this far from his family and friends. He wished that he had never agreed to that first trip with Richard and that he didn't have the last one looming before him.

And when was he going to tell her about losing the state job? He'd have to tell her before she found out, that was for sure, and yet, if he told her too soon, she'd grill him about his comings and goings. But if she found out on her own, there'd be hell to pay.

Late in the night, hearing subdued voices in Rex's room, he wrestled into his robe and slippers and went down the hall to investigate. Jim and Rex were bent over the radio. Jim had the headset and Rex was copying down what he said while Jim made fine adjustments of the dials. The gooseneck lamp was twisted down so low over the desk that the two collaborators threw giant shadows whenever they moved. Pom thought it best not to interrupt Jim's rapid dictation, so he slipped into the room and waited by the door.

"They're going to make another drop on the night of the twenty-sixth. I missed a word, the name of the pickup boat, I think. Then the position. The same as before. *Break contact if you see Sam. Reschedule drop for twenty-five hours later. Baldwin will coordinate.*'" Jim took off the headset. "Baldwin. That's the first time I've heard that name. Is there anyone named Baldwin you can think of?"

Rex was tired but excited. "No, but he could be almost anywhere between here and Cedar Key, maybe even down toward Yankeetown. He could be just about anywhere. You sure there wasn't a first name?"

"Yes, and I wouldn't expect one." Jim listened to the throaty threat of a distant owl. "For that matter, it could be a code name like Sam, which probably means the Coast Guard. It doesn't give us much to go on. But we do have the *Cristobel* and we know where she's going to be on the night of the twenty-sixth. We also know that she's going to be on the lookout for the authorities. So if the agents do go after her, they'll have to be unusually careful. The clever thing would be to draw her into U.S. waters. Then they can seize her and find out who she's delivering to. This could be very big."

Pom came into the light. "But don't talk about it yet."

Startled, Rex looked up from his notepad. "Why?" Pom put his hands in the pockets of his robe. "Find out more about Baldwin before you take up Avery's time."

Soft static came from the headset on the desk. "They've become very tight with information," Jim said. "Until the mention of this Baldwin, we hadn't gotten anything new since they started using the name *Cristobel*."

"Do we know anybody named Baldwin, Dad?" Rex was recopying the message for neatness.

Pom weighed his answer. "Could be a first name, could be a last name. Could be something else altogether."

Rex's face showed disappointment as he looked up from his copying. "So you don't think we should go to the sheriff?"

"Not just yet. See if you can't get some more details."

"But we've only got till the twenty-sixth," Rex reminded him. "That only gives us three more nights of listening."

"Tell you what," Pom said. "I'll mention it to Avery tomorrow if I see him, just to get him thinking in that direction. He's going to have to decide whether to let the Coast Guard in on this or work it out with the sheriff in Levy County. It's not as easy as you might think."

Rex's face brightened. "You suppose they'd let us go with 'em on the twenty-sixth?"

"Not on your life. That's dangerous work."

"Well, what if we went out on our own? Who do we know with a boat?"

"Maybe you and I can go in our own boat sometime, and Jim too, of course. How does that sound?"

"Get a boat of our own? I guess so."

"For now, why don't you get some sleep? You've got some catching up to do."

"He's right, Rex." Jim stood up and stretched and said good night. He followed Pom into the hallway. When they came to the door of Jim's room, he stopped and spoke in confidence. "I'm sorry. I guess I'm a terrible influence on the boy."

Pom looked away. "He just needs some sleep."

"He's so excited about these messages."

Pom lowered his voice. "There's something else I want to say to you, about Ainsley."

"About the bruises you talked about at dinner."

Pom put a hand on his shoulder and gave him a little shake. "There's nothing you can do. This has to be taken care of the right way."

"Is she safe?"

"She comes from tough stock. She'll be okay. And she's the best way we have to find Theron and get some answers. For now the best thing you can do is to keep your distance from her and don't go looking for him. The worst thing would be if you find him."

Jim started to open the door. "You're going out looking for him?"

"I didn't say that."

"I'd like to come with you."

"You know you can't."

Jim's hand tightened on the doorknob. "You'll let me know what you find out?"

"When the time comes, the whole town's going to know."

Pom and Trent spent most of the morning driving around looking for Theron in fish camps and hunting shacks. They went to a stand of pinewoods across the swamp from Kincaid's place, to the log cabin where he did his taxidermy and worked on cars. They waded through the debris of automobile parts and pressed their noses to the filmy windows, seeing only shelves of stuffed animals and a few deer heads mounted on the wall.

"He sure is around plenty when you're not looking for him," Pom said as he backed the Model T out of the rutted driveway. When he got back out to the gravel road, he hit on an idea and headed west.

"You figure he's up at the San Felasco Hammock stretching the deer-hunting season?" Trent said.

"He stretches everything else, doesn't he?"

"What you going to do if you find him?"

'It ain't him I'm after."

"You're as cagey as a fox, Pom."

"Got to be. We're in a tight spot."

When they were well into the hammock, a deep blue glinted through the scrub. Pom slowed the Model T and backed into the nearest turnoff. Then he wheeled around and drove out the way he had come.

Trent was perplexed. "You're not going to tell me you drove all the way out here just to eyeball that car, then turn right around again?"

Pom glanced over his shoulder before answering. "I just don't want Theron to know we're out here. We're going to park down a ways and hoof it back in here good and quiet."

Far away they could hear the occasional pop of rifle fire.

"That Theron," Trent said under his breath, "he's about as subtle as the 6:39."

"As long as it's way over there, it's a good sound," Pom said. "Lets us know right where he is. That's his thirty-aught-six we're hearing, isn't it?"

"Blow the damn deer's head clean off. Scares me to death."

They came to the Studebaker and Pom walked around it a couple of times. "Pretty car. Looks like he's already put a ding in it though, all along the side." He ran his finger along the crease, then pulled out his penknife and made a scratch of his own.

"Damn, Pom. His new car."

"Not so new. Good job of repainting though. Blue over green, dark green."

He tried the door. It opened smoothly. He stuck his head inside and pulled back in a hurry.

Trent made a face and spat. "God almighty. What's that?"

"It's been underwater. He could take the engine apart and dry it out and put it back together, but he couldn't keep the lake stink from breeding in the frame. The morning sun puts quite a point to it."

He went around to the front and raised the hood. "We'll have to hot wire it."

Trent pinched the crown of his fedora. "You figuring to swipe this damn thing?"

"Not for long." Pom folded the hood over and began poking around among the workings of the Studebaker. "Get in there and give me some gas, just enough to keep it from stalling."

After a few more twists, the car sprang to life.

Trent chuckled. "You'll have to show me that sometime."

"I like you better young and innocent. Hop in. We're going for a spin."

Pom backed the car around and headed down the dirt ruts.

"Just where are we going?" Trent clapped a hand over his hat.

"To any good wide place." Pom bounced the car over roots and potholes. "But I already found out what I need to know."

Inside the dashboard something was rattling. Pom came to a bend in the road and swerved. The sound in the dashboard rolled from right to left and stopped with a clank. After fifty yards, Pom turned around again and swung the car hard the other way. The sound rolled from left to right.

Trent put his ear to the dashboard. "What do you suppose?"

"I don't suppose anything," Pom said. "I *know*. It's a cat's eye marble."

"Is that so? I suppose you know the color too."

"Yellow. Now I've just got to figure out what to do about it."

Pom eased the Studebaker back into the scrub. They got out and halted in their tracks.

"Hello, boys."

Theron was dressed in colors that blended with the woods, drab green and buff. The barrel of the thirty-aught-six was wound with vines.

Pom stared at the barrel trained on his heart. "You having any luck, Theron?"

"I caught *you*, didn't I? Come on over, Trent, and stand next to Pom here."

When they were side by side, Theron stepped back and held the rifle on both of them.

"Saw your car and couldn't resist taking it for a spin," Pom said. Without the usual chuckle, his words rang hollow.

"Saw it—or came looking for it?" Theron cocked his head as if he were straining to hear the truth.

Pom stayed calm, kept still, with his hands in sight. "Came looking for it, of course. We heard you had this magical automobile."

"That so. Who told you—Ainsley?"

Before Pom could answer, Theron reached into his pocket and pulled out a pecan. He tossed it to Trent and told him to walk with it.

Trent swallowed. "What do you aim to do?"

"That's up to you. Now get on over there by that pine tree."

After about twenty yards Theron called out. "That's far enough. Now stop and face me."

Trent did as he was told. His knees were shaking.

"Now take that pecan and hold it up between your fingers."

Pom watched the barrel of the rifle come up.

Trent dropped the pecan, picked it up, and held it out as far as he could between his thumb and forefinger.

"No, not out there," Theron said. "I want it right beside your ear."

"Oh, come on," Pom protested. Further words failed him.

Theron raised the rifle to his shoulder. "Now, this gun pulls to the right, so I'm going to aim for your nose and I should hit pretty close."

He fired.

Suddenly Trent was on the ground. He got up wringing his hand.

Pom ran toward him. "Where you hit?"

Trent worked his fingers. "Nowhere. Son-of-a-bitch is a good shot. I'll say that for him."

Theron lowered the rifle. "Next time you come sniffing around, we'll put the pecan between your teeth."

CHAPTER 27

When he got back to Magnolia Street, Pom left Trent to help Jim with the wiring and went looking for the sheriff. Leonard indicated that he was with someone named Lola.

"I've heard of Lola," Pom said, "but I've never met her."

"Guess you don't move in the right circles," Leonard told him. "She does business in a cottage on Pleasant Street. He won't like being bothered."

Pom found the sheriff in the backyard of a sunny clapboard cottage next door to where a Victorian with gingerbread and turrets had burned down. Suddenly the grass was growing thick and green around the little house that had languished in shadows for its first twenty years. The sheriff was perched on a wooden stool beside a brick-lined bed of Spanish bayonets and elephant ears. He had a pink striped sheet draped over his shoulders. His big flat-brimmed hat sat on a picnic table nearby. One of his hands poked out from the sheet and held an oversized comb. The other was brushing a loose hair from his nose.

Pom arrived smiling. "Gone and left you to cut your own? You get it cheaper that way?"

The sheriff was not amused. "She got a phone call." He had a hangdog look, sitting there abandoned in the yard with a sheet wrapped around him.

"That's a very becoming color for you, Avery."

"I've got a gun under here, Pom."

"They say that Lola's pretty good at everything she does."

The sheriff gave Pom a sour look. "I don't care about everything she does. I'm just here for a decent haircut. You ought to have her cut your hair sometime."

Pom ran a hand over the crown of his head. "Can't afford it."

"Oh, come on. It doesn't cost that much."

"It ain't the money I can't afford. It's the hair."

The sheriff looked toward the cottage, hoping for an interruption, but Lola was nowhere to be seen. "Did you come out here for a reason?"

"Well, I was just out thinking of buying a new automobile."

"That'll be the day. You're wedded to that Tin Lizzie of yours. You wouldn't know how to drive—or sleep in—anything else."

"I was just wondering if you've come across any abandoned ones in the past couple of months."

"Nothing you'd want. I guarantee you that."

"And if you found one, say in a lake, what would you do with it?"

"We'd figure it was used in a crime and hold it for evidence."

"Not sell it in one of your auctions?"

"Are you kidding? You'd never get the smell out of it." The sheriff shook the comb. "Look, if you know something, you ought to come forward."

"Well, I don't. And I've talked to just about everybody but the cows in my pasture."

"Everybody but the cows, huh. Well, if *they* tell you anything, let me know and I'll get Doctor Willis to have a look at you."

"Soon as I know anything, I'll tell you. But right now there's someone else I've got to talk to."

"Is that so?"

Pom took a hand mirror from the picnic table and smoothed the wisps of hair over his ears.

"And who might that be?" the sheriff asked.

Pom handed him the mirror. "Rachel."

They met at the elementary school that was under construction northwest of town, almost to Boundary Street. It was a hulking brick edifice two stories tall, long and solid, smelling of damp mortar and sawdust. It was cold and drafty with the wind whipping through the long, high hallway. The light of late afternoon glanced off the vast windows and cast pale blue patches on the hardwood floors.

"We'd be more comfortable someplace else." Pom's voice echoed in the huge hallway. He turned up the collar of his hand-me-down overcoat.

"They wanted to meet here," Rachel told him again. "They've got their reasons."

Somewhere down the open hallway, a two-by-four fell. Kim and Carl entered at the far end and came toward them.

Kim had part of a blanket over her shoulders and Carl was wearing three oversized flannel shirts. Pom put them at ease. "Don't worry. One of these rooms is going to be the principal's office, but I don't know which, and anyway there isn't a principal yet. When I was your age I could smell one a mile away." He motioned toward the nearest doorway. "Why don't we just go in here?"

They entered an auditorium. Carl stared at the gaping room as if it were the grandest thing he'd ever seen. For a moment all of them forgot their purpose and wandered down the aisles. Rachel went onto the stage and looked out at the rows of empty seats.

Pom took advantage of the distraction and asked Carl and Kim about their parents. "I don't suppose you've got any pictures of them."

"Not as I know of," Kim said. "We move around so much. We don't have much stuff anymore."

"Well, tell me a little about what they do."

Kim had gone backstage and was poking around at the curtain pulleys and weights. "They deliver medicine mostly. That's why they need such a good car. So they can always depend on it."

"The dark green Packard."

"No, sir," Carl said. "A Studebaker. It's a Studebaker."

"Oh, yeah. You said you put a marble in the dashboard."

"A cat's-eye, a big yellow cat's-eye."

Carl vaulted onto the stage. Pom walked over to where he sat kicking his feet idly over the edge. "How long since you've seen your folks?"

Carl and Kim looked at each other. Neither spoke.

"You know," Pom said, "Mrs. Holliman hasn't seen her dad for a long time either. More than a year now."

"Well, it hasn't been that long for us," Carl said quickly. "Only since the twenty-fourth of Sep—"

Kim clapped a hand over his mouth.

"You live on a farm around here," Pom said. "Is that right?"

Kim thought for a moment and nodded. Carl shook free from her hand.

"Do you ever have any visitors at the farm? Folks coming to see your parents?"

"Sure," Carl said. "Everybody has company."

"Sure they do. You remember the last company you had?"

"Well, I don't know." Carl wrestled with his memory or the safety of what he was saying. He looked at Kim for agreement. "There was the man with the tattoo."

Pom had been studying a stress crack in the plaster. He looked up. "What kind of tattoo?"

"I'm not sure." Kim was thinking back. "A knife or something with this snake wrapped around it."

Carl was quick to correct her. "A sword. Right up here on his shoulder. We saw it that time he took off his shirt. He was dressing a deer in the barn and he had his shirt off."

"Dressing a deer?"

"Yeah. He'd shot a buck on the other side of the hill and he dragged it over to dress it. He came over pretty often after that."

"On account of he was a friend of your parents, Carl? That's why he came over to clean the deer in your barn?"

"I guess so."

"Do you know his name?"

"No, sir, I don't remember it. I don't' know as I ever heard it."

"Other than that tattoo, what did he look like?"

"I don't know. Kind of tall I guess."

Kim held her hand over her head. "Everybody's tall compared to you, Carl. Every grownup anyway."

Pom pressed on. "Brown hair, black hair, bald?"

Carl tried to be accommodating. "Kind of brown I guess."

"More like red," Kim said.

"Anyway, you'd know him if you saw him again?"

Kim shrugged. "Sure. Especially if he takes his shirt off."

"Was that the last time you saw him? When he came over to dress the deer?"

"Why, no," Kim said. "For a while he drove up to our place just about every week."

"Every week, huh? He must've liked to visit."

"Well, he helped Daddy load the medicine into the Studebaker."

"Medicine. Like bottles of medicine."

"That's right."

"Can you tell me what your parents looked—what they look like?"

When they had finished, Pom thanked them and motioned for Rachel to come down from the stage. "It's getting cold in here all of a sudden and I want to be on time for supper."

She came toward the edge of the stage. "Can Kim and Carl come?"

"Not tonight, kiddo. This wouldn't be a good night. Soon though. They're good guests. They eat everything on their plates without complaining and they help clean up."

On the walk to the car Pom asked Rachel to keep a secret.

She stopped. "Something about Carl and Kim?"

"Let's not get into that. For now, just don't tell your mother or anyone else about what we said back there at the school. It's going to come out, but there's a time for it to come out, and that time hasn't come yet."

"You should see the scarecrow Kim put up, so lifelike."

"Corn's about gone, kiddo. She could've saved herself the trouble."

"You're always so literal. She told me it's a guardian she can have watching over her and Carl whenever their parents are gone."

"Well, there's an interesting idea."

"Do you know something about their parents?"

"I'm working on it, and while I am, I'm going to be gone some, too. Better not mention that to your mother either."

She watched him pick up a piece of lime rock and turn it over in his palm. "Does all of this have something to do with Jim?"

He traced a piece of shell in the rock and then tossed it aside. "You ever pull up a rice paper plant?"

"You mean those big things that are taking over Gramma Ward's backyard? They make a big mess. You pull on one and you find out it's connected under the dirt to all the rest."

"You sure do. So, yes, Jim's connected to that talk we had back there at the school, but I don't know yet just how, and you have to keep mum till I find out."

CHAPTER 28

Richard didn't like his business calls coming to the house, but it was the surest way to get the word from Deardra that the men in Baldwin were ready for another run. Each time the telephone rang he jumped, and when he heard the familiar pattern of short, long, short, he dashed for it. He wound up talking to several of his mother's friends, including Flora, who was returning a call about the next séance. "Tell her that my house is too distracting," Flora said. "Tell her that we should try some other place. I don't think the spirits cotton to visiting my cluttered barn of a house. Tell your mother to call me back and we'll confer."

He had no idea what she was talking about.

The next caller was an old friend of his father's offering to sell some prime residential lots in West Palm Beach at premium prices.

"I don't believe Daddy's buying now." Richard coughed at the understatement and his chest began to hurt.

He was in his room, at his boyhood desk, working out the details of the final run to Baldwin, when the doorbell rang. He heard the door open and listened as his mother's voice went high the way it did when she was flustered. As he stood and listened with the model biplanes dangling around him, he recognized the other voice as Edith's. He considered rappelling out a back window, but the very thought made his chest hurt all the more. Instead he decided to make the most of what he had and, leaning heavily against the banister, he walked down the stairs and kissed his mother on the cheek.

When Edith saw the bruise on his forehead, which was uglier than ever, and the way he leaned against the doorjamb, she burst into tears.

"Oh, now, Edie, it was just a little run-in on the road. I never did find the deer. Mother, you remember Edith 'cause I'm always talking about her."

"You are?" Mavis was intrigued by Edith's loose-fitting dress.

Richard laughed. "Oh, stop kidding around like that, mother." He winked at Edith. "Now you know where I get that wicked sense of humor of mine." He squeezed Mavis' hand and joined the teary Edith on the other side of the screen door. "It's okay, Mother. We're just glad to see each other." He put his arm around Edith's shoulder. "Sorry I didn't call sooner, but as you can see, I've been a little off my game." He guided her across the front lawn to a cement bench shielded by privet. He stroked her blonde hair. "I hated putting you off. I was going to come over as soon as I got my wind back." He took a deep breath, let out a little cough, and put his hand to his chest.

"You, poor, poor thing." She touched her finger to his collarbone. "What happened? All this time I thought you didn't love me."

"It was because I love you that I didn't call. I couldn't stand the thought of you worrying at the sight of me."

Her eyes filled with tears again. "You should've called, but can you ever forgive me for doubting you?"

Her hand was on his shoulder. He kissed it. "Hey, who's your best guy?"

She smiled, nuzzled his neck, put her head on his chest. "That would be you." She sat up. "It's just that it's been so hard," she sniffed, "with me in my condition and all." Her blue eyes lit up and she pulled back. "Richard, let's get married right away."

He coughed. "Sure, sugar, sure. There's just some things I have to do first, you know, to set us up. I'll be able to travel in a couple of days." He coughed again, a little more emphatically. "Then we'll do it all."

She blinked away the tears. "We can't wait any longer to tell my father."

He smiled. "Well, you know what? I bet he'll see things our way."

"If we hurry we can still have a big church wedding, the kind I've always wanted."

He pressed her hands in his. "That would be grand, sure enough." He gave her a little hug and spoke in soft tones. "But what if we did something really thrilling? Now, just hear me out. You know, we can always throw a big party after the wedding. Big as you want. Bigger than anything you ever saw at Kincaid's. But for some real excitement, what if we *elope*?"

With the back of her pale hand she wiped away a tear. "Elope?"

"Sure, you know. I put a ladder up to your bedroom window, the whole kit and caboodle."

"Well, I hadn't thought—"

"Doesn't that sound *romantic*? I'll whisk you away in the night."

"To your tent in the desert?"

He laughed. "Something like that. Go home and pack your bags. Be ready."

"You mean you're going to surprise me?"

"You can just count on it, sugar."

He paced in his room until his restlessness got the better of him, and when the telephone call from Deardra still had not come, he put on his hat and headed for the door.

His father was on the front steps smoking a cigar. "Shouldn't you be resting up, Richard? You're shuffling around like Crazy Joan."

"I'm just kind of stiff. You know how it is. You take a hit and you feel okay at the time, and then, after a day or so, you stiffen up. I just need a little air after holing up all day."

"You get your phone call?"

Richard spun around. "What phone call?"

"I don't know. Your mother said you were mighty keen to get one. I just wondered if you got it."

Richard felt his shoulders go slack. "No. It wasn't anything important. He went on the offensive. How about you? You get any bites on Palm Terrace today?"

J.J. stepped on the head of a cast iron turtle. The shell flipped up and he tossed his cigar butt into the cavity beneath. "You know the answer to that one. Don't forget to come home now."

When Deardra saw him propped at a corner table, she pulled up a chair, set down an ashtray, and looked him over.

"I believe your work is starting to take a toll on you."

He turned the un-bruised side of his face toward her and smiled. "You still thinking of selling this place?"

She held her cigarette over the sawdust floor and tapped it with her forefinger. "Let's just say it wouldn't be the end of the world if it went up in smoke. There's a guy who wants to buy it with me in it, your friend from Miami, the one with the Panama hat."

He lunged toward her, but the pain in his chest stopped him short. "You kidding?"

"Wish I was. He's made me one of those offers, you know?"

He took in the giddy yipping of a clarinet set against the guttural squawk of a saxophone. "I don't suppose the guys from up the road have called here tonight."

She pulled a nickel-plated pocket watch from a fold in her dark green dress. "There's still some time left. If they're going to call, it's always by eight. Isn't that the deal?"

"So why haven't I heard from 'em?"

"Maybe they were detained. Maybe they're taking off for Christmas eve."

"Sure."

"So you wait."

"Yeah, or maybe you and I take off."

"Take off?" She snapped her fingers. "Just like that?"

"We'll be taking off one way or the other. Why not on our own terms?"

"Well, for one thing, I still have this place. I can't just...."

"Turn the key and walk away? Why not? It's a warehouse, Deardra. Use it like one. You could be out of here tonight. If that goon wants the place, he'll have to find you, and it's a big country. How long would it take you to pack?"

She stubbed out her cigarette in the cupid ashtray. "Back to New Orleans? Back to the sweet and shady Garden District?"

He reached across the table and put his hand on hers. "Wherever you want. That night at Magnesia Springs, didn't you say you wanted to go on a cruise? Go on your cruise and make some plans—with me."

"With you? My, my, now we *are* getting creative. We just stuff all our clothes and money into a couple of steamer trunks and jump into your car and go—is that it?"

He squeezed her slender hand. "Why not? Isn't it better than what we have now? Isn't it better than staying? Or do you like the guy with the Panama hat?"

She looked up, and the surprise in her face made him turn around. In walked Pom and Trent. They threaded their way around the dance floor to the bar, came over to the table, and sat down.

"Welcome," Deardra said. "What'll it be tonight?"

Pom smiled at the irony in her voice. "Nothing for me, thanks, and my friend here has sworn it off for life, haven't you?"

Trent looked down at the scarred tabletop. "That's what I hear."

Richard started to fold his arms, but it hurt. "We still haven't heard from them, if that's what you're here for."

"We were just looking for a couple of guys," Pom said, "wondered if you might've seen 'em in here."

"Chances are," Deardra said.

"A kind of heavyset, probably well-dressed fella with a ring on his little finger, gold, looks kind of like it came off a cigar."

Deardra pursed her lips. "I don't usually look at their pinkies, and we have lots of well-dressed men in here. You'll have to give me more to go on."

"What's this about?" Richard asked.

"It's kind of a scavenger hunt," Pom said. "Trent and I need something to occupy our minds until bigger things come along. Here's a harder one." He pointed to his shoulder. "How about a fella with a sword and a snake tattooed right about here?"

Deardra smiled. "When they're in here, they usually have their shirts on."

When he got home, Richard had another visitor. Waiting in a Nash parked on the street was Edith's father. He got out of the car, came across the yard, and caught Richard by the sleeve. He was a fury in seersucker. "You've got your nerve. I don't want you to see my daughter again."

Richard twisted free and backed away. "Well, shucks, Mr. Thompson. *She's* the one who came over *here*."

"*Professor* Thompson. Only because you've got her so confused. She spends half the time crying and the other half trying to sneak out of the house. I don't know what you've been telling her, but I'll put a stop to it."

Richard let him come a little closer and then stuck out his chin and smiled. "Well, now, prof, don't forget to tend to business. Remember, Trent Walker can't help you out anymore."

Suddenly the enraged father was on the defensive. His eyelids fluttered. "I don't know what you're talking about."

Richard held two fingers together. "Trent and I are like this. I know him real well. He thinks the world of your gift for chemistry, never thought chemistry could taste so good."

Professor Thompson tugged at his collar. "I tell you, I don't know what you're talking about."

"Okay then, here it is." Richard put his hand on the professor's shoulder as if to give fatherly advice. "You're in the bum rum trade. Moonshine. Here I am struggling to make an honest living as a real estate broker and you're coming down on me as if I'm not good enough for your daughter. The only reason I stopped coming to your house was because I didn't want to be seen associating with a woods cook. It's no wonder Edie wanted to come over here. Aren't they paying professors enough?"

Thompson shook off Richard's hand. "I'll kill you before I'll see you with my daughter again."

Richard cocked his head and smiled. "With that little silver popgun in your socks drawer?"

Something caught in the professor's throat but he managed to cough out another threat.

"With a goddam *fork* if I have to."

Across town, behind the house on Magnolia Street, Trent was chopping kindling while Pom added to the woodpile at the foot of the kitchen steps.

He paused to re-seat the ax head, rapping on the base of the handle with a sledgehammer until the blade tightened up. "Thanks for taking me in. I hope I ain't too much of a pain to the wife and kids."

Pom didn't turn around. He had found a piece of good dry oak, but it had a big knot in it.

"We're all in this together. I wish you'd call or write to Elsie and the girls."

"When I get the money, I will. Till then, she's better off without me. Now don't you give me that gnarly hunk of oak there. Splitting the last one damn near busted my arm."

Biting back a smile, Pom straightened and tossed the piece of oak to the far end of the pile. "I'll tell you, if there's one thing I've learned in eighteen years of living with one, it's that once a woman accepts you, she'll stay attached almost no matter what, and I doubt if Elsie is any different. You may be the seediest little roach that ever scuttled out of the woodpile, but still she wants you home, and if you're not home, she wants to know why. Now I want you to promise me something. I want you to promise me that as soon as we get this last trip over with, you'll take every dollar of that money and carry it home to Elsie and spend it getting your girls and that farm of yours squared up. You promise me that right here and now or you can drop that ax and trot on down the road."

"What about my trial?"

"Once those feds leave town, that trial will be small potatoes. You'll most likely get a fine and a week in the county jail."

Trent raised the ax and made a solemn vow. "Soon as we get this last trip done, everything I've got goes to putting my house in order. No more Porter's Place and no more Island Hotel."

Pom had a flash of insight. "Listen, why didn't we think of this a lot sooner? A fella dressed like that and wearing a ring on his little finger, he's not likely from around here. Doesn't it stand to reason that he was passing through? And if he was passing through, wouldn't he likely be staying in a hotel?"

They walked over to the Commercial first, formerly known as the Alachua. It was the oldest hotel in town, and it looked the part. Its weathered stucco walls and arched, rippled windowpanes were from another time, and its deep overhang was a looming peril. "I'm going to this one first because it's the only one I'm dressed for," Pom said as he spanked off the seat of his britches. The lobby was cramped and the carpet was worn. The haggard, pasty-faced old clerk who emerged from living quarters behind the counter had never seen the man Pom described, so the two searchers re-crossed University Avenue and went to the White House Hotel, a large rambling structure that smelled of fresh varnish, pressed linens, and apple cobbler. The slender tan brunette behind the counter looked familiar, but Pom couldn't place her. She was so pretty that Trent made a point of glancing around the spacious lobby so as not to stare at her. Her blue eyes went blank when Pom asked about the well-dressed man with the pinkie ring, but she reminded Pom that he had brought her cat back from the jaws of death after an encounter with a wild boar.

"I thought she looked familiar," Pom said as they retraced their steps through the large dining room. "I remember that cat now. Got around passably well on three legs."

"I'd've remembered the cat *owner*," Trent said.

"She didn't look like that when I worked the miracle for her. Everybody's growing up around here. Well, there's nothing left but the Hotel Thomas, and we'll be lucky if they don't throw us out of there on looks alone."

"You want me to wait outside?" Trent offered.

"No, we'll just act like we belong there. That's half of success, you know, just acting like you belong in a place."

"Anyway, maybe you fixed somebody's dead gopher turtle over there. Squashed flat in the middle of the road and eaten by buzzards but you taped it back together so good that it won the dance contest at Magnesia Springs."

As they found their way to the lobby of the sprawling Mediterranean villa, Pom looked up at the massive façade. "Looks kind of like Kincaid's place, doesn't it? Only smaller."

The night clerk, a crisp man in a blazer and bow tie, greeted Pom warmly.

"I knew it," Trent said under his breath. "It's the fella with the gopher turtle."

The clerk spoke lovingly of a collie that was mending nicely after tangling with a 1924 Chrysler Six Touring Car.

Even Pom became impatient with the praise. He described the well-dressed man with the cigar ring and was caught off guard when the clerk remembered him.

"It's that ring on the little finger," he said. "There was something a little…"

Pom jumped in. "Fussy about it?"

"As a matter of fact, yeah. Fussy."

"Amelia thought so too," Pom said, as if the clerk would know who he was talking about.

"He comes through from time to time," the clerk said. "Less often lately it seems. Do you know him?"

"No, but we sure hope to make his acquaintance. You know his name?"

The clerk turned back the pages in the register and ran his finger down the columns of names and addresses. "He was here about the time we had the banquet for Sigma Chi. My God, what a night that was. We're still finding—Here! How's that for a good guess? Mr. Harvey Champeau of Ybor City. That's interesting. He stayed here two nights, still owes us for one of them." He swung the register back around so Pom could see it. "Occupation—salesman."

"Cigar salesman," Pom suggested." Seeing that Trent had let his attention stray to a large round copper and silver tray on the lobby wall, he tugged at his sleeve. "Cigar salesman, don't you suppose, Trent, if he's from Ybor City and Amelia said he was wearing a ring that looked like it came off a cigar? Come on now. Work with me. I'm trying to keep your mind occupied."

Trent followed him down the broad steps to the circular drive. "Okay, but that still don't give us much to go on."

"I don't know. We've got a piece of a puzzle on this side of the table and one over there and they sure look like they go together, with maybe just one more piece in between."

"My dogs are barking. Where we going now?"

CHAPTER 29

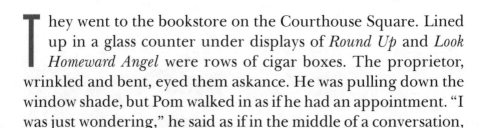

They went to the bookstore on the Courthouse Square. Lined up in a glass counter under displays of *Round Up* and *Look Homeward Angel* were rows of cigar boxes. The proprietor, wrinkled and bent, eyed them askance. He was pulling down the window shade, but Pom walked in as if he had an appointment. "I was just wondering," he said as if in the middle of a conversation, "who's your tobacco salesman?"

The proprietor was getting ready to light up one of the more expensive ones, an after-hours indulgence apparently. "What would you be wanting to know for? He won't sell directly to individuals."

"It wouldn't be Mr. Harvey Champeau by any chance?"

"If you have a personal matter with him, oughtn't you to know his name?"

Pom glanced at Trent. "I believe we've picked up a gnarly piece of oak."

Trent turned his back to the counter and muttered, "Didn't you pull his prize goose out of a bobcat's belly?"

Pom started to lose patience. "Look, friend, all we want to know is the name of your salesman. Now is it Harvey Champeau or isn't it?"

The proprietor took his time lighting the cigar. He tossed the spent match into what looked like an old artillery shell casing. "I believe that might be his name, yeah."

"Well, when's he coming back?"

"You said you just had one question."

"Oh, for crying—Look, what's this book? *Red Harvest.* I'll *buy* this book if you'll tell me when Mr. Harvey Champeau is due back in town."

"Probably about a week from Tuesday."

"Now we're getting someplace. What's the name of his company?"

"You going to buy that book or aren't you?"

"Sure! Sure!" Pom made a show of digging into his pocket.

"That other one's pretty good too—*A Farewell to Arms,* as long as you don't care about a happy ending."

"All I want is this one here. Now what's the name of Mr. Champeau's company, if you please?"

"Well, I believe it would be the Perfecta Cigar Company, Manufacturers and Importers."

"Perfecta—got it." Pom headed for the door. "Come on, Trent. We've done about all we can for tonight."

The clerk leaned across the counter. "Wait a minute, mister. How about the book?"

On his way out, Pom pulled down the shade. "Closing time, ain't it? Just put it on my tab, will you?"

"Well, what's your name?"

"You ought to know, oughtn't you, if I have a tab."

When they got back to the house, they found Jim on the floor of the front room taking directions from Flora about how to straighten the Christmas tree. As if making small talk, Pom asked him what company he had worked for in Ybor City.

Jim gave the trunk a slight turn. "It went by the dubious name of Perfecta."

Pom looked at Trent. "The Perfecta Cigar Company...."

Trent was quick to chip in. "Manufacturers and Importers."

"That's the one," Jim said. "May I ask why you want to know?"

"During our rambles today Trent and I heard about another fella who works there. I'm not sure I recall his name though."

"Mr. Harvey Champeau," Trent said with an air of importance.

Pom rolled his eyes. "Apparently my attempt at irony was too subtle."

"Harvey Champeau." Jim came out from under the tree and sat up. One hand curled into a fist. He's the worst kind of capitalist scum." He apologized to Flora for his language. "Where did you run into him?"

"I didn't say we ran into him. I just said his name came up."

"Well, he was trying to cut the workers' wages if you can believe that, cut them while he and the other fat cats continued to suck out every nickel of profit. I told him exactly what I thought of him and his idea and he went and got me fired. I think he also had me jumped as I was leaving town."

"Is that so?" Pom's voice trailed off as he linked the pieces of a puzzle.

"It sure is."

"You must've told him off good," Trent said.

"Well, yeah. I was on the platform with my book in my hand and all the leaf rollers there listening. It was kind of public. I think he took it hard."

Pom straightened a popcorn chain. "And I think I just heard something snap into place."

On the pretext of going to get some tinsel, he and Trent hurried over to the Wards to make a telephone call to Ybor City.

"It's long distance, but it's a call that's going to get Jim Rhodes off the hook," he told Richard. "I'm one step away from the guy who planted that Luger in my house and I'm going to get him."

In J.J.'s paneled office, among the yellowed photographs and staring trophy heads, they cranked up the telephone and called Ybor City and, after several leads, they found a surly sales executive who told them that Harvey Champeau had been laid off two weeks ago.

"He could be anywhere," Pom said. "How do we track him down?"

Richard coughed. "I'm going back to bed. My chest hurts like hell and those nitwits up in Baldwin are likely to call any minute. Y'all had better be ready when they do because there's going to be big money in this one."

"Big money. How much?"

"Couldn't say."

"Well, what's it for?"

Richard gave him a sleepy smile. "Special delivery I guess. Probably has something to do with New Year's Eve."

On the drive back to Magnolia Street, Pom was absorbed in his thoughts. They passed the ancient scarred tree called the lightning oak, which stood at the edge of the dismal stretch of live oaks and scrub known as Leary's Woods. To the left the thickets had been hacked back to make room for a few stone houses. "Now think about this," Pom said. "Here at one end of the rice paper plant we've got this guy whose name we know, but we don't know where he is. And he's got something to do with planting that Luger in Jim's room. Over at the other end we've got this guy with the tattoo who was running rum with those folks who wound up wired to the tree in my pasture, Carl and Kim's parents. We sort of know what he looks like but we

don't know his name, and he and Champeau are likely connected. Champeau distracted Amelia while somebody put that Luger
in Jim's room. But why? There are a lot more people passing
through town than there used to be. But this is still a pretty small
place and so I think it's all hooked up together—Champeau, the
guy with the tattoo, the dark green Studebaker that Theron has,
and that Luger, and if we can get a hold of any part of it, we'll
start reeling in the whole reeking thing."

When they got back home the house was empty. On the dining room table Flora had left a note saying that she had gone to
Nelda Ward's to pick up some sugarplums. Pom heard voices
in the backyard and they went into the kitchen to see who it
was.

"Take a good whiff of that," Pom said on his way to the back
door. He raised a cloth covering a pair of loaf pans swelling with
bread. "It's my belief that if Penelope had been baking, Ulysses
would never have left home to fight the Trojans and there
wouldn't be any *Odyssey*. I'm about ready for a quiet night at
home."

Jim was standing in the backyard expounding upon the vir-
tues of a minimum wage as Ainsley sat on the chopping block
raising objections. "The tycoons will never go for that," she said.
"You've sure got your work cut out for you."

Pom clattered down the back stairs. "Don't convince her, Jim.
You'll just get her into trouble."

Ainsley turned, smiling. "Well, his ideas are interesting. I'll
say that."

Jim stood straight with his hands behind his back, as if he
were reciting *The Wreck of the Hesperus*.

"Ainsley was just interviewing me for another article, although there are better spokesmen for the socialist cause. We
were just talking about the work force and the importance of
equal pay for women."

Pom put his hands in his pockets. "There's hardly enough work for *men* lately," he said, glancing at her healed lip. "You're looking better."

She crossed her arms as if inviting him to look her over. "I'm just fine, thanks. *You're* still looking kind of bunged up though."

"It was a hard-kicking mule. Things quiet down at the house?"

"I'd say so, yeah. We don't have anything as exciting as a bloodthirsty Red facing a murder rap."

Jim allowed himself a faint smile. "I'm glad I've got the press on my side."

"You'll have more than that if things work out," Pom said. "We know who helped put that Luger in your room."

Ainsley jumped up. "Spill it, Pom. It'll crack this whole thing wide open."

"Hold on now. We know who he is and we think we know why he did it. We just don't know *where* he is. And we sure don't want to splash his name all over the place till we rope him in."

"Come on." Ainsley held him with her eyes. "I get information in confidence all the time. I won't spoil a good story. I might even know where to find your guy. I've got my contacts, you know."

After thinking it over, Pom shrugged. "All right. But you can't tell anyone, not even your mother, or this whole thing could derail. And don't go trying to catch this guy on your own. No stunts like that."

"Pom, I cover the stories. I don't make 'em. Who is it?"

"Harvey Champeau," Trent said quickly.

Pom tossed up his hands. "So much for suspense."

"We worked at the same cigar factory down in Ybor City," Jim told Ainsley. "He had it out for me, but I don't know why he would come all the way up here to frame me for murder."

Pom fixed his eyes on Ainsley. "Well?"

"Never heard of him. Sorry."

"He comes to town every now and then, or at least he did until recently. He made selling trips up here, but he got the sack a couple of weeks ago, so that may be as far as we can follow him. But then there's another piece, and I don't know if the two fit together. There was this fella who knew the victims, used to run booze with 'em."

Ainsley swept her hair back. "You *do* know a few things."

"Well, I need to know a lot more before it does any good."

"So what about this other guy, the rumrunner?"

"We don't know much. Apparently he blended into the woodwork pretty well, except for the tattoo on his shoulder, a sword with a snake wrapped around it."

Ainsley's eyes narrowed. "Pom, is this whole thing a joke?"

"Do I look like I'm joking?"

"Then don't string me along. You know perfectly well that you're describing Theron."

"*Theron*? He's got a tattoo like that?"

"I ought to know. I was married to him for eight years. One night he came home drunk with that tattoo. He's got a pair of lips in a shadier place."

"He knew the victims. He's got their car. You sure you've never heard of Harvey Champeau? No connection between him and Theron? What might Theron have in common with a cigar salesman from Ybor City?"

"Dunno, unless Theron's been a hunting guide for him. He consorts with the best and the worst when he has a gun in his hand. What's he got to do with framing Jim?"

"Harvey Champeau kept Amelia distracted while somebody planted the Luger in my house. Champeau didn't like Jim, but once he got him canned, why come all the way up here to frame him?" He took a breath and looked her in the eyes. "But there *is* somebody right here in town who hates Jim enough to frame him."

"My God! You mean, just because I was talking to him on your porch that time?"

"And a few other times."

"I don't think so."

"Then there's another thing. That dark green Studebaker. Who put it in the water?"

"Wait a minute. Let me be sure what you're saying."

"Ainsley, that Studebaker belonged to that man and woman wired to my tree. It's been painted dark blue over the original green. If he's got that tattoo, Theron was the guy running booze with 'em, and somehow he knew that their car went underwater after they were killed."

She sat back down on the chopping block and put her face in her hands. "This is too much to believe, even of Theron."

"You said something put him on edge."

"That's a far cry from—Look, whatever you think of him, if he'd shot at those people, he wouldn't have missed, not from twice as far."

Pom turned his palms up. "You've got me there. It doesn't fit."

She pulled her hair back. "Why not tell all this to Avery? He *is* the sheriff."

He avoided her eyes. "He's going to know soon enough, one way or another. But the time isn't right yet. That's all I can tell you for now. In the meantime, just leave Theron to me, will you? You don't need to tangle with him again."

"You know you're asking me do to the hardest thing in the world—nothing."

Before Pom could reply, the telephone rang.

CHAPTER 30

They met in the office at Porter's Place to talk over the plan. Richard sat backwards on a cane chair while Pom paced and Trent sprawled on the cot. From time to time, headlights on the far side of the tracks glanced across the lacquered window. Music from the bar seeped under the door, rasping and giddy. Pom pushed aside some decaying papers and propped himself against the roll-top desk. The ceiling reminded him of the porch at home with its perpetually peeling paint. He wondered how many years had passed since the warehouse had been a place of honest commerce. He wondered how much longer it could go before Avery and his deputies knocked down the door and swept the place clean. He tried to picture the dim room full of sinners with its tin roof peeled back and God peering in.

When Deardra entered the office, he looked at the frowsy dress and feathery hat hanging on the wall and came to a conclusion. "If the place gets raided, that would make a pretty good getaway disguise, wouldn't it?"

She took up a position at the door and smiled. "Wouldn't it though?"

"The pickup's on Saturday the twenty-eighth," Richard said again. His arms hung off the back of the chair, showing buffalo nickel cufflinks. "They're giving us plenty of notice this time."

"Fine, but we'd better leave early," Pom said. "It's going to be rough out there. Forecast says two-foot chop followed by rain."

Trent shifted on the cot. "Half the time them forecasts in the newspaper are for some other planet "

"I'm just telling you," Pom said.

Richard shrugged. "The rougher it is, the less likely they are to come after us. The feds don't like getting wet any more than you do."

Pom went to the window and watched a freight train as it squeaked and banged through the littered corridor on its way to the depot. "Well, now there's a comfort. We can flounder around on the oyster bars without anyone coming after us, except maybe the hijackers."

Richard lit a cigarette. "Your sunny self seems to have taken a turn toward the dark, Pom."

"December's a bad month to be out," Pom said, still watching the train. "Trent and I are supposed to be home by the fire with our wives and kids tonight. It's Christmas Eve."

"Just bear with me now." Richard swung the chair around and brought it closer to them. "We unload as usual on the Waccasassa and pack the truck. Trent takes the boat back over to Cedar Key. You and I go to Baldwin, unload, collect the money, and get back before sunrise."

Pom rubbed his chin as he thought. "That simple. But you say it's big money. Have they told you how much?"

"Five thousand."

"Five thousand?"

"What for?" Trent asked.

Richard blew a stream of smoke. "Ours not to reason why. It'll be enough to put us all back on our feet."

"If nothin' don't happen," Trent said.

When the freight train had passed, Pom turned and came away from the window. "All right. One more thing. If I've got this figured right, we're going to be coming back to the river when the tide's just about dead low. We're going to be facing a real obstacle course."

Richard gestured toward Trent, who had sat up on the cot. "That's what *he's* for. He's going to show us how to run a maze with that boat."

The next time the phone rang at Pom's house, it was Mavis wishing everyone a Merry Christmas. While Rachel finished clearing the table and Rex helped himself to seconds on mincemeat pie, Pom was back in the kitchen polishing off a drumstick. He stood listening long enough to figure out who it was and then went back to his nibbling while Mavis filled Flora's ear with details about the golf clubs she had given J.J. Even though none of the Hollimans knew a wood from a wedge, she described each club in detail.

"Does J.J. play golf?" Flora asked at last.

"He will," Mavis assured her. "He will. It's just the thing to get his mind off of Palm Terrace. He can spend some time outdoors without shooting anything. And we're honorary members of the Faculty Club thanks to Nelda's donation. It's my way of weaning him off those guns of his. I get scared just having them in the house."

"I'd be scared *not* having them in the house," Flora said after she hung up.

Three days later, the Hollimans were just sitting down to turkey *a la king* when Richard called.

It was already well past sunset when the *Sun Dog* left the big wooden wharf at Cedar Key and punched through the chop in the channel.

"Won't anybody wonder what we're doing out here on a ducky night like this!" Trent shouted as he re-tied the string on the hat of his slicker. "This is just perfect fishing weather."

"It is for *our* kind of fishing." Richard said. He looked stylish in his black oilskins, even though they were the same as Trent's. "Look at that! Not a boat out there!" He turned around, one hand still on the wheel, and hollered at the dark horizon. "Hey there, everybody! We're going out to get some Canadian Red! Drinks are on us! Canadian Red for the poor grubbing share-cropper! Canadian Red for the fat-assed lush! Canadian Red for the little old lady who ain't been laid in a thousand years! Canadian Red for the preacher and the deputy and the whole goddam thirsty world!"

They were much quieter by the time they got to the reef. The gray Gulf looked boundless, making it hard to believe that the *Cristobel* or anything else could be waiting for them long miles out. Cold spray sparked through the arc of light from the mast, and the boat spanked along blindly by the compass. The three men huddled in the cockpit and pulled their slickers about them and braced themselves against each collision. Pom looked at the starless, moonless sky, unable to tell what the weather was going to do. He hung on, going numb while they put the miles behind them. As they approached the position, he took the binoculars from the ledge behind the wheel, steadied himself against the gunwale, and looked hard into the vague offing.

Richard slowed the boat, and the wind and the engine noise died down. Pom kept looking for the freighter. Finally he put down the binoculars. "Anybody bring cards or should we cut bait and fish?"

Trent shook the spray from his slicker. "How long do you suppose we ought to wait?"

"No boat, no dough," Richard said. "We wait till it gets here."

"Trent's onto something," Pom said. "It's just a matter of time before the jig is up for that boat. This could be the night they got nabbed. My own kid knows it's coming."

Richard had been swinging the wheel to keep the bow pointed in the right direction. He swung it too hard and they all scrambled to stay on their feet. "What are you talking about?"

"Rex has been listening to the radio every night to take his mind off the murders. He stumbled onto coded messages going to the *Cristobel,* directions as to when and where the pickups were to be made."

"Jesus Christ, Pom. Thanks for telling me."

"It shouldn't matter for now. I told him to keep it to himself till we were ready to go to Avery."

"Who else knows?"

"Just Jim. He's the one who decoded the messages."

"You think he's kept his trap shut? Hell, what if he's told Ainsley? We'll have a damn press conference out here."

"It's a leaky bucket anyway, Richard. That's why tonight's got to be the last night. Too many people know too much. Maybe they're not talking to each other right now, but pretty soon they will be. It's all going to hitch up and the whole story's going to come pounding out like a freight train."

"If that boat's full of federal agents," Trent asked, "how we going to know till we've tied up to it?"

"Well, you'll just have to cross your fingers," Richard said. "Sometimes that's all you can do is cross your fingers."

Pom took off his hat and rubbed his forehead. "My fingers haven't been *un*crossed since I got into this mess."

Trent was studying the dim horizon with the binoculars. "Well, you'd better keep 'em crossed. Yonder comes company."

They waited and watched, bobbing on the water as the light edged toward them. It turned and spread into a rough profile, then assumed the shape of the freighter. It flashed a signal: long, short, long, short.

"Getting cautious, aren't they?" Pom said.

"So are we." Richard answered by turning the mast light on and off in a more extended sequence of short and long.

"They sent us a C," Pom said, "for *Cristobel*. What was that you sent them?"

Richard turned away from the wheel and smiled. "*Shave and a haircut, two bits.*"

"Looks like they're still giving us the eye," Trent said. "They're hanging right where they are. No, here they come."

"You recognize any of 'em?" Richard handed Pom the binoculars as the freighter came into range.

"Well, they've still got that short guy with the beard, the Yankee."

Trent picked up a gaff. "I don't like the looks of 'em."

Pom was still watching through the binoculars. "We're all right. Reading animals is my line of work and I can tell by the way they move if something's off. Same for people. I'd be able to tell if they were on a string. Just take it easy and let 'em come on."

The two boats had scarcely tied up when the bearded Yankee handed a small suitcase over the side.

Richard watched Trent take the suitcase and set it on the deck. "We don't take passengers."

"You take this one," the Yankee said. "All the way to Baldwin."

The men cast off the lines and the freighter slipped away.

Trent stood with his hands on his hips. "Hold on! What about the damn booze?"

The Yankee raised a finger in warning. "Don't lose it, don't take anything out, don't even open it." He said something else that was lost in the wash as the freighter moved off to the southeast.

Pom stared at the suitcase as Trent ran his fingertips over the locks. "This is it?"

"It's locked," Trent said when the freighter's lights had faded behind them. "You want me to pop it open?"

Richard ran the flashlight over the suitcase. "Can you jimmy it without anybody being able to tell?"

"As long as it ain't rigged," Trent said. "And if it is, we'll be sprayed all over the Gulf anyway."

"That's comforting," Pom said. "I think I'll watch from the bow."

In the engine compartment Trent found some wire that suited him. He broke off a piece and bent it into a hook and poked around in the lock. He propped the suitcase on one of the storage lockers and went to work. After he tinkered and probed for a while, the lock clicked. He slid back one of the two openers, blocked the latch with his thumb, and then raised it gently. He slid back the opener on the other side.

He jumped up and the suitcase crashed to the deck.

"Jesus! Look out! It's going to blow!"

Richard threw himself to the floor of the cockpit.

Pom disappeared from the bow.

Trent slapped his knee, threw his head back, and roared. "Got you going, didn't I? Didn't I get you going?"

Richard raised himself from the floor of the cockpit, hitting his head on the wheel. "You crazy son of a bitch."

Pom reappeared at the bow, soaked from the knees down.

Rubbing his head, Richard started laughing too. "Where'd you go, Pom? Trent and I were just having a little fun here. How'd you get your britches wet?"

Pom sat dripping on the edge of the bow with his elbows on his knees. With the back of his hand, he mopped his chin

"Come on down and see what we've got," Richard said.

Trent held up a round blue and white container.

"Salt?"

Pom got up and made his way to the back of the boat for a good look. "I'm not running any dope."

With a thumbnail, Trent pried open the container and poured some of the powder into the palm of his hand. "It's dope? What do you do with it—put it in your pipe?"

"You take it like snuff," Richard said. "If it's what I think it is."

"I'll stick to what I can drink or chew." Trent opened his palm and blew the dust over the side of the boat.

Pom crossed his arms. "I'm not having anything to do with it."

"Well, you don't have much choice for now." Richard moved the throttle forward. "When we get to Baldwin, you can wash your hands of it if you don't want your share of the five thousand."

Trent slapped the suitcase shut. "Pom, it's twenty-five hundred for the two of us for one night's work."

"When we get to Baldwin with it," Richard reminded him. He rammed the throttle full forward and the boat burst through the waves. "We're here. It's here. Might as well take it and be rid of it. You can do a lot with twenty-five hundred."

"All right," Pom said, "as long as we've got it. But if it's worth that much, somebody's going to be all the more eager to get their hands on it, aren't they?"

When they finally saw the first distant lights of the coastline, Trent started to relax. "It's not like wallowing in the troughs with booze up to the roof. Even with this chop and low tide we'll be able to get in fast. And we won't even look like we're running booze, we'll be riding so high."

A crack split the darkness. Everyone dropped to the deck. Trent jerked his head down and wiped blood from his ear.

Pom yanked a handkerchief from his jeans pocket and pitched it to him. "Hold it tight."

Richard reached up and swung the wheel hard right.

A second shot passed over Pom's head.

Crouching and ducking, Richard steered in a zigzag. A third shot cut the water nearby, and a fourth.

"Who do you suppose?" Pom was on his knees beside him.

Richard turned off the mast light, grabbed at the wheel and gave it another hard turn. "You tell me."

"Kinda makes it hard to know what to do."

"The hell it does. We run like crazy all the way to the Waccasassa and get that suitcase into the truck."

Trent crawled forward, pinching his ear. Blood streamed down his fingers. "We can maybe zigzag 'em down a ways and shake 'em or run 'em aground. There's some nasty stuff down that way at low tide. Damn, that stings."

"You don't suppose we'd be better off going back out?" Pom said.

Richard jerked the wheel again. "We'd be right out in the open. Let's see who's faster." He stood up, shoved the throttle full forward, and braced himself against the wall of the cockpit. Pom and Trent rose up and looked around. Two more shots popped in the darkness but fell far off to the side. Ahead, the low dark forms of mangrove islands rose up.

Pom watched the white water peeling away from the stern.

"The first thing we do is run through that rat hole," Trent said, pointing off the starboard bow. "Go right through there, then cut hard right for a hundred yards and you'll come out in a little channel that'll take you most of the way back up to the river. After that, if they're still on us, it's going to be nip and tuck and a lot of luck, but by the look of 'em they draw more than we do, so we'll have the edge on 'em—as long as they don't have a local on board. If they've got some damn fishing guide, then we're going to have to do some fancy dancing."

"And for now," Pom said, "he's gaining on us."

Richard pushed on the throttle but it was already full. The stern rode low in the water. The waves chipped and shattered across the bow. Water blurred the windshield. Trent climbed onto the bow to get a better look and chopped the air with his hand. "That way! That way!"

Richard edged to the right, but rain began to erase everything.

Pom put the back of his hand to his stinging eyes. "They know what we're up to. They're making right for those sandbars. They're aiming to cut us off."

"Take the wheel a minute." Richard made his way to the stern and took a hard look through the binoculars.

"What do you see?" Pom didn't dare turn around, even though he couldn't tell where he was going.

"Rain!" Richard staggered back toward the cockpit and wiped the lenses with his shirttail. "But at least that's all *they* can—" Suddenly he fell forward, hit the deck hard with his shoulder, and rolled over on his side. Trent scrambled down from the top of the cockpit, took him by the armpits, and dragged him into the shelter of the cowling. Richard tried to move his right leg, but it wouldn't come. "The hell. I must've barked my shin on something."

"Yeah," Trent said. "A bullet." He crawled over and peeled back the pant leg and sock. "Right in the meat above your ankle. It went in, but it didn't go out."

"No kidding? I never even heard it. Just felt like I got hit with a baseball bat. But, now that you mention it—"

"I can't see a thing," Pom reported from the wheel.

"Just hold where you're going," Trent told him.

Richard propped himself on one elbow. "And don't slow down!"

"Damn lucky shot," Trent said. "They couldn't have seen you."

"Just luck," Richard said.

"How you doing? At least it missed the bone."

Richard's reply was high and thin. "Hey, save me a place on your damn dance card."

Trent got up on his knees. He bent back and called into the cockpit. "Back left, Pom! Just a little to the left! And remember, when we get through—hard right!"

Two more shots broke the night, both wide. Richard sat up and propped himself against the wall of the cockpit.

Trent came back for the flashlight and pointed the beam through the rain ahead of the bow. "You're dead on! You see 'em there? One at one o'clock and the other at eleven."

Pom nodded and held the wheel hard.

"Okay," Trent said. "Don't anybody so much as breathe. Here we go. Good luck to us."

(HAPTER 31

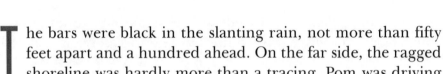

The bars were black in the slanting rain, not more than fifty feet apart and a hundred ahead. On the far side, the ragged shoreline was hardly more than a tracing. Pom was driving blind. He called Trent in from the bow and made him take the wheel. He took the flashlight from him and climbed forward to point the way between the bars. The boat took a quick turn and, all at once, one of the sandbars was beside them on the left, the white waves lapping at its crest. The other came at them just as fast. The boat shuddered and bucked and then they were free again. Trent cut the wheel hard to the right and straightened it quickly and the right-hand bank dropped into the froth behind them.

Pom laughed. "Let's see 'em get through *there*!" Over his shoulder the larger boat had slowed.

From the other side of the cockpit Richard put a thumb up. "You shook 'em!"

Trent wiped the spray from his eyes and reached for the throttle.

In the bow Pom laughed and swung the flashlight in a circle. "Let's just see 'em try to come—"

All of a sudden he was airborne, flying headlong into the rain, still clutching the flashlight. He thought there had been a loud bang and a concussion, but his musing broke off when his face hit the water. He had the sense to dive deep to keep clear of the prop of the oncoming boat, but when he came gasping to the surface, the boat was far behind him and listing badly by the starboard bow. As he treaded water and stared at the sinking hulk, something heavy tapped him on the shoulder and, when he turned to stave it off, he saw that all around him pine logs rolled and bobbed in the breaking wake of the boat. He hooked his arm around one and paddled for all he was worth toward the disappearing wreck.

Something dark and formless came splashing toward him. The far end of the log dipped under the water as Trent grabbed hold.

Pom caught his breath. "Where's Richard?"

One side of the boat rose out of the water, and then the whole thing crashed into the waves and went down in a rush of sea and debris.

Trent hung his head over the log.

Pom paddled over to the far end of the log and patted him on the shoulder. Beyond the bars, the pursuing boat was still moving toward them. "You want to sit tight and let 'em pick us up?"

With one arm around the log, Trent started swimming. "I'll ride this damn thing all the way to Key West before I let 'em take me in."

Dragging along with the log, Pom called out. "Richard!"

In a futile effort to get away, Trent swept them on for a few more strokes. The approaching boat blinked out in the rain and then came back.

Pom wished he hadn't lost the flashlight. "Richard!"

In the splashing darkness they heard a strange belching sound.

"Rich—"

Something knocked Pom in the back. "Keep it down. You want 'em to hear us? Who's got the suitcase?"

"Suitcase hell," Trent said.

Richard swept the hair from his eyes and peered through the rain. "I had it when I jumped in. It's out here someplace."

"That thing's going to get us killed," Trent said.

Richard kept looking. "*Not* having it's going to get *me* killed."

Trent continued to paddle, even though the going was very slow. "You suppose these logs just happened to fall off of a boat or did somebody put 'em here just for us?"

Richard pulled at a piece of planking. "Keep low. They're not getting us and they're not getting that suitcase." His eyes followed the drifting logs as he caught his breath.

"Well, now," Pom said, "on the one hand, the logs did sink the boat, but on the other, they're going to keep us from drowning."

Richard was already thinking ahead. "Kincaid's throwing a New Year's Eve party and I intend to be there, so let's get this thing going faster."

Trent kept looking back at the approaching boat. "You're riding a damn log and you've got a slug in your leg. How fast did you expect to go?"

"Tide's going out," Pom reminded them. "We might be on our way to Mexico."

A pale light played across the water, showing logs all around them. The big boat was looking for them, but the distance was too great and the rain too steady. The third sweep of the light came closest. Richard ducked low and waited until the brightness passed.

"Guess what," Trent said. "They ain't coming in here. They can't clear them bars and they can see these logs, so they probably figure we're done for."

"They may be right," Pom said.

Half-submerged, a gas can floated toward them, tapped a log, and drifted away. A hat, dark and shapeless, washed by brim up and vanished under the lip of a wave.

Trent spat a long stream of water. "Wish I had a fishing pole. I'd get a head start on the trout."

Pom blinked up at the sky for a sign of a letup. "I think the trout are going to get a head start on us."

They joked about how they could warm up the water and about which parts the fish would bite first, but the jokes thinned out as the cold seeped into their bones. At first the water felt comfortable compared to the air, but after a while it was all the same. Richard spoke cheerfully of the pleasant numbness that had replaced the pain in his leg. But discomfort and doubt quieted them and then dulled their thoughts so that they swam along in a mindless repetition of strokes and rests. They stopped thinking about whether they were making any progress against the tide or if it had finally turned in their favor. Even after the rain stopped, time and distance were too hard to distinguish. As the sky cleared and the stars came out, the night became all the colder, and still the three plodded on with quivering jaws and breaths coming in gasps.

They kept close for warmth, but Richard shifted constantly, looking for the suitcase.

When the first light of dawn broke through the clouds, he saw something flat glinting in the water. He rubbed the brine from his eyes and looked harder.

"Let's go. That way. Fast."

With heavy arms, they managed to steer the log within a few yards of it. Then it bobbed away.

Trent pushed off from the log and dogpaddled after the suitcase, but after ten yards he cramped up and had to fight to stay afloat. It was all he could do to rejoin the other two.

"I'm too old for this," Pom said. He pushed off and splashed hand over hand, but soon got tired and had to slow down. He floated and thrashed his way to it, threw his arm out, and grabbed hold.

Richard was too tired to cheer. He dropped his head down onto his arm.

Trent thumped him on the shoulder. "I got bad news. He ain't coming back."

By the time he was able to drag himself off the end of the log, Richard had lost sight of Pom and had to splash his way as best he could, gurgling out Pom's name as he went. From the crest of a wave, he saw a finger pointing to the sky, and he pulled toward it, trying not to use his bad leg. By the time he got to the place, one wave looked the same as the next, but he dove down blindly in a spiral until he collided with something, a hand. He dove deeper, groped for an elbow, hooked onto it, and beat for the surface with his free arm and his good leg. When that wasn't enough, he kicked with his bad leg, too, until he and Pom broke the surface and sucked in the sweet morning air.

Pom puked water into the surging waves and coughed. "Good to see you."

Richard hadn't heard him. He was feeling for the suitcase. It had come open. One after the other, the boxes of counterfeit salt rolled toward the bottom of the Gulf.

He felt one going, stuffed it back in, and clamped the suitcase shut. With failing hands, he secured the clasps.

Pom was still coughing water. "Damn, we're done for."

"Not yet." Richard told him. "Hang onto this and I'll tow you back. Whatever you do, don't let go."

Richard's fingers had cramped shut on the suitcase by the time the brightening sky and the high whining of a small boat engine revived them. They got up on the log as best they could, flapping and making a racket with throats hoarse from seawater. The deadly forest of flotsam was nowhere to be seen, and the plywood husk of the boat buzzed right to them.

The man at the tiller was tanned and ropy, and looked at ease, as if he'd been working on the water for most of his thirty-some years. Bundled up beside him was a skinny girl of eight or nine. She kept her thin hands tucked into the sleeves of an over-sized jacket, but from time to time she pulled at a tam-o'-shanter atop the stringy blonde hair that flew about her face.

The castaways were so cold and stiff that they had trouble working their hands to drag themselves into the boat. Richard hauled himself onto the log and got the suitcase aboard, but the man had to haul him in the rest of the way. The girl shrank back as if the dripping men were monsters plucked from the secret depths of the Gulf.

Her father laughed and tugged at her hair. "It's all right, Billie! Nobody looks good first thing in the morning." He adjusted the floppy hat strapped to his chin. "How long were y'all in the water?"

Richard sat on the gunwale and gripped the suitcase. "Long enough."

"We sure do thank you for picking us up." Pom's voice quavered in the wind as the boat gained speed.

Trent smiled at the girl, then turned his back to the wind.

The man and his daughter lived at the edge of a little stretch of mangrove beach, in a Cracker shack with a dustpan roof, three rooms, and a deep open porch. He gave the wet men a few rags to dry off with, a mug of strong coffee to pass around, and a box of limp saltines. They picked at the weevils in the crackers as they dried themselves in front of a flickering wood stove.

"You're welcome to stay as long as you need," the man said. He introduced himself as Marlin Barlow.

His guests used just their first names.

"Y'all picked a hell of a night to be on the water," Marlin said.

Richard was in no mood for pleasantries. "We need to get up to the Waccasassa. You got a car?"

"When it works. Last time I had it out, it took a team of horses to get it home, and all this rain just puts it right to sleep."

"I could maybe have a look at it," Pom said.

While Richard sat under a spruce pine, clutching the suitcase, the other men bent over a rusting Hupmobile Runabout, pulling at wires and shaking their heads.

"Your friend over there's kinda partial to his luggage," Marlin said.

"He likes to look his best," Pom replied without turning around.

"Pom here's a miracle worker," Trent told Marlin. "He can bring anything back to life, whether it's a critter or a contraption."

"What's the matter with his leg?" Billie asked. She held both hands behind her back as she looked at the engine.

"He's just kind of wore out," Trent told her. He smiled and she turned away.

"This is one of those Lazarus cars," Pom said after he'd had a good look under the hood. "Nobody but Jesus could bring it back to life. And anyway, we can't get everybody in it."

Richard thumped the suitcase. "One way or the other, let's get it going, friends."

"Even if we can get it going, it won't be safe," Pom said. "The gas tank's got a leak in it."

Richard pulled himself up with a stick and hobbled over to the car. "Patch it with cement if you have to. We've got to get out of here."

Pom poked his foot at a mildewed tire. "Well, just where are we?"

"About halfway between Crystal River and Hudson," Marlin said.

"*Hudson!*" Pom looked at his host in disbelief. "We won't get back to the Waccasassa this year."

"It's going to be longer'n that if we don't get this thing start-ed," Trent said.

Richard called Pom over to the tree. "What about his boat? It's fast enough."

"You'd have to fill it top to bottom with gas and then steal it," Pom said. "Assuming we even could even find enough gas."

Richard nodded toward the Hupmobile. "Then let's just get that thing going till we can get to something better. I think that guy's up to something."

"Who, Marlin? He's okay. He's helping us out, isn't he?"

"He keeps asking about the suitcase."

"Oh, come on, he's just curious."

"Keep your eye on the girl too."

"The girl! What can she do?"

"She can blab."

"You okay, Richard? How's the leg?"

"It'll be a lot better when it's in Baldwin."

"In *Baldwin*? We've long since missed the train."

"There'll be another one."

"Richard, the—the salt's all gone."

"There's one left. Now let's get going."

After an hour of tinkering with tools more fit for a carpenter than a mechanic, Pom and Marlin brought the car to shudder-ing life.

Trent brought his hands together. "You done worked anoth-er miracle."

Pom wiped the grease from his cheek. "If we get five miles on these tires, *that*'ll be a miracle. You okay to move, Richard? Let's go."

For the sake of keeping his leg free, Richard perched in the back, on the spare tire, most of the way to Homosassa, when the back right wheel fell off and spilled him and the suitcase into a ditch. They waited half an hour under a cabbage palm while

Marlin and Billie went into town looking for a relative who could help out.

Richard found a place in the shade and sat down. He patted the suitcase as he watched the road. "Keep an eye out. We don't know who's going to be coming down that road."

"It's likely to be a while," Pom said.

"If they're on the level," Richard replied, tapping.

Pom was looking down the road now too. "It's just a Cracker and his little girl. They don't know what's in that suitcase."

"I didn't get this far taking people at face value."

"Wait a minute. What's the date today?"

"It's the twenty-ninth, Pom, the twenty-ninth of December."

"Damn. When's your payment to the collector due?"

"Night before last."

An hour later, Trent elbowed Pom out of a nap. "Take a look at this. Our ride's done come."

Pulling up to the palm tree was a Cadillac hearse, its carved painted panels and whitewalls blazing in the afternoon sun.

Trent rubbed his eyes. "Comin' for to carry me home."

Pom read a church advertisement stenciled onto the passenger door. "Communion Wafers Made *Flesh* Daily."

With the aid of a pine stick, Richard wrenched himself to his feet. "Come on. We don't have all day."

Marlin called through the open window. "Better get in. It's real good at going but not so good at stopping, Hop in the back and we'll be there before you know it."

Trent wasn't so sure. "Ain't nobody in it, is there?"

After a rumbling *harrumph*, Marlin spat into the road. "Not as I know of."

They had him drop them off where the Otter Creek highway crossed a road to the Waccasassa. Pom and Trent hiked to the truck while Richard waited out of sight.

Trent looked from tree to tree as they approached the landing where the truck was stowed.

"That fella never did ask what we were doing out there in the water all night."

Pom pulled at a shirt still sticky with salt. "A wrecked boat, a game leg, and three shady characters out in lousy weather He probably figured we weren't after grouper."

Trent looked itchy in his damp clothes. "You suppose he'll snitch on us?"

"To the sheriff? No, but I imagine he's already telling all his friends. Richard's probably right about that much."

"What's Ward the wonder boy going to do now? He's got no boat, no money and no goods and plenty of people that want a piece of him."

"Richard's got something up his sleeve."

"You know what I wish, Pom? I wish I was setting back at my still right now with the whole day stretching out like a path, not hardly a care in the world. I went wrong when I threw in with that Professor Thompson, but I've been sweating circles ever since I got mixed up in this. Nobody was after my damn hide before. I could've quit on Monday and been home with Elsie and the girls by Tuesday. Those days look mighty good right now."

Pom was walking on the high grassy ridge between the sandy ruts of the road. "We've got all these lines tangled underneath the boat and I'm trying to figure out how they all connect. And in the meantime, that suitcase might yet get us all killed. It's already got Richard so ratcheted up that he doesn't trust his own shadow."

"What if we just ditch the whole business and hitch a ride back to town? Richard can drive with one good leg if his life depends on it."

They had come to the truck, which was hidden in a thicket of pines and palmettos. Pom walked around it to satisfy himself that it hadn't been tampered with. "We're in this thing together now. Let's see it through together. Richard didn't *have to* pull me out of the water to get the suitcase." He smiled and patted Trent on the shoulder. "Think of it as a lark and you'll enjoy yourself a lot more."

"Oh, sure," Trent said as they got into the truck. "Just a lark."

They picked Richard up and, as the road improved, Pom drove hard despite the recent mishap with the deer. When they got to the Packard, Richard tumbled into the backseat, still hugging the suitcase. As they came into town and the blinding sun flashed through a procession of trees, Pom thought that the vast shaded university campus, fields, and distant spires looked like a haven from the troubles they had seen and expected yet to see. But he concluded that the danger was all around and that their final encounter could take place, not just on desolate country roads, but in neighborhoods of neat hedges and red curbs or even in Kincaid's trimmed gardens.

Richard stirred in the backseat. "Don't take me to that damn hospital. Take me over to Dr. Willis' house."

They passed the 2:15 on its way to the depot and rumbled over the railroad tracks that ran up the middle of West Main Street. When they passed the prosperous Duck Pond neighborhood, Pom turned left onto a street lined with shade trees and well-kept Victorian homes. He pulled up at one of the older and smaller ones. When the three got out of the car, Richard leaning heavily on Trent and Pom, they set two or three dogs to barking and became all the more uneasy. They argued for a while about which door to use. Pom was for going up to the front porch, but Trent remembered going in the side door. It was closer, so they climbed the steps and turned the bell, which had been painted over. Trent and Pom argued a little longer about what to do and then dragged Richard up to the front door and rang the bell there.

Fumbling with the knob and muttering, Dr. Willis let them in. He looked old and sleepy. "For God's sake," he said, "was that y'all making the racket at the side door? I ought to have that thing boarded over. Haven't used it since they built the hospital. Y'all look like the wrath of God. What's the matter?"

The three shifted their weight. "Richard here has hurt his leg," Pom said.

"Well, come on, come in. Let's have a look at you."

He led them through a stuffy front room smelling of kerosene and rose water and into the cluttered office. Once he had Richard's leg propped up on a chair, he put on a pair of wire-rimmed glasses and wasted no time in his diagnosis.

"Hurt his leg? On a damn bullet." He stood up and rinsed his hands in a basin. "But then I suppose y'all know that. You go to the hospital right now. I'll telephone over there and tell them to expect you."

Richard kept his leg on the chair. "I could do without the fuss. There's not so much to taking out a bullet is there?"

"There is to that one. It's in pretty deep and you've got a lot of swelling. It's going to take some digging and we've got that nice new hospital sitting over there for just this kind of thing."

"I'll go to Jacksonville if I have to," Richard said. "But you can get it out, can't you?"

The doctor peered over his glasses. "They're discrete over there, Richard, if that's what you're worried about."

Richard gripped the arms of the chair as if to get up. "I tell you, I'll go to Jacksonville if I have to. Can you get it out or can't you?"

The surgeon issued a challenge of his own. "You're talking to somebody who got by on three hours of sleep last night. You still want your bullet out?"

Two hours later, they laid Richard limp and sweaty in the back of the car. Pom turned around and looked at him from the driver's seat. "You got a plan?"

"Never mind," Richard mumbled. "It's going to look a lot better tomorrow."

"He ain't making sense," Trent said. He twisted around as Pom backed out of the doctor's driveway and looked at the form slumped in the backseat. "You want us to carry you off somewhere? Ain't they going to come looking for that suitcase?"

Richard pulled himself up on one elbow "Count on it. And they'll get it, too, but not till I'm ready. Then let 'em come. For now I'm going to do a little cooking. Stop at the Leary store, will you? I want to pick up some salt."

CHAPTER 32

When Pom and Trent got to the house on Magnolia Street nobody else was home. They changed clothes and picked up as if they had never been gone. They went back to work on the wiring.

"You've got a peculiar way of getting along," Trent said. "Before all this trouble, if I was to come home a couple of days overdue Elsie would rip my hair out."

Pom sneezed at the dust he had stirred up. "Well, Flora can't grab hold of my hair anymore, but you can be sure there'll be an accounting," He went back to his measuring. "At least we're done chasing around with Richard."

"Five thousand dollars. That's a laugh. We damn near got killed and didn't turn a nickel."

A passing car prompted Pom to look toward the street. "Richard's working on *something* and I kinda feel like we ought to be looking out for him till the deal's done."

"You can't take care of everybody. Especially somebody as slippery as Richard."

"For whatever reason, he half killed himself to fish me out of the water. Flora hasn't yet come to terms with her dad dying out on the reef. She sure didn't need her husband going down too."

When she finally came home, Flora was surprisingly cordial, to the point of making Pom uneasy.

"You've been out and about," he said.

"Yes, out and about. I did a little shopping. Went to see Mavis. Richard's under the weather, cut his leg pushing his car out of a ditch on the way back from Ocala."

"That Richard and his car. I don't suppose you know where Jim is."

Flora ran her hand along the new wiring Pom had fastened to the frame of the wood room door. "Ainsley talked him into taking her on one of his song hunts."

Pom looked at Trent. "Any idea where?"

"Oh, off toward the Millhopper. You know how he likes to poke around in those little colored settlements up there in the woods. I can't believe Ainsley went with him."

"Call it a hunch," Pom said, "but Trent and I ought to go up there. If Theron finds 'em, it's going to be heads knocking."

Flora patted the doorframe. "Well, maybe I'll see you again someday."

"Now, come on, we'll back in an hour, two at the most."

Flora turned toward the stairs. "Oh, take what time you need. I've got a few things to do myself."

It took them a few tries to get the Model T started and Trent bruised the back of his hand cranking it, but before long they were rattling down the Millhopper Road.

"We ought to've taken a gun or two," Trent said as he scanned the pinewoods to the east.

Pom swerved to avoid a garter snake. "The last thing I want to do is get into a shootout with Theron."

"Well, going up against him unarmed again wouldn't be so healthy either. You suppose that Luger in your house was his?"

"If not, I imagine he knows where it came from."

"You think he shot them two that was wired to your tree?"

"I just don't know. I can see Theron flying off the handle and shooting somebody, but I can't see him taking the trouble to set 'em up and take pot shots at 'em—and then miss."

They passed the old church with its green gravestones and came to a sandy track that entered the road from a vast stand of oak woods. Pom stopped the car and looked down the corridor of ancient branches hung with Spanish moss.

"I can't see Theron going down there. Those woods are honeycombed with colored people, one little shack and pen after another."

Trent looked off to the west. "We could try some of the hunting camps up toward San Felasco. We found him there before."

For a few miles, the narrow gravel road dipped and rose from one hill to the next, and the massive live oaks gave way to scrub and thickets rutted here and there by wagon wheels and tires. "Flora's dad and Ainsley's dad had a phosphate mine up here back in the nineties," Pom said. "I remember Mr. Larrabee telling me they thought they were set for life, and then practically overnight it played out."

Trent had been listening for gunshots. He lowered his hand from his swollen ear. "They say the next big money's going to come from tung nuts for paint. Them in the know just can't plant the trees fast enough."

"Trouble is," Pom said, "you've got to get the trees from China and then you've got to baby-sit 'em for a few years before they produce. Then you've got to hope the bugs and the freezes don't get 'em. Maybe you still don't believe me, but you're better off with your farm."

"I don't blame you for telling me to buy, Pom, never have. If it hadn't been the farm, I'd've spent my inheritance on something foolish. Your advice was good. We just had bad timing, all of us."

"Well, you might've done okay with the guano boat."

"Them guano dollars come hard. How long do you figure before the fellas from Baldwin come down here looking for their suitcase?"

When they gave up on the hammock and went to Porter's Place to look for Theron, they found out that the men from Baldwin had paid Deardra a visit.

"It was last night at closing," she told them. "They were looking for a suitcase. But they were willing to settle for Richard's last name."

"Did they hurt you?" Pom asked.

"No, but the clothes horse offered to give me a scar just like his."

"What if they come back?"

"Well, one day at a time."

"You'd be safer coming with us," Pom said. "We need to tell Richard those guys are looking for him. He'll want to hear what you have to say. Did you get a look at their car?"

"It was a Duesenberg, a red Duesenberg."

"Same as the one I saw in Baldwin," Pom said.

They called the Wards. J.J. answered and said that Richard had taken off somewhere. "A couple of hours ago he could hardly get down the stairs and now he's off dancing the Charleston somewhere. Tell me how much sense that makes."

They squeezed into Pom's car, skirted the potholes in the parking lot, and turned east on University Avenue.

Deardra took out a compact and touched up her lipstick. "Do we know where we're going?"

"Ever been to Magnesia Springs?" Pom asked.

"Yeah, with Richard one time. Just to see if I could get his car up to speed."

"Well, it's not New Orleans, but Richard told me he goes out there to bury himself in the crowd when the creditors come prowling."

Trent looked over his shoulder at the empty road. "If they'd followed us we'd know it by now."

Deardra swept a strand of hair from her face. "What if they find out where he lives and go to his house?"

"Then they'll have to deal with J.J.," Pom said. "A man with a bad temper and a cabinet full of guns."

They passed the solemn courthouse and highborn Victorian houses and bounced over seams and washouts for a quarter of an hour and then Pom turned off the road and drove through a gravel parking lot. "I'm glad *somebody's* had a good year," he said as they jostled into a yard thick with late-model automobiles, one of which was the familiar Packard.

Trent walked the grounds looking for Richard while Pom and Deardra hurried toward the dance hall. They squeezed through the crowd as if they owned the place and followed the general flow of people past the green oval swimming pool.

"Did you bring your suit?" Deardra asked Pom as they came to the water's edge.

He smiled. "I went swimming last night."

They found Richard upstairs in the billiard room with Edith. He brushed chalk dust from the sleeve of his navy blue blazer as Edith leaned over the table, concentrating on a bank shot. She jabbed the cue ball and watched it spin off the six, which shot into the pocket.

"Hi-ho, everybody. I think we've discovered a talent here." Richard lowered his cue stick and limped toward the table. "We could take it on the road and make a killing."

"I don't suppose you two have met," Pom said. "Deardra, this is Edith."

"We haven't met," Deardra said, "but I've seen you at my warehouse. We have friends in common."

Edith looked up and smiled, having failed to catch the innuendo. "Isn't it a lovely party? Quite the bash."

Pom put his hands on his hips. "We need to pull Richard aside for a minute and talk a little business." He seemed perfectly at home, even though he was in mended work clothes and everyone else was in their pressed Sunday best. He was no longer self-conscious about the bruise on his forehead.

Richard patted Edith on the crepe shoulder of her loose-fitting dress. "Sugar, why don't you go see what they're dancing out there while we talk shop? We'll come get you in a twinkle."

Edith forced a smile. "You better." With a toss of her blonde waves and a backward glance at Deardra, she slipped past them and disappeared into the crowd on the dance floor.

Pom came forward to be farther from the noise. "Richard, your friends from Baldwin are in town. They showed up at the Porters Quarters looking for you last night."

He set his cue stick down on the table. "What did you tell them?"

"They got your last name out of me," Deardra said. "I'm sorry. I needed to buy a little time."

He took her by the shoulders. "That was all? You sure?"

"That was all. Richard, they want that suitcase."

"I'm sure they do. And they're going to get it too. You sure nobody followed you?"

"Relax," Pom said. "I'm positive. But you can't string 'em along forever."

"I don't intend to. Just till day after tomorrow."

Deardra took a breath. "They're very unhappy with you. They're not going to wait that long."

Richard cocked a brow and smiled. "Except that they still want that suitcase and I'm the only one who knows where it is."

Pom reached for Deardra's elbow. "Will you do me a giant favor and go find Trent before he finds something to drink?"

She was quick to read between the lines. "Glad to. I'm sure it'll take as long as you want."

When she had left, Pom gestured toward the door. "Did I miss something back there in the Gulf of Mexico or did—"

"I'm telling you, Pom, don't worry about Ralph and Archie. They're amateurs. The collector's the one to look out for. He kills people for the fun of it. We just need to keep a jump ahead of him for two more days."

"Play straight with me, Richard. Those people in my pasture. Was it the collector?"

"Now, how could I—"

Pom grabbed a billiard ball, and bounced it off the floor.

"Sure it was the collector, the damn collector."

"How do you know?"

Leaning on the pool table, Richard came toward him. "He told me, Pom. He wanted me to know he was serious about collecting from *me*."

"Why haven't you told Avery?"

"'Cause I've got no proof. I've never even seen the goddam Luger. So how's Avery going to hold him? He'd just get him mad, and the guy wouldn't mind killing me as it is. I just want to pay him off and go."

"Pay him off with *what*? You don't even have a boat now."

Richard came so close and spoke so softly that Pom could scarcely hear him above the dance music. "I'm going to pay him with money from our friends in Baldwin, who are going to pay five thousand for their suitcase."

"You going to turn one box of salt into six?"

"Like the fishes and loaves."

"They'll never fall for it."

"They won't have to, at least not for more than a few hours. Back in October Kincaid offered me a business loan. If I can come up with five thousand by New Year's Eve, he'll match it. So he doubles their five. If they catch me somehow and squawk about the salt, I can pay them back with sincere apologies and use Kincaid's five to pay the collector, minus your cut, of course, with some left over."

"But you'll still owe five thousand to Kincaid."

"He isn't going to come after me with a Luger, Pom. He'll give me a month or two before he even asks questions."

"Sounds too easy Then what?"

"Then I'm up in the wilds of North Carolina where Kincaid can't find me. At least not until I actually have the five thousand."

"What do you want us to tell the guys from Baldwin when they come around again?"

Richard listened to the music for a moment and then his face brightened. "Tell Archie and Ralph I'll meet 'em at the house on Palm Terrace at nine o'clock on New Year's Eve. That's when they can pick up their suitcase."

CHAPTER 33

After Pom and Trent dropped Deardra off at Porter's Place, Pom looked out through the windshield. "A red Duesenberg. Can't be too many of those around town. You want to go hunting again, Trent?"

"We giving up on finding Theron?"

"For now. This is even more urgent."

"It's kinda dark, ain't it?"

"That could be good."

After driving through all the hotel parking lots and checking a boarding house or two, Pom got a hunch and drove to Richard's house. As they came to the hill, he slowed the car and looked down the side streets. Only every now and then did the lights of a house glimmer through the oak trees.

"Well, they ain't at his house," Trent said.

Pom drummed the wheel. "Neither does a panther come right out in the open. He stalks his prey, especially if closing in on it might be dangerous. If they know about Richard, chances are they know about J.J."

"Well, *these* damn panthers drive a red Duesenberg," Trent said. "So where's it at?"

Pom stopped the car and stared into the dark oak woods that stretched most of the way down the hill. "They could park on one of those lover's lane trails in the Leary Woods and be out of sight but still have a good view of Richard's house."

"And a lot more. I hear that Jake Jolly all but lives in there just aching to get an eyeful."

They doubled back to the rambling clapboard Leary Store, parked beside one of the painted oaks in the lime rock lot, then crossed the road and walked into the woods. About fifty yards down one of the meandering sand tracks, Trent stopped and caught Pom by the sleeve. Ahead of them was the red Duesenberg.

"Kind of like gathering eggs, isn't it?" Pom whispered. "And we just found a big one."

Trent pulled back into the shadows. "Now that we've got 'em, what're we going to do with 'em?"

Pom dropped down on his haunches behind a low-hanging branch draped with moss and studied the Duesenberg. He smiled. "You just keep an eye on 'em and I'll be right back." By the time he returned, the big man had gotten out of the car and was pressing his hands to the small of his back as he gazed through the trees toward Richard's house. Pom watched him for a moment. The big man stood by the car, as broad as a gas pump. Pom handed Trent a rock wrapped in paper. "You still got a good throwing arm on you?"

Trent hefted the rock. "You want me to kill him?"

"No, I want you to deliver the message to him. Soon as you do, we beat it for my car."

"You want me to knock him out?"

Pom pointed at the big man. "Don't get fancy on me, Trent. Just see to it that he knows what hit him."

"Be more fun to bust it through the window and hit that other fella."

"Maybe, but more dangerous. Now just—"

Trent cocked his right arm and let the rock fly. When they heard the hollow knock and saw the big man's head jerk forward, they ran all the way back to Pom's car.

Once they had the Model T started, Pom looked over his shoulder at the vacant track. "We'd better tell Richard they know where he lives."

Trent continued to look back. "All we've got to do is find him again."

When they got back to Pom's house, they had company. Ainsley was in the front room with Jim and Flora. Jim was repositioning the fireplace screen. In one hand he had a tight grip on the poker.

Pom took off his jacket and tossed it onto the round table in front of the fireplace. "Hey, Ainsley. We've been looking for you, but I didn't expect to find you here, not at this time of night. I hope you haven't come around for more table-tipping."

She rose from the wing chair. "No such luck. Truth is, Mother and I had another visit from Theron."

"What did he want this time?"

Ainsley joined Jim by the fire and stared at the sparks that rose from the popping pine logs. "He came down there looking for me. He wanted me to go away with him in that stinking car of his. When I told him no, he said something about Jim and took off like a firecracker. When the coast was clear, Mother and I made a beeline for Nelda's. I left Mother over there."

"Where do you suppose Theron is now?"

"Probably working himself up to come after Jim."

Pom put his hands on the round table. "Good thing we got here ahead of him."

Flora was sitting in the Morris chair to one side of the fire. She'd been working on a latch hook rug that lay curled on the floor at her feet. "I wouldn't call it luck to have a wild man coming our way. I wanted to call Avery, but Ainsley's dead set against it. I can't talk sense into her."

"You've got to be careful pulling at rice paper plants," Pom said, "or you'll tear up your whole yard."

Flora snatched up her rug. "More riddles."

"Rex and Rachel around?"

"Rachel's at Roberta's and Rex hasn't come back from selling peanuts at the 6:39."

"Good." Pom went over to the stairs and cranked the telephone and asked to be put through to J.J. Ward. "Tell Richard we delivered his message," he told J.J. in a loud voice. He paused, wanting to warn him that the house was being watched, but he knew that he had to get to Richard first. "He'll know what it's about. Tell him as soon as he comes home, will you? Tell him I'll be up late, so he can call anytime. You have a good night now. Say hi to the missus for us."

"So what do we do?" Trent asked. "Sit here and wait?" He took out a piece of string and started a Jacob's Ladder.

"I'm too tired to do anything else," Pom said. "You and I are going to take turns."

"You can count me in on that," Jim said. "I got you all into this."

Pom shook his head. "Don't take credit for all of it."

Trent was over at the window by the piano. His hands stopped. "I got news for you. Won't neither one of you have to wait up. Yonder comes our boy now."

After a hurried argument, Pom got Flora and Ainsley to go upstairs. The three men waited inside the front door as the dark blue Studebaker stopped at the front gate.

"He's looking mean—and sober." Trent said, watching Theron flip the latch.

"Yeah, but at least he isn't carrying a gun." Pom pulled away from the door as Theron strode down the brick walk.

Jim took his glasses from his vest pocket and set them on the mantel.

Theron took the steps two at a time and landed on the porch with a thud. He steadied himself against the wall, coughed, opened the screen door and tried the knob. With a rattling of wood and glass it unstuck, and he stepped into the front hall. Suddenly he was facing Trent, Pom, and Jim.

He swore under his breath.

Pom made way for him, nodded toward the front room. "Come on in, Theron. We've been looking for you."

He headed for the stairs. "I'm looking for Ainsley. Tell her to come down."

Pom blocked his way. "What makes you think she'd be here at this hour?"

Theron raised his nose and sniffed. "'Cause I can *smell* her. After eight years of sharing a bed with her, you'd better believe I can smell her out." He brushed past Pom and put a hand on the newel post. "Now call her down or I'm going up to get her."

Jim grabbed his shoulder and spun him around. "The hell you are."

Theron swung hard and hit him on the cheek with enough force to stagger him backwards, but Jim recovered, swung at Theron's chin, missed, and caught him in the throat, slamming him onto the stairs and falling forward with him. Theron hammered him on the jaw and Jim crashed to the floor as Pom and Trent jumped back to make room. Theron stomped on him, but Jim grabbed his foot and twisted, throwing him off balance, and in an instant they were both on the floor, snatching and kicking. Grabbing hold of the wicker chair, Theron struggled to his feet, but went over backwards when Jim came at him low and butted him in the chest. They fought their way into the front room, knocking over chairs and tipping the round table as they rolled and punched. The screen fell away from the fireplace, and they fought jerking on the scattering coals. Theron snatched up a piece of fat pine from a copper tub, swung it, lost it, and sent it crashing into the fire in a shower of sparks. He caught Jim a good one in the mouth, but Jim came back at him low and butted him into the Christmas tree, which went over in a welter of popcorn, cranberries, and tinsel. Jim yanked him by the ankles and Theron dropped hard, his head bashing an ugly chord on the piano as he went down. When he came back up, Jim was over him and let loose a punch to the cheek that pasted him to the rug. Theron came up again and Jim caught at his collar and threw him down, ripping his shirt away to the elbow, exposing the blue outline of a snake twisted around a sword.

Jim hovered over him, fists doubled, flushed and panting.

When Theron came up on his elbows, Pom put a foot on his chest and pinned him to the floor.

"As long as we're visiting, why don't you tell us all about a Luger and where you got that dark green Studebaker?"

CHAPTER 34

———

Richard was in the back room at Porter's Place having a smoke. When the telephone rang, he took time for another puff before picking up the receiver. He waited for the man on the other end to speak first.

"That you, Richard?"

He winked at Deardra and let out another curl of smoke. "The same."

The big man was more than a little annoyed. "You're becoming quite the pain in the tuckus. You know that?"

"You got the message about the delivery, I trust?"

"Yeah, we got it. Sure we got it. You goddam near knocked me out with it. So you know we've got your address."

"My *former* address, Archie. I just moved. The current resident there is a gun collector."

"We'll see about that. You want us to meet you at Palm Terrace. The house being built at the end of the street. Tomorrow night at nine. Do you mind telling me what the hell is wrong with *tonight?*"

"Archie, it's late. I've had a long day. Tell you what. Let me talk to the boss. Put Ralph on."

"Drop dead. How do we know you won't have somebody else there waiting for us?"

Richard rocked back in the swivel chair and propped his feet on the roll-top desk. "Well, practical concerns like money aside, you have my word on it, my word as a gentleman—my word as a *southern* gentleman."

"You and I know what your word and a plugged nickel is worth." The voice on the phone became distorted as the big man got too close to the mouthpiece. *"Be there."*

"Wouldn't miss it for the world. See you tomorrow night at nine. Oh, and Archie?"

The big man's breathing came thick over the phone.

"You sound all wound up. Are you grinding your teeth again?"

When he hung up, Deardra took the cigarette from his hand and put it between her lips. "I think you pushed him too far."

He patted her hand. "It'll be all right. They're going to be happy. They're getting what they want. I know those two. They're going to go speeding back to Baldwin just as soon as they get the salt, as he calls it. I'm almost going to miss that Archie."

"What about the money? What if they just take the goods from you?"

"They might do that, but they're more likely to shortchange me for being a pain. They know that if they stiff me completely, I'm likely sic Avery on them."

"It sounds dangerous to me, Richard, damn dangerous."

He took her cool slender hand and pressed it to his chest. "That's part of the fun, isn't it? If you've got a fast car, do you drive it like the old lady going to the library?"

"What if the timing's off? What if they're late?"

"They won't be."

She slipped her hand away and smoothed the frowsy black dress on the wall. "You'd better hope it takes them a while to find out the stuff is fake."

"Don't worry. By the time they figure it out, I'll be halfway through Georgia."

"So why are you making them wait?"

He crossed one Argyle ankle over the other and laced his fingers behind his head. "Because I don't want to give them time to look too close at the salt before I take their money to a New Year's Eve party."

In the beams of the Packard's headlamps, he looked like a conjurer at some sylvan ritual, playing to an audience of pine saplings, wheelbarrows, and a skeleton house. He laid the suitcase on a pine stump and waited in the open with outstretched hands.

At nine o'clock, there they were. The red Duesenberg bobbed over ruts and potholes as it came around the sinkhole pond.

The big man got out of the car and looked around. Seeing nobody but Richard, he knelt at the suitcase and tested the locks.

"This thing looks like hell," he said. "What've you been doing with it?"

Richard glanced over at Ralph, who was squatting by the Duesenberg, poking at something with a stick. "It was murder out there, Archie. Ask the guys on the *Cristobel*."

The big man took a key from his hip pocket and tried the lock. "You pulled a switch."

Richard smiled. "Your hands are shaking. Want me to get it?"

Archie pounded the suitcase with his fist and tried the key again. The suitcase popped open, revealing neat rows of cylindrical salt boxes. He broke the seal of one, poured a pinch of white powder into his palm and sniffed.

"Okay."

"You want to try another one, Archie? I've got all night."

"Yeah, well, I don't." He pulled a fat envelope from his inside coat pocket and handed it to Richard. "Don't ever be late again."

"I promise, Archie. Never again. You have my word."

Cappy Kincaid's New Year's Eve party displayed the remnants of an opulent Christmas. A giant North Carolina Fraser fir decked with tiers of small blue electric lights still dominated one end of the banquet hall, which echoed with jazzy tunes and laughter and the clink of colliding glasses. Even though a cold front had moved in during the afternoon, the French doors at the ends of the hall were open, and the partygoers found their way onto the terrace by the light of Japanese lanterns, crossed the shadows of tall pines, and entered the vaulted courtyard that embraced the glittering pool.

Someone near the deep end was drawing a cluster of men. Thinking that it was Cappy Kincaid, Richard led Edith that way only to find out that the attraction was Buddy Cole, splendid in an old-fashioned wide lapel tux and tails, with a purple ribbon splashed across his chest. He was taking bets, writing names down in a notebook.

"What've you cooked up now?" Richard asked, reading the gold letters on the purple ribbon: *Happy New Year 1930.*

The broad face lit up. "Diving for dollars, twenty bucks a comer. Not bad for five seconds of work, all of it downhill."

"Have you tried it out?"

"Nope. That's the deal. One dive, blind."

"You've got more guts than I do. How many takers?"

Buddy glanced at the notebook. "Upwards of thirty. Six hundred smackers. With one jump. Wish I'd thought of this a year ago."

"Is there enough water? You got it all figured out?"

Buddy put an arm around him and leaned in close. "Yeah. A kid could do it. Dive flat."

"A belly whomper? Damn."

"Painful but legal, safe—and profitable."

"Well, good luck. We'll be watching."

The guests talked of bank failures and cascading stock prices and Wall Street suicides. They spoke in envious murmurs about the rumors that Kincaid had sidestepped all of it and remained prosperous by selling most of his stock before the collapse.

"He's probably better off now than he was last summer," Richard told Edith as he smoothed the lapel of his blazer and traced the edge of the envelope in his inside pocket. "There are so many bargains you can get now. In fact, I need to talk to him about one tonight, but don't you worry, it won't take long."

She clung to his shoulder and blinked up at him. "Will we be seeing dear Deardra again tonight?"

He smiled and patted her waved blonde hair. "Hey, like I told you, that was business. And as soon as we swing this last deal, she's out of the picture."

"She had a look in her eye, Richard, and it didn't say business. She's not from around here, is she? She sure doesn't dress like it."

They were going against the current of partygoers now, most of them pushing their way toward the swimming pool. Richard made way for a large woman wearing a chinchilla stole adorned with a live chameleon tethered to a stickpin.

"She's from New Orleans. That's practically all I know about her, except that she inherited that warehouse from her great uncle, an old-timer named Bobby LaRue. That's the only reason she's in town. She's been trying to sell it, but the best she can come up with is an offer from the Baptists, who want to rent it while they get the roof fixed on their church."

Edith struggled to stay stuck to his arm. People were pouring through the banquet hall to get to the vaulted courtyard. She put her free hand up to protect her domed hat. "Looks like Buddy's getting ready to dive. He looks kind of nervous."

Richard turned and looked up at the balustrade above the deep end of the pool. "It's acting mostly. It's just a matter of building up the suspense, then hitting the water flat and milking the suckers."

She tugged at his arm. "Come on, let's go root for him."

"You're not going to see much," he said as they crowded into the echoing courtyard. "The place is packed."

Everyone jockeyed for prime positions around the pool. The band in the banquet hall played a fanfare and a drum roll as Buddy climbed onto the stone rail of the balcony and straddled it.

Edith unpinned her hat to get a better view. "Gosh, he looks like a prince up there."

Richard glanced down at her. "He's fancier than an undertaker's funeral. He's putting on quite a show."

"I don't know. He looks nervous to me."

"It's part of the act, I tell you. By gauging the height, he knows he'll come out okay."

The crowd laughed. Buddy swung his other leg over the balustrade, braced himself, and looked out at the columns and the water and the people watching him. The balcony was jammed shoulder-to-shoulder with revelers. Hands dangled over the abyss. Somebody up there started tossing pennies as if to show how far the drop was. Buddy licked his lips a couple of times and took off his jacket. He handed it to Cleveland the cook, who was making a few extra dollars as a waiter. He loosened his white bow tie and unbuttoned his collar.

"The watch!" A sunburned man bellowed through cupped hands from the far end. "The watch!"

"We came here to see a dive, not a striptease!" someone shouted as Buddy unhooked his watch and handed it to Cleveland.

Buddy unlaced his shoes, pulled them off, and handed them to someone behind him. A few helpful hands got him standing up and balanced. He hugged a column, swallowing and looking down at the light-struck pool. The voices trailed off, and suddenly the only sound was shifting water echoing in the vaulted ceiling. With his free hand, he pulled at one of his white suspenders. His stocking feet curled down and gripped the balustrade. He turned slightly, said something to Cleveland, and smiled, wiped his forehead with a white handkerchief that slipped from his fingers and fluttered down to the pool. He crouched, still hugging the column. He perched there, looking out over the shimmering blue water. He glanced up at the dark skylight. He swallowed. He rubbed his hand on the column, got a better grip, and eased his way back into a standing position. His free hand went out for balance. He edged away from the column, now touching it only with his fingertips. He gazed at the upturned faces, nodded, and broke into an angelic smile. He bent his knees, and before anyone quite knew it, he was gone, twisting as he dropped, his arms spread as he fell face forward toward the shining water.

He hit with a slap that threw the laughing and shrieking crowd back from his tidal wave.

Richard straightened his tie and started toward the bar. "Looks like a bull's-eye to me. Wish I could make money that fast and easy. Let's go get a drink before a line forms."

Buddy burst from waist-deep water and held his hands high. The crowd surged forward, cheering and applauding. The band played a celebratory flourish. Then the diver's hands came down. He turned and dropped back under the churn.

A voice came through the confusion of the crowd. "What's he up to now? Diving for those pennies?"

Richard threw off Edith's hand, pushed back through the onlookers, and jumped into the pool. He thrashed through the water and brought Buddy's face up as the laughter gave way to murmuring and then screams. Cleveland went in without taking off his white jacket and helped lift the limp body onto the terrazzo floor.

"Careful," Richard said, "we don't know what's wrong with him."

With the tenderness of a father putting a child to bed, Cleveland straightened Buddy's listless arms. "It was too shallow."

Repeated calls brought Dr. Willis in from the terrace. He came through the circle of onlookers, tossed his cigar away, and dropped to his knees beside Buddy. As the crowd pressed closer and closer, he touched his fingers to Buddy's throat, then to his wrist. He peeled back the dark wet eyelashes, put his ear to the purple ribbon, tore open the collar and shirt and pressed his palms to the unresponsive heart. "Clear these people out of here," he said without emotion. "Where's the telephone? I need to call the coroner."

It dawned on Richard that he was staring into the face of a dead man. He got to his feet and started pushing people away from the body. Cleveland got out in front of him and took a more gentle approach, asking everyone to go home. When they were finished, only two other people remained in the courtyard. Edith continued to stand on the far side of the pool, watching the flashy water wash back and forth over the terrazzo. And on the balcony above the deep end of the pool, Cappy Kincaid stood smoking a cigar as he ran a hand over the column that Buddy had clasped as he gazed down at the crowd.

Without lifting his eyes from the water, he spoke to Richard.

"If you're here to collect for him or anything else, come back in a couple of days."

He threw his cigar into the pool, turned, and walked into his den, closing the door behind him.

The news swept through town like a thunderstorm. Rex dreamed again of the tree in the pasture and woke up sweating despite the raw air pouring through the open window. He saw himself riding slowly down the deserted road, Lucy's white mane flowing like breath in winter. He thought for a moment of getting up and banishing his fear with the radio. But the cold kept him in bed, and the thought of that mysterious boat, the *Cristobel,* was in itself something dreadful. So he settled more deeply under the quilt, a darkness of his own choosing, and worked over in his mind what he had to do regain control of his life. He lay in the darkness, listening to the wind in the pine trees, hoping that Jim would come padding down the hall to suggest a conversation about the most mundane of daytime things or even to speculate about the strange goings-on in the Gulf. But the only sounds in the house were the hissing radiator and the rhythmic tapping of the screen outside the kitchen door. At night the familiar sounds became sinister, and not even the quilt could keep them out. He felt the beating of his heart and thought about poor Buddy Cole, suddenly dead amid the life and glitter of the New Year's Eve party. He wondered if Buddy would be buried in the tux and tails and purple ribbon proclaiming a Happy New Year. He wondered if Buddy, gliding down dark streets at night, now knew the secret of the corpses wired to the tree.

He felt his willpower losing the upper hand in an arm-twisting with his fear, and he knew that he'd be shivering here night after night in the deadened house unless he met his fear head-on and wrestled it to the ground.

He remained paralyzed and alert, heard the front room clock strike one and two in hollow brassy tones, knew that the first gray rays of dawn would show that he had lost his match with fear. As much as he dreaded the cold and the terror, he dreaded more the thought of losing his self-respect and freedom. He threw back the quilt, dressed, passed down creaky stairs and over groaning floors, opened the tapping screen door, and, pulling on his grandfather's overcoat, fluttered into the night.

He kept to the middle of the shrouded street to avoid setting off the neighborhood dogs, stopped, and clung to a magnolia as a milk truck clattered over the tracks on West Main Street. In the looming shadow of the silver-shingled courthouse, he walked north past vacant stores and silent churches, past the massive sandstone Masonic Hall and grand turreted houses on wooded lots, until he came to the paddock where Lucy dozed on locked legs. He squeezed through the barbed wire, took the makeshift bridle from a bait bucket, and buckled it around Lucy's neck before she had quite come to her senses. He pushed open the old shambles of a gate and climbed onto the horse's sagging back.

She was not one for disciplined night travel. She was not above jumping the fence and roaming on her own at night, but bending to the will of a nightrider was a novelty, and he had to kick at her with pointed heels before she would take her first faltering steps. Getting her as far as the path was like walking through tar. It was as if she were in league with the forces he had come to fight, but finally she began to put one heavy hoof after the other, and she settled into a grudging rhythm on the margin of the road.

After a hundred yards, railroad tracks came in from the east, and he left the seamed pavement to follow their silver sheen due north and then in a slow curve toward the west. His continued his forced ride over the crossties and through pine scrub and palmetto, feeling heavier and heavier as he approached the place where the road and the tracks came together again. And just beyond it, sooner than he expected, were the rough white ruts that ran from the road to the gate. He wanted to make this ride different from the other, different enough to make it his own doing rather than the accident the first ride had been, and so he remained mounted when he lifted the chain loop from the gate, and he worked the horse with his knees to keep her clear of it as he reached low and pulled hard.

He nudged her through the gap and guided her past the place where he had dismounted before, kept her going down the slope until they were in almost total darkness. She refused to go farther. She threw her head and tried to turn around, tried to leave the path and bolt for the road, but he held her fast with the belted reins. Then the leather gave way and she jerked her nose forward, wheeled, and threw him. He thrashed in the blackberry bushes, got to his feet and watched her trot toward the gate. When he looked back around, he was staring into the darkness. Only the vaguest outlines of pasture and woods and the dim huddled forms of cattle showed just beyond the fence. He followed the slope down, smelling the frost in the air, until he saw the broad black outline of the tree, its twisted branches dropping low, as if to scoop a furrow in the hardening ground.

His steps shortened as he approached it, but suddenly he was where he had been when he had seen the swollen dead. He stayed there, feeling the faint sounds of the night— movement in the blackberry thicket, distant beating wings. He wasn't the boy that had come here at the end of summer. He was a lifetime beyond that boy, but he had not yet freed himself from the fear that had bound him to this place and that past life.

He stepped forward, close enough to distinguish the deep grooves in the bark, the dug-up bullet holes and dark stains. He stretched his fingers toward the form but found himself a foot shy of the mark. With his hand still extended, he took a short step and another, stretched his fingertips and planted them on the tree. He patted and petted it, ran his fingertips through the rough grooves, wrapped his arm around the trunk, pressed his face against the cold bark and kissed it.

(HAPTER 35

M avis declared that they had been going about it all wrong. She cited an article in the Sunday supplement that, as she put it, dropped the scales from her eyes.

"I never did like that expression," Ainsley said. "It's kind of ludicrous when you think about it."

With unusual determination, Mavis persisted. "We don't need a medium. We need an *empath*."

"Oh, for God's sake," Ainsley drawled, "who writes that stuff—and how much do they get paid?"

Mavis tapped a spoon on the table to shush everybody. "You see, an empath is a person who can feel what others are feeling—or have felt—even after they're dead—and can speak for them."

"Sounds kind of crowded to me," Ainsley said. "It would be like hearing everything that everybody's ever said. I mean, blah, blah, blah."

They were sitting at the round table in front of the fireplace. Mavis laid the spoon down. "Now, darlings, please. Let's just think about this for a minute. The talent in the Leary family is not for something so common as dabbling with a Ouija board. You know how they say Joan's mother foresaw the yellow fever epidemic of 1888? She had a fever dream."

"Because she'd been eating the wrong kind of mushrooms," Ainsley said. "She wasn't called Mad Mary for nothing."

"Never mind that. The point is that she *felt* what was going to happen. She felt the—the psychic energy in the air."

"She was nuts, too," Flora said. "That probably helped."

Mavis appealed to Rachel, who had been sitting quietly the whole time. "You see what I'm getting at, don't you? It was the *emotion* that Joan's mother was reading."

"Well, the thing I don't get," Rachel said, "is how she could read the emotion before it happened."

"Don't you see, child? There's this thing called the—the collective spirit that senses things before they happen—and that's what Joan's mother was feeling. Now, as I was saying, if Joan's mother could feel the emotion in events *before* they happened, how much easier must it be for Joan to read them *afterward*?"

The fire had baked Ainsley on one side and left her cold on the other. She turned her chair around even though she had to look at Mavis over her shoulder.

"I still don't get it. Isn't that what we've been trying to do all along?"

The fire popped, startling Mavis. She shifted to the other side of Flora. "Yes, of course, but we haven't been doing it in the right *place*. Don't you see, it's the *place* that's connected with the emotion and it's the emotion that brings out the spirit voice? Your best chance of finding Valentino wouldn't be *here*. It would be in his mansion or on the set of *The Sheik*."

Flora looked at her with raised brows. "Are you saying we're supposed to go out to that pasture to, what, commune with the spirits?"

Ainsley laughed. "You mean, like joining hands and dancing around the Maypole?"

"I'd leave that to Joan," Flora said.

"Or is it more like a dowsing rod," Ainsley said. "Joan walks around in the pasture and, as soon as she finds a spirit, her head jerks down."

"You laugh if you want," Mavis told them, her voice going shrill above the merriment, "but as surely as those two people had spirits, those spirits have things to tell us from the other side. I suggest that we start with a session in the parlor just to get acquainted, you know, to take the edge off."

"With the spirits or with Joan?" Flora asked. "Which has more of an edge?"

"I sort of wish we had stuck with playing bridge," Ainsley said. "This is getting to be a little strange, even for me. I mean, a field trip—with Crazy Joan?"

Mavis spoke slowly to get her voice back. "Well, now, as a journalist, shouldn't you be more open-minded? I mean, haven't we been saying all along there could be a story in this, a big story, of a murder case solved from beyond the grave?"

"Oh dear." Ainsley dropped her hand to the table. "I suppose so. But I've got my doubts about the advisability of a bunch of women visiting a murder scene in the dark. You just might run into some spirits from *this* world."

"I'd take along a man or two," Rachel said.

Mavis winced. "Which men did you have in mind? Can you picture Mr. J.J. Ward attending such an outing? He'd have us all committed!" She turned to Flora. "And Pom—he'd be cracking jokes the whole time."

Flora turned sideways to the table and studied a mended popcorn chain askew on the off-kilter Christmas tree. "Well, you can count me out regardless. It was one thing when we were playing parlor games. This is something else."

"Jim would be good," Rachel said. "He can sure take on anything out there. You should've seen the way he beat up Theron the other night, right here in—"

Flora cut her off. "That's not the kind of thing a lady should talk about."

The tawdry incident distracted Mavis from her spiritual schemes. She asked if Theron had been charged with anything.

"Poaching," Flora said, "but that was just for starters. We still don't know exactly what the fight was all about. We heard Pom say something about a Studebaker, but he won't tell us what he meant. Whatever it was, though, for once he was dead serious."

"I can't wait to see him," Mavis gushed. "I want to hear the whole story."

Flora put her chin in her hand. "Knowing Charles, you might wait a long time."

J.J. Ward was always uneasy when Mavis had the car. At his mother's house she had knocked out several yards of picket fence with it, and on a rainy afternoon she had swerved into the steep bank of the Sweetwater Branch, where three men and a mule had worked for hours to get the car out of the mud. The bumper never had been the same. He figured she was safe enough on the short drive to the Holliman house, but once she had gone, he started to get edgy and irritable. So on this night, as she was off for cards or one of her fool table-tipping sessions, he couldn't concentrate on the account books, and they were bad anyway. He slapped the warped ledger shut and went into the front yard for a smoke.

Part of his restlessness came from a phone call of the night before. Kincaid had told him to come over and fill in the fatal swimming pool. "The wife and I are leaving for Europe tomorrow and when I get back I want to see a terrazzo courtyard where that pool is, smooth and pretty enough for dancing. You've got four weeks. That ought to be enough, especially since there's some money in it. As for that house in Palm Terrace, I don't like the way it's going up. If you expect me to buy in Palm Terrace, pull the damn thing down. I'll talk to my own architect when I get back. Got that?"

J.J. was on his second cigar when he saw a familiar figure shuffling up the hill and out of the sunset. He had known Joan Leary all his life. Although she walked hunched like a brittle spinster, she was only a year older than he was. They had attended high school together. The other kids used to make fun of her because she seemed to live in a world of her own, nodding and humming to herself at the back of the classroom, regardless of what everyone else was doing. She smelled bad. She had a habit of sucking on her middle fingers and, when her peers teased her on the street, she would pull her fingers from her lips and shake them as if sprinkling her hecklers with some kind of unholy water. Now that she was fifty-three years old, she had outgrown some of her quirks, but she had taken on others. Day in and day out, she carried that coat over her arm, on the hottest day of summer and the coldest of winter. No one had ever seen her wear it. It was always riding on her arm as if she were about to get into a knife fight, and although her conversation was often unintelligible, she liked to startle unsuspecting pedestrians by asking completely baffling questions through her small under-developed teeth. Sometimes, on a bet, boys would rush up to her and ask nonsense questions of their own and then run away laughing. Sometimes, on a dare, smaller boys would run up to her and touch her in a one-sided game of tag. It was a mark of sophistication among adults not to cross the street when she approached and a manifestation of great worldliness to commune with her as if she were more or less normal. Apparently the upcoming séance in the Holliman parlor would be the only time in living memory that she had been invited into someone's house.

As he smoked his cigar and watched Joan work her way up the hill, J.J. was feeling feisty, feeling like stirring things up a little, so as she approached his house, he hailed her cheerfully.

"How you doing tonight, Joan? How are things at the store?"

She was shaking her head and mumbling.

There was a legend that just down the road, at the lightning oak, Flora's mother and Aunt Caroline, then teenagers on horseback, had encountered Joan's mother, Mad Mary, and had ridden off in terror. Old-timers said that the experience had inspired Caroline to become a great actress before she, too, went a little loopy.

Was Joan's family madness contagious?

There was a recurring story that Joan was the unacknowledged daughter of the late John Howard.

J.J. was in no mood for such speculations. He hailed her again.

"Where you been, Joan? I thought you were over tipping tables at the Hollimans."

This time she looked up. She stopped in the middle of the road, stared at him, and then started shuffling toward him.

He found himself puffing a little hard on the cigar. He let out a long, relaxing stream of smoke and stood his ground. After all, there was nothing she could do to him. Even though it was only a hundred yards down the road, he hadn't been in the musty old store for years, but he knew that it was a very ordinary rundown place and no witches' den, and yet he was surprised when he got a close look at Joan. The sun had browned her face, had made the skin thin and wrinkled like a spoiled apple, but her gaze was that of a much younger woman. It was as if her face were falling to ruins around those two stony eyes.

"I seen a man and a woman," she said. It was an ordinary statement but she gave it extraordinary significance. "I seen 'em wired to a tree."

The cigar tasted sour in his mouth. J.J. held it between two fingers and watched the spark languish. "Hell, Joan, that's old news. We've put that behind us by now."

She gave no indication that she had heard him. She raised a sinewy hand to the sky. "There was a tree, a tree and a creek and a pond and the bones of a house."

He put the cigar back in his mouth for a moment, hoping to get it going again. "It didn't happen quite that way, but as I recall, you never were worth a hoot at geography. There's no creek out by Pom's pasture. Must be you're thinking of the railroad track. And there isn't a pond or a house either one. You've been getting bad information from the haunts."

Her hand came down from the sky and she went scraping down the road toward the store, sputtering and shaking her head as if she were arguing with some unseen companion.

"It's those damn mushrooms," J.J. said to the empty air.

Later that night his misgivings about the car were confirmed when Flora brought Mavis home. J.J. came into the driveway to hear the bad news about the Chevrolet.

"Charles is looking at it now," Flora said. "That dogwood on the corner was okay in the horse and buggy days, but the Poinsetts really should have taken it down twenty years ago."

Mavis gathered her fox fur boa around her neck to avoid getting it caught in the car door. "Honestly, J.J., I think that car pulls to the right."

"I don't doubt that it does now," he said. "Is it out of the street, Flora?"

"Charles and Jim and Trent pushed it onto the boulevard. Charles thought maybe he could get the kinks out in the morning."

J.J looked down the street. "He doesn't need to do that. I'll be by first thing."

"We can send the horse over in the meantime," Flora said.

J.J. took her seriously. "No need for that either. Just tell Pom I'll be over in the morning."

Later that night, after his parents had gone to bed, Richard stubbed out his cigarette and decided that he had pushed his luck far enough. His leg was still plenty sore, but he could drive if he didn't have to change gears too often. And anyway, Deardra was damn fine behind the wheel of a car. She wouldn't say just what they were, but she had made some kind of arrangements for Porter's Place. Apparently the collector and the men from Baldwin had scared her enough that she was willing to drop the place and go. Kincaid was nowhere to be found. They were two days into the new year, five days late, and the collector could turn up at any minute. The time was ripe. It would be safest just to hit the road, not even tell his parents where he was going. Just call them after things had cooled down.

He was putting his belongings into the backseat of the Packard when something white seemed to float through the darkness of the woods across the road. He watched the spectral thing for a moment, but it disappeared back among the oaks before he could identify it.

He drove to Porter's Place, went around back, and rapped on the lacquered window.

"Usually I don't mind being fashionably late," Deardra said when she had let him in, but don't you think we should be on time just this once?"

He looked at the dowdy black dress hanging on the wall. You leaving that here?"

She smiled. "As a welcoming gift for the new tenants. I'm sure it'll suit one of them."

"You still okay with going back to New Orleans?"

"Sure, but wouldn't Miami be faster?"

"Well, it's a little hot down there."

"Suit yourself."

"The boat to Calais?"

"Yeah. The slow one."

"Fast car, slow boat. I like it." He hesitated. "Mind one stop on the way out? I thought I'd take leave of the folks. Not let on, you know, just say *so long.*"

When they got to the house, he kissed her and got out of the car. "Don't get lonesome without me now."

"You won't take all night?" She sounded almost childlike. She climbed out of the car and followed him up the walkway.

"I'll take the back door," he whispered. "It's quicker."

When they rounded the corner of the house, they bumped into the man with the scar. Thrust forward in his bony fist was a Luger.

"*Jesus.*" Richard glanced past the azaleas in the side yard and saw the red Duesenberg parked by the road. He tried to cover his surprise with a quick smile. "You guys are quiet."

The big man came out of the shadows. "Sometimes death is, Rich, like a thief in the night."

"Don't be sore, Archie. I got taken, same as you. He put his hand to his breast pocket. "I was on my way to find you just now, to give you your money back."

The big man rifled through Richard's pocket and jerked out the envelope. He motioned toward the Packard. "So where's the real suitcase? Were you stupid enough to try and sell it to some-body else?"

"Look, Archie—"

The big man slammed Richard's head against the white brick wall. "Let's get going. It's time to finish the game. Ralph's going with you two, I'll follow along and we'll get this deal done once and for all."

Ralph nudged Richard and Deardra with the Luger as they walked toward the Packard. "So, Rich, when I get to know somebody, there's something I get curious about. You want to know what it is?"

"Sure, tell us what you get curious about."

He tapped Richard on the back of the neck. "Tell you when we get there. How about that? You make us wait, we make you wait."

As they left, Richard looked over his shoulder for some sign of life in the house and saw only black windows.

From the dark upstairs bedroom, J.J. watched the strange procession as it left the yard. The mishap with the car had made Mavis take more than her usual quota of sleeping pills with a chaser of sherry, and she was down like a sinker. She had never heard a thing.

He went to the gun cabinet and found it locked. For the first time in years, the key was nowhere to be seen. He hadn't been able to find anything since Mavis had fired Amelia and taken on the housecleaning herself. His faithful Winchester and his father's ancient Colt rifle were in there. So were his Enfield and the shotgun and the handguns. He was about to give Mavis a good shaking when he remembered the .22 standing in the closet. He stuffed himself into his britches, pulled up his suspenders, grabbed the rifle and a box of cartridges, and hurried outside before he realized that the Chevrolet was gone. He ran around to the backyard and saw in the distance the lights of two automobiles heading north, Richard's Packard and some other car. He had no idea what he was going to do. Then he saw the white apparition. As he stared into the woods, the cloud took the form of a horse. It plodded toward him, crossed the side road, and meandered up to the azaleas.

"Come here girl, come on, Lucy." He lowered the .22 and coaxed her with the cartridge box as if it were a large lump of sugar. She stood where she was, arching her neck and waiting for him to come to her. He stepped carefully and held the box toward her. She moved her nose toward it a bit, but lost interest and turned her head away. He came toward her a step, two steps, and caught the halter at her cheek, then the remaining belt of the bridle. She began to pull away. He steadied her, grabbed a handful of her mane, led her to the stone bench, and vaulted onto her sagging back. She flinched but stood still as he caught his breath. He stuffed the cartridge box into his coat pocket, guided her with his free hand, and gave her a quick double kick that left no room for resistance. For the first time in a quarter century, he had a horse under him and a rifle in his hand, and he was ready to go to war.

CHAPTER 36

Richard was bumping down the dirt road to the pond with Deardra beside him and Ralph in the backseat of the Packard with their luggage, covering them with the Luger. He turned just enough to be heard.

"So did you kill somebody fair and square for that gun or did you steal it?"

"You don't care about that," Ralph said, tapping the back of Richard's neck with the mouth of the Luger. "In fact, after to-night, you don't care about much of anything."

Deardra made a point of not looking at him. She was watching Richard. "What's he talking about?"

"With Ralph it's usually hard to tell."

The Luger came forward and glinted in the pale blue light. The sharp, minty smell of schnapps preceded his words. "Where's the real stuff, Richard, the stuff the guys on the *Cristobel* gave you?"

"It's in a safe place, ready for you to pick up."

The Luger poked into his neck again. "We'll get the real story out of you in a minute."

The wet road spattered the car as they rounded the sinkhole pond dark in the shadows of arching oaks. Behind them the big man followed in the red Duesenberg. Ahead, the skeleton house was faint against the trees and sky.

"Looks like this is it," Ralph said. "Dead end road, ain't it? Everybody out."

He had Richard leave the headlamps on. Their twin gleam showed fragments of trees, the husk of the house, a leaf-strewn yard. Richard and Deardra walked in the general direction of the doomed dwelling with Ralph jabbing his weapon at them. The big man followed.

Deardra drew closer to Richard. "That gun's a Luger, isn't it, same as the one that killed those two people in September?"

"You ought to see the guy I got it from," Ralph said. "You think I'm a mess."

"A war hero," the big man said.

"Just take it easy and everything'll be okay," Richard told her.

"Oh, sure."

"Okay, hold it there," the big man said.

Richard and Deardra stopped and turned around. The big man was a stone's throw away, counting the money in the envelope. "Did you really think you were going to get away with it?"

"I tell you, I was on my way to pick up the real stuff," Richard said. "The guys on the *Cristobel* were putting one over on you."

The big man snatched up a green pinecone and popped him in the face with it.

When he came to his senses, Richard blinked and smiled. "Hell of a throw, and now I know where I've seen you. Eight, ten years ago. Homecoming. Fleming Field. I sneaked a seat on the forty-yard line and got a good look at the game. You sacked our quarterback."

Archie tugged at his cuffs. "He was a pushover."

"The guy was flat on his back and you—"

The big man was grinding his teeth. "He was disrespectful, just like you. Rich. He paid."

"You stuck your thumbs in his gullet. You damn near strangled the guy blue before they pulled you off. After that stunt, your team dropped you like a turd, didn't they? I hear the damn bus left without you."

Archie rubbed his jaw and yawned. "We won that game. Now let's talk about you. You tried to sucker us. That was disrespectful. That was disloyal. It's time to pay."

Ralph came up behind him. "We got the money back. We got no time for games. We're going to get out of here. Now get in the car. Hop to it."

The big man stayed put. "Ralph, why don't you get some wire?"

Richard put on a smile. "Tell you what. Keep the money and I'll tell you where the real stuff is, free of charge."

Ralph's hand twisted on the Luger. "The hell you want wire for, Archie? Get in the damn car."

"Well, Ralph, do you think the Wallers *glued* themselves to that tree? While you were sleeping off that bender in Jacksonville, Theron and I were down here tending to business."

The Luger jerked wide. "*You* knocked off the Wallers? What the hell for?"

"Lack of respect, Ralph. And lack of loyalty. They were going to betray us."

Ralph didn't know where to point the gun. "You've really gone over the edge now. I tell you, this time when the feds come after you, boy, you're on your own."

The big man smiled. "But they won't come after me. It was your Luger that killed the Wallers. That very gun you're holding, that now has your prints all over it. Theron and I borrowed it while you were in blissful repose. The Wallers became very respectful."

Ralph jabbed his breastbone with a hooked forefinger. "Since *I'm* the boss, how about showing *me* some stinking respect and getting in the goddam car?"

The big man pulled a .38 and pointed it at Ralph's chest. "There's a new boss. Now give me the Luger and go get some wire."

Ralph backed away, stooped, and laid the Luger on the ground like an offering. "Okay. You want to shoot 'em, go ahead. Shoot 'em. You got my permission. But skip the frills and let's get out of here."

"Not yet. I want a warning to others who think about crossing me. Now, go get some wire."

Ralph tugged at the knot of his silk tie. "This tears it, Archie. This time I'm telling the old man."

"Go ahead, if you live long enough. But with four people killed by your gun and nothing to show for it, don't you suppose Ralph Senior will finally wash his hands of you? After enough screw-ups, brains trumps blood, don't you think? Now get the wire."

"Okay, okay. We'll get this figured out later." Ralph turned and, with a backward glance, scuffed through the leaves to the lip of the slope overlooking the creek. He found a roll of rusty barbed wire hanging from a tree where the house builders had cut away the old cattle fence. He took his time bending it free.

"I thought you were in a hurry," Archie said. With the .38 he gestured toward a large oak. "Over there, kids. And keep calm. I don't want any screaming and squirting this time."

Richard backed toward the tree, stumbling when he bumped into Deardra. "You guys would have to be crazy to give up a load like that when it's practically next door waiting for you. Just let us out of here and it's yours."

Archie watched Ralph pull at a piece of wire long enough to circle the thick oak tree and a couple of bodies. "Richard my friend, you've strung me out so long that now I'm ready to string *you* out, with the mademoiselle thrown in for free. To hell with your salt. At least we have most of the money back." He watched Ralph come toward them with the barbed wire. "So now do us all a favor. Shut up and take what you've got coming."

Settling into the new pecking order, Ralph herded them against the trunk of the tree and rubbed the back of his hand against Deardra's cheek. "So, now you want to know what I get curious about, when I get to know somebody? I get real curious about what they look like dead. And, girlie, I'm looking forward to seeing a lot more of you."

"I don't suppose you have a cigarette," she said to the big man.

He shrugged. "You wouldn't have time to smoke it."

Ralph wrapped one end of the barbed wire around Deardra's arm. He pulled it tight and began binding her and Richard to the tree. The wire cut through her black silk dress and across Richard's white Arrow shirt and blue blazer. For the next circuit Ralph passed the wire across Deardra's breasts and up to Richard's throat.

Archie pulled a handkerchief from his coat pocket and blew his nose. "You probably won't need gags. You strike me as a quiet couple."

Ralph looked at his handiwork. "Not as quiet as they're gonna be. Let's put her in the backseat after."

"Let's not, Ralph. Maybe you'd like to have her mailed to you. You with me now?"

Ralph stroked his salmon pink tie, over and over. "Sure, count me in, Archie. Your call."

The big man told him to put some extra twists in the back to make the binding more secure. Then he came around to the front of the tree.

"Well, Richard, we have arrived. You think there's an afterlife?"

Richard was gazing out across the leaf-strewn lot, past the shell of a house to the rough sand road beyond. The Packard was on the grass as if parked for a moment's errand. "Those two you laid out back in September, they've sure had an afterlife. They've been the talk of this town ever since."

Archie was so close now that Richard could smell salami on his breath. "Yeah. And they're going to fry the wrong man for doing it."

"Sure," Richard said. "It ought to be your name in the papers, the star of the gridiron."

The big man wiped his hands on Richard's coat sleeve. "Not me. I didn't kill them. Theron did. But I told him to. Thank me now because I'm going to tell Ralph to shoot you from just a few yards away. He's probably a miserable shot, you know, because he isn't really a war hero. In fact, I doubt if he's ever fired a shot at a person." He turned toward Ralph. "Have you?"

"You kidding?" Ralph threw out his hands. "I was in the war for God's sake."

Archie came up to him until the .38 was aimed point blank at the center of the salmon pink tie. "So you say, over and over, but you didn't really get your scar in hand-to-hand combat with a Hun, did you? More likely a piece of garbage hit you while you were whimpering in a trench, because you're a coward. You like to see things dead, but you don't have the guts to *make* them dead." The big man's eyes lit up. "Well, rejoice. Here's your chance to show your bravado."

Despite the cold, Ralph was sweating. "You've really lost it this time, Arch."

The big man moved behind him and punched the .38 into his back. "Pick up your Luger and shoot them, Ralph, or *I'll* shoot *you*. Hop to it now."

CHAPTER 37

Ralph brought the Luger up and shook it in the general direction of the tree.

"Do us all a favor," Archie said. "Shoot straight. It took Theron a whole clip to settle the Wallers down. Maybe you should stand even closer."

Ralph raised the Luger, steadied it, and fired.

Richard heard the bullet thud into something. He turned his head as best he could. "Deardra?"

She let out a breath. "Present."

"Next stop, New Orleans," he said. "Car's all ready to go."

"Oh, sure. Let's go."

"You're not trying," Archie said. "C'mon, Ralph, give it your best shot."

"When I kill 'em, then what? You going to shoot me, Archie?"

With a twitchy hand, Ralph took a second shot that whistled past Deardra's ear.

"Won't have to. I'll just drive away with a carload of money and leave you here with two stiffs. Who knows? If they catch you, maybe I'll find a way to collect the five-hundred-dollar reward. In absentia, of course."

Richard laughed. "There was no other Richard."

Deardra let out another breath. "Don't fall apart on me now. If I'm going, I want to go smart."

He laughed again. "The collector. He made up the whole damn story. There wasn't any garden, no roses."

"Why don't you just move in closer, Ralph?" Archie spoke with the casual courtesy of a golf instructor.

A shot barked as it hit barbed wire.

Deardra flinched and let out a breath. "He really is a lousy shot, isn't he?"

Richard's voice went high and thin. "If he uses up the clip, we should get a turn."

A tear ran down Deardra's cheek. "Oh, damn."

"We'll hit the road tonight, leave everything behind and not stop till we're on the boat to—where is it?"

She sniffed. "Calais."

Ralph came a few steps closer, moved his head from side to side for a better fix on his targets, raised the Luger again and fired.

Richard felt Deardra stiffen.

He tried to turn toward her, but couldn't. "The open road. Anyplace you want to go."

After too long a silence, he heard his own words, as if from far away.

"What do you say?"

That silence again. And then a voice, calm and low. "Can we go now?"

"You bet," he said, strangely happy. "Ready?"

He felt a rushing in his ears and the next shot sounded distant. He waited with his eyes shut, a good long time, listening for a sigh, a whimper, a breath cut short. He looked in time to see the marksman shake his head, apparently disgusted at having missed again. But instead of raising the Luger for the next try, Ralph let off a wild round and pitched face down onto the ground.

Archie disappeared.

Richard strained at the wire, trying to make sense of what had happened, trying to get free before Ralph got back up. Squinting past the fallen shooter, he thought he saw a white cloud moving among the trees across the road. He ached to rub his eyes for a better look.

The cloud took the form of a horse and vanished.

From the woods across the road, a shot flashed.

J.J. wedged himself against the grid of what would have been the living room wall, pushed another cartridge into the .22, and rammed the bolt home. A shot went through the window hole beside him and skipped through the timbers. Whatever handgun the other man was shooting carried at least six rounds. The .22 was powerful and more accurate at a distance, but carried only one small bullet at a time.

A second shot flipped a two-by-four propped against the stud beside him, and it clattered to the unfinished floor. J.J. thought back to his long-dead friend Jeremy and what it must have been like for him in the battle at San Juan Hill, with the bullets chopping through the brush. He had always envied Jeremy that adventure, the test of courage, had tried to enlist in the army with him at Port Tampa, but had been turned away because of his missing fingers. He had long since learned to shoot game with his maimed hand, but he also knew what it felt like to get shot, which made him all the more gun shy when the game was shooting back.

Running from tree to tree, the man came toward the house shooting. He was going to reduce the range and flush J.J. out with multiple shots before J.J. could reload. Crouching, J.J. ran deeper into the house and took up a position to the side of another window hole. The man stopped behind a stump and dropped to the ground. Three fast shots splintered the window frame, forcing J.J. back through open walls at the rear of the house. He stopped behind the row of wheelbarrows in what was to be the backyard and perched, winded and scared, trying to keep his hands steady.

He shot at a moving shadow, which gave away his position and, an instant later, two shots grazed a wheelbarrow, just inches from his face. He pulled back, stumbling over a loose board, and a third bullet skipped across the lip of a wheelbarrow an inch from his face. Breathless and fumbling with the box of cartridges, he reloaded. The man had stopped to take aim or reload, but now he was on the advance again. J.J. steadied the .22, fired at the gun flashes, reloaded, and listened over the sound of his pulse and breath.

Had the man run out of ammunition? J.J. moved along the line of wheelbarrows and back into the house. From a window frame, he looked into the darkness in time to see a shape rise up from the ground, a strange form with a jutting arm.

J.J. sat back, leaning against a skeletal wall, listening, jerking the rifle toward one open end of the house, then the other. He leaned toward the window hole to get a better look into the yard. His ears tightened as he tried to pick a noise out of the stillness.

The window frame exploded as something like a bear burst through it, throwing J.J. back so fast that he dropped the .22 and threw his hands against the studs to keep from going over. The thing in the man's hand came at him, a hatchet, in a vicious downward chop, and the blade bit into a timber where J.J.'s missing fingers would've been. The big man, thinking he had hit flesh and bone, was startled and confused for an instant

when J.J.'s hand came at him unbloodied, yet regained his senses quickly enough to rip the hatchet free. But J.J. was on his
feet now, gripping the barrel of the .22, and he brought the butt
down on the big man's hand. With a growl, the bear came down
on him, hatchet in hand, and, trying to keep him at bay, J.J.
raised the rifle as the big man lunged.

The .22 went off, and the man, creased in the cheek, came
down at him screaming, his face spattered red, as the flared
blade flashed at J.J.'s throat. A jab with the rifle barrel brought
the attacker down, but a hard punch to the ear knocked the .22
out of J.J.'s hands, and the big man grabbed the rifle, raised it
by the barrel, and swung. In the sweep of his fingers as he tried
to pull himself off the floor, J.J. felt his left hand close over the
hatchet. He heaved it so hard that he fell over backwards and hit
his head on the cement floor.

He tried to get up and fight through the ringing in his ears,
but before he could lift his shoulders, the rifle banged his chin
and Archie Packer collapsed on top of him.

A drop of sweat from the dead man stung J.J. in the eye. He
pushed the body off and got to his knees. When he had caught his
breath, he wiped his face on his coat sleeve and let his gaze drift
to the slop oozing from the side of the corpse's head. He stood on
unsteady legs and waited for the dead man's jaw to stop quivering.

Muttering meaningless words, he made his way out of the
house. He halted long enough to take a breath and pull his
thoughts together. Then he went to the tree and started untwist-
ing the wire.

Richard coughed and put a hand to a cut the barbs had made
in his throat. "It was just the two of them. What do you suppose
we ought to do now?"

J.J. finished unwrapping the wire. "You ought to leave town
tonight and not come back for a good long time."

"There's a considerable chunk of cash in their car. Someone
ought to do some good with it."

"Go on now. Get going before somebody else comes down that road looking for them—or you. But they're not going to find anybody and neither is Avery. As for your mama and me, we don't know where you've gone. You were always taking off. Now go on and do what you've got to do so I can get to work."

Richard warmed to the idea. He kissed Deardra on the cheek and put his arm around her. "Ready to go?" He gestured toward the Packard. "The road starts right there."

She swept a strand of hair from her mouth. In the half-light her eyes looked black. Her breathing was rough.

He brushed off his lapels. "If we leave now we—"

She put a slender finger to his lips.

"No, Richard."

He kissed her finger, pulled it away, held it. "Nothing has to change."

Her smile was sad. "Richard, you're a sweet boy and I love you to death, but right now I just want to be that woman in the frowsy dress, sitting on the bed drinking a warm beer in some crummy little hotel room, and I don't think I'd ever have that with you. You're so damn good-looking and hardheaded you're bound to get any girl in trouble. So you just run along and I'll wish you all the best." She placed a trembling hand on his shoulder and kissed him on the cheek.

He smiled. "It sure was fun."

"It all happened way too fast."

He walked over to Ralph and poked the body with the toe of his wingtip. He nudged the Luger out of the leaves. Then he turned to his father.

"You ought to give Amelia her job back, if she wants it. She may be a snoop, but she didn't steal that silver."

"Go on now," J.J. said. "Go on while you can. Don't waste a second."

Richard looked at the dead man on the ground and the red Duesenberg at the edge of the yard. "What about all this?"

J.J. put a hand on his shoulder. "Your mama and I have been cleaning up after you ever since the morning you were born. I don't see why tonight should be any different." He put out his hand. "Good luck to you, son. Godspeed."

Richard limped over to the Packard, pulled out Deardra's trunk, and started the engine. "There's one more thing I wish you'd do. Would you say good-bye to Gramma for me?"

"What will you do?" Deardra asked when Richard had driven away.

J.J. spoke as if listing the routine for the coming day. "I've got some cement to mix. There's a man that wants me to fill in a swimming pool. If I were you, I'd take that Duesenberg over there and drive it to the next depot. Then get on a train. It's faster."

CHAPTER 38

—⌒●⌒—

First thing in the morning on Friday, January 3, 1930, Pom and Trent walked over to the jail.

Avery had already been working on Theron for most of an hour. The two of them were in the front office and seemed to be having a casual conversation, except that Theron was hand-cuffed to a heavy wooden chair.

The sheriff sat at the desk with his black boots resting on an open drawer and one elbow propped on an ancient typewriter "You want to hear it all again? I've got plenty to keep you in while we add more charges—poaching, violating the Volstead Act, driving a stolen automobile, and I suppose I can get you on assault if I talk to Ainsley again. Sooner or later, planting false evidence. So any way you look at it, you're not going anywhere for a while. You'll have plenty of time to talk." He got up from the scarred desk and stood behind the accused. "It's anybody's guess how long you're going to be in here, probably through the duck hunting season, the turkey hunting season, and all the way around to the next deer hunting season at least. You want me to go on? Am I leaving out some critters? The sooner you talk, the happier we'll all be. So let's take it from the top again. Tell me about Mr. Harvey Champeau and the Luger that ended up behind the books in Pom's house."

Even after several days in jail, Theron was bull-headed. He sat with his feet spread and his head high. His tongue bulged in a purple cheek. "What a man says to get out of a fight don't have nothing to do with the way things are. I don't know who you're talking about."

Sheriff Mecum walked back to the desk and lit a cigar. "All right. Let's come back to Mr. Champeau a little later. One more time, what do you know about a couple by the name of Waller who were renting the Cobb farm last summer? Before you answer, I'll remind you that we have two witnesses that place you at the farm repeatedly during the summer and into September."

Theron looked up at him with a crooked smile. "Why, hell, sheriff, I get around all over the place. I've been to a lot of farms."

"Yeah, but on this one they were trafficking booze until they got themselves shot to death in Pom's pasture. They drove a dark green '27 Studebaker—just like the one you painted blue. Where'd you get that car of yours?"

Theron shrugged. "Like I said before a hundred times, from some guy up in Alachua. I didn't get his name."

The sheriff stood up. "I guess I've gotten everything I can out of you."

Theron held back a smile. "I guess you have."

"You've plain outfoxed me."

In victory the prisoner became modest. "Ah, well, I don't know."

The sheriff put a hand on his shoulder. "So now a couple of federal agents would like to talk to you, Thorndike and Lamar. They're real interested in anything to do with liquor." He bent down and looked Theron in the eye. "*They* send men to prison,

Theron, northern prisons. You ever been north of the Mason-Dixon Line? They've got prisons up there big as the Courthouse Square. And they don't bother with chain gangs and work release and amenities like that." He turned an imaginary key. "They just pitch folks in there and let 'em serve their sentence, their whole sentence, making license plates or some damn thing that doesn't require daylight. Of course, they don't have so many poachers up there, mostly just big city nigras and perverts. I imagine they'd lick their chops to see a good old hickory-smoked Southern boy like you. They'd think you were something special, kind of a *delicacy*."

Theron bit his lip. "If that Champeau put the Luger in Pom's house, you ought to go after *him*. I hardly know the man. I'll tell you that much."

Avery slammed a ruler on the desk. "You'll tell me a damn sight more than that. We know that Champeau didn't put the Luger in there. He kept the maid busy while somebody else did. There was a dog across the street barking her head off at him the whole time. Wouldn't take you but a minute and a half to get in and out of there. Now, that in itself isn't so big a crime, but if that Luger really is the murder weapon, you'll have a lot more to answer to. Accessory at least, Old Sparky if you did the shooting. Makes bunking down with the colored boys look pretty good."

Theron's face reddened as he strained at the cuffs. "A good lawyer can get me off."

Avery brought down his cigar and leaned in close. "You got the money for one? Well, of course, there's always the public defender."

The prisoner wagged his head and tugged at his bonds. "I won't go to any northern jail."

"Let's start easy, Theron. Who's Harvey Champeau?"

The prisoner rolled his head till his neck cracked. "He's out of Ybor City."

"How do you know him, from rumrunning?"

"Hell no. He worked at some cigar factory down there. He and some other guys have been coming up here every year to hunt. When they're in town they live pretty high on the company dime. They're always talking about the agitators down there, and when I told 'em there was one up here making time with Ainsley, they knew just who he was. We all wanted to get him. They made a special trip up here to run him out of town. Champeau was a wrestler, said he could make quite a mess of the Red. We caught up with the guy on the Millhopper Road, but Pom's kid got in the way and they botched it. Harvey hated getting beat by a Red, so he decided to get serious. He got a Luger from a dealer down there. Just to frame him up for a few days and scare him off. We figured it would take a week or so for somebody to find it. We couldn't believe our luck when that maid jumped right on it."

The sheriff shoved a chair in front of Theron and sat down. "All right. Now what about the Wallers?"

"I met 'em when they wanted heavy springs in their car. One thing led to another and after awhile I was running some of the stuff up to Baldwin. I spent some free time up there at the farm. Took a shine to the missus, but she treated me like a damn shoeshine boy. They both did. So I decided to put one over on 'em. Just a joke to get even."

The tip of the sheriff's cigar glowed hot as he let the words wash past. "What kind of joke?"

"I told Archie the Wallers were laughing at him, making fun of his bad back."

"Archie? Who's Archie?"

"He's a big guy, but he talks smart. Used to be a college ball player. Got a hell of a temper that he hides most of the time. But when he starts grinding his teeth you'd better—"

"Okay, but who is he, Theron?"

"He and this guy Ralph, they pay the rumrunners who bring the stuff in from the Gulf to the freight yard in Baldwin."

"So you and Archie—"

We caught up with the Wallers just this side of Paradise. They didn't suspect a thing. Thought it was some kind of a deal. Archie pulled the gun on 'em and one of us got the idea of tying 'em up with the wire and just leaving 'em there for a few days. We knew somebody'd come along sooner or later. But once we had 'em wired up, Waller said something to Archie. Something about football sounded like. Whatever it was, it sure set him off. He had his back turned and he spun around and took a shot at him."

"With a Luger."

Theron nodded. He bit his lip. "He swiped it when Ralph was sleeping off a drunk. The guy's hooked on some stinking peppermint liquor."

"Did Archie keep on shooting?"

"A couple more shots I guess." Theron bowed his head. His shoulders twitched.

The sheriff bent down, came in closer. 'There were more shots fired, Theron, a whole clip. What happened?"

"Jesus Christ. They were jumping around like hell on that tree."

"Who finished them off?"

Theron's face twisted. "Archie *made* me do it, held a gun to my back and watched. But, hell, they were done for. You'd put down a horse, wouldn't you? Or a dog. Doesn't a man deserve as much? Or a woman? I couldn't stand it, couldn't stand it. They were done for."

Avery drew back. "And that way, if you got out of hand, this Archie could say it was you that killed the Wallers. He'd have your prints on the Luger."

"There was blood spattering everywhere. He told me to get rid of the car, the Studebaker, and I was running so crazy I was at Lake Santa Fe before I knew it. I even forgot to get out of the damn car before I ditched it. I spent half the night wandering wet till I came to my senses."

The sheriff sat up. "And started thinking about that Studebaker."

"It's a hell of car."

"Why'd you stick around, Theron? Why didn't you take off, disappear?"

The prisoner's face came up. "It was that damn Ainsley. I couldn't get her to come with me." A look of something like pride lit up his face. "And anyway."

"Anyway what?"

"It worked for the fox, didn't it? He ran right through us and we never did find his track."

The sheriff reached around and tapped a long ash from his cigar. "Now tell me where we can find these men Archie and Ralph."

(HAPTER 39

A day later, Pom swayed in the porch swing as he read the story in the newspaper. The January afternoon was warm and the sunlight seemed to be melting the paint right off the clapboard walls of the house on Magnolia Street.

"You want to read about it, Trent?" He glanced over his shoulder to make sure nobody else was within earshot.

"No, you tell me." Trent lounged against the porch rail, listening to a handful of crows fighting over chicken bones in the street. "Just point it at the ear that ain't wrapped up."

"Rex and Jim got their names in the paper. *Informed Sheriff Mecum of mysterious coded signals going to the ship* Cristobel *near Seahorse Reef in the Gulf of Mexico, which subsequently was seized in a joint operation involving federal agents and the Coast Guard.*"

"Probably took all of 'em just to find their way out there," Trent said.

With a slap of his hand, Pom flattened the newspaper. "Apparently there was some argument from the *Cristobel* that the Coast Guard seized them outside of U.S. waters."

Trent shrugged. "Why hell, Pom, you can't trust *anybody*."

"Tracked the signals to a radio setup in a house near Cedar Key. The feds collared the guy who was sending the signals to the boat. Then they tracked the whole thing up to Baldwin and found all that booze hidden in lumber cars, picked up a couple of guys from New York."

"But not the big fella and the one with the scar."

"No. They flat out vanished. Quite the bonfire they had up there at the rail yard. Fourteen thousand quarts. When are you going back to Elsie?"

"As soon as you tell Flora about losing your state job."

"Don't wait for that. I feel like the man dangling from a runaway zeppelin. I've waited too long to let go, but the longer I wait, the harder I'll fall. You get right down to it, I've been lazy."

"Are you kidding? Running all over the state working two jobs is lazy?"

"Yeah, because I did it on the sneak. I could've figured out a way to do it by the rules. And I let everything go around here. I haven't even gotten that dog head out of the icebox."

"Well, won't anybody beat you to that."

"Yeah, and I shouldn't've wedged it in on top of Flora's chocolates. Now here's the part about the murder weapon, a nine millimeter Luger that turned up on Sheriff Mecum's desk, one that was a good match for two of the slugs taken from the deceased in my pasture."

"And a perfect match for the slug in the cow."

With his thumb, Pom thumped his chest. "Why didn't *I* think to look at the cows? *I'm* the damn veterinarian."

"Well, Avery said he got the idea when you told him to question the cows that were out there that night."

"Yeah, but I was *kidding*."

"Who'd've thought it was all connected like that, from the *Cristobel* out there in the Gulf to them bodies in your pasture and the train men in Baldwin?"

Pom put his heel up to stop the swing. "Didn't I keep saying it was like a rice paper plant? You pull on one end—"

"I bet everybody in town wishes they were as smart as you, Pom. That must be why old Mr. Howard made you his executioner."

"The word is *executor*. And I'm not even going to think about where that eighty-three hundred came from, except I don't believe the signature on that will was his. I doubt if I'll ever know who mailed that little bundle to me. What are you going to do with the thousand he left you?"

"Sometimes I think I could spend twice that getting that weasel hole of a farm fixed up, but the fruit flies are over with, and the hog cholera. So it'll get us through the tough spots. I haven't told Elsie and the girls yet for fear it's all a dream."

Pom put the newspaper in his lap and started swaying again. "Don't go spending any of it on firewater now."

"Go jump in a lake, Pom." Trent stood up and scuffed some loose paint off the gray porch floor. "How much did he leave you? You're the one that took him in."

"Well, the note's kinda vague as to just who's supposed to get what. And anyway, cash just slips through my fingers. It's probably just as well that I work mostly in trade."

"He left it all up to you, didn't he? Ain't you even taking a cut?"

"You ever heard of something called a conflict of interest?"

"All right, if you're going to be that way."

Pom folded back the newspaper and smoothed it. "Sounds like the federal men did it up brown in the Porters Quarters the other night. Came busting through there with their guns drawn and their axes raised and tore up the whole warehouse on the way in." He sat back in the swing. "Avery told the feds he'd look into it, but they wouldn't wait, just went charging right in."

Trent stopped scraping paint. "Smashed the place up and flushed out a whole congregation of Baptists."

Pom bit back a smile. "Must've spiced up the old prayer meeting." He swung forward and propped his feet on the porch rail, an uncomfortable luxury. "I haven't seen Deardra for a few days now."

"Not her and not Richard either one. What do you suppose?"

Pom watched a brush salesman thread his way through the yard across the street, setting off one dog after another. "You know who else I haven't seen for a while—that blonde girl that Richard was scooting around with."

Trent stopped his scuffing again. "Her dad was working on his hooch recipes right there at the college, you know."

"Just doing it for a lark, you say."

"Some people got to have risks in their lives every day or they get fidgety. Some of 'em walk on the wings of airplanes and some of 'em make booze and run rum."

"Some get away with it," Pom said, "and some don't."

"Too bad about them kids," Trent said, "losing their folks that way."

"Kim and Carl? At least now they're going to know." Pom nodded toward the parlor behind him. "That's one reason I'm out here and not in there."

"Flora telling 'em?"

Pom listened to the sound of footsteps and muffled voices in the house. "She was the best one to do it. In fact, I think she *had* to do it. In a way, she's losing her own dad today. When she went in to talk to those kids, I think it finally hit home to her that old Mr. Larrabee won't be coming back. She's in there facing the facts the same as they are."

"Rachel told me they kept quiet about their folks being gone because they was afraid of being put on one of them orphan trains."

"I saw one back in Missouri, in Lamar, about 1910. What worried little faces."

"Kept up the scarecrow for the sake of appearances, but ski-daddled if anyone came to the door. What do you suppose is going to keep 'em off the train now?"

Pom folded the newspaper again. "John Howard."

Trent looked down the street. Rex was bringing Lucy back from another escapade, leading her by the chin with the halter. "It's just too damn bad them killers got away."

"There's that Luger on Avery's desk," Pom said. "Kind of like a hunting trophy. So maybe they got away and maybe they didn't."

It soon became common knowledge that Professor Thompson did not get away. Reading about the crackdowns on moonshining in the county, a fellow faculty member passed over for tenure by a committee chaired by Professor Thompson caught wind of his aromatic chemistry experiments and sent an eloquent if overwrought note to federal agents in Jacksonville. On a Saturday morning, the heavily-armed agents charged up to the chemistry building in two marked cars and found a cup of coffee still steaming on the counter in the professor's fragrant laboratory. They also found a small black ledger full of fascinating names and sales figures. They split up, ran slipping through the freshly waxed corridors, and found no Professor Thompson, but they did spot a man jumping into a Nash Roadster. They clattered back down the corridor, tumbled outside, and gave chase. Off they went, speeding down the tree-lined lanes of the campus and out of town with a startled motorcycle policeman pursuing all of them.

They sped past the Leary Store, nearly knocking over old Joan as she shuffled along with her coat over her arm. Professor Thompson disappeared down a side road and suddenly was a couple of miles ahead, congratulating himself for saving his skin, until he got to the prairie and saw the cattle spread across the road.

The Campions were at it again, bobbing along at their sleepy pace when he roared up, honking the horn and shouting.

"Move those cows, boy! Move those goddamned cows off this road right now!"

Tom Campion reined in his big slow-moving draft mix and counted to ten before turning around. "Sir, if you'll just give us a few minutes, we can keep 'em in good order and we'll all be on our way."

"I don't *have* a few minutes, you plodding yokel." Professor Thompson waved his hand as if to erase the cattle from a blackboard.

Tom looked down the road to his brother, hoping for some support in his effort to keep his temper, but Tim was pointed the other way, prodding a calf out of the drainage ditch.

"Sir, just give me a minute or two and we'll have 'em off the road. Sorry for the inconvenience."

The professor leaned on the horn. A couple of calves trotted nervously into the scrub.

"Hey, please don't do that, mister. Car horns make 'em jumpy."

Seeing that it seemed to have at least a small effect, the professor leaned on the horn again.

Tom's horse jumped and swung around, throwing him off balance. He grabbed at the saddle horn and regained his posture, but lost his temper. He counted to about three-and-a-half before pulling his .45.

"It was your fault," the professor sputtered. "You shouldn't have—"

A blast from Tom's gun threw the professor to the seat of the convertible. When he heard the second shot and realized that he was still alive, he sat up in time to see Tom trot around to the back of the car and shoot out the third tire. He glanced back and saw two cars and a motorcycle descending the slope into the prairie at high speed. The horse and rider eclipsed his view of his pursuers and then a fourth shot settled the car onto its rims.

Tom tipped his hat. "I imagine we won't be holding you up no more. You have a good day now, sir."

A day or so later, the schoolyard pirate Ollie Holiday had a mishap of his own. He had cornered Rex at the fence and rifled through his lunch bag for the treasured pecan pie. Late in the afternoon, as he was on his way home through the Leary Woods, still picking his teeth, he stopped at the sound of somebody running through the brush. He was standing on a carpet of leaves, listening, when he caught sight of a pie box in the path a few yards ahead. He hurried to it, raised the lid, and was reaching for a fistful of mouth-watering pecan masterpiece when he felt his feet jerk out from under him. He hung by his heels, twisting and jackknifing in a vain effort to reach the fallen pie or even to get a look at the perpetrator. He wasn't about to compromise his warrior status by crying out for help, at least not for the first hour, but pride departed with daylight and he bawled like a calf until Jake Jolly gave up his lonely vigil in lover's lane long enough to come and cut him down.

That was the story circulating at the depot when the Hollimans went to see Jim Rhodes off on the 6:39. Rex had put up only a token protest when Jim thanked them all at supper and announced that he would be heading to Milwaukee to write for *The American Socialist*. Rachel had just put a song on the Brunswick, a piece of questionable respectability called *The St. Louis Blues*.

When she heard the news, she stopped winding the turntable. As the tune ran down, she picked up the needle and closed the lid.

"Now that I'm free to come and go again," Jim was saying, "I'll be getting out of your hair. I imagine it's time for your family to be a family again."

So a few days later they hiked over to the depot, Rex carrying Jim's duffel bag and Rachel his guitar, and they stood on the platform beside the steaming locomotive, strangely at a loss for words beyond small talk. Jim seemed to be looking around for someone.

"I hope you'll tell all my friends and supporters thanks and good-bye for me." He craned his neck for a better view of the platform. "I was sort of hoping to see Ainsley."

Pom chuckled. "Like most women, she moves in mysterious ways, Jimmy. Thanks again for all the help with the wiring. The light in the parlor is all but blinding. If ever you come back, you'll be hard-pressed to recognize our little town. We're getting that fancy."

Jim smiled. "Some things don't change and I'd like to think that all of you and this place are among them."

Rex looked away, scanning the cars all the way to the locomotive. "Maybe some night I'll tune in a northern station and there you'll be with more songs."

Jim shook hands with each of them and accepted a parting hug from Rachel.

"It's going to be a lot less interesting around here without you," Pom said.

Jim was about to say something to Rex when a conductor came through telling the passengers to board. He snatched up his duffel and guitar and made his way to the steps the porter had set down. A fellow passenger asked him if he wasn't the famous Shirtsleeve Troubadour and the two of them were talking as they climbed into the train. When his face reappeared in a

forward window, the family waved and he raised his hand in sa-
lute. The train let out a blast of steam and pulled forward. Rex
turned away, but Rachel continued to wave as the light-struck
cars passed from view.

Pom laughed and the others turned to see what had set him
off. He was waving at someone smiling and blowing kisses from
the breezeway between the last two cars.

"I've never seen Ainsley look so pretty," he said. "She must be
onto the story of a lifetime."

Two days later, Kim and Carl left too. Pom had worked his tenuous
connections with the First Presbyterian Church and arranged
for Preacher Gordon to hold a graveside service for Roy and
Leslie Waller, for whom Flora had secured a plot at Evergreen
Cemetery. Beneath the arching branches and drooping moss of
live oaks, the couple got their names back and went into the
sandy soil attended by their children and a circle of posthumous
friends. The angular brother of the late Roy, tall and taciturn,
pressed hands with the attendees and, within a couple of hours,
was ushering his young charges onto the very same 6:39, for the
first leg of a trip to the family farm near Elmira, New York.

Standing on the platform as a downdraft shrouded the train
and well-wishers with smoke, Rex felt as if his whole life were
suddenly taking to the rails. It was an awkward good-bye. On
her way into the car, Kim turned and smiled at him, but he was
already walking away, and when he looked back, she was gone.

When Saturday morning came around, Rex was restless. Pom
asked him if he'd like to go for a ride. "I've got something to
show you," he said. "It's not a radio, but you might take a shine

to it." When they got to Lake Santa Fe, the boat was in the water beside one of the new piers. They walked out to it and stood there looking at it while the water lapped at its polished hull.

Rex eyed the tall varnished mast and long boom. "I've never seen anything like it. Whose is it?"

Pom ran a hand over his thinning hair. "Well, it's yours—if you want it."

Rex's jaw dropped. "Mine? How?"

"I've been kind of chipping away at it some of those late nights—not all of 'em, but some. I wanted to finish it for Christmas but I got held up. Got to be careful though. It's the kind of thing that makes you late for supper. If you fall in love with it, you just might be at odds with any woman in your life."

The sunshine was warm and bright and a breeze kicked up sparks in the water. Rex looked at the lines of the boat again, the upward curve of the bow, the sharp cut of the stern, and the bright finish of the hull that reflected the blue of the lake.

"How does it go?" he asked.

"Get on in and I'll show you. You'll have it crisscrossing from shore to shore before you know it."

It was true. The wind built gradually behind them during the afternoon. Rex loved the way the boat heeled in response to it, forcing them to sit on the high side so that they wouldn't tip over. By late afternoon, they were off Breezy Point and comfortable with the violence of coming about in the puffs that rolled across the water. They spoke little except for matters of sail trim and steering. Pom watched a trickle of water sliding from side to side in the bottom of the boat, talked of what he might do to seal the hull better, and suggested that it was time to turn around, but Rex talked him into one more passage along the far shore, and as they came about, an errant gust caught the mainsail and threw it hard from one side of the boat to the other, jerking the mainsheet from Rex's hand, and sending the boom hard against one of the side-stays that held the mast erect. The stay snapped, with a squawk the boom swung far forward, and the unbalanced boat rolled over, dumping the sailors into the chilly drink.

For a moment Rex was turned around, but then he fluttered his way through the floating acreage of the mainsail and grabbed hold of the hull. The first thing he heard was his father's laughter.

"For a while there we were having a grand old time!" Pom said. "We knew just what we were doing and where we were going. For a while there, we were really roaring!"

The boy blew water from his nose and watched the orange sun fold itself into a flat, icy cloudbank.

"We're going to be late for supper tonight," Pom said. "It's only our first trip and we're already going to be late for supper."

Over their shoulders, one of the first stars of evening winked beside the cradle of the crescent moon. Pom patted his son on the shoulder. "You're learning, and you're a quick study." He grabbed hold of the hull. "In a little while this'll all blow over and we'll kick this thing right back to solid ground. We'll set her back up and get her going proper tomorrow."

CHAPTER 40

On a cold rainy evening in November of 1942, Pom Holliman pulled his Ford pickup onto the shoulder of the road for a closer look at the hitchhiker huddled against the wind. He rolled down the window and stuck his head out as the man hurried toward him.

He laughed.

"Richard! Richard Ward! Last time I saw you, you were traveling in higher style."

The man came closer, set his suitcase down and gave the driver a going-over. "I'll be damned, Pom! What are you doing up here?"

Grinning, they pumped hands through the window. "I've been looking at cows up near Camp Blanding, false alarm on some brucellosis. What'd you do, Richard, park that Packard of yours in a tree somewhere?"

The hitchhiker wedged his suitcase into a jumble of bait buckets, tackle, and toolboxes in the back of the truck and came around to the passenger door. "I sold it to a rumrunner in Georgia twelve, thirteen years ago. I hear that he and the car missed a mountain curve and took a dive, along with a lot of good booze. You get your state job back?"

Pom smiled as Richard climbed in and sat down beside him. "The guy who had the job enlisted in the Army, but he's a lot safer than I was when I told Flora they'd canned me. Has it really been thirteen years? Where you been?"

Richard took a stick of gum from his raincoat pocket and went to work on it. "Up around Wilmington, North Carolina, mostly. I'm thinking to come back home though. Edith's had another baby."

"The blonde girl? I never heard you were married."

"We eloped the night I left town. Kind of sudden."

"Town's been kind of quiet without you. You thumb all the way down here?"

"Just since Atlanta. I ran out of ration points. Been cold and wet as a duck's ass ever since. This gas rationing's a bitch, ain't it?"

"I see your dad from time to time. He's as crusty as ever."

"I'm sure he is."

"I miss your grandma. She was one of a kind."

"How's Rex doing? He must be in college by now."

"Shoot, Richard, Rex is married, got a couple of kids. He's in the Navy out in the Atlantic somewhere on a destroyer, giving the U-boats some of their own. Flora and I are on pins and needles every day."

"Shooting at the Germans all over again. You'd think they got enough the first time."

"We're hoping he'll be home for Thanksgiving, but I've got my doubts, Christmas maybe."

"How's Flora? She still locking you out when you come home late at night?"

Pom smiled. "Some things don't change, even after thirteen years. I've got a better vehicle though. More room to stretch out. You been in touch with your folks?"

"They drop me a line every now and then. I call 'em up sometimes."

"They know you're coming?"

"I figured to surprise 'em."

"Well, you always were good at surprises. Real good."

Richard wrestled out of his raincoat and stuffed it onto the floor. He slouched against the seat with his hands behind his head. The rain picked up and Pom poked around with the vents to keep the windshield from fogging up. The wipers jerked back and forth, showing blurry semi-circles of pastures and pine trees.

"He had a couple of hard years, your pop. But he got those houses put up from one end of Palm Terrace to the other. Got his money back out of the Dixie Hotel too. It may be empty but it sure is a monument."

"Yeah, it's a monument all right."

"Your pop did just what a whole lot of other smart people did."

"So how can a guy make a little money down here these days? Sell a little black gasoline under the counter?"

"Damn, Richard, with this war on—"

Richard stopped chewing and smiled. "I was kidding, Pom."

"Same old Richard. Did you see that they're going to start making pennies out of steel so they can use the copper for shell casings?"

"Before you know it, you'll need a damn ration card for your pocket change."

"I tell you though, if it keeps the destroyers in business, I'm all for it."

"It sure is coming down out there. It's one sorry-ass night. This heap beats your Model T by a mile, doesn't it? 'Bout a '35, isn't it?"

"Thirty-four. If this cloud's as big as it looks, it'll keep the wolf packs off the prowl. When the moon's out, it gives 'em a perfect silhouette of our ships. The bodies from the freighters wash up on the beaches down here, you know."

"Good reason to live inland."

Pom smiled. "It's pretty quiet here in the hinterlands. The occasional shot fired in anger. But nothing as chilly as those two bodies in my pasture."

Richard gave Pom a good long look. "That was a while ago. A lot can change in thirteen years. People change."

"Did you know that Deardra Morrissey's back in town? I can never remember what her married name is though. Her husband's an eye doctor, a quiet kind of fella, wears glasses."

"Good advertising."

Pom chuckled. "They've got a nice little piece of property way out toward the Millhopper. Keep horses on it."

"I never figured that Deardra would be settling back here," Richard said, "especially married to somebody quiet and respectable."

"Like you say, people change."

"Some of 'em."

"How did you manage to dodge the collector at the end there?"

Richard smiled. "I took a page from your book. Spent a night sleeping in the car."

Pom chuckled. "Well, I'm glad I was a positive influence."

"I'll tell you who I've been wondering about lately—Kincaid. He still throwing parties at his hacienda on the top of the hill?"

Pom waved as he approached a wet-faced farmer driving a rubber-tired wagon with a team of mules. "Mr. Kincaid has not been with us for quite some time. Not long after you left, we got word that he met his maker when he was in France. Choked on a pheasant bone."

Richard sat forward, looking for a landmark that would be the first sign of his homecoming. "Well, so he changed too."

"His son's moved onto the property. Spencer. Takes after the old man in charm. Theron did some time in Raiford, you know, but they never caught those other two guys, Archie and Ralph."

Richard rolled the window down just long enough to throw out his gum. "Maybe *they* settled in town too. You never know. You might even find 'em at Kincaid's. On the floor for every dance."

An Army truck pulling onto the road forced Pom to slow down. "Soon as we get this war over with, we'll all be up for some dancing. It sure is good to see you again, Richard. I know your folks are going to be whistling Dixie to have their boy back."

Richard stuck out his chin and smiled at his reflection in the rain-streaked window. "You know, Pom, if you're tired of driving, I can take over. I bet we can get this thing going a lot faster."

Acknowledgements

Thanks to all who helped to bring *Midnight Catch* to life: Karl Schmidt, Kelly Wimmer, Patricia Gilliland, Florence van Arnam, Jim Haselden. Sara Rath, Frank G. Caruso, Alistair Sewell, Kim and Tony Hokaj, Stephanie Dickerson, David Stluka, Trevor Stephenson, Darren Hill, Matthew Roth, Jesse Eells, Jake Scholz, Tim Olsen, Mickey McBryde, Ernie and Milena McFeeters, Frances Theisen, Orennia Goetzinger, Cheryl Rot, and Erika Nielsen. Thanks also to Amanda Gilliland for going through the manuscript when it was still in its adolescent phase and hadn't yet slimmed down and discovered who it was and what it wanted to be.

Norman Gilliland grew up in Gainesville, Florida, and began a career in broadcasting there as a host and producer of classical music programs for radio. Since 1983 he has been a producer at Wisconsin Public Radio. His previous books include two volumes about classical music–*Grace Notes for a Year* and *Scores to Settle*–and the award-winning historical novel *Sand Mansions*. His audio productions include *Beowulf: The Complete Story—A Drama* and *Oedipus Rex*. He appears in the 2005 Oscar-winning documentary *A Note of Triumph: The Golden Age of Norman Corwin*. He and his wife have two sons and live in Middleton, Wisconsin.

13882871R00204